A STALKER SERIES NOVEL

WHO

Published by MM Publishing LLC
Edited by Jenny Sims
Proofed by Tina Rucci, Lynn Mullan, & Carol Agnew
Cover Design by Shayne Leighton of Shayne Leighton Designs
Who, Stalker Series, Novel 1
All Rights Are Reserved. Copyright 2018 by Megan Mitcham
First electronic publication: October 2018
First print publication: October 2, 2018
Digital ISBN: 978-1-941899-35-9
Print ISBN: 978-1-941899-36-6

A STALKER SERIES NOVEL

WHO

To dogs. To my pups and yours. To the pups without someone to call their own. You are the best of us. We don't deserve you. Thank you for putting up with our humanity and continuing to love us unconditionally.

~ 6.5 Million pets enter US animal shelters every year.
~ 1.5 Million of them are euthanized every year.
Statistics from the ASPCA.

SPAY & NEUTER, please, for the love of dogs (and cats), and if you're looking for a new friend, consider adopting a shelter animal. They make the greatest companions. I know from experience. You can check my Facebook feed for proof.

ONE

THANK HEAVEN FOR SLUM NIGHTS. Larkin's fingers smoothed over the red gold of the Montblanc fountain pen atop the glass conference table on the seventy-ninth floor of the Ashford Building, balancing the weight of it easily between her thumb and index finger. She zeroed in on the target three seats away on the right. A pulse danced in the old man's temple, proving he wasn't as heartless as his air indicated.

Genevieve's ultra-red pout turned the slight shake of her head into a homing beacon, demanding Larkin's attention. Her dear friend cocked a brow as only New York's premier hotshot attorney could. Larkin smiled. After all, this whole mess was Gen's fault. She'd demanded their inner circle abscond the gilded cages of White Street, Glass House Tavern, and Monkey Bar for body-brimming dance clubs or foam-serving pubs at least once a week.

Had Larkin known she'd earn the title of undefeated darts champion, she'd have expanded her horizons years ago. So many Manhattanites deserved a fountain pen to the temple.

Larkin gave Cornish Gleeson's brain bull's-eye one last glance before checking the time. Six thirty. She turned her gaze to her assistant. "Reagan?"

"Yes, Miss Ashford." Reagan stood from her chair against the wall with her digital pad and stylus at the ready.

"Please cancel my reservations at Le Cirque and have a good night." Seven delectable courses scrolled through Larkin's mind as each distinct flavor wafted across a well-trained palate. She swallowed her pooling saliva, along with her amusement at the disgruntled look on Genevieve's face.

Should've let me kill him.

Across from Gen and to Larkin's immediate right, Marlis's lower lip quivered ever so slightly. Larkin's other dear friend either hadn't noticed the contemplation of murder in her eyes or had agreed. She could plead insanity.

"Yes, ma'am." Reagan's slight British lilt perked with the edict of freedom. If only Larkin could give herself the decree. The slight woman nodded and fled the room as though the seven people around the table aimed to have her for their meal instead.

"Just perfect." Gleeson flicked a wrinkled hand. "Let the minutes show Miss Ashford's…" He dragged out her honorific as though it were an insult, and then stalled with a contemplative tap of his wrinkled chin. "Yes, let it show her complete and total lack of respect for the board assembled here."

Irritation rooted at the base of her spine grew thorny offshoots that threatened to sprout out of her skull as sharp horns. The smile curving her lips died.

"Objection," Gen shouted.

"I second that." Tarin Blakely's thin arm shot into the air. The board treasurer never said much unless it pertained to numbers or her two children.

Larkin assumed she didn't converse much because heavy caseloads at her prestigious brokerage firm and her loving but overbearing family wore her to the bone. The small gesture of solidarity shocked the hell out of her. And not just her. Marlis's mouth fell open on a gasp.

Next to Mar, Benjamin Daily smoothed a hand down his tie and straightened in his chair. Larkin hadn't thought it possible. The guy was the definition of uptight even though he was far too young to be so stuffy.

"Cornish." Brice Beauregard planted two palms on the table and leaned over the glass. The seams of his charcoal gray suit bunched but not at the buttons where most men his age needed it let out. It stretched the material over his chest and at his shoulders. Genevieve licked her lips, also noticing the way the salt-and-pepper-haired man reigned over his body and the room.

"You don't speak for me, old friend. Nor do you speak for the rest of the board. You speak for yourself." The ruler of the Beauregard fortune eased back into his chair and turned a sultry smile on Larkin. She seriously tried not to feel it between her legs, but she had a thing for older men.

Daddy issues.

Mr. Beauregard turned back to Gleeson. "Cast your grievance. Keep your crotchety attitude."

"Fine," Gleeson growled. "Your dinner plans prove you're not taking this board seriously."

Seriously? Was this guy serious?

Everything she'd worked for her entire life rode on the shoulders of this board and their decision. Every weekend and night for the past fourteen years, while not with her girlfriends, was spent working toward her goals.

Larkin painted on a smile and clung to the calm that confidently carried her through life.

"Mr. Gleeson, my dinner plans prove that I expect this board to work efficiently." She wouldn't call him out on his snide remarks about a woman-owned company or a woman-dominated board. She didn't have to. "My dinner plans prove that I expected to celebrate a decision and the culmination of work that began while you were still barking people around on the floors of Willhelm Media."

She stared him down, daring him to speak. He bit his tongue—literally, by the look of the lump in his cheek.

"I asked each member to present their data-backed opinions this afternoon. If anyone has disrespected the gathered board, it's you, sir, because you neglected to share your report."

Larkin braced for the impact of Gleeson's balled fist. It came from behind his shoulder and descended like an anvil, rattling the thick glass table.

You break it. You buy it.

Tarin jumped several inches from her seat and landed with her arms drawn across her face and chest.

Gleeson sneered at Brice Beauregard. "Why I let you talk me into this, I'll never understand. You can't talk sense into a woman who doesn't have a man standing for her."

Anger, usually stowed neatly in an overhead compartment, combined with irritation and rained down in the turbulence. Warning: Oversized baggage. Delayed luggage. Heaps of unchecked shit hammered into Larkin.

"You're saying this to number one hundred two on Forbes list?" Genevieve sliced a manicured nail at Larkin and then swung it to Mar. "Hell, Marlis will pass you by next year." Her red point turned on the son of a bitch whose momma never taught him how to respect a woman. "You're hanging around the four hundreds, right, Gleeson?"

Genevieve crossed her arms over her ample rack and pushed the blouse-covered thing at Gleeson. "I'm the baddest bitch prosecuting attorney the city's ever seen. And guess what? We've done it all without a man standing for us. If there were men in our lives, they'd be at our sides." Gen stood and smoothed her hands down her sides, accentuating the swells and dips of her goddess body.

Larkin held her breath for the fatal blow. Gen always had one.

"Except, of course, when their faces are buried between our legs." Her friend nodded at the other men in the room. Brice hid everything behind a mask of impassivity. Benjamin, on the other hand, tugged at his tie as though the silk strangled him. "I move to close the meeting." Gen smiled sweetly.

"Second," Brice choked out.

Gen flashed Larkin a wink, grabbed her briefcase, and headed for the door. "Share your driver with me, Mar?"

Larkin wondered if she meant the car or the actual driver. Neither would be a first for her friends.

Marlis shoved a stack of papers into her crocodile Givenchy and primped the formfitting houndstooth wool to her knees. Her gaze glanced over Benjamin before finding Larkin. She blew Larkin a kiss and hurried after Gen.

"Meeting adjourned." Larkin gently placed the pen atop her folders and stood. Sweat trickled between her breasts. It tickled across her belly and charioted away her reserve. The walls swelled, threatening, at the most, to suffocate her but at the least to make her look like a fool in front of the city's premier CEOs, her board members.

"Thank you for your time, ladies and gentlemen," she wheezed.

Larkin hit the button on her chair at the head of the clusterfuck.

"Yes, Miss Ashford?" The masculine voice rumbled

through the speaker and caught the attention of everyone who remained.

"Lucas, Reagan has gone for the day. Kindly show out my guests?"

"Yes, ma'am," her senior bodyguard said as she rushed through the private entrance to her office.

The door closed behind her with a thump. Larkin tried for a full breath, but each was syphoned through an ever-tightening airway. It'd been too long since her last hit. She squared her shoulders and stalked to her desk. From behind it, she ran the world—her slice of it anyway. Her hands smoothed over the cool marble top, grappling for composure. Fragrant gardenias floating in the low crystal vases on her desk may as well have been dead rats for the effect they had. Zen music filtered in from unseen speakers. It sounded like nails being dragged across the length of a brand-new Maybach.

Highs and lows of a day spent with the tech department congealed with the fallen hope she had for the board meeting. They'd combed through the upgraded apps she planned on releasing within the week for her biggest moneymakers, her foundation, her babies—Duo and Ditto. There were major kinks and little time to fix them.

Stress clamped down on her airway. Panic shredded reason—the thing she used to get through even the toughest days—into bloody ribbons.

Larkin bolted from her desk. Leaving the work she always toted home, her purse, and her phone, she ran. The door at the entrance to her secret stairwell weighed three times heavier than normal. Sharp clacks echoed in the glass and metal box. The frantic pace made a mockery of her usual grace while the impact demolished the spikes of her blush Louboutins.

On the penthouse level, she darted past the door of her apartment to the end of the short hallway. She fought for a lungful of air at the bottom of the maintenance ladder but couldn't gain headway. Her fingers and hands trembled on the rungs, but she fought the rise of panic and pushed ahead. One lever turn and a hoist of the metal cover revealed the deliverance she'd denied herself for too long.

The sky was an inkblot, vast and black, yet light shone like glitter. It shimmered from a thousand upright structures, dancing through a million windows. The city created its own dawn. A rise of light that shrouded her in darkness and peace. Larkin shoved out of the manhole. Biting wind slapped her cheek, stealing the breath she hadn't realized she'd possessed. She sucked in oxygen in greedy gulps. Vehicle exhaust and food wafted in the air. Horns and the bustle from the heartbeat of the city carried on it. Steam billowed from vents to the left.

Familiarity wrapped around her, smoothing down the jagged edges. But the absence of her protective spines left her exposed, raw. Tears pricked her eyes. With God as her witness, they were a reaction to the violent, near icy gusts and no more. Weakness equaled defeat. A backward old man and a technical glitch wouldn't ruin her.

But a phone call from her father could.

Larkin wrestled out of her red jacket, hating that it was tailored so snugly. Though that's exactly how she'd wanted it when the world wasn't falling down around her. The fabric slipped from her fingers as she pushed toward the raised ledge. A chill kissed her bare arms and neck. She yanked the blouse from the prim tuck at her waist and pulled the pins from her conservative chignon. Wind carried her hair away from her face. Why not her troubles too?

The low wall stopped her momentum with the unforgivingness of a thousand-foot concrete barrier. Her hands trembled so, and she dared not look over the ledge. Instead, she stared at the soldered bands of gold and diamonds on her right ring finger. It called her a fool. Bile and panic churned her insides.

Why?

She ripped her mother's wedding set from her hand and clutched it in the center of her fist. A scream, long and brutal, ripped from her throat. It cursed the sky and the stars, the land and the water, and the blood flowing through her veins.

With rage came not only tears but also sure hands. Larkin slapped the streams from her cheek, hiked the pencil skirt as high as it would go, and hopped her almost exposed ass onto the ledge. The concrete threatened to freeze her to the spot. Carefully, she turned and faced the city. In her palm, the rings burned a hole.

Time to release the past, but first, she had to confront it.

Larkin lifted her fist into the air, reared back, and—

Imposing arms banded Larkin's waist and yanked her from the wall. Skin and patent leather scraped across the gritty surface. The torso her back slammed into was as unrelenting as the concrete. Her replenished supply of oxygen exited her lungs in a whoosh ... without so much as a goodbye.

A fresh form of panic took hold. Larkin screamed, but no sound left her gaping mouth. She put the fancy shoes to work, kicking indestructible shins. Her fists met with muscle-hardened brawn. His free hand pinned her right arm to his side.

"Lady, you picked the wrong rooftop." The stranger shook her.

If only she'd brought her purse, she'd have her gun. But no. Maybe she could play cooperative until an opportunity to escape presented itself. Christ knew screaming wouldn't do any good, even if she had the breath for it. That was why she came up here when the world got too rough—so they couldn't hear her release.

She could see inside a thousand windows—and if someone in any one of them looked, they would see her—but they wouldn't hear her. Her office and apartment had spectacular views, but she never took the time to study or truly appreciate them. Not until she came up here. And look where that had gotten her.

"Stop fighting," the man's low voice demanded.

The cold suddenly imposed a threat to her life. Who the hell could survive a frozen spine? It must have frozen because, as he commanded, she stilled. Her mind continued to run rampant, calculating angles and dismissing them in rapid fire.

"I have money." Larkin's throat hardly allowed the words to pass.

"Well, thank you." He stepped away from the edge of the building, carrying her along with him.

Hope bloomed.

"You reaffirmed my lifestyle choices."

Then the madman laughed, and her hope died.

"Let me go." Larkin poured as much demand into her voice as she could muster.

"So you can splat your brains on the pavement and the cops can pin it on me? No thanks."

"What are you talking about?" Larkin tried to turn her head, to get a better read on the crazy person who held her in the unbreakable grip of his arms, but shadows shrouded his features. "Who are you?"

"Your guardian angel, sweetheart."

His deep baritone rumbled in her ear. He didn't feel like a guardian angel. And then a far-off bulb lit. Larkin's hair smacked her cheeks with every vehement shake.

"I'm not trying to kill myself."

"Right."

"Are you going to rape me?"

He scoffed, and the heat of his breath coursed down her neck. "Lady, I just saved your life. I'm not going to hurt you."

"Then let me go."

The stranger turned away from the view. His heavy boots took another step in the direction of the manhole. He lowered her what seemed like three feet, and her quaking shoes hit the ground. The cuff of his arm slid from her waist.

Larkin held perfectly still, afraid it was a trick. Her knees conspired against her, shaking and rattling her bones together.

"I hope your night gets better," the stranger said from just behind her.

On wobbly heels, she turned her head to look up at the man who scared the shit out of her and could have done her real harm. Her gaze lifted higher and higher, shot wider and wider still to encompass the mountain behind her. The collar of a leather jacket flipped up points to a stubble-covered jaw. Dark, almost black eyes studied her from under the brim of shaggy onyx hair. A jaw made for crushing bone flexed.

His head tilted, and light caught the edge of his face. Bubbles and recesses lined the other side of his face from the point of his dark eye to the hinge of his jaw. The red scar was the stuff of horror movies. But the intensity of his gaze forced her heart into her throat, blocking her screams yet again.

Larkin eyed the manhole, twelve feet away, and ran for her life.

TWO

HER SLICK-BOTTOMED SHOES skittered over the first two rungs. Only her sweat-slicked grip kept Larkin from plummeting the twelve feet to the floor below. Her ribs and lats screamed at the overextension, but she didn't dare pause or look up. Fear of him standing over her in the open manhole was too much. She repositioned her feet and half shuffled, half slid down the ladder.

The clack of her heels slamming into the marble-tiled floor reverberated inside the empty hallway. Shock of the impact shot white-hot pain up her heels, calves, and thighs. Her breaths echoed loudly in the eerie silence.

Only ten feet away, her slick white door and its ornate gold knocker beckoned. She supported most of her weight on her left foot and hobbled the distance as fast as she could. Her ankles throbbed and wobbled. No sound except the pounding of her pulse and the whooshes of her breath stood out. He could be right behind her. His approach on the rooftop had been silent. So too could he be now.

Larkin collapsed against the shiny, cold door and wrenched the knob. Of course, the damn thing was locked, and she didn't have her key. A sob threatened to crumple her to her knees right there. Liking old-fashioned things—like actual paper notes and fancy keys in locks—would get her killed.

Thank the heavens above for Lucas. Five months ago, her head of security had suggested keypads, in addition to her ancient key lock, be installed on all her doors for an added layer of security. She pounded in her entry code as well as a security alert.

When the mechanism released, Larkin chanced a look down the hallway because the last thing she wanted to do was lock herself inside her apartment with a man like that. Still, the hallway remained empty. She wrenched the knob, flung herself inside, and slammed the door closed behind her. The electronic lock slid automatically in place. A flip of the deadbolt shored her nerves enough to stand. Automatic lights flicked on behind her through the sitting room and kitchen, giving warmth to the cool, modern surroundings.

Metal on metal trilled.

Larkin's feet left the floor. Every nerve ending short-circuited, making her legs and arms shiver. She whirled to the right in search of the sound. The antique phone on the high table next to the door rang again and again while she stared at it and struggled to calculate what the hell was going on. Her jittery hand reached for the ivory handle and lifted.

"Hello?" she squeaked.

"Miss Ashford, I'm headed up as we speak. Are you all right?" Lucas's concerned voice poured through the phone. He used her formal title, which meant he brought backup. Good. Lucas Backstrom was lethal, and nothing about him was small. Judging by the size of the stranger on the roof, he'd need backup.

"I'm ..." *Shit.* She could think but apparently, speaking was too much to ask. "I'm ... I'm ... okay. I think."

"What's the problem?" he demanded. A month ago, she'd liked the command in his voice, but now, it seemed intrusive, and she didn't exactly know why. "Do you have ... company?"

Ah, and there was the reason it irritated her. He hocked the word company. It landed on her cheek and slid to the floor like the unwelcome accusation it was. Anger stiffened her spine, and calmed her fear and the rush of blood in her ears.

"There was a man on the roof," she snapped.

"On the roof? Did you bring him up for the view?"

The thunder of her heartbeat returned but for an entirely different, much more manageable reason. Give her irritation over gut-churning fear any day. She'd spoken of the view to Lucas but had never taken him or anyone else up there. And she never would.

"I went up for air, and he was there. He scared the shit out of me," she snapped.

"Hold tight. Lock your door. We'll take care of it." The line died.

Like she was dumb enough to leave her door unlocked. Hell, she'd gotten herself away from the man and in here without Lucas's help.

"Dipshit." Larkin dropped the receiver into the cradle and teetered past the sleek fireplace, the white and gray seating area, and the glitter of the New York City night through the wall of windows.

Her palms splayed on the wet bar built into the wall as her gaze pinged across the labels. She reached past The

Dalmore and other expensive liquors and went straight for her run-of-the-mill vodka—the liquor that would burn the worst and, she hoped, settle her nerves. The bottles clacked and rattled as much as the stack of rings on her pointer finger.

"The ring."

God, she was an idiot. She'd abandoned her mother's ring and her jacket. The jacket didn't matter. The ring … It was worth a sizable fortune. She wanted it back so she could toss the damn thing off the building.

Larkin ripped the crystal stopper out of the bottle filled with vodka, ignored the shelves of glasses, and tipped the liquid to her lips. The first sting did little to knock away the haze of terror, so she tried another gulp. Liquid fire burned its way over her tongue and up her nose. A hiss sang between her teeth.

The tremors in her fingers and heart regulated. Her stomach churned. It had been too many hours since she'd eaten, yet the thought of food ignited a flash fire across her skin. She set the bottle on the white granite counter next to the other bottles. No need to compound her issues tonight. Her hand fell to her belly, and she sighed.

"Breathe, Larkin. You've been through worse." Emotionally worse, yes. Physically? Not even a play-yard scuffle. Nothing remotely dangerous had ever crossed her path and revealed itself.

No one had the audacity to touch her without her permission, much less attack her in the night, in her favorite place on the top of her building.

Her fingers slipped from the quieting rumble of her stomach up to her ribs. She closed her eyes and felt his thick arm banded around her. People were always so delicate with her, even her lovers, even when she hadn't wanted them to handle her with kid gloves. The stranger used a barely hinged force she'd never experienced. Between his compulsion, her fight to get away, and her easily marked skin, she'd bruise by morning. Even now, her skin ached.

She found her reflection in the mirror behind the shelves and glasses. Sections of formerly ordered hair hung loose around her face and neck. Thick black lines of melted mascara formed a pool under one eye and ran down her cheek on the other. It looked as though she'd cried. She hadn't. She didn't. Though the evidence stared back.

Larkin ignored the disarray for the moment and lifted the thin material of her wrinkled shirt until the underwire of her lace bra peeked out. A wide red swath marred her porcelain skin. She let her fingers ease across her upper ribs and then down to within inches of her belly button.

He'd been savage with her. At the same time, his parting words replayed in her mind.

I hope your night gets better.

The words were kind. Shit, if she could take a step back from her shock and fear and look at the situation with her usual collected calm, she could see it from his perspective. A crazy woman scampers up the manhole that no one except him and a maintenance man or two had ever been through. She rips off her jacket, screams at the night, and rushes headlong at the ledge.

"Sweetheart, I just saved your life. I'm not going to hurt you." His words whispered across her cheek.

Her shirt slipped through her fingers and covered her gym-tightened stomach. The stranger had been so solid and immovable it caught her unaware. Most men she'd been with had been fit by reps and metal weights, but that guy …? The world had honed his body into a lethal force she couldn't reckon with.

Larkin smoothed her shirt with a disgusted huff. She kicked off her scuffed and beaten shoes and stormed through the seating area. A wall of glass fronted cabinets, neatly decorated with wine glasses and china she never used, and the massive granite slab atop the kitchen island created the hallway through the kitchen to her bedroom. At her presence, warm light eased on in the bathroom and closet, creating twin funnels of light that illuminated her king-size bed. It beckoned her, but her stomach refused the invitation.

Makeup slowly dried like cement around her eyes. She needed it off, as well as the feel of the stranger's arms. The thick band hung around her middle. His hot chest molded to her backside. Her fingers trembled over the first button of her shirt.

"Dammit, Larkin. Get it together." She gritted her teeth and unfastened it, and then another. The boiling water from the shower would wash the night away. It had to. No way would she go back to the pills.

A solid double bang reverberated through the apartment. Her breath clogged her throat, and her head snapped away from the glass and marble shower ten feet away to the long, dim corridor.

Why hadn't she had them program those lights?

"Because you are not afraid of the damn dark."

The heavy knocks came again, insistent as ever.

She hadn't expected the guys back from the roof so soon. Had they taken down the stranger? Her feet moved hesitantly down the hallway. What if the stranger was standing on the other side of her door? What if he forced his way inside?

Damn, if only she had her sidearm.

Beside her, the refrigerator's compressor hummed to life, and she startled. Jesus, she was well and truly falling apart at the worst possible time. Her company needed her now more than ever. Her hands balled to fists, and she squared her shoulders, marching to the door.

It loomed large and foreboding.

Three more vicious knocks shook its frame. "Open the door. It's Lucas."

He'd never been so demanding, but she'd never been in real danger before. Up until now, his job consisted of managing the building's security staff, shooing away unwanted advances, and sitting around bored to death for hours on end.

Larkin wiped the makeup from under her eyes, drew a deep breath, and let it out slowly. When her fists eased enough to allow blood flow, she stepped to the door, opened it, and stood in the doorway, faking the hell out of her cool demeanor.

Lucas's crystalline blue gaze assessed her top to bottom and back again. His wide jaw worked his lips into a sneer.

A lump formed in her throat. She'd never seen this side of Lucas.

"Did he hurt you?" Lucas pointed at her chest.

Her head shook as her gaze dropped to the swell of her breasts on display between the two open buttons on her rumpled, untucked blouse. "No." She choked on the lump and grabbed the fabric together.

"You sure?" he insisted.

"No. He just surprised me. No one is ever up there. Maintenance during the day occasionally, but no one at night." She needed to redirect and fast. "Did you find him?"

Lucas's longer than a military buzz, but not by much, hair clung to his head as he shook it. "Carl and Dan are doing a floor-to-floor sweep on each end of the building, but no one was on the roof."

"Oh." She didn't know how she felt about that. He hadn't hurt her. He hadn't even threatened her.

"What was he doing up there?"

Fuck if she knew. Stargazing? Howling at the moon?

"I don't know."

"What did he look like?" Lucas's gaze narrowed.

"What?"

"Pressed and ready in business casual?" Lucas's large hands turned toward the heavens, and he shrugged. "Was he dirty, drunk, and hanging his legs over the edge of the building?"

"He was ... none of those things." Larkin shrugged and tightened her grip on the material.

"Well, what was he then?" His tone slashed and grated at her withered patience.

"He was there. Just there, okay?"

"Like he appeared out of thin air?" Doubt scrunched Lucas's light brows.

"It doesn't matter. He's not there anymore." She let her grip slide down the door to the handle. "I need a shower and sleep."

Lucas took a step forward. "Are you sure he didn't hurt you? If he did, there's nothing to be ashamed of." He reached for her shoulder. His hand eased to her elbow and then fell away. "It happens every day, and women don't report it."

"He didn't even touch me," she lied. Why, she had no idea, but suddenly dealing with Lucas drained her more than the stranger had.

"Do you want me to stay?"

Lucas was hot, knew how to fuck, and was a blue-blooded hero for goodness' sake. He'd dragged a gut-shot comrade off a battlefield through a hail of bullets. If this were a romantic drama, they would have rolled the credits months ago. But Larkin didn't do romance. She didn't do overbearing. She did business and men but never interchangeably. Well, never again. Lesson learned the hard way.

"No. I'm fine, thank you."

"It's been a long time, Lark. I thought we were good together."

"We were." No need to deny it.

"So?" He leaned in, almost imperceptibly.

"You wanted more than I can give." Larkin backed farther into her apartment and eased the door between them.

His hand met the door and stopped it cold.

Larkin's pulse revved.

"Come on. If you'd just let me in …"

"I don't do that. It's for fairy tales and movies, not real life. Good night, Lucas." She shoved the door.

Again, it didn't budge.

"Wait."

"No." Sickness churned in her stomach and rose into her esophagus.

"You forgot this stuff out here." Lucas crouched, stood, and offered her the items he'd picked up off the floor next to her door. Her neatly folded jacket lay in his palms, and her mother's ring sat at the center of the fabric. "Good thing you didn't take this up there. The guy would have tossed you off the roof to get that rock."

Larkin stared at him for a long second. She thought he'd retrieved them from the roof, but … if he didn't, did the stranger?

"Larkin, are you sure you're okay?"

"I'm fine. Thanks for this." She accepted the items he shoved through the small opening between the door and frame.

After a long, hard look, Lucas lifted his palms in surrender and eased away. When the door met the latch, Larkin slid the bolt into place and melted onto the floor.

THREE

———

"MISS ASHFORD?" Larkin's intercom beeped, pulling her gaze from the computer monitor she'd been staring at for the past ten minutes. At least it was an improvement from staring out the window at her building's image in the reflective finish of the windows in the Crenshaw Tower across the street and wishing it was taller. If it were, she could see the roof and maybe—

"Miss Ashford?" Reagan's voice pitched.

"Yes, Reagan?"

"Your car has arrived."

Larkin straightened and hit the mouse pad, pulling her computer from the monotonous batting around of her most prized logos. Duo shined in glossy white, its D formed by an engagement ring. Ditto glittered in a pale pink with the dots above the I and slashes across the T's in blue. A boutique-style rattle formed the Ditto's D.

The blinding white screen with hundreds of tiny numbers pulled the projected launch numbers into focus. After months of staring at the data, she knew them without looking. A click of the calendar blocked the numbers. If only she could do that with the massive and very abstract file in her head that was sucking up all her brainpower.

She scrolled through the calendar but saw no appointments. "My car?"

Her cell phone beeped on the desk and flashed a text message. The girls had been blowing up their group text all morning. They were filling Libby—their only bestie not on the board—in on what went down over the glass table, each voicing their outrage. They were probably still ranting. Her friends did it well.

"Yes, ma'am. Your lunch date at Per Se."

The hint of hunger toying with Larkin's stomach at the mention of lunch turned rabid as soon as the memory of making the plans cemented. Its teeth sank in, shook, and refused to release its sickening grip. More than anything, she wanted to cancel, but she'd already negotiated the date down from dinner and the theatre. No way would she get off the hook—not as long as her last name was Ashford.

Maybe it was time to find a family to adopt her. Too bad she was too old.

"I'll be down in a moment."

"Yes, ma'am." The intercom connection dropped.

Larkin grabbed her phone and read the line of texts.

Libby: I can have the forensic accounting department look into Gleeson.

Another message popped up.

Genevieve: I can round up a slew of his female employees and work up a sexual discrimination suit against him.

Marlis: Great. I'm not an FBI agent or a lawyer. What can I do besides give him the evil eye?

Genevieve: Mar, you're too nice to even give a good evil eye. You can keep the rest of us from going straight to hell, and that's why we love you.

Larkin jumped in. There's no hope for me today. I have lunch with capital D.

Libby: Going into meeting. Muting. Good luck, Larkin. I have bail money.

Genevieve: He's too slimy for me to touch.

Marlis: Tell me where you're going. I'll have my driver accidentally run him over.

Larkin: Thanks, but I can't have you going to jail. Maybe that means we're all going to hell together.

Genevieve: I'll bring the booze.

Larkin: I'll bring the boys.

After closing the numbers on the launch and the spreadsheet weighing the pros and cons of going public—the only things she needed to focus on at the moment—she left her haven and met the angry day. It greeted her in the form of Lucas's stoic face outside her office door and compounded out the massive rotating door with icy sheets of rain and hundreds of bustling New Yorkers. They jostled along the sidewalk with scarves and slickers pulled tight, their scrunched faces intent on the ground in front of them.

"Miss Ashford." Douglas, her driver of fifteen years, held a large umbrella open at the edge of the glass canopy.

"Larkin," she chided the gray-haired man as she had every day for the past five years.

"Yes, ma'am." He offered her his elbow and a smile, then ushered her to the back door of the blacked-out Town Car and inside without a cold drop on her head.

"Thank you, Douglas."

He leaned in conspiratorially and flashed her a wink. "I poured you one finger of liquid courage."

"You're the best." And Lord, she meant it. The man

was more a father to her than the man with whom she shared a name and blood.

"No less than you deserve." Douglas closed her in tight and left Lucas in the icy rain without a glance to fend for his own door in the front passenger seat.

Larkin set her purse on the seat beside her, snagged the glass of scotch out of the holder, and eased back against the plush leather. She took a deep sniff of the whisky, letting it settle in her lungs. No way was she an alcoholic on days like this. Pre-noon drinking or not. What awaited her warranted the entire freaking bottle, if not more.

The city passed by in a slog of cars, bikes, and bodies. Like zombies, they walked to and from the lives that chained them to their small corner of the world. The chains held them to it, bounded them, and enslaved them without their knowledge. And wasn't she one of them?

She kicked back the drink and let it sting its way deliciously down to her belly. Her fingers danced along the button on the door, and she gave into the compulsion. Hair be damned, she lowered the window. Muffled sounds of the city she loved and hated in equal measure became nuanced yells, tired grumbles of old cab engines, and the screeches of brakes. Food cart fat and oriental takeout wafted in on the air. She breathed it in as deeply as she had the scotch, and a tiny smile curved her mouth.

Those guys had to be freezing their asses off.

Too soon, the car pulled to a stop in front of one of New York's most famous see-and-be-seen overpriced eateries. Her smile fell to the carpet. What she wouldn't give to grab a street dog and eat it over her computer while toiling with the decision she had to make.

"Miss Ashford." Douglas stepped back and held the umbrella out for her.

"Stubborn old coot." Larkin stood and pecked his cold cheek. "Wish me luck."

"I'd wish you bravery, but you have it in spades. So luck it is." He walked beside her to the restaurant door where Lucas held it open.

"Keep it close and running." She smiled at Douglas. "If I kill him, I'll need a getaway car. Are you up for the task?"

Douglas's strong jaw tightened for a moment. Then his eyes narrowed and shifted beneath his eyebrows. He leaned in close. "You know, I've always had a fantasy about being the Transporter." His deadpan beat all others.

A genuine laugh started in her belly. It rolled through her chest and extremities, making it all the way to her lips. The thing only the two of them knew was in his heyday, the former CIA operative had made the Transporter look like a schoolgirl. Amusement energized her enough to shoulder the task ahead. She swatted his arm and nodded her thanks.

At the edge of the portico, Douglas folded the umbrella and watched her ignore Lucas as she walked through the door he held open. She wondered if the intelligent fellow noticed the tension that collected like bricks for a building's foundation on her shoulders. If only her and Lucas's weirdness last night was the only trouble.

The twentysomething model-pretty hostess assessed Lucas head to shoulders and back again. Her cheeks pinked, and her mouth gaped. Her guard stood watch in an inconspicuous corner of the foyer where he'd stay through the meal. Larkin stepped to the podium and waited her turn.

"Hello, may I have your name please?" The hostess's breathy lilt would have steamed her glasses had she worn any.

"Ashford." Larkin ignored the girl's eye bulge and the prattle about how she was new and should have known such an iconic New York face, which really meant money.

Instead, Larkin pointed at a notepad and pen on the podium. "May I?"

"Of course." She passed over the items. "As soon as you're ready, I'll take you to your husband."

Larkin's hand froze in midstroke. How disgusting that people in this convoluted city assumed an older man and younger woman were married because they had the same last name. Her gaze slashed to the young woman's, who would probably happily accept a proposal from a man old enough to be her grandfather as long as he was loaded.

And there Larkin was, making snap judgments about someone else when all they'd done was give her the courtesy first. Damn, she was jaded for a girl in her twenties—the last year of them—but the twenties all the same.

"He's not my husband." She finished writing the digits and name on the paper and pulled it off the stack.

"I'm so sorry. I—"

"Don't worry about it. I'm ready."

The girl looked from Larkin to Lucas and back with a question in her eyes, but she grabbed a menu and headed up the short central staircase. When they were out of earshot, Larkin handed the hostess the note with Lucas's name and phone number. She slowed, but Larkin's momentum kept her moving.

"Ma'am?" The hostess eyed the paper.

"He's my bodyguard, and that's his number. His favorite drink is a draft beer, and he likes live music." Bands, not opera. Larkin nodded to the young woman and hoped she'd take Lucas's mind off their non-starter fling.

"Thanks." She blushed.

"Larkin, darling. You look as stunning as ever." The bastard couldn't be troubled to stand, but he lifted his arms and opened them, though not wide enough for a hug. He always did one of those very European air hugs and double kisses. As though he was receiving her spirit, not her, his daughter.

"Father." She smiled as sweetly as their past and present would allow and took her seat.

"I ordered you a Glenlivet."

The moment the words, "I ordered," were off his tongue, Larkin's stomach corkscrewed its way to her little toe. After eleven years of the fucked-up tradition, it shouldn't hurt this much. No matter how she tried to prepare, it wrung out her insides. No matter how many times she told him she hated the sight of the stuff, and no matter how many times she explained why, he insisted it was just a drink engrained in their family through the generations.

It hadn't done much for her mother's generation. Then again, she hadn't been blood. She'd married into the Ashford clan. Fuck, they were English anyway, not Scottish.

He slid his own off the table and held it up for a toast. "To a good year."

Her father didn't wait for her to join him. Years ago, he'd learned he'd die of thirst before she'd cave and let that shit pass her lips. It tasted just fine, but the picture of that bottle in her mother's hand would be forever seared in her brain.

"How's business?" he asked through a satisfied hiss and blindingly white teeth.

"Busy. How was Italy?"

A server stepped to the table with a pleasant smile and a warm welcome. He suggested the nine-course chef's tasting menu for the day.

"Of course." Her father placed his hands together and bowed like he was a guru or ancient oriental. He was a white guy from very old—not existed in decades—money. "Lovely. That'll be just lovely."

The server turned to leave.

"Pardon me, but I'll need to change that to the five."

"Nonsense." Her father shooed her words away. "I haven't seen you in months."

"A year and a half," she corrected. They'd been the most peaceful of her life.

The server's blue eyes bobbed back and forth between them, patiently awaiting an answer.

"It'll be the nine." Felix Ashford nodded as though his word were final.

"Then I'm afraid it will be dining for one." Larkin stood. "I really do have work to do, and I don't have the time for nine courses." Neither did she have the inclination to endure a nine-course chef's tasting menu with her father.

"A workaholic, my daughter." His white hair shook. "Five courses then," he conceded, and the waiter scurried away before they could change their order again. After all, if she left, who'd pay the bill? The short answer was she would, one way or the other, which was why this meal irritated her so. It was guaranteed to cost more than his high-dollar caviar and oysters and her cheese plate.

Larkin had a mind to ask for seating in the salon and a one-entree meal. Five courses were four too many with him.

Silence settled over the table. Her father stared into his emptying glass.

"How was Italy?" she asked again.

"It was ... complicated." He grinned.

"How so?" Larkin took a sip of her quadruple distilled water and waited and waited.

"Deidra left me."

Another divorce. That was why they were here. Another negotiation. Another settlement.

He grew bolder with age. They'd gotten down to business before the first course arrived. Maybe he was just running out of bullshit. Hard to believe since the man wallowed in it. Then again, he'd once wallowed in money, more than she'd managed to amass with hard work and determination.

There was something to be said for earning your fortune the old-fashioned way as opposed to inheriting the piles from your great-great-great-grandfather. When you earned it, you weren't so quick to throw it away.

Larkin slipped her phone from her purse and discreetly texted Douglas to ferret out the details on her father's most recent split. She wouldn't get them from her father. He twirled around the ice in the glass of whisky he'd ordered for her, planning his next move.

"Was it the gondolier or the pool boy this time?" She took another sip of water, feeling a bit more confident about the course of the meal and its likelihood to stay inside her stomach.

"Shhh." Her father's head tilted this way and that, looking to see who was in eavesdropping range.

"Really, Father." Larkin pressed her elbows to the table and lowered her voice. She didn't want to embarrass him. She just wanted him to understand what she'd been telling him for years. "There's nothing wrong—not one single thing—with being attracted to men except when you insist on marrying women."

His back stiffened, and his age showed for the first time in the way his large frame didn't quite reach the stature for which he'd been aiming.

"It's time to stop living a lie," she pressed.

"Larkin Gwenette Ashford, this is hardly the place."

"Then invite me to the house the next time you want to discuss the terms of your impending divorce and how much it will cost me." Larkin's fingers squeezed her phone.

The server tripped into the tension with dainty salads and their light courses. Her father waited until he left before picking up his butter knife and pointing it at her.

"I haven't said a thing about money, you greedy little

girl." His upper lip curled into an ugly sneer.

What the actual fuck?

In all her dealings with Felix Ashford, not once had he ever been vicious. Adrenaline, akin to that of her presumed attack last night, dumped into her veins. Sweat gathered at the high collar of her formfitting dress. He snatched the oyster fork from the fine linen and flipped it over time and again, end to end. The small tines grazed his palm more aggressively with each pass. His reaction scared her. Fear incited by her father whipped up enough anger to override the fear.

"You haven't mentioned money yet, but that's only going to last as long as it takes the check or the divorce papers to arrive. Did you tell the lawyer to serve you here, like last time?" Larkin pushed her seat back. "And you call me greedy? I'm greedy? Says the man who whored his way through several billion dollars because of secret lovers need secret hideaways. Greedy, says the man who drove his wife to suicide and left his daughter to fend for herself at thirteen."

Larkin shoved her phone in her purse and stood.

"Sit down." Felix pressed the sharp end of the tiny fork against the starched white tablecloth and pressed down so hard the points sank below the surface into the hardwood.

Alarm bells clanked and whirled in her ears. She looked for Lucas but didn't see him anywhere. A large hand wrapped around her wrist and pulled her down with a bite she'd never experienced. Well, not until last night.

"Listen to me." Felix plastered on a fat fake smile and leaned across the table so far, his tie pressed close to a pool of vinaigrette. "I couldn't help the ill timing and lacking couth of Beverly's firm."

Judging by the lack of circulation reaching her fingertips, she really should keep her mouth shut about the ugly divorce with his second wife. Sixteen years of taking care of herself wouldn't allow her father to swoop in now and issue commands.

"Right," she spat. "Just like you couldn't help sticking it to the gardener."

"In case you were wondering where you inherited your promiscuous ways, you were screwed on both sides. Your mother did her fair share of lover hiding."

Shock released the hinge on her jaw while rage gave her new cunning. "You will release me this minute or so help me God, I'll make the biggest scene you've ever witnessed. I'll tell every gossip rag willing to pay for all our family secrets every last detail, and I'll give the proceeds to charity."

Her father's gaze lifted over her shoulder. His grip loosened, and his sneer morphed into a stately smile.

Blood rushed into her fingers, threatening to burst them like over-watered grapes. She snatched her hand into her lap and prepared to hide behind Lucas while she told her father never to contact her again. Her sentinel had to be the reason for her father's abrupt metamorphosis. When she reached with her good hand for her purse, her fingers met empty air. The damn thing had been in her hand. Where the hell was it?

"Larkin Ashford, you've made my day." Bronson Beauregard, her CFO's handsome-as-sin son plucked her clutch from the floor and offered it up with a dapper smile.

Her head spun as though someone had set her on a Tilt-A-Whirl against her will. Lucas hadn't changed her father, Bronson had. Nausea, confusion, fear, and irritation played a hard game of poker in her belly. Somehow, they all won.

When seeing Bronson—face to face for the first time since they were kids—it wasn't the type of reaction she'd expected. Then again, too many things were happening too fast, and no one played their usual roles.

Over the years, she'd tracked her childhood playmate's progress through a European boarding school and college, and then his climb from the bottom of his father's company to the top. She'd drooled over his bare-chested spring break pictures and swooned over the African safaris and mid-ocean stargazing dates he'd procured for girlfriends. Larkin fancied herself a strictly business anti-romantic, but she'd daydreamed about their reunion. In each one, her father was nowhere in the landscape, and the whirling in her stomach had been from the heat of his presence. Not this craziness.

"Thank you." She took the purse with a weak nod and set it on the edge of the table before she dropped it again.

"Two times in as many days. Lady Luck has smiled upon us." Brice Beauregard offered her a nod, clapped his son's back, and stepped around him, extending a hand to her father. "Felix, it's been a while."

Her father waved over the server, then stood and puffed to his full height. He was a tall man, taller than the two Beauregard men. Next to Brice's and Bronson's healthy broad shoulders, he appeared weak and unavailing.

"Brice, too long, my friend." Her dad extended a firm hand to Brice, and then pointed at the chair next to him. "Please, join us. We're just starting our courses."

The men continued with their polite I-don't-mean-to-intrude, oh-it's-no-intrusion conversation, but Bronson caught both her hands in his and pulled her up.

"Larkin Ashford." Bronson held her hands wide and made a show of inspecting her. He wasn't overtly sexual, but she caught a devious sparkle in his green eyes. "You look ..." His stunning gaze shifted back and forth and then landed on hers. "Gorgeous." He pulled her in for a big hug. Unlike most others, she went willingly. After all, they were friends.

His strong arms settled around her waist and cinched tight. A moment later, her feet left the ground, and he whirled them about. Her fingers locked around the back of his neck and held fast while she prayed she didn't vomit all over them both.

"Bronson," his dad chided.

A satisfied chuckle rumbled from Bronson's chest and shook hers. The room stopped spinning, and her feet found purchase. Her gaze found Bronson's full lips spread into a mischievous smile. His sun-blond hair hung over his brow, and his lively green eyes searched her face.

"Just wow." He stole a peck from her cheek and stepped away.

Larkin laughed to cut the tension that built around her organs. "The last time you saw me, I had braces and pigtails." And a mother. She kept the last buttoned in tight and shrugged. "Nowhere to go but up."

"I liked your pigtails." He winked.

"I recall you liked my braces. They gave you something to tease me about." Finally, Larkin felt a playful smile on her lips. It cooled the tension baking her insides.

"I was a boy. It's our sworn duty to pester the girls we like." Bronson pulled her chair out for her. "My lady."

"Ha." She covered her mouth.

"What? You didn't think I'd forget, did you?" His mouth quirked. He bowed and flourished his arm toward the chair.

When they were young, they played king and queen of the castle nearly every day. He'd order his friends to slay the dragons, which her friends played. Then they'd live happily ever after at the top of the treehouse in his father's backyard.

Her father and Brice talked quietly about setting up a game of golf later in the week if the weather slacked off.

Bronson waited for her to sit. With no graceful exit and less will to leave than she'd had five minutes ago, she sat. He helped her into the seat, took the one next to her, and allowed the waiter to serve him the first course of what was suddenly their nine-course meal.

In for the long haul.

Felix reached across the table and patted her hand, but he never broke eye contact with Brice. The urge to stab it with the salad fork overwhelmed her. He'd won this round, but no way in hell would she stand for his behavior again. He ruined the threadbare truce they'd had. No way would she meet with him again without a lawyer or security team at her side.

Bronson leaned close, shielding his mouth with the back of his hand. "Not a chance a king forgets his queen."

"Oh, I'm sure you have a gaggle of ladies vying for the title these days." Larkin grinned and toyed with the hem of her collar.

"Ah, a few. There was one who came close several years ago, but none of them compared to my first and truest." He settled his focus on her with a sexy smile that batted around her alarm bells like an innocent kitten. Years ago, Bronson may have been innocent, but these days, he looked downright beautiful and cunning.

"I didn't know you were in town. How long are you stateside?" Diversion was the safest route until she knew what she was dealing with. A playful flirtation she could handle. But a true-blue knight in shining armor? Not so much.

"You didn't tell her?" Brice smirked as he heaped caviar onto a cracker.

"I've only been here for twenty-four hours." Bronson split a look between them, huffed playfully, and then turned back to her. "I'd planned to pop in to see you, but your receptionist said you were booked today and tomorrow."

"You could have just called. My number hasn't changed in years." Larkin caught her father's nosy stare out of the corner of her eye. Grabbing her cup, she sipped the tepid water just to have something to do. The longer she sat under his leer, the more uncomfortable she became. He looked too smug about the turn of events.

"I wanted to tell you in person. Out of all the people I knew in the city, you're the only one I've really kept in touch with through the years." He smoothed a manicured hand down the front of his tie.

"Tell me what?" She abandoned her glass and leaned forward, dying to know and afraid of the answer at the same time.

"Unless I royally screw up in the next year, I'm back for good." His smile stretched from ear to ear.

"Oh my goodness, that's great news." She couldn't help but mirror his excitement. It filled the air around him with tiny sparks and cut the tensions that lingered from her fight with her father.

"I sent you to those schools around the world to pre-pare you for this. You won't fail." Brice lifted his glass to his son. "To my son, the future of Adorn. May you both prosper for generations to come."

"Here. Here." Felix raised his refilled Glenlivet and drained half.

"Congratulations, Bronson." Larkin clinked her water glass to his, sipped, and turned to Brice. "Are you plan-ning to retire?" Both her father and Brice were getting on in age, but the diamond supplier for most of the world for the past five decades didn't seem the type to let go so easily.

"In a year, after Bronson learns his role at the top. He's done well from the ground up. I don't see a reason for him to falter now." He nodded. "Bitsy and I want to see the world—like your old man—while we can still get around."

"Well, congratulations to you both." It was great for their family, but immediately, Larkin's thoughts flew to her newly formed board and the man at the heart of it, who was retiring in a year.

"Don't you start worrying." Brice patted the table. "I can make time for quarterly board meetings. After we get things ironed out, I'm sure that's all we'll be meeting."

"Am I that transparent?" She smiled to keep from frowning.

"That business minded," Brice corrected. "It's not a bad thing, but too much work isn't good for the soul."

Her father spouted off about how much his travels had eased his burdens. As though the man had worked hard a day in his life. Larkin tuned out the men and stared at her plate, totally disinterested in the fare.

"I have another reason for wanting to see you in person," Bronson whispered.

"Oh, yeah?" She grinned, happy for the distraction.

"It'll help in the soul saving department."

"Sounds illegal. Aren't us rich kids destined for the devil?" She giggled to mask the truth of the matter.

For most of her friends, money meant dealing with absentee parents and all the troubles that accrued. One of them had OD'd before her eighteenth birthday. Another had been raped by her uncle from the age of nine until she killed herself at fourteen. Only the strong and lucky made it to adulthood without a major addiction or criminal records. Brice had been wise to send his son away.

"No." Bronson scooted to the edge of his chair and grabbed her hand. "My family is throwing me a welcome home party Saturday at the Waldorf. Be my date?"

Whoa, she hadn't seen that one coming. Hell, she hadn't seen any of this coming. What harm would attending a party with one of her oldest friends do?

"I thought it was closed for renovations," she hedged.

"It is." His smile was bright and radiated arrogance, but somehow, it worked for him.

"But when your dad is the patriarch of a diamond business who has sent thousands of newly engaged brides to the Waldorf's doorstep for gluttonously lavish weddings, they make accommodations."

"Something like that." He chuckled and placed his other hand atop hers. "What do you say?"

"If you promise to slay any dragons we come across."

"It'll be my honor." He raised her hand to his lips. His hot lips pressed against the back. A long sweeping gaze assessed her.

Men had appraised her over every day of her life since puberty. Some ogled. Some looked for the angle to her money. Some sized her up as a business opponent. Some scoffed at her position in her company until she proved she'd earned it.

This look was none she'd seen before. It scared her almost as much as her father's newfound anger.

"Success looks good on you, Larkin."

"You haven't seen me pre-makeup and caffeine." She chuckled.

"Not yet, but I'd welcome the pleasure."

FOUR

LARKIN WALKED TO HER DESK, carrying a steaming cup of double espresso complete with the fern leaf cream design. No steaming hearts for her. She couldn't operate many kitchen tools. The one that mattered, though, was the one she made sing like a barista at Le Peloton Café. Judging by the wall of black windows that reflected the pre-dawn New York hour and her puffy-eyed appearance, she might need to go up to her apartment and craft another cup before Reagan made it in to the office.

She drank deeply and sat in front of her computer. As the liquid life-bringer cascaded down her throat and worked its magic, she woke her computer. The background picture temporarily blinded her. She blinked at the image of her and Marlis grabbing the Wall Street Bull by the balls. Gen and Libby had insisted on grabbing its horns and acting like they were punching it in the nose.

It suited them. That damn bull represented the men who held the keys to the free world's finances since damn near the birth of its creation. And by God, they were leveling the playing field in one way or another.

When her eyes adjusted to the light, she entered her passcode and opened the report from the head of her tech department. She had exactly five hours before her nine o'clock meeting to read through the nearly seventy-page report and try to understand it. No trouble at all. It'd only taken her six years to learn French. She could master another foreign language in about as many hours.

Right?

Larkin sucked down another gulp and leaned toward the screen to find out.

Hours passed. Her espresso drained dry. Still, she read and re-read sentences, willing them to decode. Her best friend Google helped. Her shoulders hunched. Her brows pinched. Her lids squinted.

A knock reverberated through the room.

Larkin's hands shot out, palms extended, to ward off an attacker. Her entire body jerked.

On edge much?

She braced her hands on either side of her chair and regulated her breathing. Daylight poured into the once pitch-black windows, and the cityscape of concrete, metal, and glass filled her view. Her building's image reflected in the Crenshaw Tower instead of her own. The tick of her heart kicked up again with the realization that the world had continued spinning, and quite quickly, while she'd immersed herself in tech jargon.

Another knock sounded at the door. Her gaze found the time. There was still enough time left to tackle the last few pages, though not as in-depth, and get to the sixtieth-floor tech department.

"Yes?"

The door opened. Reagan stepped inside and closed the door behind her so forcibly it announced its closing to the entire floor. The young woman yelped. Her hands covered her heart, which held nothing else. Not the coffee she brought every morning without fail, nor the iPad she used to discuss the day's schedule and make notes. Reagan shoved a lock of hair behind her ear.

"Is everything okay?" Larkin had never seen the woman so out of sorts.

"I'm sorry about the door. I'm sorry to bother you at all." Her gaze shifted toward the door.

"It's fine, Reagan. What can I do for you?"

"Not me." Her head shook vehemently. "I know you have a meeting with Mr. Torres in seventeen minutes. I saw your light on when I got in at seven thirty, and judging by the amount of muffled cursing I've heard, you've been in here for a while working quite diligently."

Great.

Her assistant judged her depth of work by her cursing. It was an accurate measure she hadn't realized she possessed. The office needed soundproofing.

"It's Mrs. Blakely." Reagan huffed. "I tried to get her to make an appointment, but she insisted she must see you now. Not later today. Not when you had an opening. Not when—"

"Thank you, Reagan. I know you tried. Send her in." It would take less time to find out what the treasurer of her board needed than to calm Reagan.

"Yes, ma'am." An eye roll indicated Reagan's irritation that Tarin had gotten her way.

"I appreciate your effort," Larkin soothed.

"Thank you." Reagan opened the door and left, presumably to fetch the woman from the reception area. That, or tell her to take a flying leap.

While she waited, her gaze drifted out the window to

the building's reflection yet again. She should be thinking about the meeting ahead or the innuendo Bronson left her with the day before. Stubbornly, her mind returned to the rooftop as it had for the long hours of night until sleep stole her away for a short time. Worse still, she hadn't told the girls about the incident. They'd worry—for good reason.

The man had been big enough to shove her to her death with one hand. She'd been alone with him in her sanctuary. A place no one would have thought to look for her body.

Larkin stood, straightened the skirt that covered her thighs all the way to her knees, and shook her head. There was nothing to worry about, but as her hand traveled to her ribs, the tender skin contested. Despite the bruise across her middle and the scrape down her thigh, the man hadn't meant to hurt her. His intent, if she believed it—and, stupidly, she did—had been to save her life. He didn't steal her mother's diamond engagement ring. The thing was worth more than Larkin's shoe collection. He hadn't stolen anything except her ability to focus ... on anything other than him.

Reagan knocked lightly on the office door.

"Yes."

The door opened an inch at a time. Her assistant smiled sweetly and lifted a hand, gesturing inside. Tarin Blakely rounded the corner and walked into Larkin's office—a place she'd never been before—as though she visited regularly.

"Darling, thank you for seeing me on such short notice." Tarin's arms opened wide. Both shoulders of her boxy, black power-suit lifted to her ears. The woman Larkin had only met four times continued past the guest chairs, around her desk, and toward her.

Larkin didn't hug anyone. Her best friends exchanged

single cheek kisses. Her father stole hugs. Only Bronson had received one as of late. It had been nice, but that one was stolen as well.

Sure enough, Tarin stopped just in front of Larkin, wrapped her arms around her middle, and squeezed. The bruises over her ribs wept. She held her breath and clamped her lips. Too many seconds passed before the woman released her, but she didn't retreat as much as common courtesy demanded. The treasurer had two small children, so maybe she'd forgotten social graces in the touchy-feely world of toddlerdom.

"Thank you, Reagan." Larkin waved her assistant off and turned her gaze to the woman sharing her oxygen. "Tarin, how are you?"

"I'm great." Her grin was so wide that Larkin realized she'd never seen the woman smile in a meeting. Sure, she'd given cursory niceties but not the fully bloomed joy that radiated from her now.

The lady standing in front of her was a completely different person than the one she'd met before. Larkin got it, of course. In a business setting, you projected the person people expected or needed you to be. Tarin obviously felt comfortable enough around Larkin to lower her armor.

"That's good to hear." Larkin smiled. "I have a meeting at nine, so if I can help you in the next few minutes, I'd be happy to. Otherwise, we'll have to set up an appointment to talk further."

Tarin's smile dropped. "I didn't mean to interrupt. Of course. I know you're busy."

"What can I do for you, Tarin?" Like Reagan, if she didn't get to the point, her time would be gone before the pleasantries were out of the way.

"Oh, I didn't need anything." Tarin's hand covered her heart. "I came to check on you." Again, the smile came, bold and bright.

"Me?"

"Yes." Tarin nodded. Her short blond hair swished around her face.

She didn't elaborate, and Larkin had no idea—that Tarin would know about—why she needed checking on. "I'm fine."

"You don't have to put on a brave face in front of me." Tarin chucked her arm. The slight woman hid some power under that square suit. "Men have no idea how hard we work. They'll never understand the pressures we face. Marriage. Motherhood. Careers."

Two of the three didn't apply to Larkin, but she didn't interrupt. Tarin's cheeks blushed bright, and her words refused to slow.

"Not to mention menstruation." The woman's hands shot high and wide.

Menstruation? Larkin talked about it with her friends, but she didn't know this woman beyond business pleasantries and the bit when she mentioned her children and husband for one reason or another.

"If men had to deal with cramps and bloating, the world would grind to a screeching halt. If they—"

A small ding ended Tarin's tirade and not Larkin, though she'd wanted to. Her gaze slid to the cell phone on Larkin's desk next to the computer. It held there for a moment. Finally, she returned her attention to Larkin.

"Do you need to get that?" Her smile was gone. A look of concern or irritation—she couldn't be sure—occupied its space.

"No." She needed to get Tarin out of her office so she could make her meeting.

"Oh." The vibrant smile returned. Her hand swatted the air between them. "Well, you get my point. Cornish Gleeson is beyond a bastard for what he said to you the other night, and I just wanted to make sure you were okay."

"Thank you, Tarin. Really, I'm fine."

Larkin's phone shot three rapid-fire beeps, drawing the woman's attention again.

"I can wait if you want to tend to that," she offered again.

She walked around the desk, flipped it to silent, and set it on the stack of papers, praying the damn thing wouldn't make any more noise to railroad her bid to get Tarin out of her office. Knowing her friends, though, it wouldn't happen. When they got going, look out phone bills.

Larkin hurried around the desk, sidled close to the distinguished accountant for several massive corporations, and hoped she'd follow Larkin toward the door. "I appreciate you thinking of me enough to come by and check in."

Again, the phone went into fits, and Tarin's gaze narrowed on it.

"I really have to get to a meeting." Larkin made a show of looking at her watch. Crap! She only had enough time to gather her things and get to the meeting.

"I understand." Tarin smiled meekly. Stopping a few feet from the door, she turned to her. "How about lunch?"

What about "in a hurry" did this woman not understand?

"I'd love to on another day. I have plans today and am pretty booked until I make a decision about going public." Larkin pushed ahead, knowing Reagan would be right there to escort Tarin out as soon as she opened the door.

"Surely, you have to eat." The woman huffed. "Unless you're on one of those diets where you only take vitamins, powdered meal replacements, and drink water with the proper pH."

Just wow.

Larkin didn't have time for this shit.

"Yes, I eat. I usually do it at my desk. Not dropping food on my keyboard is a trick, but I get a good bit of work accomplished." Larkin cleared the last few steps to the door and opened it. "Thank you again, Tarin. I appreciate your concern."

The woman stayed put and studied her up one side and down the other. Tarin's study homed in on her arms. "You're more athletic than I thought."

She usually wore sleeves in a business setting, but somewhere through the hours spent hunched over her computer, she'd shucked her jacket. Her brain searched for the proper response. It came back empty-lobed.

"Clearly, you eat. You must work out too." Tarin's odd smile returned.

Words refused to form in Larkin's mouth. The conversation had taken such an unlikely turn. Tarin was a numbers savant but socialization, not so much.

"Miss Ashford, you need to leave for your meeting immediately." Reagan stopped in the open doorway and offered Larkin her morning coffee. "Mrs. Blakely, I'll show you out."

Tarin looked back and forth between them as though she wanted Larkin to intervene on her behalf.

"Thank you for the visit, Tarin. I hope you have a lovely day." Larkin snagged the coffee and sent her assistant a knowing look. "Thank you, Reagan." The young woman's hiked brow said she understood all too well. Larkin nodded her final goodbye to Tarin and rushed to her desk without a backward glance.

The room emptied, and the door closed quietly behind them. She didn't have time for a cleansing breath before gathering her laptop and other meeting accoutrements into her bag, abandoning her coffee after only one gulp, slinging on her jacket, grabbing her phone, and heading to the service elevators. The last thing she needed was to run into Tarin again.

Every impact of her purposeful strides echoed off the

glass and marble surfaces until she shoved through the rear door and those surfaces devolved into cinderblock and laminate. Her phone shook twice in rapid succession. Larkin pressed the call button for the elevator car and grabbed the possessed device from her bag.

Several messages littered her screen. Each one was from her BAB text loop. BAB, stood for Bad Ass Bitches, of course. Yes. Yes. They were all highly educated women who knew badass was one word, but the inspiration had come to them on a night of particularly overt hedonism. Then they'd reasoned that they were badass and that their asses were pretty bad. Hence, BAB.

Libby: I can't make our lunch date. Hate to miss it!

Genevieve: What the fuck?

Marlis: No! Why?!?

Libby: I shouldn't say.

Genevieve: But you will.

Marlis: Because you love us and know we'll worry more if we don't know what's going on.

Genevieve: And never leave you alone until you tell us. Tell us!

Minutes passed in strings of texts as she'd been dealing with Tarin.

Genevieve: Give it up, Libby, or I'm coming to your office.

Marlis: You know what happened the last time she came to your office.

Genevieve: I wasn't the only one coming. Winky-smiley face.

Libby: He still asks about you. Eye-roll face. I'm in a meeting. Shut up! Larkin is too, based on her no-comment.

Marlis: You started this …

Genevieve: You know what it takes to shut us up.

Libby: I got a lead on the gun trafficker's case I've been working on. Going to TN.

Marlis: That's wonderful!

Genevieve: I want a pic when you get them in handcuffs.

Libby: Shut up already.

Larkin: Congrats, Libby. Be safe and tell us everything when you get back.

She closed her phone and stuffed it inside her bag, but not before seeing that she was now one minute late for her meeting. The elevator car still hadn't arrived. She looked left and then right. A florescent light flickered horror movie style. Unbidden, a chill zipped up her spine.

"Seriously?" Larkin rolled her eyes at herself, as she should. She'd been living alone in NYC since she was fifteen. Boogeymen didn't exist. Criminals did, which was why she employed a security team.

Her gaze found the readout above the elevator door. The panel was blank. No bright lights told the car's location. Even the call button remained dim. Surely, she'd pressed it. It was an automatic action when stepping up to an elevator. If six people were standing, waiting for the car, the Pavlovian response to step around them and press the button took hold. She stepped forward and depressed the button again for good measure.

Nothing happened.

Not nothing. That damn light flickered again.

Her phone beeped. She yanked it out of the bag.

Libby: Thanks! Now really, shut up!

"Three minutes late." Larkin tossed her phone into her bag, glared at the elevator, and then looked down at her sharp-toed, sharp-heeled pumps. "This is going to hurt." Her shoes marked her decision to take the stairs with boisterous clacks. She shoved past the door into the stairwell. Cool, dank air slapped her cheeks and tried to frizz the hair she'd pulled into a high, tight ponytail.

Before she hit the first landing, the door slammed onto its frame, shocking her eardrums again and again as the explosive noise echoed down the hollow concrete column. The metal banister cooled her palm. She gripped it tightly and plowed ahead. With her office and home occupying the top two floors of the eighty-story building, getting to the sixtieth on foot would take forever dressed as she was.

There was no turning back now. It would take her just as long to reach the main office elevators and wait for one to reach her. Another sharp bang filled the stairwell somewhere below. Instinct forced Larkin to quiet her steps and strain her hearing. She didn't hear the familiar strike of stilettos nor the heavy tread of dress shoes. In fact, not a whisper came from the depths.

Larkin leaned over the railing. Row after row after row of ugly black banisters, concrete steps, and space carried on infinitely. It seemed. She didn't see a hand gripping for balance. She didn't see anything. Maybe someone had thought better of it and opted for the elevator as she should have. One gentle step at a time, she descended. Her breaths ceased. Her heart pounded against searing lungs.

Maybe she needed to see her shrink. The attack—non-attack—had affected her more than she realized.

A laugh, feminine and full, lifted from the depths, freezing her in place. Her grip on the railing tripled. The jolly sound shouldn't sound so sinister in her ears. Her throat collapsed in on itself.

Just when her hysteria hit critical mass, the comfortable strikes of high heels ticked their way down one flight of stairs and the smack of another door echoed from below.

She sagged against the railing in relief while simultaneously berating herself for foolish fears. This was a building filled with businesses. Some hers. Most not. These people rented blocks of floors on which they conducted business. This was not the back alley of a run-down building. This was her building. She was fine. Late for a meeting, but fine.

Larkin jogged ahead with purpose.

At the seventy-fourth floor, she toed off her shoes and

held them. At the seventieth floor, she questioned her sanity. Tarin hadn't been all that bad. She could have ridden down nineteen stories with the woman. At the sixty-seventh floor, she thanked the inventor of the elevator. At the sixty-first floor, she stopped and took a moment to dab her forehead, pull in three deep breaths, and slide her shoes back on her feet.

She completed the last flight of stairs—maybe ever in her life—smoothed the front of her dress, and pushed into a long hallway. The short carpet welcomed her tired feet, and she hurried toward the reception area.

Tom Harron, the youngest man in the tech department, stood to the side of the elevator with an iPad in his hand. His eyes jumped from its screen to his iWatch and back, to the elevator readout—which worked—and back to his iPad. He'd been her liaison for this latest launch. Larkin snagged a look at the clock above the receptionist desk. Ten minutes late. Her stomach knotted.

"Mr. Harron?"

The man whirled to face her. His mouth bloomed into a sweet smile, and he shoved the glasses up his nose. If she ever mixed business and pleasure, she would have tried it with Tom on their first meeting. The guy was intelligent, personable, and hot in that geeky, finally-grown-into-his-body-but-wasn't-sure-what-to-do-with-it way. Alas, he had a girlfriend. He'd mentioned Jenny in every one of their face-to-face meetings.

"Miss Ashford?"

"Hi." She extended her hand. "How's Jenny?"

"She's fine." His gaze slid down the hallway and then back to her. "You rode the service elevator?" He shifted his device into his other hand and shook hers with a steady but non-crushing grip.

"I wish." She laughed.

"The stairs?" His voice raised an octave.

Larkin nodded. "I'm sorry I'm late." Their hands separated, and she motioned toward the rows of offices. "Please, lead the way."

"Of course." He strode ahead down a long row of glass front cubicles and into a conference room where three other senior members of the tech staff, as well as the head of the department, Daniel Torres, sat, and a freaking Power-Point gleamed on the far wall.

Humiliation nudged her cheeks, but she refused to let it. "Ladies. Gentlemen. I apologize for my tardiness."

"It's your money, Miss Ashford. However you see fit to spend it is of no consequence to us." Mr. Torres dismissed her with a turn of his head. His slick, long black hair held perfectly still thanks to a salon's worth of product in his hair. He picked up a remote control, straightened his gray sweater and the points of his Oxford undershirt, and clicked the first slide to life.

The other eyes in the room widened.

Larkin had expected no less from the man who was crotchety before his time.

Mr. Harron mouthed an, "*I'm sorry,*" and pulled out the chair at the head of the table. When she took it, he sat next to her—a nice buffer between her and Torres. She felt bad for the kid. Sitting between her parents at a dinner table had been shitty. Now, she'd give anything for the uncomfortable theatre of it all.

Torres read bullet points from the presentation and expanded only enough that everything he said had been included in the seventy-page report he'd emailed to her and the rest of the people in the room. Talk about wasting money.

She left him to his yammering and looked around the room. Every set of eyes roamed. Some took immense interest in the ceiling while others gazed at the walls opposite them and some even their crotches. Even Harron's eyes flicked between his hands, which fidgeted atop the table, and the farcical excuse for an educational presentation.

"Mr. Torres," Larkin interrupted.

"I'll answer questions at the end, Miss Ashford." The man didn't bother to look at her. "We have a great deal of material to get through and fifteen minutes less to get through it." He clicked for the next slide.

"I, and everyone else in this room to whom you sent the report, read it." Around the room, people nodded.

Torres turned to face the room. "Well now, that's a surprise." He shrugged. "In that case, I'll take follow-up reports from everyone in my department before you leave for the day." The collective groaned. "If there's nothing further, meeting adjourned." The collective reached for their laptops.

"I have some points of clarification." All eyes turned to Larkin.

"Such as?" Torres's right brow pierced the sky.

"The report states that once complete, the app will take up to a month to clear for sale on the vendor platforms."

Torres nodded with both brows up and one eye rolling into the back of his head. "Yes." His yes sounded more like *no shit, dummy.*

Fine. If he wanted to be a dick, he'd better prepare to get his balls kicked. "Is that a standard turnaround?"

Again, he gave the *no shit,* "Yes."

"Great. I want that time cut in half." Larkin smiled.

"It's standard and out of our control," Torres snapped. "They review our security measures and firewalls placed in the app to keep the consumers' phones safe from hackers. They must monitor for malicious software."

"It may be standard, but we're not average. Are you average, Mr. Torres?"

"No," he scoffed.

"Perfect. If the standard for any thirteen-year-old with

a calloused right hand and a laptop is a month, our department should be able to contact the app departments at these vendors and plead our case. If that doesn't work, I'll contact the people I know on the boards of those vendors and get things moving faster." She mentally ticked that off the list and moved down. "Now, why is the iOS app taking three times as long to develop as the Android?"

"If you'd let us go live with Andr—"

"I want them rolled out at the same time. You know this."

Harron shifted his chair toward Larkin. "Android follows the same programming code with which—"

"Why are you even bothering?" Torres growled. "She won't understand what you'll tell her."

Larkin stood.

The rest of the room squirmed.

She kept her features schooled and her voice calm. "I appreciate that you all understand technology on a level that I never will." Her gaze narrowed on Torres. "It's why I pay you so well." Larkin let that declaration hang in the air, reminding this asshole who paid for his stuffy sweaters and super computers. "I'd like to understand, at least in laymen terms, what's going on in the technical aspect of my business."

Torres stood and pointed at the people who ran the different branches of the department, then motioned to the door. "Out. And I want those reports by day's end." People scrambled except for Harron.

Larkin seethed.

"If time is of such importance, they don't need to hang around here waiting while you get an elementary lesson on coding and software." Torres powered down the projector and grabbed his laptop. "For that matter, neither do I."

The pompous man power-walked his way to the door.

A list of things trampolined on the tip of her tongue, but she let him go. No good would come of a rash, "You're fired." No matter how good it would feel at the moment.

"I'm so sorry," Harron whispered. "He's gotten worse each day closer to the deadline."

"Don't apologize for him. He's a grown man who will deal with the consequences of his actions soon enough." Larkin drew a deep breath and turned to Harron. "Please finish your explanation that was rudely interrupted."

"Android follows the same programming code with which we're all familiar. iOS requires Swift coding."

She was pretty sure it didn't have to do with the only kind of swift she was familiar with.

"So Torres is having to learn Swift before he can code for the iOS."

"He could have just told me that or put it in the report." Larkin shook her head.

"He's a proud man." Harron rolled a pencil between his fingers. The relic seemed completely out of place in an environment with Bluetooth, scanners, and lighter than air computers.

"Are you a proud man, Mr. Harron?"

He rolled his pencil and let his eyes wander for a moment. "Not too proud to explain something to a person with a desire to learn."

"Last question."

"Okay."

"Are you ready to take Mr. Tor—"

Harron coughed so loudly it made her jump in her shoes. His eye widened with an indiscernible message. "Yes, I'm ready to take you to the elevators." He stood and motioned her to follow.

Larkin hoisted her bag and rushed ahead to catch him. It wasn't until they reached the bank of elevators that they were shoulder to shoulder.

"Torres records the meetings," he whispered without looking at her. "He records more than that, if you ask me."

"You know what I was about to ask you?" She breathed.

"I ... don't know for sure."

"You do." Larkin nodded. "Are you ready?"

The elevator doors opened, and three people poured out.

"Connie," Harron called over his shoulder, "I need coffee. Do you want anything?"

A short woman behind a tall desk peeked her eyes over the top. "No. Thank you, though." The balls of her cheeks turned red.

"If you change your mind or need me, text." He motioned Larkin into the elevator and followed. The doors closed. "I can't believe you like Florence and the Machine. You'll love Vagabon. Laetitia Tamko. She's local and well, just listen."

What the hell?

Larkin didn't dislike Florence, nor her Machine, but she hadn't a damn clue what they had to do with their current conversation.

He pressed several buttons on his iPad. A hauntingly sweet melody enveloped the empty space around them. Laetitia sang about being small and surrendering. Harron turned to her, placing his back to the camera. "You can't fire Torres."

"Why not? Sure, you're young, but you're a leader. You're knowledgeable. Most importantly, you're willing to listen and give feedback without ego."

"Beside the major fact that I'm not ready?"

"Which is why I want you there."

"Aside from that, if you fire Torres right now, he could cripple your app before he leaves. It'll put you a year behind. Starting over."

Laetitia sang about how she was a small fish and Larkin was a shark.

"He signed non-tampering and non-disclosure agreements."

"Men and women swear until death do them part every day …" The look on his face said he no longer believed in happily ever afters.

"Jenny?"

"She wants some time."

"I'm sorry."

His eyes rolled. "She said I was the shark." He huffed. "Clearly, I'm the fish."

The elevator dinged. When the doors opened, they revealed Reagan and her iPad ready to destroy today's to-do list. Her eyes brightened, and she rushed forward. "Vagabon. I love her!"

"New York women are haunted," Harron groaned.

The song ended sweetly.

"By the ghosts of our pasts, for sure." Larkin grabbed the doors to keep from getting stuck on a long elevator ride. "We like the same music. We need to talk more about it."

"My girlfriend liked that music. I think it's a terrible tune."

Larkin stepped off the elevator. Harron waved and pressed a button. The doors closed too soon, taking any further explanation with it. Was it her or the moon? It seemed everyone she interacted with today left her with more questions than when the conversation started.

Shit, she longed to escape. She longed for the roof.

FIVE

—

MARLIS'S JAW HIT THE SMALL, high-top table they sat at in the corner of a crowded bar. Actually, her entire face met the lacquered surface. "No!" She thrashed, gasped, and laughed simultaneously. "You didn't."

"Of course, I did." Genevieve signaled the waiter for another round. "That was the third time that rat fucker tried to blackmail me." She drained the last of her crafted beer from a mug almost too heavy for her to lift. Gen's face scrunched, her shoulders slumped, and she coughed like the lecherous old judge presiding over her latest case. "Let me shove my hand in that honeyed pussy, and I'll see he does sixty to life." The voice that exited her pretty mouth was more foul than the dumpsters they'd passed to get into this place.

"I might throw up my crab cakes," Larkin admitted. "Please, don't ever do that again."

"I won't." Gen straightened and grinned. "He won't either."

"Isn't it illegal to tape someone without their knowledge?" Marlis's shoulders bobbed. "I'm not the lawyer, but I swear I've heard that before."

"It is," Gen agreed with a grin. "But the recording of his crass proposition, along with the boast of power in his position, is enough to keep his hands far away from my ass and his rulings on my side of favorable."

"You're blackmailing him back. Which is also illegal." Mar pointed out the obvious.

"The way of the world, sweetie." Genevieve shoved Mar's half full or empty—depending on one's perception of the world—mug toward her. "You're falling behind, short stack."

"I'm not short," Mar snapped.

Larkin leaned over, prayed she wouldn't tip the table, and grabbed Mar's ankle. She lifted. Five inches of high heel threatened to maim any person who ventured too close. "Not with these weapons, you aren't."

"Christ, Larkin, you'll show off my goods." Marlis wrangled her foot back and straightened her skirt.

"Maybe I'll get you a date with an actual man." Larkin gagged. "These yuppie types you've been entertaining are too ..."

"Prissy to give it to you good," Gen offered.

"Bull's-eye." Larkin drained the rest of her beer and shoved Mar's toward her again.

Marlis picked up the mug with both hands and tipped it up. It took several long gulps, but the golden liquid drained. She slammed the thick glass onto the table. In any of their usual establishments, the sound would have screeched everything around them to a halt. In the ruckus of jukebox music, at least fifty flesh and blood men—none of whom were sporting skinny jeans, nor manicures—and the ten or so girlfriends or hangers-on with them didn't pay the noise any attention.

"I dropped the last of Marc's things off at his office this morning." Marlis sighed.

"Honey, he ran away from a street beggar and left you behind to deal with him." How many times could Larkin gag in one night. "What if he'd been a mugger instead?"

"That asshat would have left you to save his own over-moisturized skin." Genevieve snarled.

"Then he yelled at me for giving the man a gift card, saying that he could spend it on booze just as easily." Marlis planted both hands on the table. "Fuck him."

"Yes!" Larkin fist pumped the sky and instantly regretted it. Her ribs ached.

"That's my girl." Gen high-fived Marlis and yelled at the waiter to hurry with their refills.

Thank goodness their late lunch had turned into an early dinner. It sounded like they could all use a drink or five. She was also grateful for this night. The last thing she needed was to run into another pompous asshole. She needed a man. Not for forever. Hell, not even for the night. Just a few minutes would take the edge off her clawing desire. Her gaze scanned the room. There was a thicker guy in a back booth who looked like he rode a motorcycle. Too bad he had the ponytail to go with it. A man at the bar leaned over to grab his drink from the bartender and exposed a nice bicep. Too nice. He probably wrestled with a 'roid needle on the regular.

She needed someone to make her stop thinking about the man on her roof. When she closed her eyes, she felt his unforgiving forearm band around her waist, yanking her against an impenetrable wall of muscle. He locked her against him. Under the table, her thighs thrashed. Moisture gathered. The folds of her sex pulsed.

It shouldn't be like this. She should be scared. She was

scared. But horny too. No one had ever handled her the way he did.

She should leave now and speed dial her shrink.

"Quit holding out on us, Larkin."

"What?" She choked.

When Larkin came back to the present, Gen had her lawyer's gaze narrowed. "We've let you be quiet long enough. Spill it."

"Spill what?" How had Genevieve found out about her man on the roof? Libby? No, she hadn't reported it to anyone. There's no way they could know. She should have told them by now, but ...

Mar clapped. "Yeah, what'd I miss?"

"Ladies, sorry it took so long." The too young, too thin waiter plopped down their third round. How'd he manage all those mugs with no muscles?

"Thank you," Marlis cheered.

"Thanks," Larkin offered.

Genevieve grabbed hers and chugged.

Maybe that would occupy her long enough to forget that Larkin had been at the interrogation table. Nope. She wiped her mouth with the back of her hand and leaned in. Her breasts pressed against the lacquered wood, shoving her full cleavage higher still. "Bronson Beauregard and his fine vagabond ass is back in town."

Relief drained the nerves from Larkin's body.

Marlis squealed and then swooned, placing the back of her hand to her forehead and everything.

"And," Gen stabbed an accusing finger at her, "you have a date with him."

"What?" Marlis's eyes gleamed like disco balls.

"It's not like that." Larkin waved them off. "How'd you know, anyway?"

"Forget about how I know." Gen rested an elbow on the table and propped her chin atop it. "I want details first." She chased the proclamation with a gulp.

"We both do," Mar interjected.

"It's nothing really. He's back in town. I saw him and his father—"

"Yum, times two." Genevieve licked foam from her upper lip.

Larkin rolled her eyes. "I saw them at that horrible lunch with my father. His family is throwing him a welcome home party, and he asked me to go as his plus one."

"When?" Mar shouted.

"Easy there." Larkin calmed her with both palms out as she would a rabid dog. "The party is Saturday."

"This Saturday? What are you going to wear?" Marlis grabbed her cheeks. "God, it's a good thing we have a spa day already scheduled tomorrow."

"It's not like that," Larkin reiterated. "I'm not sleeping with him."

"I expect the last thing you'll be doing with him is sleeping." Gen cackled as though it was the funniest thing she'd ever said.

Mar joined in.

"Oh, that reminds me. I pushed our appointments to six. That way Libby will be able to make it, and we'll get a full day of work in." Larkin grabbed her phone and shot them all a quick text. Who knew what they'd remember once tomorrow hit.

"Yay, Libby!" Mar squealed.

"I'm glad for Libby, but I was looking forward to blowing off a half day of work." Gen syphoned off the last of her beer.

"I didn't say you couldn't." Larkin clanked her mug to Gen's and then Mar's. "Hell knows, you deserve it."

They drank, paid, squeezed into the back of Mar's Town Car—sans men—and before Larkin knew it, they were in front of her building.

"Sweet dreams about having Bronson Beauregard's baby," Gen singsonged.

Larkin stepped out into the cold night and looked back at Marlis. "If I pay your driver, will he smother Genevieve in her sleep?"

"No," she whispered. "Mine's not as good as Douglas."

"A shame." She grinned and blew them each a kiss.

"See you tomorrow," Marlis called.

"Mrs. Beauregard," Gen taunted.

Larkin slammed the door in her face and turned toward the building. Her ankles wobbled, and three extra-large beers sloshed around her equilibrium. Great. She searched the street left and right. Nights were quiet in this part of town. Offices filled the structures surrounding her. No right-minded person lived where they worked. Obviously, she was lacking in some corner of her brain.

A hooded jogger paid his dues, renting his fitness and shuffling one foot in front of the other. Cars thundered through the street, utilizing the lower traffic flows to get across town in half the time.

She drew a deep breath, focused on the destination, and walked slowly. The jogger drew near. Each step brought them closer together. Larkin focused on the glass front doors and the light pouring from the interior. His footsteps challenged the concrete. They churned and propelled him. Closer. Her gaze strained to make out his features. His hood was long. It encompassed his face, leaving only a shadow where eyes and a mouth should be.

People jogged these streets all the time. Every day. Men. Women. Fast. Slow. Short. Tall. This man was tall. Taller than any she'd seen before. Thicker too. As thick as the man from the roof.

Larkin swallowed, but nothing moved down her parched throat. Her hands shook, so she shoved them in her pockets. Instinct cried for her to reach for her purse, for her gun, but she shook her head. No. This was just a panic. She was a New Yorker, born and raised, and a jogger would not scare her.

"Good evening," she managed.

He didn't speak. His feet continued churning, propelling so close that the scent of his sweat permeated her nostrils. Her heart rate revved.

The jogger broke even with her, pressing between the few feet from her and the door. Music, harsh and wailing, sank its beats into her eardrums for a second, maybe two, as he passed. As quickly as the tunes came, though, they disappeared.

Larkin stalled. After only a few strides, darkness enveloped the man's broad back. There was no moon. Only the darkest night. A gust of winter air seeped through her coat, and chills cascaded over her entire body. The desire to run after that man and make certain it wasn't her man from the rooftop warred equally with the desire to run inside and seek warmth and safety.

"Miss Ashford?" Lucas stood in front of her. Behind him, the rotating door spun. How had she not noticed his approach? "Is everything all right?"

She blinked and focused on his face. "Yes. I was just enjoying the changing weather before I turned in for the night."

"I'll wait with you." His sweet smile curved. "It's not safe for a woman to be alone ..." He stalled so long, she thought he was leaving that sweeping generalization at her feet. "Not out here, at night." Good for him, he didn't.

"I'm ready to go in." She motioned him ahead.

"Ladies first," he insisted.

"Thank you." Larkin hurried ahead, hoping her bubbly beer haze could keep up. She pushed through the doors, past the deserted main lobby to the mouth of the elevator bank.

"Miss Ashford?"

Damn. Her strides slowed to a stop. Blame the beer and politeness, but she turned.

Lucas walked her way with two large bouquets in stunning crystal vases. "These came for you this evening."

"Oh." Her mind struggled with the calculations. Two vases plus two arms equals no hands with which to open her door. Still, she reached for them. Flowers cheered her up even on the shittiest of days. Today didn't rank that high on the scale. Otherwise, she'd have stopped off for her own damn flowers.

"I'll carry them up." He sidestepped her and walked to the elevator before she could rebut.

"Really, that's not necessary."

"There are over a hundred flowers, two gallons of water, and twenty pounds of crystal in my arms. Don't argue, Larkin. Press the call button."

"Bossy on the late shift." She jabbed the button. The thing lit like the star atop a Christmas tree.

"Last I recall, you liked it." He adjusted a vase cluttered with flesh-pink calla lilies to the side and gave her a questioning look.

Drunk or not, she wouldn't be baited into this conversation. "The service elevator didn't work today."

"I never received any calls about it," he grumbled.

"Surely, I wasn't the only one to have trouble with it." Larkin stepped forward and stabbed the button again. What the hell? The car should be on the bottom floor, waiting, like usual.

"Why were you taking the service elevator?"

"I didn't. It was broken."

"Where were you going?" He hitched a vase of red roses and weird white bulbs with black dots in the center higher on his hip. "I didn't know you knew there was a service elevator in the building."

It was her building. Of course, she knew there was a service elevator. Service stairs too, which she'd taken. The elevator dinged, and the doors opened.

"Never mind." She stepped inside, pressed the button for the top floor, and entered in her passcode. Soon, they were closed inside together. Maybe she'd pass out standing up and not be expected to carry on civil conversation.

"So you're fucking Bronson Beauregard." His gaze cut to hers.

"Excuse me!" Her bubbly beer haze evaporated in pure indignation.

"You could have just told me there was someone else. I'm man enough to understand that you'd want someone with money and homes around the fucking world, instead of war stories he'll never tell you."

"I'm not fucking anyone. Not that it's any of your business."

"Come on, Larkin." Lucas shook the vase of calla lilies. "He dropped these off himself. Not a florist shop delivery guy. Bronson fucking Beauregard. A man doesn't do that unless he's in deep."

"Bronson dropped them off?"

"I'm surprised you didn't see him. He left less than a minute before you stalled at the front door."

She hadn't seen him, but she might have seen HIM. Which they weren't talking about.

"I get it. He's on your level. I'm not." Lucas shrugged, and the flowers bobbed.

"Christ, Lucas. Bronson and I have been friends since we were young. He just got back into town, and we saw each other at Per Se. I haven't ever fucked him, and I'm not about to start. Fucking people you come in contact with on a regular basis fucks you harder every day after, until it's unbearable." She growled the last word, making certain there was no room for misunderstanding.

"I didn't mean to … Damnit, Larkin. I'm sorry. I just …" He looked at his shoes. The elevator continued its infinite rise.

She relished the silence. And the smell of the flowers. The roses really filled the dank space. "Who sent those?" She held up a hand. "I'm not fucking them, whoever it was."

"I don't know. It was a delivery guy."

The doors opened, and Larkin shot out of the car and to her door. She unlocked it and stopped in the doorway. "I'll take them from here." He hadn't been lying about the weight. She hefted the roses into her arms, walked them to the kitchen island, and then returned for the calla lilies. Luckily, he'd stayed put outside.

"Thank you for carrying them up. I wouldn't have been able to manage them both." She took the remaining vase.

"Let me come in." He stepped forward and leaned one thick shoulder on the doorframe. "I'll make you forget the day and all the stupid stuff I said." His fingers grazed her cheek, brushing a strand of hair that had fallen from her ponytail behind her ear. "Then I'll go."

Larkin might be the only woman in the history of women who hated when men pulled that move. Who gave them the right to shove hair behind someone's ear? It was uncomfortable, belittling, and possessive. If she wanted hair behind her ear, she'd put it there. The irritant was enough to take the edge off his proposition. It gave her perspective enough to look past the screaming orgasm he promised to the added layers of shit she'd have to deal with days after.

No matter what he promised in the late hours, he wasn't the type to fuck and forget. She'd already learned that the hard way. Never double down on a bad bet.

"Good night, Lucas." Larkin gave him a friendly nod and closed the door. The electronic lock did its job without trying to fuck her. Why couldn't Lucas? She flipped the deadbolt. It thunked into place, and she hurried to the counter. The flowers were heavy.

She set the calla lilies next to the odd arrangement and shucked her jacket onto the back of the sofa. Her fingers tore open Bronson's card first. An embossed BBB scrawled the front of the card. The interior …

Larkin gasped.

"Looking forward to Sunday morning. Love, Bronson." Larkin bit her tongue. "Seriously?" There weren't any more provocative flowers than skin-colored calla lilies. The flowers, in any color, looked like a vagina. The card could not be any more suggestive. She dropped it onto the counter. "I will not sleep with Bronson. I will not sleep with Bronson."

While she chanted her plan, she opened the second card and pulled it out. The front was blank. The interior …

Larkin gasped.

Her heart flipped inside out. With every beat, it compressed her veins until they might explode. She'd been called worse in her life, certainly, but never in quite this way. Her lips refused to give the word more life than it had in her hand, in her home, on this card. Her gaze found the morbidly shaped berries that looked like eyes, then the word.

CUNT.

SIX

"MISS ASHFORD."

"MISS ASHFORD."

Douglas stood on the curb in front of her building in the waning sunlight as unassuming as ever, but this man was a weapon. He'd been hardened over time and tasks. The one she'd given him last night was child's play. Even Lucas could do it but asking a favor of him would cost a price she refused to pay.

"Larkin," she chided, but it lacked the heart of days before.

"Yes, ma'am." He offered his elbow. Today his smile was on vacation too. In its place, he wore a no-nonsense scowl.

"Wait up!" Lucas ran from the rotating doors. "Why didn't you tell me we were leaving?"

"Because we're not." She gestured between the three of them. Her finger shifted to her and Douglas. "We are.

It's spa day."

"But—" Lucas began.

"I think my heart can handle women running around in robes all evening, Lucas. And, if not, I'll die a happy man." He shooed the younger man away and waved Larkin forward.

When she grabbed Douglas's sturdy arm, he ushered her to the back door of the blacked-out Town Car. She steered him toward the front. "I'm sitting with you today."

"No, ma'am." He stopped their progress cold. The man was strong for fifty plus. "It'll look suspicious."

"I don't care," she snipped.

"Which is why you pay me to care." He walked her to the back door and opened it wide. "I poured you two fingers of happy Friday."

"Stubborn old coot." She tossed herself onto the back seat.

"Brat."

If the shoe fit.

Douglas closed the door, climbed in behind the driver's seat, and soon pulled away from the corner. At the front door of the building, Lucas stood sentry, a pissed sentry. He'd wanted to ride along every day since the attack, non-attack on the roof.

Oh well.

"Went and shat where you eat, didn't you?" Douglas's wise voice carried from the front of the car.

"What's that?" Larkin cupped her ears. "I can't hear you from all the way up there."

"Oh, child." His gray head shook.

The car crawled through Friday afternoon traffic. Larkin waited for him to speak. Stubbornly, he refused until she broke.

"Do I have to beg?"

"No. You have to promise never to sleep with Lucas

Backstrom again, or, at the very least, fire him before you do."

"I promise." The glass of whisky beckoned. She tossed it back. The liquid burned just the right amount. "I learned my lesson."

"Let's hope so."

He drove in silence.

"So? Flowers? The card?"

"The woman who owns the flower shop won't betray clients by giving out information unless it's in the form of a warrant from the police."

Larkin groaned.

"Do you want me to get one?"

"No." The last thing she needed was the police sniffing around her life. She didn't have anything to hide, but she had a lot to lose, which made good people grabby. "The card is harmless, really."

"That's what I thought." He turned onto East 76th, the street on which The Surrey lived, which housed her spa of choice.

"That it's harmless?"

"No." His groan reverberated around the front seat. "That you'd say leave the cops out of it. Otherwise, I would have already called a friend in the department."

"Oh." Larkin rolled the cup between her palms.

"Want me to persuade her in other ways?"

"No," she chided.

"I wouldn't hurt her." Something in Douglas's monotone didn't reassure Larkin. Scaring the woman to the point of spilling her guts wouldn't leave a scratch on her exterior, but she knew from experience that the interior was another story entirely.

"No. It was a stupid card. I've gotten hate mail before."

"Facebook comments don't count." Douglas eased the car into the far-right lane and jockeyed for a position at

The Surrey's main entrance.

"Could you tell that to the world or the thirteen-year-old girls whose hearts are broken on a daily basis by internet trolls?"

"Yes, but they won't listen. Just like you're not listening." He pulled in front of the intricately carved scrawled concrete awning.

Larkin set the cup down, leaned forward, and poked her head through the open partition. "I'll not have you torture an innocent woman to get information. Those days are behind you. It's fine."

Douglas placed the car in park. He turned his wide shoulders to face her, the day's scowl still in full effect. "It was flagrant and personal."

"Maybe I pissed someone off. It happens, you know."

"Oh, I know." He patted her cheek ever so briefly.

Her chest warmed. The move was so protective and endearing. Fatherly, almost. Her father had never made her feel that way. She closed her eyes to keep from tearing up. A smile stretched across her face. When her eyes opened, the fear of exposure had passed, but Douglas had caught the vulnerability.

His wise gaze studied her more closely. "What's wrong?"

"Nothing. As long as you leave that poor woman alone."

The car door opened, and Tony, the doorman, offered his hand. "Miss Ashford."

Larkin blew Douglas a kiss and got out of the car.

"Hello, Tony. How are you today?"

"Just fine, miss. And you?" He closed the car door and opened the one leading to bliss, where she could forget about cunts and cocks for a while.

"I'm better now, Tony."

"Glad to hear it, Miss Ashford. You have a swell day,

now." Tony waved her off through the foyer.

Her feet never carried her as fast as when she booked it to the spa entrance … except when she ran from an attacker, non-attacker.

Nope.

This evening wasn't the time for thinking about that or HIM. *Relaxation, here she comes.*

"Hi, Larkin." Tabitha, the spa's director, greeted her with air kisses and a flute of champagne. The woman had to be in her mid-to-late sixties. Tabby was old and worldly enough to call her by her first name. She'd worked in the spa industry on one level or another since LBJ was in the White House. But you couldn't tell it by looking at her perfect porcelain complexion or the way she whisked from room to room, assuring everyone had everything their hearts desired.

"Tabby, how are you?"

"When will you stop asking? This is about you, darling." She whipped Larkin into the crook of her arm. The director's jet-black ponytail cascaded over her shoulder and settled halfway down her back. Together, they marched.

"Never."

"Well, you're late," she whispered, using proper spa voice past the reception area.

"Am not." Larkin glanced at her watch. "I'm right on time."

"Then your posse is early. They're awaiting you in the Superior Couples Suite." Tabby shooed her into the pied-à-terre-style locker room. She felt more at home in the French minimalist enclosure than she did her own homes.

"Thank you, Tabby."

"Shoo. Shoo." The woman scolded her as though she was a child.

"Thank you, Tabby," she mouthed.

Tabitha waved over her shoulder. Her long ponytail swished behind her while her hips sashayed out of the room.

Larkin and her friends didn't get the special room because they were better than anyone. They'd been given that room years ago upon their first trip to the Cornelia Spa, actually, when the staff figured out their "spa voices" were about ten decibels too loud for the near silent establishment. She chuckled to herself while she stripped off the bindings of the world, placed them in her locker for safekeeping until she was ready to face it again, and pulled on the fluffy robe and slippers.

When she opened the door to the suite, she found Marlis and Genevieve on the long white sofa refilling their flutes from a chilled bottle of Laherte Frères, Rosé Ultradition. Libby sat on one of the two massage tables in the center of the room, ostensibly claiming her spot in the rotation. A messy bun of brunette hair sat atop her head, and she clutched a full glass with two hands. Red weaved a web across the whites of her eyes, muddling the usual green pop of her irises.

"What'd I miss?" Larkin shut the door in a hurry and offered the top of her flute to Gen who filled it without question.

"Us pestering Libby to give us details about her big case." Marlis tucked her legs under her and turned her intent brown gaze on Libby.

"It'll only take you two glasses to crack, lightweight. You might as well spill it before they separate us," Larkin prodded.

"You bitches are the worst," Libby snarled.

"And the best," Gen sang.

"Seriously, they should hire us to interrogate people." Mar patted Gen's shoulder. "Give us an extended wine budget and half the day. Ha! They'd know all they needed to know without any bloodshed."

Libby buried her face in her hand.

"Drink up, Lib. You know they have a point." Larkin walked to her friend, planted a kiss on her cheek, then propped a hip on the edge opposite her.

"I do, which is the problem." Libby downed the entire flute in two gulps. "Fine, I've officially met my quota to talk." She crisscrossed her legs and turned to face the group. Her eyes brightened. "I didn't get the lead I was hoping for, but I was able to cross some people off my list."

"What are you looking for again? People? What'd they do?" Marlis rambled.

"I'm looking for one person in particular. He's collecting the largest private stash of weapons the United States has ever seen." Libby's head flopped from one side to the other. "Well, not seen yet, but heard about."

"Who is he?" Genevieve begged. "A prepper or a terrorist?"

"I don't know." Libby sighed.

"Yet." Larkin lifted her glass.

The familiar knock of handsome devils coming to do the work of angels fluttered on the door.

"To Libby finding her guy," Larkin finished.

On the sofa, the girls cheered. Whether for Libby's success or the start of the massage, soak, steam rotation, she wasn't sure.

"Come in," Libby called.

The door opened, and Eric stepped inside and closed the door behind him. She had to give it to the new guy. He was a quick learner. "Ladies, are you finding everything to your liking so far; room temperature, champagne? Are we ready for some amuse-bouche?"

"We'll wait until later to amuse our mouths, love." Gen delivered the line with her signature half-lidded gaze and sexy smirk.

The other girls giggled.

For crying out loud. They were determined to get kicked out of the spa or sued one day. At least they knew a good lawyer.

"Everything is perfect, Eric." Larkin straightened. "Thank you."

"Wonderful." He pointed outside the door and then to himself. "Clive and I will be your masseurs this evening. Will you and Miss Irish be taking your massages first?"

"Yes," Libby announced.

"Very well. I'll give you a few minutes to undress to your comfort level. Please lie face up under the sheet." He turned to Gen and Mar. "Ladies, if you would please make certain to close the door to the bathroom fully this time."

Marlis's cheeks burned as red as a winter fire.

"Of course. I certainly thought I had last time." Genevieve crossed her legs. The terrycloth robe fell open, revealing a wealth of skin from painted toes to upper thigh.

"Of course." Eric's trained gaze hit the ceiling. Cocks, though, couldn't be trained as well as the eyes. His grew until it pressed a handsome outline against the front of his pants. He nodded and rushed from the room, still careful to close the door without a whisper of sound.

Libby fell forward cackling.

Marlis fanned herself with a group of pamphlets about spa services. None of which included a happy ending.

"Genevieve Holst." Larkin walked to the side table, set down her flute, grabbed a towel, and tossed it over Gen's legs. "Stop trying to expose yourself to the staff. You'll get us kicked out."

"You've already gotten me kicked out of heaven." Marlis stabbed the air between them with a pamphlet. "You better not get me kicked out of my happy place."

"Don't blame your proclivity for yuppies and married men on me." Genevieve stood and strode for the bathroom for an aromatically infused soak or a turn in the steam shower.

"I didn't know he was married. There was no ring." Marlis tossed down the pamphlet and stomped after her. "Not even a ring tan line."

"What's your excuse for the yuppies?" Libby slipped her naked curves between the sheets.

"Match point." Larkin untied her robe.

Another soft knock sounded on the door. The room fell silent. Narrowed gazes slid around the room from one to another. Staff here always gave them more than enough time to get into position for their services. It kept the likelihood of a peep show to a minimum, or as close to the minimum as they would come with Gen there. Her friend stepped forward, still robed luckily, and opened the door.

Eric appeared in the slit. "I'm sorry to bother you again, but this came in from Miss Ashford's company."

"And it can't wait until after?" Genevieve propped a hand on her hip.

"It was labeled urgent. I apologize." Eric handed over a small envelope and bowed his head. "I'll give you ladies a few extra minutes to get situated."

"Thank you, Eric." Gen took the envelope, closed the door, then turned on Larkin. "Seriously? Can they not wipe their asses without you?"

"Most days." She expected any urgent news to come in a large envelope. A contract that needed her signature. A termination form that needed her initials.

Gen handed over the greeting card-size envelope embossed with her company's logos, and then huffed toward the bathroom entrance.

"I thought we said no work stuff on spa days?" Marlis huffed.

"Some of us live in the real world," Libby piped. "Real world shit doesn't care whether you're in the middle of a screaming orgasm or in the supermarket restocking the kitchen that hasn't seen a real vegetable or fruit in over a month."

"Speaking from experience, I guess." Gen shook her head. Surely, lamenting the orgasm interruption.

Larkin ignored them and ripped the edge of the envelope. The moment the plain white card cleared the encasement, she knew what it was. Her fingers froze to the unfeeling exterior. The moisture in her mouth turned to dust. She opened the edge with stiff extremities to find the word she'd known would be there, as decisive and defamatory as it had been the night before.

"Who do you have to fire now?" Gen's commanding voice filled the room.

"What?" Larkin jerked her gaze from CUNT and blinked the girls into view.

"What's wrong?" Marlis's soft eyes begged for understanding.

If the girls knew about the card—or now cards—they'd freak out. Libby most of all. They'd demand heightened security, which was the last thing she needed. Lucas at her side 24/7.

No way.

Larkin cleared her throat, shoved the card inside its sleeve, and stuffed it inside the pocket of her robe. "Nothing and no one." At least, she hoped she didn't have to fire anyone. The stationery had come from her office, but surely that didn't mean it was someone who worked for her. Anyone could get their stationery. Couldn't they? If they could, what did that say about her security? If they couldn't, what did that mean for her—that she worked with someone who tormented her? To what end?

"Then why'd they bother you now?" Libby's eyebrows crinkled.

"Just incompetence." Larkin slid the open robe off her

shoulders and hung it on the rack near the door.

"Anyone have a tampon?" Marlis whined. "I'm good for now, but I used the last of my briefcase stash."

"You really need to change your birth control," Genevieve barked.

That was one way to get past the envelope interruption. She needed to think without their wise gazes honed on her.

"I know. I know," Mar hissed. "Who has time to …"

When Larkin turned, every eye in the room was locked in her direction.

She was naked with these women at least once a month. They were all naked or at some point of undress together on nearly a daily basis. The birth control she used to regulate her body offered the lovely side effect of no period, so she didn't have to worry about a junior high school bloody legs situation.

"What?" Larkin turned, giving them a full frontal, and shrugged enough to make her boobs bounce. The bruise across her ribs drew her attention to the thing they were all fixated upon. How had she forgotten? The fucking envelope, that's how.

"Larkin?" Marlis squeaked.

"Holy shit!" Genevieve bellowed.

"What the hell happened?" Libby held the sheet to her chest and sat. Her gaze cataloged the length and width of each anomaly.

"Calm down." She used her spa voice to accentuate the point. A surprise impulse to cover up took hold, and she hurried to the table and slipped under the cover.

"Explain now," Libby demanded.

Larkin sat forward, holding tightly to the sheet. She should have come up with an alternate story. Something that wouldn't scare them as much as the truth. Her cheeks filled with air. Slowly, she blew it out.

The whispered knock sounded on the door. Marlis rushed past the table and opened the door a crack. "I'm sorry, but we're going to need a few more minutes." Mar didn't wait for a response. She closed it just as quickly and hurried back to her spot.

"I'd ask if you can promise not to freak out, but I know that's not possible." Her gaze traveled to each of her friends.

Marlis stepped forward. "Honey, did Lucas—"

"No!" Her nose crinkled at the thought. If he laid a hand on her, she'd have him in jail or at the bottom of the Hudson.

"So just tell us," Libby pushed.

"Lucas and I were just a one-time thing." She huffed and corrected, "A couple of times thing. We're not now. It's really nothing."

"That's not nothing." Libby gestured to Larkin's entire body. "You look like you've been body slammed."

"Are you getting into that kinky shit?" Genevieve asked as straight-faced as she ever was. "If you are, you be the one with the whip. It's more fun that way."

"No. You have to promise you'll try not to freak out." They shrugged or nodded to one degree or another, and she told an abbreviated version of what happened on the roof.

For several seconds, they were silent. The spa staff probably thought they'd died because there was a knock on the door. Marlis rushed to it again, begged for ten more minutes, and promised they'd be tipped well for waiting. When Gen didn't toss in a lewd comment about showing her gratitude, Larkin realized the seriousness of the situation.

Marlis walked to her side. Her friend's cold fingers rested on her shoulder and squeezed. "I know the roof is your happy place, but why were you so close to the edge?"

Her question was quiet. Too quiet.

They were all quiet, waiting for her to answer.

"I just lost it a little after that meeting." Larkin blinked tears away. Shit. She hadn't been this quick to cry since her mother … "Everything came to a head, and I needed out."

"You weren't trying to …?" Genevieve couldn't complete the thought. Thank goodness.

"No." Larkin shook her head so hard, her ponytail flopped.

They took a collective moment.

"Some fucked-up knight in shining armor shit." Gen plowed a hand through her loose red hair.

"I don't want or need one of those," Larkin explained.

"You don't even need us." Genevieve hugged her arms around herself, clutching the terrycloth with both hands.

"What does that mean?" She kicked her feet off the side of the table and sat straighter.

"She doesn't mean it in a bad way." Marlis fanned the air as though trying to eliminate a foul odor. "It's just … you didn't tell us about a potentially life-altering situation in which you were involved. You're so independent that it sometimes feels like you're pacifying us."

Larkin had no idea what to do with that. She was independent out of necessity. It was how she'd grown up. It was how she'd survived. "I was in shock. I thought he would kill me."

"He could have," Libby interjected. "You need to carry your gun on you at all times.

She flipped the sheet back, revealing her bare ass to the collective. "All times?"

Libby flipped her sheet back. A leather strap hugged her otherwise naked hips.

"I bet you don't take it into the steam shower or tub," Larkin countered.

"No." Libby's green eyes rolled. "But it'll be in easy

reach."

"Sorry, but I'm fresh out of garter belt gun holsters and whatever you call that thing around your hips." Larkin pointed at her friend's ass.

"Ah." Genevieve shucked her robe. "I don't think she has to worry about Bronson killing her."

"I don't think I have to worry about being naked with Bronson," Larkin countered.

"I'm calling bullshit." Marlis untied her robe and followed Gen into the bathroom and closed the door completely.

Libby stared at her. "Bronson? What else did I miss?"

"Do you want a massage or more gossip?" Larkin lay on the table, straightened the sheet over her breasts, and relaxed her arms.

Libby did the same and looked at her. "I want both."

SEVEN

WALKING THROUGH THE WALDORF ASTORIA'S grand Park Avenue entrance had always been a treat. A slice of old New York. A reminder of more decadent and unhurried times. When architecture was art and art was life. Tonight, the majesty of empty corridors and stunning art deco opulence lodged itself in her throat.

"Amazing, huh?" Bronson smiled.

He should have been looking at the perfection of design from the gold leafed carved molding, to the steel inlayed windows, to the details in the circular "Wheel of Life" floor mosaic crafted from hand-cut marble tiles. She couldn't pull her gaze away from the building nor keep it still for more than a few seconds. There were so many things to see that she'd never taken the time to catalog.

Why she had to do it tonight was beyond her, but it felt as though it'd be her last chance. Things were changing, but change didn't scare her. If handled properly, it bred opportunity. Would the project renovators take care to preserve the history in these walls? Would she take care to ensure her business succeeded in the choppy seas of the public market?

"Come on. We'll be late." He tugged her through the lobby to the elevators.

"I've never known you to worry about punctuality." She almost snorted.

Bronson shifted the bow tie strangling him and studied his distorted reflection in the metal doors. His fingers ran the boundary of his coiffed blond hair, ensuring every strand held the line. After everything was just so, the doors opened. He ushered her on, holding too tightly to her silver-gray woolen cape.

"For a long time, I wasn't concerned with it. A watch. Clocks." He pressed the button for the third floor but held fast to her back. "They were superfluous accessories. I came and went as I pleased."

The man sharing the car with her was a different one than who she'd known years ago. A different one than she'd seen in his safari pictures. His hair had never seen a comb, much less hairspray, in his months spent on the South African coast. The sun had licked his skin and the wind whipped his hair to Mother Nature's will.

"Those times are behind me. Now, I'm honed in on my future." His gaze dropped to hers. All the playfulness he'd possessed days ago looked as though they'd never had a home in his piercing stare.

"Do you feel burdened by your father's expectations for you and the company?" The kind of pressure Brice Beauregard could place on a person was enough to make anyone act outside their character.

"No. Beauregard's is my legacy. I'm ready to make my mark on it. To bring it into the 21st century. To secure its place in the world for my children."

The elevator dinged and opened on the third floor. Transition kept Larkin from tripping over her tongue.

His children?

Women were supposed to be the ones with biological clocks, not men. Hers wasn't making a peep, and she thanked the heavens above. Bronson's, on the other hand, sounded a gong.

He hustled them to coat check and stripped off his overcoat. Larkin did the same with her cape, and then handed it over to the woman behind the counter. While Bronson requested the coats be put in a special spot for quick retrieval, she stepped away. His pampered persona made her queasy. This Bronson wouldn't slay a subway rat, much less a dragon. Which was all well and good because she wasn't screwing him. Not tonight. Not ever. She hadn't expected that sticking to her guns would be so easy, but …

"Holy fuck."

Larkin turned to see Bronson's gaze honed in on her body. It stroked her up one side and down the other. She stood straight and waited until he met her eyes.

"I expected you to look lovely, as always, but this." He used both hands to mold the air into the swell of her breasts and the curves of her hips. "Good night. That is the dress to end all dresses. You wear it with such intent the world will come to heel, willingly."

She looked at the silver sequined double plunged top that seamlessly morphed into silk lace flowers, and then again into flowing rose gold tulle. The neckline and high-waisted slit were boisterous. All the important parts were covered, though. It held the art deco elegance she'd wanted to honor the Waldorf with. Judging by Bronson's sure steps to her side, the arm he offered, and the sideways eyeball fuck, he fully assumed she'd worn it for him and him alone.

Perhaps she had. Every girl wanted to be desired, even if her intentions were purely platonic. She needed to find a buffer soon.

He paused at the closed ballroom doors.

When have they ever been closed for a party?

"Ready?" he asked with a wicked grin.

"Always," she hoped aloud.

Bronson nodded to a man she hadn't noticed earlier who then spoke into a headset. Music on the other side of the doors simmered, and a voice took its place. "Now for the guest we've all been waiting for. The only child of Brice and Bitsy Beauregard. Heir to the Beauregard fortune, returning to stake his claim on the world after studying it for ten years. Bronson Brice Beauregard."

His last name hung on the man's lips through the uproarious applause, through the WTF rant in Larkin's head, through the doors bursting and a spotlight blinding her. She wasn't ready. Not for this. Not at all.

Her date pulled her forward into the grand ballroom. Tables bursting with people and high-topped vases overflowing with white flowers surrounded them, sucking up every bit of the oxygen in the place. People patted her on the back, as though she'd done some great thing by placing one foot in front of the other. That probably was a feat. Every instinct in her body told her to stop, turn, and run. Well, maybe stop and punch Bronson for not warning her about the wedding reception style entrance, then turn and run.

He hoisted their interlaced hands into the air as though they'd just made it official. The crowd reached a fevered pitch. He wasn't a New Kid on the Block, and she wasn't Posh Spice. This wasn't a concert. This wasn't a union of any kind. This was all wrong. She was Pissed Spice.

Larkin moved deeper and deeper into the rabbit hole

because of her inability to form a single word or apply the brakes. Bronson pulled her up onto the stage. The leader of Emerald City Band egged him on with a massive smile and hopping feet.

Her inner monologue ran on both sides of the fence and barked pros and cons between the slats like frantic dogs.

Fuck this. Don't make a scene. I'm going to kill him. It's a public venue, so people will see. You won't fare well in prison. What an asshole. He didn't know it would be such a production. Screw this, I'm leaving. If you go public, you'll want these people's backing. To hell with going public ... I'll do it on my own like I have been for years.

Everything internal and external locked up when the band member handed Bronson the microphone. Business mode took hold. She knew how to command a room. Despite Bronson, she'd show these people exactly why she ran a successful business and would continue to, regardless of whether she went public.

She set up jokes for him to slam home. She played the attentive date. She worked the room. For two solid hours.

"Larkin, darling."

"No," she hissed under her breath.

"Felix." One of the men in the group of bankers she and Bronson had been conversing with lifted his hand and offered her father a sideways salute.

"Gentlemen." Her father nodded to each man. "If you don't mind, I'm going to steal my daughter away for a few minutes."

None of them minded.

Jerks.

"Darling." Like a caring father would, he looped her hand through his arm and strolled her away at a leisurely pace. "How are you?"

Tired of bullshit and hungry enough to eat it. "I'm

well. And you?"

"Oh, I'm just trying to figure out why you're here as Bronson Beauregard's plus one, and I knew nothing about it."

"Seriously?" She steered them to a server carrying hors d'oeuvres. Larkin swiped two canapés, tossed the tiny things into her mouth the moment the waiter was out of sight, and maneuvered toward another server with flutes of champagne.

"Yes, seriously." He pulled on her arm to slow their strides. "I received an invitation only yesterday because I spoke with Brice at The Club."

The Club stood for The Metropolitan Club New York. It was started by newly monied men at the turn of the 19th century, boasting such names as Vanderbilt, Morgan, and Roosevelt. Her father had no business maintaining a membership, especially since he couldn't afford another divorce.

"If you have an actual question, I'll answer it if I can." She plucked two glasses of bubbly from the server and thanked him.

Her father immediately reached for one of the flutes. The plan had been to demolish both and chase down another server for two more, but she handed it over.

"When's the big day?"

"Excuse me?" Larkin choked. Carbonation fizzed its way up her nose.

"He introduced you to all of New York as his. I assumed you two were planning a formal engagement announcement, and that, again, I'd be the last to know."

"No. We're not even dating. And really, you can't talk to me about being the last to know things." She set her flute on the nearest table. "You were in Monaco celebrating the honeymoon of your second sham wedding before I knew about it."

"Larkin, really." Her father's gaze scanned their immediate surroundings. Every eyeball was transfixed on the larger-than-life band and not their familial drama.

She pinched the bridge of her nose, willing the pounding behind her eyes to stop. It didn't, but one thing could. This back and forth with her father could stop tonight. She drew a deep breath and grabbed both his hands.

"I don't want to fight with you anymore. You're the only family I have. So from now on, I'm going to put forth effort. The past is in the past, but it haunts me. Your inability to admit some basic truths haunts you. Let's … I don't know. Let's meet with a therapist together."

"What? No!" He pulled away as though she'd announced to the room that her father likes cock. Only a handful would be surprised, and those were the same people who still thought white bread was a wholesome food.

"Why not?"

"I'm not discussing personal matters with a stranger." Her father dropped into the nearest chair. His elbow dug into the table, and he rested his head in his hand. Larkin pulled out the chair next to him and sat. She leaned in.

"It wouldn't be someone you met on the street. These are professionals with expertise in human emotion and psyche. They're also a neutral party."

"We're not having this conversation. Especially not here." His hand made a small shield between them.

"Fine." She grabbed the champagne flute back from her father, gulped down the liquid, and discarded the glass. "I'll come to the house. We can talk over tea if that will make you feel better."

"It won't. You're not invited to the house." He straightened. His blue eyes and indignant scowl pierced her heart. The words hurt too.

"Why?" The question left her lips as a squeak. It was

lost among the first few titled words of Montell Jordan's "This is How we Do It."

"This is our song, princess." While Larkin's jaw still scraped the silk tablecloth, Bronson rounded the chair, grabbed her hand, and pulled her to her feet.

"You kids have fun." Her father waved them off as though he hadn't just crushed the hope and determination blooming in her chest.

Bronson weaved them through a sea of sequins and skin, undulating hips and pumping fists that hadn't yet caught on to the change in tempo from Journey's "Don't Stop Believing." He stopped near the center of the dance floor, and she stared at him blankly. Her brain wasn't inside her skull. It was back … under the heels of her father's Italian leather shoes.

"I won't let him ruin your night." His fingers tightened around hers. A genuine smile played across his full lips.

"Can you stop him from it? I can't."

"Please." Bronson tugged her closer and pointed at his chest. "Dragon slayer. Remember? If I can take out dragons, that clown is nothing." A svelte arm curved against her back. "Less than nothing." He winked. His hips found the upbeat rhythm.

Suddenly, her brain was back between her ears, snapping the room into focus. Smiles surrounded them. Joy and excitement radiated in the crush of gyrating bodies. Her date became the center point of that elation. Tension fell away, pushed out by the music. They'd danced to this song in elementary school and had no clue what the words meant. The only thing they knew was they'd liked the beat and the, "La ra ra ra ra ra."

"There's the smile I know." His arm loosened, and he backed up with a side-to-side slide in time with the music. When he popped a move or two from the music video, she lost it in a fit of giggles.

They danced—song after song—and the world disappeared. For a little while, she was a kid again. She hadn't been one for long. When she had been, though, Bronson had been there with his early release Xbox and collection of Adam Sandler movies. Movies her mother didn't approve of. They hadn't understood them, but they watched anyway. Just to be able to tell the kids at school they had. Here he was tonight, making her crazy and causing her to swing from outrage to delight. Much as they had as kids.

Brittany's "Toxic" faded away. She blotted at the fine sheen of sweat coating her brow and grinned.

"Thank you, Bronson."

"It's my pleasure." He slid from his jacket, tossing it to a guy she didn't know.

A voice whispered over the speaker, "Get up. Get up. Get up. Get up. Wake up. Wake up. Wake up. Wake up." Marvin Gaye took his turn singing sweetly about getting down tonight.

Bronson moved close, swaying his shoulders from one side to another. He hooked an arm around her waist and pulled them pelvis to pelvis.

"Oh, no." She laughed.

"Oh, yes." His hips ground side to side.

Before she knew it, Bronson's sexual healing invaded the minimal space between them. Hard. Long. Invasive. He leaned close. The tips of his fingers bit into her shoulders, forcing her forward. Their chests brushed together. His breath cascaded across her neck.

"Bronson?"

"Yeah?" His lips brushed the crest of her cheek.

"We're friends, right?"

Just friends.

"Hell, yes." His dick ground against her as though it were trying to find its way in.

"Do you know the fastest way to ruin a friendship?"

"Everyone does. Fuck your friend." He kissed her neck just below her ear.

"Exactly." She stared at the gold cord looping from one balcony to the next. "Since you know, I shouldn't have to explain to you this isn't a thing we're going to do."

His hand slipped to the dimples in her lower back. He leaned away only enough to clash their gazes. A mischievous glint flickered deep inside those emerald greens.

"Maybe I don't want to be your friend."

Her brow hiked so hard it almost tossed a cramp in her forehead.

"Maybe I want to be your lover."

"I don't take lovers. Lovers turn into husbands or enemies. Both, in time."

"You're too young to be so cynical, Larkin."

"I've lived a lot, and you know it."

The overwhelming lust in his expression dampened. "I'm sorry I moved away when you needed me most."

"Me too."

Bronson lifted her hand to his shirt. He probably intended for her to feel his beating heart, but she felt only cotton, buttons, and silk.

"Larkin." His voice patted her name as though it were a pet. "We travel in the same circles."

"When you're in the country, we do," she agreed. "That hasn't been the case for a long time."

"We're both ambitious. We both enjoy life."

Not as much as she enjoyed work for the oblivion it brought.

"It's possible we'd never make it to enemies." He stared, a challenge brewing in his gaze.

"I need a drink."

"You need my cock inside you and my tongue down your throat."

Her cheeks flamed despite herself and her no-fuck-

Bronson stance. He knew how to work the ladies. He'd been practicing for a while.

"Go get a drink." His hold loosened. "It'll tide you over."

Larkin opened her mouth to argue about not needing to be held over because they were never going to happen, but the self-assured expression on his face kept her quiet. She'd show him. No need to debate a non-issue. She liberated herself from his arms and meandered her way through the crowd toward the nearest tray of champagne.

EIGHT

The flask of whisky she'd fleeced from Douglas had yet to wet her lips. She stalled with the flask just below her nose. Years and aged perfection wafted up her nostrils, tempting her taste buds, but she couldn't drink it. She couldn't have a minute to herself. This was the main reason Larkin's partying days were behind her. Everyone had something to say. She longed for the bustling quiet of the rooftop, but it wouldn't come tonight.

Larkin set the flask on the high-top table then turned to witness Brice Beauregard's approach. Of all the animated statues that blew hot air into the ornate room, he bothered her the least.

"Why, thank you. You don't do too poorly yourself." She offered him a spot at her claim and a kind smile. He sidled up to the table. Even in heels, Larkin craned her neck to meet his gaze.

"I hope that grand entrance didn't throw you for too much of a loop. My Bitsy has a flair for the dramatic. And where our son is concerned, everything is dramatic."

"I'm not going to lie. It was more than I anticipated." She stole a sip of whisky and relished the flavors marbling in her mouth.

"Bitsy is more than most people anticipate." He patted his heart. "I knew what I was getting myself into, which only makes me question my sanity every other week."

"I admire you two. Your marriage has lasted where most have failed." Larkin offered Brice the engraved silver container.

"It's not without its efforts." He took it, downed a hefty gulp, and handed it back. "That's some genuine whisky."

"My driver's private collection."

Brice nodded. "The key is finding your person. When you find the right one, nothing will stand in your way."

He nodded but ignored her plea to shift the conversation from relationships to liquor. Liquor she could speak about intelligently. Relationships, not even close. She placed the cap on the flask and screwed it on tightly. Her gaze leveled Brice's.

"Please don't tell me you're here to lobby for marriage. Especially not my marriage. Your friend Cornish is more than enough to handle on that front."

"I apologize for his behavior." He sneered.

Her business couldn't progress with two of the biggest figures on the board opposing her, so his sneer offered comfort. She snatched it up like a freshly cracked cask of Macallan. After the proverbial beating she'd taken from her father and tailspin Bronson put her through, the welcomed relief washed over her drawn shoulders. It eased them from her earlobes and guided the flow of air through her lungs once more.

"Thank you, Brice. Really." She hugged the flask between her palms.

The night wasn't a waste, after all.

Brice rested an elbow on the table top and turned to face her. His kind gaze searched hers. The hood of his brows narrowed.

Larkin waited. For what, she didn't know.

"Cornish hasn't the tact, but he has a point."

The reconstruction of her night gave way. A landslide. The ground beneath her shifted. Doom.

"Think about it," he whispered conspiratorially. "With the Duo branch, you run a company that sets trends for brides. With Ditto, you sway mothers-to-be on everything from feeding regimens for their unborn children to the perfect shade to paint the nursery."

"And?" Her fingernails clung to the bark of the last standing tree.

"And you are unmarried and childless."

It gave way with the others. They shifted, careening down the mountain. The mass gathered speed. It gathered more debris. It tumbled. It crashed. She lay at the bottom of the pile, unwilling to give up the fight.

"I am not the face of my company. For those reasons you stated, I explicitly branded the company without my likeness. It stands on its own with the market, and product researchers I employ speak to trends as well as the health and well-being of brides, mothers, and babies."

"True. You're doing an amazing job."

The concession felt like an intro, rather than a pure offering. "But?"

"You can't tell me the public doesn't pay attention to your life."

"Sure, they do. With articles about the self-made millionaire." She kicked the sentence at him as though it were a ball of success, straight to the face.

"And the series of men you're dating."

"I don't date." The ball grew heavy and cumbersome. The whisky turned to poison in her stomach.

"Exactly. And the people know it." He gestured around the room "So many of them are here tonight only to see what we'll reveal to them. What they can share on the internet or with a reporter to gain a buck."

Where the fuck was Genevieve? Her friend had promised she was coming tonight, and she'd seen hide nor red hair. She could use that hair at this juncture because it would distract a man like Brice. No matter how much he thought himself above others, above the moral deterioration, Larkin had seen the way he looked at her friend when he thought no one was looking.

"When you go public, it is no longer about how that affects you. It's about how it affects your bottom line. It's about how it affects your investors' bottom lines."

Larkin stood, wane of speech and full of bile.

"I hope I delivered my thoughts more appropriately than my friend."

"Much more so," she choked out.

"Wonderful then. I'll leave you to it. Good evening, Miss Ashford."

"Good evening, Mr. Beauregard."

"Just call me Dad."

"Dad?"

A thousand times throughout her life, Larkin questioned whether her father was, in fact, her biological half. Even with her father's proclivities, she'd never given real credence to the notion. But was Brice saying …

"It has a nice ring to it." Brice smoothed a hand over his double-breasted tux and leaned closer. "Think about it. Bronson, the head of the world's premier diamond supplier. You, the head of the world's premier wedding and family media empire. Together, you two could own the world."

So, not her father, but Dad. Her bile vanished. In its place raged the lumen power of the sun. It radiated through her stomach, up her esophagus, and spewed between her lips. "I have no desire to run the world, nor marry your son."

"Think of the power. Think of all the good you could do with that power. The social changes you could back. The lives you could improve."

He raked in almost twice the amount of money she did, and her charitable giving was more than double his. Brice Beauregard cared nothing about the lives of those beneath him except how they could bend them to his benefit. At the moment. Hers, in particular.

"Just think on it." He waved wildly to someone across the room and took off.

Larkin shoved the flask into her clutch. Her feet thundered toward the exit. How had every man managed to shit on her in the span of a few days? All except for Douglas. She shoved through a side door and rushed to the bathroom. Tulle flared with each stride. Her breaths hissed. She didn't slow for the door. Instead, she lowered her shoulder and wished she'd been born a huge fucking man. Then people wouldn't question her decisions at every turn. Her work, as opposed to her marital status, would show her credibility.

"What a presumptuous piece of trash."

The door swung wide and fast. Its backside smacked the stopper and rebounded quite viciously. She grabbed the door's edge. The will to slam it back once more pulsed in her veins, but the sound of running water killed the impulse. What would the public think? Headlines the next day would read: UNWED BUSINESSWOMAN ON RAMPAGE IN NYC. Her eyes rolled skyward.

A crystal chandelier and gold medallion ceiling reminded her exactly where she was and what was expected of her. The elegantly dressed woman in the reflection of the ornate vanity nook sneered at her.

"Oh, you must be single," she hissed quietly.

The reflection liked the sarcasm. Its smile peeked through the anger and resentment marring her features.

She rounded the vanity and stalled in the entryway.

Water ran full throttle in one of the three marble basins. Air bubbles blasted into the brimming water and rose from the depths. They frothed at the top and poured over the edges, creating a smoothly flowing waterfall. The constant stream forged a small lake in the center of the bathroom. It rippled and pressed its edges wider and wider as she stood in slack-jawed bafflement.

Finally, her gaze thawed. Slowly, it searched the gilded area and heavy wooden stalls. Each stall door hung open and empty, save for one. On the far side of the water, the floor-to-ceiling door stood closed.

"Hello?" Larkin's voice bounced off the hard surfaces and echoed hollowly in her ears.

Where was the bathroom attendant? There was one in every high-end venue throughout the city. Sometimes two or three but never none. Hell, even Yankee Stadium had bathroom attendants.

Maybe they'd gone to contact maintenance.

Larkin grabbed a handful of fabric and hiked it high. She pulled the sparkling Jimmy Choos from her feet and set them to the side. The marble floor cooled her residual anger, and she eased forward.

Cold. Ice cold water flash froze her toes, stealing her breath for a split second. The next, it forced gasps through her lungs. She leaned forward, expecting to find a broken lever. Under her light touch, the frigid water ceased. Behind the cold metal, the drain plug had been pulled taut. Her fingers depressed it. The lever gave way, but the plug remained in place. She eased her hand into the bowl. Icicles pierced her skin, and chills shot up her arm and spread through her body in a rapid plague. Water breached the edges again, hitting the floor and splashing her bare legs and the tops of her feet.

Larkin grabbed the lip of the plug and pulled. The pipe guzzled the water in deep, greedy gulps that rattled through the room.

A warning crawled from the deep, arcane part of her brain. It screeched and bellowed for her to run.

Someone had plugged the basin, turned on the water, and left it.

Why?

Her gaze jerked to the mirror in front of her, and she fully expected to see the face of the boogeyman looming. In a flash, she relived the night on the roof; only her mind twisted it, and this time, there was no safe release.

The stalls leered like monsters in the night. Especially the closed stall. There were no faces. No boogeyman. But a suffocating silence filled the cold space.

Larkin pulled her hand from the sink and turned, confronting the closed stall.

"Hello?" she demanded. "Is anyone in there?"

The silence grew until it threatened to break her.

She stepped forward. Water rippled. Her ankles quivered, but she pushed on slowly, steadily, coming closer to the stall until she stood in its shadow. When she reached for the door, her fingers trembled. Disgusted with her fear, she curled them into a fist, held her breath, and knocked on the stall.

Un-oiled hinges creaked. The door opened, allowing a sliver of light to shine through the hefty wood.

"Shit." Larkin jumped backward and dropped the edge of her gown to cover her mouth. She hadn't expected the thing to move.

Heart clogging her throat, Larkin stepped forward and pushed the door. It opened only a few inches before hitting something and stopping cold. Her heart stopped too.

Through the crack, Larkin stared in horror at a woman's prone leg. Words and thoughts and screams collided in a heap of helplessness. Her gaze searched desperately for someone, something. There was only her and this woman, who needed help more than she did.

Larkin pressed the door open enough to stick her head inside.

"Oh, God."

Pills lay on the floor like confetti at a party. Toilet paper hung from the roll and gathered on the floor. The woman sprawled belly down across the closed lid of the toilet. Her short, curled bob hung across her face. The hair didn't move. The woman didn't move.

A medicine bottle remained clutched in her hand. That ominous sign was the only thing giving Larkin hope that she wasn't dead.

"Miss? Miss, can you hear me?"

She offered no response.

Larkin wedged herself through the narrow opening. The jewels on her gown scraped against the stained wood. She exhaled and wiggled and finally broke through. With a bare foot, she moved the sequined end of the silver gown and stood between the woman's sprawled legs, one of which blocked the door from opening properly.

In all her years spent on earth and all her schooling, why the hell hadn't she taken a first-aid course? The information would certainly have come in handy now because she hadn't the slightest clue what to do. She pressed her hand to the woman's back and prayed for movement of any sort. Hell, she'd take a startled screech or a full-on attack to the chilly silence.

One. Two. Three. Four. Five. Six. Seven.

She didn't know why she was counting, but ...the woman's chest expanded.

"Oh, thank you." A shiver of relief washed over Larkin, and she sagged. Sure, the breaths weren't as strong or full as they should've been, but they were there.

The woman needed help, but at least there was help for her. Larkin reached for the purse she always carried around her body, but tonight, it wasn't there. She'd left it in the car, sure she wouldn't need her money, identification, or phone this evening.

Dread crept up her spine. She had to leave her and go get help.

The woman's body shook. It flailed violently from side to side, startling Larkin. The woman's strong legs smacked into Larkin's and tossed her off balance. She fell back. Her arms shot wide and slammed into the stall while her shoulder met the door. It was all too much. Too fast. Before she could blink, she was on her ass, staring into the white face of Tarin Blakely, the treasurer on her board, the stuffy mother of two, the woman who worked numbers for so many international power companies.

"Tarin?"

Maybe she suffered from seizures? Had she come with her husband? Would he know what to do? Larkin scrambled up with a new sense of urgency. She knew this woman; she wouldn't let her die.

"I'm going to get help. I promise. I'll be right back."

Adrenaline dumped into her bloodstream, making her limbs shake, but she wrestled her way out of the stall, ran through the water—dress be damned—and sprinted for help.

The hallways seemed longer than they'd ever been as her bare feet pounded the floor. She ran past the ballroom entrance and down the main corridor to the coat check.

"Please. Help me, please?" Larkin begged between

breaths.

Behind the counter, the woman's eyes bulged and searched the surroundings for danger.

"Do you have a phone?"

The woman stared.

"A phone? Give me a phone." Larkin thrust her open palm at the woman.

The young woman thrust the hotel phone into her hand and scrambled back.

Larkin pressed 911 and placed the phone to her ear.

"I need security at coat check, now." Coat check lady clutched a walkie-talkie to her chest.

"There's no danger. There's a woman unconscious in the bathroom," Larkin explained, while simultaneously strangling the phone. The damn thing wasn't working. "Why isn't the phone working?" She pulled the cordless thing from her face and stared at the tiny digital readout to see if it was even operational.

The woman stepped toward the coats. As if they could save her from the wrath about to rain down upon her.

"Do you have to press a number to get out? Nine? Eight?" Larkin hung up the phone, clicked it on again, and tried dialing nine before the number for emergency services. Nothing happened.

"Tell me how this damn thing works," Larkin bellowed at the girl, now completely behind a rack of coats. She gave up and dialed again, trying eight this time.

"Damn you. What's wrong with this thing?" She whacked the phone against her hand.

"What's going on here?" a deep male voice demanded.

"She's acting crazy." The coat girl emerged from her hiding spot and pointed an accusing finger at Larkin.

"Miss?" Five firm fingers gripped Larkin's upper arm. "Is it time to call your car? How much have you had to drink tonight?"

Larkin whirled on an average-size fellow with a larger-than-life authoritarian complex. The badge on his chest was too shiny. His glare too eager.

"I haven't had nearly enough for this. I'm trying to call an ambulance. There's an unconscious woman in the bathroom." Larkin pointed down the long corridor. "Past the ballroom." She tossed the phone at the coat wench. "Why don't you make yourself useful and call an ambulance."

She wrenched her arm from his hold and started down the hallway. "You can tackle me or follow me, but I guarantee my lawyer is better than yours."

"I'm sorry, miss." The security guard jogged beside her. "I've had to escort a few people to the exits already this evening." He hollered over his shoulder, "I'll call the ambulance." They hustled ahead, and he depressed a button on his shoulder. "I need first-aid to the rear woman's ballroom restroom and the ambulance on standby."

"Ten-four," crackled over the radio.

"What happened?" He huffed as they strode up the hallway.

"I found her in a stall. There were pills everywhere. She's breathing but not well."

"An overdose. I've seen it before." His nostrils flared. "Ain't pretty."

Not at all.

Larkin's stomach threatened to bail. She'd seen it before too. A tear slid down her cheek. Her lids blinked furiously to banish it and the memories away. This was a different time. A different place.

They rounded the corner, and the security guard stalled as though the women's sign was a bright red octagon. She shoved into the bathroom, not waiting a beat to invite him. They'd already wasted too much time. Tarin could be … Nope, she refused to wander that path because no good would come of it. Tarin would be fine as long as they transported her as soon as possible.

"Watch the water." Larkin slowed only enough to keep from wiping out in the large puddle and skidded to a stop in front of the stall door.

Why was it closed? She hadn't closed it. Dread that Tarin had endured another seizure flowed over her like the bathroom sink had on the floor.

Larkin shoved the door open and stared.

"Miss? The lady you were talking about?" The security guard rolled his eyes from one side of the vacant stall to the other.

"She was here sprawled across the toilet on her stomach." She stared into the perfectly tidy stall. The toilet paper boasted perfectly folded creases as an attendant would were there one here. Gone were the confetti pills. Gone was the woman.

Never had Larkin doubted her sanity, but it was as if she'd fallen into some sort of alternate reality. Where she was insane.

"You sure it was this bathroom?" His hands hiked high and wide in an exaggerated show of sarcasm.

"Yes." She turned away from the stall, searching for proof that she wasn't nuts. The glimmer of water caught her eye, and she clung to it. She pointed at the mess scattered across the floor. "I found the water running in the plugged sink before I found her."

"Well"—he scratched his head—"I guess she caught her second wind. It happens." His uneven shoulders bobbed. "They take another hit, and they're at it again. She's probably out on the dance floor." His tiny thumb smashed the radio. "Cancel that ambulance and first-aid call. False alarm. I need maintenance to the rear ballroom bathroom."

While he worked out the details with the operator, Larkin looked around the room for any sign of where

Tarin had gone. The water on the floor was too much of a cluster to track her footsteps. There had been no sign of her in the hallway.

"Well, if we're all good here …" He hitched a thumb toward the door. "I should probably get out of the ladies' room."

She didn't know what to say, so she kept quiet while he backed out of the space with an awkward wave.

Larkin leaned against the stall and hung her head. The water turned the bottom two inches of her dress a deeper shade of pink. She didn't dare look at the underside of her feet. They were probably ruddy with dirt.

"What a night."

Music bumped through the walls as though she hadn't had a year scared off her life. As though they hadn't almost lost a soul tonight. As though nothing had happened at all except the snap of her sanity.

She needed to find Bronson and get out of here. Only, they couldn't leave until the party was over. He was the reason for the extravaganza.

Larkin straightened and leaned into the stall—where she'd just witnessed an acquaintance fight for her life—and pulled off a length of tissue. Then she saw it. Another piece of evidence that proved stress wasn't making her lose her mind. A small pill lay between the back of the toilet and the wall.

Larkin pulled up the hem of her dress, then dropping to a knee, she pinched the medicine between her index finger and thumb, and stood. The white pill had been stamped with the label APO on one side. She flipped it over and read the other side. OLA 5m. It meant nothing to her, but she could find out what—

The door opened. Roaring voices and music poured into the bathroom, causing her to startle for the hundredth time that night. The innate reaction disgusted her. Before she could focus on self-loathing, the tiny pill slipped from between her fingers, bounced off the open toilet seat, and plunged into the water.

"Great." She glared at the ceiling as though it or the big guy could help. Ha. "APO. OLA 5m. APO. OLA 5m. APO. OLA 5m."

A two-woman cleaning crew cackled their way into the bathroom, paying little-to-no attention to the mess she was or the mess on the floor. Music radiated from a small speaker connected to a phone atop their cart. Their hips swayed. Their mouths worked fast and furiously in a language Larkin didn't understand.

She used the length of toilet paper in her hand to rub the mascara from under her eyes. Next, she wiped off each foot in turn, using nearly a quarter of the roll. Disgusting. The blackened clumps of paper floated in the center of the bowl, mocking the finery of her gown.

Larkin toed the button. A whirl of water and a gush of sound carried away the remnants. If only it would take with it the disquiet in her mind. She dragged a lungful of too clean air for her surroundings, and then edged out of the stall and around the lake the ladies had yet to address. One at a time, she slipped on the fancy shoes that in no way matched her mood. The regal things carried her as far as the vanity before she crumpled into a chair. Her reflection gave nothing away. The jitter in her hands and the vivid images assaulting her mind made the night all too clear. She'd never been one to hide from the masses, but tonight was an exception in so many ways. Why not this one?

NINE

"AH, THERE SHE IS!" Bronson's voice carried above the din. The dwindling crowd of partygoers clogging the Waldorf's vestibule parted, revealing the man of the hour. He clung to two leggy blondes. Twins, from the looks of things. Then again, it was hard to see past the stage-worthy layers of makeup, conspicuously perfect breasts, and matching fire engine red gowns.

Larkin waved. An unexpected rush of relief washed over her, taking with it some of the night's turmoil. Bronson was distracted. She was thrilled it hadn't taken half as long as she'd thought.

The threesome weaved their way toward her, stumbling and snickering at their own inability to walk in a straight line.

"Larkin! I thought I'd never find you again." Bronson released the two women and fell to his knees in front of her seat. His arms clung heavily to her thighs as though he was grasping for dear life.

"It's okay. I'm fine." She grabbed his shoulder to keep him upright and her dress in its proper position, covering her not-so-perfect breasts. "Did you have fun?"

"No." His floppy blond hair shook. "I spent all night looking for you."

Not all night. She was with him for more than half of it.

"Where have you been all my life?" Bronson wrapped both arms around her waist and pulled her close.

Dear Lord, if she didn't get a hold of this situation, he'd knock them both on their asses. Larkin grabbed a hunk of his hair and turned his eyes to her. They were glassy. His pupils looked as large as the moon.

"You're being rude, Bronson. Introduce me to your friends." Larkin pointed at the two women now clinging to one another to stay upright.

"Oh!" He jumped to his feet and grabbed their hands. "Ladies, this is the love of my life. The woman I was telling you about. This is Larkin Ashford." His gaze swung back to her. His feet teetered for a second but held. "Larkin, this is Brinley and Ashley Vincent. Their father is—"

"Larry Vincent." The most notorious small games dealer in Manhattan. His game of choice was big bet, big Texas poker. His method of choice for house winning collection was blackmail.

Larkin's perma-chills from earlier returned with a frigid vengeance. She'd liked these two girls five seconds ago when they could distract her friend. Now, when they could ruin him with an iPhone pic, she didn't like them near as much. Even as children, Bronson knew how to get himself into deep shit. Seemed not much had changed.

"It's a pleasure to meet you." Larkin stood, grabbed Bronson's hand, and looped it through her arm. "I'm only sorry it was at the end of the night, and I have an early morning tomorrow. Until next time."

The women stood window-eyed—not much going on inside—with hollow smiles showcasing bleached teeth.

She pulled Bronson along, using every bit of muscle she worked to keep on her frame to maneuver them safely through the gaggle of people as intoxicated as her friend. Despite the gusts of fall wind that infiltrated the doors every time someone exited, a sweat broke out down her back. When the doorman opened the door for her, she welcomed the arctic blast.

"Miss Ashford." His driver rushed forward from the car she'd ordered fifty minutes ago for when the party actually ended, and she'd expected to find Bronson in the mix. The driver's eyes widened and the rush of his steps said she looked as desperate for help as she felt. "Here. Allow me."

"Thank you, Ricky." The weight of Bronson off her shoulders allowed the fresh and full flow of oxygen into her lungs.

"Guys. Guys. I'm fine. I've got this." Her friend shoved off Ricky and listed toward the concrete.

"I know you do, sir. I just like to help, you know." Luckily, the driver was a large man all the way around and caught Bronson before he had a hard meeting with the New York City sidewalk.

"Keeps you employed." Bronson patted his shoulder and nodded.

"Yes, sir. It does," Ricky agreed.

"Come on, Bronson." Larkin opened the door and crawled in to the far side of the limo.

"Right behind you, babe." Contrary to his words, it took the men nearly a full minute to work Bronson safely inside the car. He braced both hands on the seat and leaned his head against the headrest. "Why are you all the way over there, babe?"

"Bronson, look at me." She waited for him to lift his head, as though it weighed as much as his ego, and find her.

"I am."

"Good. I'm not your babe, and those girls aren't your friends." When he just stared, she continued. "I'm your friend. Not your babe. And those girls are dangerous. Not your friends. Their father will destroy you without good reason if the mood strikes him. If your attitude strikes him wrong. If you screw over either one of his daughters."

"Babe, you worry too much."

"And you listen too little."

Ricky climbed behind the wheel. Larkin turned to the open partition and eased her head close. "I know my building is closer, but please take him home first. I need to know he goes there and nowhere else tonight."

"Of course, miss." He nodded.

"Thank you."

"No trouble at all."

She turned toward the back to hit him with the hard question but found him leaned over on the seat. Her heart lurched.

Larkin scrambled back, landed on her knees in front of Bronson, and pressed her fingers to his neck.

His eyes cracked open. "I've been trying to get you on your knees all night."

"I've been trying not to strangle you all night." She shoved his shoulder. The rest of his body followed, lying fully on the seat.

He offered a weak chuckle, and then his eyes slid shut again.

"Bronson, tell me the truth."

"I've loved you my whole life. Whole ..." His lids closed, his mouth joining it. Several beats passed. "Whole.

Life."

"You've loved and lusted after Ava Cory all your life. Besides, that's not what I was talking about, and you know it." She shoved his shoulder. "Do you owe Larry Vincent money?"

"Nah, babe. It's not like that."

"What is it like?"

A soft snore offered the only answer she'd receive tonight.

She stared at her lifelong friend and felt … nothing. There was no spark, no intrigue, no desire for a great connection. Brice Beauregard was right. She peddled marriage and babies but felt no compunction to experience either. Her dear friend wanting her—as flawed as he might be—gave her nothing but the urge to tuck and roll.

Larkin eased onto the bench seat and watched the city blur past. There was her connection. No matter how crazy it became, she'd never leave the hustle and bustle. The architecture. The people. The stories in each of them intrigued her even on the most maddening of days. This had been one of them. The week. It started off with madness and had carried on the ruckus. Her gaze rose to the tops of the buildings where gargoyles and pigeons called home. Where she called home. Where HE had been.

What seemed like seconds later, the car stopped in front of the Beauregards' Upper East Manhattan home. Ricky opened the door and smacked Bronson's cheeks. The severe sound alone of flesh meeting flesh should have roused her friend, but even the contact didn't gain more than a light stirring.

"I can get one arm," Larkin offered.

"No, miss. I hate to say, but I've had more than my fair share carting Mr. Beauregard up to his bed. It keeps me young." The driver winked and hooked his arms under Bronson's to hoist him.

She imagined Ricky dragging him corpse-style up the front stairs and through the house and didn't know if it'd make her laugh or gasp. It wasn't to be, though. Once out of the car, he stood Bronson upright, buried his shoulder in her friend's belly, and tossed him over his shoulder. Her lips pressed together to keep the amusement in check.

"I'll be back in a jiffy, miss. Don't worry. You'll be safely locked inside." Ricky tipped his hat.

"Take your time. I'll be fine," she reassured.

"Thank you, miss, for all your help." He closed the door before she could say anything and headed up the stairs, holding tightly to the black iron railing.

Larkin gawked at the building's ornate shield and vines carved into the entrance's concrete exterior. These pre-war works of art told the most stunning stories with their mixture of art deco and classic colonial inspirations. Of all the architecture in the city, she loved these the most, which was why she'd bought a home three blocks from here. She never stayed in it because it was too far from her work and too close to conformity for her tastes.

A movement outside the car window caught her attention. People called NYC the city that never sleeps. Oh, it sleeps, and hard. From the hours of three a.m. to five a.m., it wasn't unusual to go without seeing another soul on the sidewalk. If you saw anyone, they were probably passed out or being lugged around like her friend.

The massive figure emerged from the shadows two buildings away on the same side of the block Ricky had just hauled Bronson from. On her side of the car. Something about the way he moved drew her gaze. His sheer size dwarfed the wide sidewalk, yet he prowled with the grace of a tiger on a scent.

Larkin's pulse revved. Everything about him screamed danger as her fingers flew to the lock. Even though the driver said he'd locked the doors, she slapped at it, ensuring its locked position. The sound echoed in the quiet confines, competing with only the roaring of her heartbeat.

He stopped even with the car. His head canted slightly toward the car and the noise she'd made.

Her tongue swelled, blocking oxygen from entering her body.

When his face turned oh-so slowly, it paralyzed her. As if she looked into the face of certain death. She should look away, but the near black of his hair, the scruff covering his thick chin, and his mere presence hypnotized her mind.

Their eyes met.

No.

It wasn't possible. A layer of thick and heavily tinted glass stood between them, but it was as if there was nothing. No steel. No shield. No mercy. His gaze bore into hers.

His shoulders shifted. The light from the apartment caught his face and the scar that ran the left side from cheekbone to jaw.

Larkin cried out. Oxygen flooded her system. Synapses fired left, right, and center.

It was HIM.

HIM who didn't toss her off the top of her building. HIM who had a chance to pawn her mother's ring yet returned it safely. HIM who'd haunted her dream, sleeping and awake, for the past five days and nights.

She slapped a hand over her mouth, but it was too late. He turned away from the light, away from her.

Larkin's fingers grappled with the handle. She pulled and tugged and finally managed to shove the door open. Her tired feet clamored for stability on the unforgiving concrete. His footsteps quickened.

"Excuse me?" She hauled herself upright.

His stride didn't break. He hustled down the side of the building.

Gathering two handfuls of tulle, Larkin hurried after

him. Cold slipped between her legs and fanned the dress high behind her. It slapped her cheeks and forced tears from her eyes, but she forged ahead.

The faster she walked, the farther he stretched the gap between them. Soon, she lost sight of him for moments at a time as though the shadows shrouded him at will.

"Please, sir?" Larkin's feet pounded the sidewalk until she ran at full tilt toward him. Icy wind burned her lungs.

He turned left down an alley.

Every New York instinct inside her screamed for her to stop and return to the car. Alleys equated to disease at the least and death at the most, but she carried on. The closer she came to the alley, the harder she ran. Her legs churned so quickly, she almost ran past it. She skidded to a stop, clinging to the far alley walk for stability. Her lungs heaved. Her eyes scanned.

This wasn't the alley of her nightmares. Each trash receptacle was neatly stowed at the edge. Bright streetlights illuminated every nook, revealing no cat-size rats, no drug deals in progress, no homeless scrounging for a meal, and no hint of the man she'd been chasing after ... like a crazy woman.

"How?" She walked hesitantly into the mouth of the brick walkway. Several doors lined the back of the building to the right. Bronson's building boasted a myriad of windows but no door that she could see. At the end of the alley stood a ten-foot fence she couldn't vault over with a pole and a week's worth of lessons.

Feet protesting, Larkin walked to the first door with her fingers outstretched. Her heart beat against her chest. Whether from the run or the prospect of finding HIM, she didn't know. She wrapped her fingers tightly around the knob and twisted. The worn silver knob didn't budge.

"Miss Ashford?" The driver's panicked voice ricocheted off the bricks. She looked toward the main road and then down the empty alley. There was nothing to catch here but a cold. Defeated, she headed slowly back to the car.

TEN

"WHY DO YOU DO THIS EVERY TIME?" Douglas's gray brows furrowed as they tried to pin her through the mirror over the distance of the car.

"I could ask you the same thing?" She tossed her arms over her chest and stared out the window. Frozen rain battered the cars and streets.

"I do it because I care about you," he retorted.

Larkin offered an exaggerated groan.

"You drown yourself in work. Someone has to pull you up for air."

"I went to the party Saturday." *And received threatening messages before that, found a colleague inexplicably half dead in the bathroom, then vanish, watched my friend hit on me, then pass out, then I ran after HIM like a lunatic.*

"And haven't come out of your office since."

"I was working," she snapped.

"Through the night? Nights?" He dragged out the s, emphasizing his point. "It's Monday, for the love of all that's holy."

Larkin shrugged and looked at the pre-war homes that had prompted her seclusion. It wasn't the homes themselves, but the man who'd been lurking around them. HIM, and the fool she'd made of herself.

"You can't drown yourself in work whenever life gets too hard."

"Says that man who did just the same." She found his gaze in the mirror.

"Learn from my mistakes, child."

She couldn't seem to learn from anything these days. Had she, Sunday would have been spent telling Douglas about the second CUNT card and the mess at the ball. Instead, she pored over the tech, financial, and production reports again and again.

"The next board meeting is tomorrow. Since we didn't finish our business last time, I needed to familiarize myself with every aspect of each outcome of the decision I have to make."

"You need a break from all that nonsense or you won't make the right decision."

"What is the right decision?" she begged.

"I don't know. It's for you to decide ... after you've had some time away."

"The meeting is in ..." She consulted her phone. The 6:00 p.m. readout brightened the car's interior. "Twenty-three hours."

"I suggest you use that time wisely."

Larkin unlocked her phone screen and pressed the icon to open her email.

"That is not wisely," Douglas barked. "Shit!" His two sentences nearly merged. The car lurched.

The phone dropped to the floor. She grabbed the oh-shit handle and wished like hell that she'd heeded his advice and put on her seat belt. The car skidded ever so slightly before it slammed to an abrupt stop. Pedestrians darted in front of the car, clutching their umbrellas and the front of their raincoats and paying the car that nearly slammed into them no attention.

"That's not wisely," Larkin choked out.

Douglas grumbled a string of curse words to himself, then quieted. They both sat in silence through the light and then the next. They caught the unlucky timing and the string of lights between them and her uptown home.

She ignored her phone and stared out the window at the architecture she loved as they moved slowly from one light to the next. Several blocks from her home, they pulled up to the red light. A single man stood in the freezing rain, awaiting the proper signal to cross the street. Had it not been directly under the light of the crossing, had he not been so unique in the world of suits and ties, she wouldn't have seen HIM. But it was, and she did. He wore a leather jacket, a blatant fuck you to the cold and the world. Jeans—not skinny chic, not runway ripped, but good old-fashioned work-worn jeans—clung to his ass. Frozen rain melted at his touch.

"Whew! It's not a night to be caught out in this." Douglas whistled.

Her heart pounded against her chest. She swallowed.

"Pull forward just a little, Douglas, and wait. Please?"

He did as she asked. The man turned to assess the car that'd pulled even with him as though it were a challenge. It was.

Larkin gathered her breath and opened the door. Their eyes locked. No metal, glass, nor tent obscured their view. "Get in."

His head canted ever so slightly. Water fell off the cleft of his chin, running in rivulets down his dark hair and the taut skin of his neck.

"Please." She hated begging, but she'd get on her knees in an icy puddle to get her questions answered.

He pivoted toward her and took two steps. The long strides put him in arm's reach of the car. His gaze narrowed on her, and then the seat. He grabbed the edge of his jacket and shook it, causing droplets to sail through the air. "I'll ruin your seats."

"Here. Lay this down." Douglas's calf-length raincoat hit her feet, jerking her gaze from HIS.

She yanked the jacket from the floor, scooted to the far side of the car, and spread it out.

The giant stranger waited the longest eight count of her life before stepping off the curb and wedging himself through the open door. The car shifted ever so slightly under his weight. When he sat, the bench seat submitted to his form, dipping in and cratering the edge of Larkin's side. She gripped the side of the seat to keep from sliding toward him. He closed the door behind him, and it created a vacuum in the confined space.

Silence sucked the air out of the car or maybe just her lungs. One of his wet boots, built for ass kicking, occupied carpet only inches away from her fur-lined winter ones. His hulking thigh was only a twitch away.

He'd been large on the roof, but in the back seat, he was a giant. Heat radiated from him despite the cold he'd just come from.

"I assume you know this fellow," Douglas asked without asking.

With him this close, her lungs and mouth refused to operate. Confronting him consumed all her mental function.

"We've met," the stranger's voice rumbled so low it shook her bones.

"Well, Mr. ..." Douglas let the second question hang

in the air.

Larkin was just as eager to hear the answer. Hell, more so than her driver.

"Beckett," the stranger offered.

"Nice to meet you, Mr. Beckett. Where to?" Douglas tried again.

"My place," Larkin blurted.

No way would she let him out of her sight. She had so much to say to him and didn't know exactly why.

Dark eyes, darker than she'd ever seen, sliced to her and bore down.

She held the unrelenting gaze and straightened in the seat, reclaiming a bit of the space he'd stolen. Their knees touched. Through their pants, cold and wet, a mysterious energy poured, rendering her speechless once more.

"Sir?" Douglas wouldn't take the man anywhere he didn't approve of, no matter her request. Unless she wanted them dead. She had a feeling he'd take them somewhere quiet. Not that she'd ever ask. Especially not with this guy. As capable as Douglas was, this man epitomized lethal. That, and she didn't want him dead. She wanted him. Period. No explanations. No equivocations. She had neither.

His gaze held hers for several seconds more, and then he nodded.

A car horn sounded behind them, followed quickly by another. Douglas ignored them while he situated himself in the driver's seat and then gently placed the car in Drive.

Larkin cataloged every inch of the man, who'd scared time from her life on the roof that night, visible from her forward-facing position. She didn't want to spook him by a full-on frontal evaluation, though she suspected it would take much more than just her to scare him.

Besides, her side appraisal gave her enough to handle. The connection of their legs scrambled her usual dispassionate approach to men and her sexual relations with them. Attractions had always been based on the physical or on her intoxication level. She hadn't had even a sniff of whisky today. He, Beckett, wasn't pretty. He didn't boast charisma nor infectious enthusiasm. He was danger. He was the unknown.

The sheer size of his hands baffled her. They hung loosely between his legs, relaxed and, at the same time, ready. One could span her throat and squeeze the life from her with little effort. His leg, if put to use, could splinter a door or crush a skull, probably both simultaneously.

Too soon, they stopped in front of her house. She still had so much to inventory. Frozen rain pelted the ground with no signs of letting up. Without pause, Beckett opened the door and stepped out before Douglas placed the car in Park. He shrugged off his jacket, revealing a sopping long sleeve that clung to etched biceps, a full chest, and well-formed abs. While she was distracted by his body, he'd draped the leather over his arm. It created a makeshift umbrella that did little to cover him. He extended his hand without a word.

She slid her fingers into the cradle of his palm. Either the heat of his skin or the frigid air robbed what little breath she'd managed to gather riding over the last blocks. His fingers tightened around her hand and gently hoisted her. Nose to nose, the winter sky cried around them. Its pieces pinged off the roof and pelted the back of her coat. It clung to his exposed shirtsleeve. He remained still, almost oblivious to the weather. Those dark, reticent eyes tested her once more. They asked not a thousand questions, but one. *Can you handle this?*

Probably not but she'd die trying. Her thousand questions were too much not to fight for some answers.

"Come." She dipped under his arm farther into the shelter he'd created for her, held fast to his hand, and tugged him toward the door.

He followed but not because she pulled. She couldn't move his mass if her life depended upon it. Larkin fumbled in her purse for her keys. On nights like this, she wished she employed a doorman. The cost of maintaining a place she rarely used was enough without it.

"Mr. Beckett?" Douglas stood in the winter mix without his usual coat and umbrella. Rain pelted his face, but he didn't flinch. His face read a stony cold blank she'd seen only once before. When her father had gotten out of hand with her.

"Yes?" He addressed her driver with what seemed his full attention. Yet his hand slid the key ring from her frozen fingertips, slipped the single key inside the lock, and opened the door. "Get out of the rain." An easy push at the small of her back had her feet shuffling inside.

Douglas stepped close. Her driver's head barely cleared Beckett's shoulder. "I never forget a face. Harm a hair on her head, and mine will be the last you see."

Larkin's mouth gaped. Her heart crawled up her throat to peek at the action.

Beckett extended his hand. "You can't pay a man for that kind of loyalty."

"No, you can't." Douglas shook the hand Beckett extended.

The two men made some sort of chest-beating, gaze-slicing truce and parted. Douglas's blue gaze found her. He nodded and offered her the sweet face she'd come to know and love.

"Thank you." She smiled.

He turned and headed to the car.

The stranger, for all intents and purposes, closed her door. The streetlights disappeared, leaving them in total darkness, and her pulse ticked up a notch.

"You should leave some lights on."

Metal scraped metal. She recognized it as the bolt sliding home. The moisture in her mouth multiplied when
it should be drying. She was locked in the dark with a
stranger, but all she could remember was the last time she
was in the dark with him, and she'd been wrapped in his
arms. She'd thought he'd meant her harm when he hadn't.
He didn't now. Every move he made had her best interest
in mind.

Hadn't he?

ELEVEN

"I HAD THEM SET ON A TIMER, but I haven't been here since the time change."

The air shifted. Sounds of her breaths reverberated to her more quickly than they had a second ago. His fingers caressed the outside of her hand until they reached her fingertips. He cupped her hand in his. Her breaths came faster. Cold metal settled into the well of her palm.

"You don't live here." It was more of a statement than a question.

"It's my house, but I live in the building where I …"

"Where you met me." Sarcasm laced his voice. She waited, knowing he'd say more. "You shouldn't invite strange men into your house even if you don't usually live here."

"You are strange," she admitted.

"The strangest." His hand closed around hers, cupping her keys inside, then released her.

Not knowing what to say, she stepped back and felt along the wall. "Let me find a light." She felt her way through the foyer and into the living room to the right. Her fingers found a table lamp. With one click, the room came into view. The chaise and sofa, magazines and glass coffee table, the books lining either side of the fireplace were as she'd left them. As her housekeeper had left them, actually. Her guest, though, hadn't followed. She dumped her purse and keys on the small table.

"Beckett?" She stepped into the foyer, and there he stood in a small puddle just inside the door, clutching the dripping leather jacket in one hand. "Just one second. Don't leave."

Larkin rushed down the short hallway between the stairs leading up to the left and the sitting room on the opposite side into the dining room. She looked around for a towel of some sort but found only linen napkins. A run down the staircase led her to the kitchen. She pulled a hand towel from a drawer and hurried back. When she rounded the corner, the man stood where she'd left him.

His right brow furled. "Surprised?"

"Yes." She moved slower toward him. "I expected to see the door open and you gone."

"The thought occurred to me."

Larkin stopped at his puddle and handed him the towel.

He buried his face in it. Then he dragged it over his hair several times.

"But?" she prodded.

"I gave you the key." His wide shoulders bobbed.

"Like a lock would stop you."

He didn't offer a courtesy laugh.

"Why'd you stay?" Larkin couldn't keep the words inside her mouth. She wanted to know everything about this man. Especially why he'd come with her, a lunatic who—in his mind—wanted to throw herself off a roof a few days ago.

"Curiosity."

She just waited. Maybe not just waited. Her eyebrows did some extreme stunts.

"I need to know what you want with me."

"I don't want anything from you." Larkin offered her palms in a wide shrug.

"Then I'll be on my way." Beckett nodded and turned toward the door.

Larkin shocked herself by running around him and throwing herself between him and the door. Her chest heaved with adrenaline and overwhelming, unexplainable lust.

His head canted to the side.

"Fine. I just want to talk about the other night." It was part true. "Please, come in. Let me get you some tea."

He groaned.

"Coffee?"

"Better, but I can't." His gaze hit the puddle at his feet.

"Oh. Let me take your clothes." Larkin covered her mouth, sighed, and tried again. "I can dry them."

"They'll just get wet again."

"Are you homeless?" No matter how she tried, she couldn't cork her mouth around him.

"Yes and no." He offered the first hint of a laugh, but it was gone so quickly she could have hallucinated it.

"Care to explain?"

His head shook.

"Why were you on the roof the other night?" she tried.

He simply stood and watched her.

"How'd you get up there?"

"You said a lock wouldn't stop me."

"Fine. Fine. You won't come in. You won't let me dry

your clothes. You won't answer my questions." Larkin yanked off her coat, glad for the working thermostat. At least he wouldn't freeze for as long as she could keep him inside. She sidestepped him and hooked her coat on the rack. If she was going to get this out, she couldn't look at him. The sight of him all big and fucking sexy as hell muddled her brain. Her feet carried her from one side of the foyer to the other.

"That night on the roof ... I wasn't trying to kill myself."

When he didn't protest, she looked at him. His gaze followed her, calculating her again and again like a high-functioning computer. Reading and reading and not asking a single question.

"I know it looked that way. I know, now, why you acted the way you did, but it scared me. No one is ever up on the roof. It's my place to get away from ... everything. I hadn't been up there in a while. Too long. Things were pressing in on me. Work. My ..." Why was she blabbing so much to him? He didn't give a shit. He was probably worried about where his next meal would come from. What did he care about her problems? Which really weren't problems at all in the grand scheme of the world. People lived not knowing where their next meal was coming from. People lived without proper clothing. Without proper shelter.

Beckett didn't look homeless. He wasn't malnourished in any way. His clothes were used but clean and well maintained. The scruff on his face wasn't more than three days growth.

"Your ... boyfriend?"

She stopped pacing and found his gaze. "I don't have those. They're ... messy."

"Husband?"

Her face crinkled. "Even worse."

"Finally, someone who understands."

"So many people don't." She nodded and walked, studying the intricacies of the woodwork and the fibers of the entry's rug.

"They're needy."

"And you don't need much, do you?" She stole a quick glance at him. His head shook.

"So who was it that night?"

Her gaze dropped to the ring on her finger. "My family."

His fingers came into view. They grazed the thick band and large stone.

"It was my mother's." She hated the words as soon as they were out.

"Why are you mad at a dead woman?"

Her gaze flashed to his. He stood over her, eyes warmer than before. She hadn't said a word about the rage that boiled inside her bones for her mother, but he was smart. Smart enough to add her action that night and her words tonight and ask the one question she wouldn't answer.

Larkin's head shook, jarring loose the tear she'd been fighting back.

"Seems we both have our boundaries." His thumb wiped the tear from her cheek, dragged it down her face, and smoothed it over her lips. They parted for him. He took his time tracing the high arch. The salt from his fingertip bled into her mouth as the pad dragged over her lower lip and pulled it wide. "Unlock the door and tell me to leave."

"No." Her tongue slid along the path with his finger. "You ran away from me Saturday. I'm not going to let you do that tonight."

"It's what I should do." His thumb left her lip and joined the rest of his fingers at the side of her neck. He tilted her face up. "Tell me to stop." His face, scarred and angry, neared hers, open and intent.

Not a sound passed through her lips. She grabbed his jacket, only inches from his hand, and tugged. His hold broke. The cold exterior chilled her fingertips. The weight of it forced her muscles into action but not for long. She dropped the thing on the ground behind her, toward the wall and away from the door. Her gaze never left his. His gave nothing away.

He was too tall for her to lift up onto her tiptoes and press her lips to his, and he didn't move from his battle-ready posture. She could climb him like a tree, but if this was going to work, he would have to give ... just a little.

Toe to toe, she studied him as blatantly as he did her. A healthy pulse swelled the veins of his thick neck. His gaze narrowed and cooled as though begging her to lose interest. Not a chance. Every inch of him intrigued her. Even the ugly scar that hid in the shadow of the foyer. She reached up slowly. His head shifted higher into the stratosphere of her entryway.

"Don't tell me a big guy like you is scared."

His jaw worked back and forth. "Cautious."

"I won't hurt you. Don't think I could if I tried, but I won't."

His head lowered.

Larkin grabbed his chin. It barely fit in her hand. The short hairs pricked her fingers. She turned his face to the left and held her breath. Webbed and raised skin slightly darker than the rest of his face gleamed with a waxy smooth finish in the lamplight. Its dips and rises spread wide from a point just below his eye to encompass the hinge of his jaw and a two-inch swath of his cheek. It was fully healed but not an old scar. Her fingers slid up the side of his face. She mapped the ridges of scarred and unmarred skin alike.

He moved under her touch, not visibly, but energy

hummed under her fingertips. She dragged her touch down over his scar, his neck, and gripped the collar of his shirt with both hands. Cool water seeped from the fabric, running through her fingers.

Hunger flashed in his eyes.

She pulled his face down. Her heart beat against her chest, urging her to take his mouth, but determination made her wait. He had to give. Saliva pooled. Her breasts ached. Oxygen, so skittish before, heaved in and out of her lungs as though she was chasing him down the street again. If he broke down her door and ran away, she'd chase him again. This wasn't like her. She took what she wanted. Men gave it freely. But this man just looked at her.

"What?" she broke. "What are you waiting for? It's like you're looking for something?" Her fists squeezed his shirt tighter.

"Your motivation."

Her mouth fell open. Nothing came out.

"You said you only wanted to talk."

"I lied."

"Don't lie to me again." He said it with such finality, such assurance, that she believed he'd know a lie the moment it left her lips. As though he'd known all along that it had been a lie.

Larkin nodded.

"What do you want?"

He might as well have stripped her bare on the street corner. She felt as open and exposed. She held on for dear life because if she let go, he'd vanish.

"I want to know your name. I want to know where you're from. Where you live now. Why you were on the roof that night. Why you pulled me from the edge. Why I always see you on the street. How you got your scar. Who hurt you."

His jaw hinged so tight the muscles controlling his jaw

flexed.

She drew a deep breath. "I want to know everything about you, and I never want to know anything about anyone. But more than that ..."

"Could there be more than everything?" he growled.

"I want you to fuck me, to fuck you out of my mind. I need you to scratch this itch. Take the mystery away. Make me stop looking for you on every rooftop and street corner."

His fingers bit into her hips. Then his eyes lowered to her level. "After tonight, you'll never see me again."

"I won't need to," she promised.

"Poor Larkin. Have your past lovers impressed you so little that you have eternally low expectations?"

"You know my name." The words came in a gasp. She was surprised her slacked lips moved at all.

"I don't get into cars with strangers. You shouldn't let them into your house." His mouth came down on hers hard, stirring her shocked lips back to life and driving away the questions that revelation created.

His tongue tasted of whisky. The good stuff. Cigar tobacco scented his hair that hung unruly and dark around his nape. Her fingers released his collar and delved into the wet locks. Water turned to steam, rolling off the back of his neck. It warmed her fingers that dug in and tugged him closer. Trapped between the confining cups of her bra and the promise of his touch, her nipples tingled. His hands gripped tightly, holding her perfectly still while his mouth assumed authority over hers.

So often she set the pace of her carnal encounters. She led them where she wanted them, how, and when. This man didn't wait for cues. He ransacked and found them for himself. When she expected him to break for breath, his tongue swept deep inside her mouth and mated with hers. His invasion reeled back only long enough to bite her lower lip and then trace the marks he'd surely left with the tip of his tongue. She opened wider, relaxed into his hold, and prayed the assault on her senses would never end.

She had no cause to trust this man she knew so little about, yet she did. At every turn, he treated her better than she had any right to expect.

The unbreakable grip he held at her hips loosened. Before she could lament the break in pressure, his gigantic hands rounded her hips. Large fingertips sank into her gym-sculpted butt, causing a yip to slip from between her lips. He didn't flinch. Instead, he used the salacious hand-holds to hoist her off the floor. Her jeans-covered crotch dragged across the swell of his thighs, then an appendage nearly as big. She nearly choked, but it morphed into a moan. Her hips rolled on their own volition, savoring the length and girth.

"Stop that." His words were deep and grave.

She ignored them, used his muscled shoulders as leverage, and worked her aching clit over his cock.

The most erotic, guttural sound she'd ever heard launched from his throat.

"Yes," she moaned. Her legs wrapped around his waist. The heels of her boots dug into his ass.

"You don't take direction very well." Beckett's mouth attacked her neck. His hands molded to her bottom and shifted her up and down along the unyielding bulge locked inside his pants.

"I usually give them." Her throat quivered. Her orgasm approached like a locomotive cresting a mountain. It was too soon. Not enough, yet too much to stop the force from collecting inside her.

Larkin's fingers gripped the top of his shirt. Her face grazed the side of his. Stubble scraped her cheek. Her eyes shut, and her body seized in the tumult. Everything quivered except the man. He stood stock-still, save for the breaths that whooshed against her neck and the heartbeat that thumped against her chest.

When she finished, her body melted against his.

He set her on her feet and pulled away.

Larkin stood blinking. Where were they? The foyer came into view. A cold, stark difference from the warmth in which she'd just been engulfed. Her chest heaved. Her body throbbed. Suddenly, she was five feet away from the man she wanted to be on top of. A chill swept over her cheeks. Was that shame? Fuck no. She wasn't ashamed of the way she'd acted. He'd wanted her just as much as she'd wanted him. Still did, by the looks of the swell in his pants and the heat in his eyes.

"Bedroom," he barked.

Her legs shook beneath her. Her heart beat so fast it might spontaneously combust. She just stared at him, completely bewildered.

"Lady, if I let you set the pace I'd be passed out right now. I need a minute to keep from fucking you on the floor in my rain puddle. Can you walk?"

She continued to stare at the animation coming from a face that until then had given away so little.

"Christ." Beckett stepped forward and hooked an arm behind her back. The other scooped her shaking legs from under her. "Where to?" He didn't wait for her to answer before starting up the stairs just to the left of his rain puddle.

They arrived on the third-floor landing in no time as though he weren't toting a hundred and thirty-five pounds. Her bathroom lay in front of them, inviting with the continually flickering light of sconces that framed a large claw-foot tub.

She motioned left toward the bar-brick archway. No light poured in through the floor-to-ceiling windows of her bedroom, yet he moved confidently through the space.

Did he have echo location or some other form of night vision, not gifted to simple humans?

He set her on her feet at the end of the bed and turned away without a word. His darkly clothed form melted into the darkness. Her ears pricked, listening for the sounds of his movement, but there were none. Her breath caught in her throat. If she breathed, she might miss what he was doing.

Light blinded her for a split second before her eyes adjusted to the lamplight of her bedside table. He straightened. His gaze roved over her, then slid to the bed. A hint of a frown yanked one side of his face. She couldn't even toil over what the problem could be. He stepped to the bed, grabbed two handfuls of pillows, and tossed them onto the floor on the other side of the bed. Next, he peeled back the fluffy duvet, leaving only a gray fitted sheet hugged tightly to the mattress where a neatly made bed had been.

Her mouth watered. Her palms itched. Her thighs rubbed together in an anxious dance of desire.

His hands moved to his belt buckle but stalled. He stalked toward her, fingers moving slowly across the metal clasp and soaked leather. Leaving the buckle, the hide popped the air.

Larkin bit her lip and balled her hands into fists to keep from touching him. She had a feeling she'd gotten away with all the missteps he'd allow. No way did she want him bailing before she got her fill. She watched his eyes, awaiting a command. His zipper screamed in the quiet room. Her clit pulsed. That zipper and the flesh behind it had done more for her already than some had done the entirety of their short stay.

Cool air seeped in from under the edge of her sweater. Warm fingertips grazed her flesh; hipbone to belly button. He yanked the snap of her jeans open and worked her zipper down more slowly than he'd done his own. Rough palms scraped up her midriff to the edge of her bra. Her breasts heaved, begging to be manhandled. His palms rounded to the back and yanked her top up over her head.

Need sizzled across her skin like electric pulses, trying desperately to get the message out. *Touch me. Kiss me. Fuck me.*

His gaze touched her as though his fingers did the job. It roved high over her face to her collarbone, down over her swollen breasts to the erect nipples that reached for attention, then down across the plain of her abdomen to the open V of her zipper and the lace panties that peeked out from below.

He picked her up, much as he had before, then tossed her onto the bed. His fingers made fast work of the laces, boots, and socks. With her on the bed and him standing at her feet, he looked like a giant. His breadth ate up more than half the width of her king-size bed.

"Cute."

"What?" Her eyes shot wide. She couldn't believe a giant like him even knew the word, much less used it.

Beckett gently pinched her pinkie toe between his thumb and forefinger and wiggled it. Then she remembered the tiny cherry design Marlis had talked all the girls into getting on their pinkie toes at the spa.

"My girlfriend talked me into it." Her cheeks warmed under his scrutiny.

"It means you have a playful side."

"Do you?"

He grabbed her ankles and pulled her to the edge of the bed. His hands worked their way up her jeans to the pockets. "Nope."

"Don't lie to me." She didn't believe him. Sure, it was buried in there beneath layers of muscle and the ashes the world had left him under, but it was there.

"Don't delude yourself into thinking I'm something

I'm not."

The seat of her pants left her ass with remarkable speed. He tossed them onto the floor along with everything else he'd littered it with.

"I don't know enough about you to think anything."

"Good." He toed off his boots and peeled off his socks. His hands moved to the hem of his shirt. His gaze bore into hers, and then he heaved the long sleeve off his body.

A lump formed in her throat.

His gaze never left hers. Only the shirt obscured his line of sight for a split second. Long enough for her to see the continuation of the scars that started on his cheek. They encompassed the bold muscles of his left shoulder, bicep, and thick forearm. They stretched down across the left side of his torso and abdomen and disappeared into the side of his pants. His expression dared her to say anything about them.

What could she say?

I'm sorry that happened to you. It must have been so painful, but it doesn't stop me from wanting to lick every inch of your body. It doesn't stop me from wishing you were on me and in me now.

"What are you waiting for? You can't fuck me with pants on." Larkin's thighs rustled together bent up to her middle to keep them on the bed and to torment herself, stoking a fire that needed banking not stirring.

Larkin marveled at the stark differences between his two sides. The right was frothy with dark hair on his arms and chest, delineated with every muscle fiber beneath the skin. The left was slick with ridges and valleys obscuring the perfect definition of muscle tone but not obstructing its devastating abilities in any way.

Beckett shucked his pants and boxers in one defiant swipe. His lower abdomen pointed to the very thing she wanted so desperately. Her body begged for it, weeping until her panties were wet with desire. His sex lolled wide and long, pink and full. Only a hint of the scar hugged his left hip. The rest of him was untouched as he had been before whatever had stolen time from him in exchange for unparalleled pain. Her need to touch him drove her onto her elbows.

Before she could sit, his head shook. "You had your fun. It's my turn now."

He dropped to his knees on the floor and grabbed her ankles. His gaze winked on her decorated toe again, then drifted up her calf to the crook of her knees to the swell of her thighs. Where his eyes traveled, his hands followed slowly behind.

Inside her chest, her heart quivered, vibrating every vein from head to toe. He stroked just as he stared—with such intensity the whisper of his touch would stay far past the physical. The study his hands made of her flesh wasn't gentle. His hands molded her skin, sculpting it to new life.

She relinquished control for the first time and watched him learn the curves and sways. He surveyed with fingers and breaths, hands and lips, tongue and teeth all over her skin until every part of her hummed, the places he had yet to touch most of all. After so much time had passed that she'd forgotten her goals with him, with life, he pushed her legs wide and pressed his mouth against the crotch of her panties.

Her head thrashed as his did the same between her legs. The tips of her nails scraped the tight sheet. Oxygen rushed in and out of her lungs. He pushed and prodded until she stood at the top of the mountain with her arms stretched wide. The wind whipped her hair and the horizon begged her to jump.

His mouth and hands left her too abruptly, and she teetered on the edge of oblivion for several seconds. He stood over her watching, waiting. When her breaths settled to a pace that wouldn't leave her unconscious, he leaned down and threaded his fingers inside the waistband of her panties. His hard, sun-kissed hands contrasted with the silky fabric of the pale lace.

A swift yank rolled her onto her belly. His grip on her lace vanished.

"Crawl to the middle." The command was low and concise.

Larkin never crawled anywhere, not for anyone. She scrambled to her hands and knees. They wobbled but obeyed the order.

He muffled a curse. Then another. The zero motion, high-end foam mattress dipped and rocked her under his weight.

"Breathe." His chest grazed her back. The breath of his simple word warmed her arm. Her head canted toward his, seeking his mouth.

Fingers twisted in her hair, pulled her face higher, and their mouths collided in a frenzy of lips and tongues. Somehow, he yanked the panties from her hips and unfastened the clasp of her bra all while tormenting her mouth and mind. He released her lips with a growl and worked the last of her undergarments free of her limbs.

With one arm around her middle, just under her breasts, and his dick nestled lengthwise between her ass cheeks, he pushed her forward with his hips. She collapsed flat onto the bed. The hold he kept on her chest kept her from crashing ... physically. Emotionally, she was a violent ball of nerve endings. She'd never been taken from behind. She didn't like the domineering quality. The object of his pleasure. Her body, on the other hand, howled in thanksgiving. Anything to quench the empty need between her legs.

Damn him, but he didn't enter her. His hands toyed with her breasts and sculpted her bottom. Sharp teeth nipped at her shoulder and hiked up her neck. Pants filtered into her ear. Hers. His. The fullness of his cock pressed against her bottom. Her hips flared in response. She rocked them against his smooth length in blatant invitation. The back and forth skimmed her swollen clit across the cotton sheet. Her nipples thrummed under his fingers. Once more, her breathing sped, and fingertips tingled, and her orgasm was a breath away.

One firm, hot hand gripped her hip and tilted her, opening her. The head of his cock pressed against the slickness of her entrance. She rolled into the intrusion, coaxing it, begging for it. He eased in. Just the tip stole her breath for only a second before he left her empty and wanting.

His unyielding grip flipped her onto her back. The world spun with her. Suddenly, she was face to face with the god of her body; the man who'd scared her and rescued her all at the same time; the man who tormented her days and this night.

Veins hugged his every swollen muscle. His chest heaved. Sweat coated his abdomen. He was feral with dark wild eyes. Hunger etched his features.

"Condoms?"

It took her a second to comprehend what he said. "Drawer. Bedside table."

The bubbled lines of his skin showed more vividly in the lamplight while he wrenched the dainty drawer wide in search of protection. A wide, jagged scar more than four inches long ran along his back just under his ribs. She felt along the uneven line, wondering how his stunning body had received such abuse.

Beckett released a gruff exhale, but she didn't remove her touch. Instead, it roved higher over the burn-scarred skin she'd touched on his face.

"You like pushing boundaries? Running up to the edge like you'll toss yourself over?" His gaze sliced to hers and held. His hands ripped the foil package and rolled the latex over his hard, smooth cock.

"Not usually. Every once in a while, I can't stop myself."

She waited for him to grab her hands and shove them over her head. He burrowed his full weight between her legs and pressed his mouth to hers. His full lips were insistent but tender. It wore on and on until she forgot about his scarred skin, and it became a part of the complex creature driving her to the brink. Their lips parted.

"Me either, apparently." He positioned himself at her entrance and worked himself slowly inside.

Their breaths and bodies mingled. Pants and grunts filled the high ceilings. Time shrunk and stretched as they consumed one another in almost every way one could absorb and be absorbed in the process.

Her body gave under the extreme weight of focus, his and hers, time and again. Each time, his followed suit but soon revived for more until nothing was left in either of them.

Too soon, the sun teased the sky with light. Beckett stood. He retrieved the duvet he'd dumped onto the floor and pulled it up over her shoulder. His wide frame leaned close, and the whisper of his lips brushed over her brow. He turned, grabbed his clothes from the floor, and headed for the exit.

"What about the door?" Larkin's voice was rough from use.

He stopped bare to the butt and turned with a question on his dark face.

"It's locked, and you don't have the key." She swallowed, releasing the feel of his hands on her throat even though they were no longer there.

"Like a lock would stop me." He offered her the first glimpse of a wicked smirk and turned away, leaving her

with her own words. Her own words and her body molded by his hands.

Larkin grabbed a handful of the comforter, pulled it
close to her breast, and snuggled into the sleep only utter
satisfaction could bring.

TWELVE

Her skin jumped from her muscles and suspended around her for a beat before snapping back into place. A scream crawled up her throat and ricocheted around her office. The papers that'd been in her lap scattered around her feet. She gripped the pen in her hand as though it were a ten-inch kitchen knife and whipped toward her assailant.

"Christ Almighty, Larkin!" Marlis's hands flew high in surrender. Her feet shuffled back several paces. "It's me."

"Marlis? Shit! You scared me to death." Her chair continued to spin. Larkin braced her feet on the floor and breathed.

"I scared *you*?" Her friend clamped a hand over her heart. Inside it, she clutched a snow kissed beanie. "I thought you were dead."

"Dead?" Larkin set the pen on the table and straightened her capped-sleeve blouse.

"I knocked when I walked in, then I called your name twice. With your chair facing the window and no response or movement." Marlis shrugged. "It always happens that way in the movies. The hero or heroine turns the chair around and ..." Her sweet face crinkled, and her tongue lolled.

Larkin's head shook, and a smile stretched her mouth.

"Then ..." Marlis's brows shot wide. "I learned the hard way that you weren't."

"Sorry to disappoint you." Larkin winked.

Marlis chucked her beanie. Larkin caught the thing before it smacked her in the face. "Hey!"

"You earned that." Marlis pulled the scarf from her neck and peeled off her jacket. "It's about a hundred degrees in here, Grandma."

She'd cranked the heat early this morning. When she'd set foot in the office, the place had felt unusually cold and unfeeling. At first, she had chalked it up to being absent the day before, but the longer she sat in her chair, behind the desk from which she ran her world, she realized the cold had been the absence of his warmth.

When she woke that morning, things had been just as she liked them. Her hope had been empty, save for her. The house had been locked up tight. Her day and duties stretched out before her, unfettered from the evening's activities. The only signs of the fun night before had been the soreness between her legs. As her day progressed, she realized more and more that things were not as she liked them.

Thoughts of him, thoughts of them polluted her mind and disrupted her life. Which was why she hadn't heard Marlis enter and why she'd yet to review the reports she knew by heart one last time before the board meeting in two hours.

"You're here early." Larkin crouched from her seat and scooped up the tech and financial printouts.

"Sweetie, are you okay?"

Larkin stood, laid the stack atop her desk, and looked at Marlis. "I'm fine. Why?"

"I'm five … now seven minutes late for the meeting." Her friend grabbed her Givenchy from the couch and her pile of fashionable winter gear.

"What?" The hands on her watch confirmed Mar's story. 5:07 p.m. "No." She gathered up her papers, laptop, and pen. Why hadn't she realized the time? "Why didn't Reagan remind me?"

This was why she didn't date or do relationships. Men turned perfectly competent women into bumbling idiots with a swing of their smile … and other things. Larkin growled at herself and turned toward the conference room door.

"She's always standing at her desk, greeting people before the meetings, but she wasn't out there when I walked past. The main door to the conference room was open, and I could hear Genevieve in there arguing with Cornish about punctuality and appliances, which is why I slipped in here to make myself presentable since I couldn't help my tardiness at this point." She said the last with a sneer.

"This is sure to be a lovely evening." Larkin rolled her eyes and left all thought of Beckett in her private domain. After all, she was about to see the woman she dreaded seeing since Bronson's welcome home party. What was she supposed to say to the woman who'd overdosed on some mystery drug—she really had to remember to look that up—the last time she'd seen her? Larkin wasn't a mother and never planned to be, but if she were, she'd never ingest a substance that could potentially take her away from them. And Tarin was the least of her worries.

She shoved into the fighting pit. The room quieted.

"Sorry we're late. Unforeseen business detained us." Larkin sat at the head of the table, and Marlis continued past on her left. The silly woman strived for a nonchalant wave at Benjamin Daily as she passed, but the instant redness of her cheeks gave her away.

"Don't worry about it," Tarin offered in a stage whisper. She didn't have to whisper. The woman sat to Larkin's immediate left and leaned so close that if Tarin fell, she'd land in Larkin's lap. Tarin tapped the massive screen of her mobile phone. Two beautiful children with stunning blue eyes and almost white-blond hair sat on a flannel blanket surrounded by leaves in Central Park. Big sister wrapped her arm protectively around little brother. Their outfits looked more styled than Larkin felt at that moment.

"Wow," was all she could muster. She was stunned. When Tarin talked about her children, Larkin instinctually pictured two snot-nosed petri dishes with chocolate milk stains around their mouths. She didn't see all kids that way. Something in the way her colleague spoke about them showed the effort it took to raise humans.

"You gave me time to view the proofs from our fall session. This one is my favorite." The woman beamed as brightly as she'd ever seen her.

"It's lovely. Your children are precious." Larkin smoothed her outfit and straightened in her seat.

"If you don't mind, I have dinner plans at seven." Cornish Gleeson leaned both his elbows on a thin leather portfolio. His demeanor read calm and collected. The glint in his eye said smug son of a bitch.

"Of course. I've been anxious to hear it since last Tuesday when it was due." She offered him the floor.

To her right, too close for comfort, Brice Beauregard's white teeth gleamed. Her only allies in the room sat at the other end of the table, too far to bolster her position.

"I would, but where's our secretary?" Gleeson shrugged.

Sure enough, Reagan's post near the door was empty. She pressed the call button for her assistant's desk. The hollow tone rang through the room, unanswered. Larkin used her phone and called Reagan's cell. Once again, the call went without a response. Not even the flirty and feminine request to leave a message punctuated the call.

"Benjamin, would you mind taking the minutes for this meeting? The board secretary is unavailable at the moment." Larkin looked at her phone to ensure she'd tried the correct number.

"I, uh?" He wiggled from his rigid position and looked around the room. "I don't really know how." His search continued until it landed on Marlis. "Maybe you'd like to take the minutes?"

Genevieve leaned close to Benjamin but didn't know how to whisper when offering a killer blow. "Breasts don't come with a how to cook, clean, and take meeting minutes manual."

Brice cleared his throat.

"Gen," Marlis scolded her friend and turned ten shades of red.

"I don't mind taking the minutes. Just give me one minute to get caught up." Tarin opened her laptop with a smile and began typing.

"Thank you." She bit her lips to keep from smiling at Gen's keen observation and sent Reagan a message while they waited in the cold and conversation-less room.

It wasn't like her assistant to vanish. Even on the rare sick leave or sick day, she reported in or begged on in the appropriate manner.

"Okay," Tarin cooed.

"Cornish, the floor is yours." Larkin bowed.

The old man wrestled his tie and then began a long,

laborious talk about tradition and the history of marriage, how it's changed, and how her company fit into that narrative today. "Your company is a part of a great tradition. It promotes the ideals of the great bond between a man and a woman, and its importance in the perpetuation of the species."

Clearly, in all the research Cornish blathered about, he hadn't thought it pertinent to click on even the home page of Duo or Ditto. Had he, he would have seen at the top of the page, in a sort of pick your adventure menu, the options for bride/bride, bride/groom, groom/groom. Had he dug a level deeper, he'd have found the same sort of options for Ditto, only more with gender neutral, gender bent, and so on.

At the far end of the table, Genevieve rolled her eyes but kept her mouth shut. Marlis hadn't even caught the snafu for her staring/not-staring at Benjamin.

When Gleeson said, "And I've come to a conclusion," everyone tuned in to the man's droning. He looked left and right, pausing for dramatic effect to ensure he held the attention of the room. "If Larkin marries, she'd firm up the company's position in the global free market."

"What?" Genevieve shrieked.

"How did everyone else present on facts; economics, tech, finance, the market, and social change, yet you base your decision on Larkin's marital status?" Marlis pointed a sharp finger at Larkin.

The room ignited. Everyone spoke atop of one another. Brice tried to start in with his "I have a great candidate" speech, but no one listened. Tarin rambled about family and blah, blah, blah. Benjamin wanted to know what was so wrong with Larkin marrying. And her girls, whew, they lit into Gleeson as though he was a crisp, clean kindling.

"People want to trust what they're buying. They'll buy burgers from a fat guy. They'll buy liquor from a drunk," the man bellowed above the din.

"He has a point."

The room quieted. Every set of widened eyes centered on her. Larkin stood. They all waited to see if she was really that agreeable to tossing her life to the side in the name of business, or if she'd lost her mind completely. After last night, maybe.

"However, if I were married, I would also open the company to liability. How many companies fold under the weight of scandal or a hard-fought divorce?"

"Not with the right prenup." Genevieve shook her head and a manicured finger. "Not that I'm agreeing with this shitshow in any way. We don't live in the forties."

Benjamin sat forward. "But we live in a time of major weight to public opinion and the reign of social media."

"I cannot believe you just said that." Marlis gasped.

"It's true. Where do people get their news?" Benjamin didn't wait for an answer. His gaze swung from Mar to her. "Facebook. All it would take is one viral post to bring attention to the fact that you're not married. They'd sentence you; judge, jury and executioner."

Gleeson pointed at Tarin. "You're the only woman among us who has children and a husband." He shook a finger at Genevieve. "And before you get started, I'm not saying this to be sexist. It's a fact that Duo and Ditto customers are ninety-eight percent female with the desire to marry or have a child." He sought Tarin again and waited.

Her mousy blonde hair bobbed.

"Do you care if the person you buy diapers from has a kid?" Gleeson shook his head before he even finished the question. "No, you don't. It's an item, a good. Duo and Ditto don't just sell goods, they sell the ideas." His gaze searched the room, looking for allies. He gained a nod from all the men in the room. "Now, Tarin, would you listen to advice about your child's diaper rash from a person who has no children of their own?"

Larkin couldn't swallow her irritation. "You said it yourself, Duo and Ditto sell the ideas. I don't give them the ideas. A team of experts in different areas, from licensed and practicing therapists to professional decorators, give their advice. I simply own the companies."

He didn't even look in her direction. His beady little eyes bore into Tarin, willing an answer.

"I've never thought about it the way you posed the question, Mr. Gleeson." Tarin toyed with what looked to be a raw cuticle bed. "I suppose, if they were brought to my attention that two companies proposing the ideals of married with children, and one was married with children and the other wasn't, I'd go with the one who has experience on their side." The cuticle seeped fresh red.

Larkin's stomach twisted. She didn't know if the sick woman's words had done it or the sight of her blood.

"With the right partner, you could avoid all this hassle." Brice didn't move. He didn't have to fidget or slam fists on tables to gain the ear of the room. They'd all heard loud and clear what he was proposing. Her friends did, at least. Their eyes rolled and mouths pursed.

"Not to get into the same firestorm as our last meeting," Gleeson strived for a genial tone and fell short, "but it's worth thinking about. If you go public, everything about you will be scrutinized more closely. Your investors' money, their livelihoods, and their families will depend on your decision and the consumer's faith in those decisions."

She should be spitting mad, but these men were doing what men had been doing for centuries. A sense of peace and calm poured over her. Her mind drifted for the briefest of seconds to Beckett's hands and the way they played her the night before. One stroke could whip her into a frenzy while another eased every ounce of tension in her body.

Larkin drew a cleansing breath. "Gleeson, thank you for your findings. I will take all your reports into consideration before making my decision."

Benjamin and Gleeson gathered their belongings and headed for the door. Brice stood, but instead of following his friends out, he headed her way. She rose to meet his gaze, unwilling to have him towering over her.

"When can we expect that decision?"

"Expectations lead to disappointment, Brice. You should live in the moment." She offered him a smile to take the edge off her words. Who was she kidding? She curled her lips to piss him off.

Brice's salt and pepper brow dropped the pretense of civility. "That's all Bronson is trying to do. Live his moments with the woman he loves."

"Love?" Larkin chuckled. "It sounds a lot like business to me. Good night, Brice. Give Bitsy my regards." She turned away before he had a chance to respond.

Tarin's wild eyes and flushed face greeted her immediately. The woman was so close Larkin brushed her shoulder and almost knocked her back a step.

"Oh, I'm sorry." She steadied Tarin.

"No." The accountant's small hands waved away the apology. "My husband always says I'm a ghost because I sneak up on him without a sound. It's my fault. I should make some noise when I approach. Maybe I'll put a bell around my neck."

Larkin couldn't stop the surprise from warping her features.

"Oh, you're a tried and true New Yorker. You probably don't know that in the old days, farmers put bells on their animals to help keep track of them." Tarin's laugh was high and pitchy. "I'm not really going to put a bell around my neck."

"Of course not." She agreed and hoped it showed. Her

gaze kept jumping to the girls huddled at the far end of the room in discussion. She wanted in on that conversation, one she knew how to navigate. One that even if she made a pitfall, she wouldn't feel like an ass about it. "Thank you for taking the minutes. I appreciate that."

"Words were nice for a change. There are so many numbers in my life."

"I bet. You take care of some of the biggest accounts in the world. I couldn't begin to undertake that sort of task."

Tarin smiled and stared as she worried her cuticle.

"If you would, please email the group a copy of the minutes. Reagan will be back next time to take over the job. I don't know what's taken her away, but knowing her, it's something she couldn't help."

"No. I expect not." Tarin giggled. "She always does such a good job with the minutes and keeping your schedule tight. So tight that drop-ins are frowned upon."

"Yes, well. I'm sure your schedule is equally busy." Larkin ignored the bait about Tarin's pop-in the other day. "I don't want to keep you any longer. I know your beautiful children will want your attention."

"Actually, they're out of town with my husband, visiting his family in Boulder."

"Oh, no. I hope this meeting didn't keep you from joining your family."

"Not at all. His mother did that all on her own." The snap in Tarin's voice turned her friends' heads.

"I'm sorry to hear that."

"We've come to an understanding and an eighteen-hundred-mile boundary between us." Her smile spoke of malice.

"We have to go." Genevieve cut through the eerie tension Tarin emitted like odious perfume.

"Can we walk you out?" Marlis grinned at Tarin. Genevieve averted her face, curled her upper lip, and rolled her eyes.

"Actually, I was going to see if you ladies wanted to grab dinner. I made reservations at Blue Ribbon."

Larkin's mouth watered for sushi, but her stomach curdled at the thought of her dinner companion. Something was off-setting about Tarin. The face down in a toilet bowl and scaring years off her life was the first demerit, but it was far from the last.

"Can't," Genevieve spouted. "I have a date."

Marlis turned on their friend. "You didn't think that tidbit deserved top billing?" She gasped. "I mean, you don't do repeats, and this is a double repeat."

Gen rubbed a thumb over her lower lip. "When it's really good …" A moan ended the thought and began many others.

"How about you?" Tarin's inquiry to Marlis was bubbly almost.

"I have a flight so early tomorrow that it might as well be today." Marlis shot Larkin an apologetic pouty lip.

The fact that her friend was going to London for a social media convention as the main stage speaker wouldn't get her out of dinner with Tarin. She'd have to do that herself. "Thank you for the invitation, but I have a lot weighing on my mind right now. I wouldn't make good company."

Tarin nodded, sympathetically.

"I'm glad you understand." Larkin grabbed her things from the table and thanked the stars the woman did the same with her laptop and briefcase. She stepped around Tarin and embraced each of her friends in turn. "Safe travels. Both of you."

"Always." Gen winked.

"Uh-huh." Mar shoved Gen toward the door. "Love you."

"Love you both." Larkin waved them off.

Tarin stopped so close to her waving arm she almost

smacked the poor woman. "We could order in, and I could try to explain why experience matters."

Anger burned Larkin's cheeks. She had plenty of experience in more important areas that pertained to running a business than this woman. The day she needed spit-up-stained blouses and 2.5 liabilities to do what she'd been doing since she was fourteen was the day she'd accept advice from an unstable human. She didn't need this chick OD-ing on pills in her apartment.

"Good night, Tarin." Larkin turned and headed for her office. Tarin could see herself out of the conference room or order her meal and take it in there for all she cared.

Her phone vibrated from on top of the pile in her arms. She scooped it up and answered without looking at the screen.

"Babe, I'm sorry about the other night. Forgive me?" Bronson's boisterous, most likely drunk, voice nearly exploded her eardrum. She'd expected Reagan to be on the other end of the line, not her childhood friend turned unfortunate Romeo.

"Don't be. I'm not sorry. I had a great time"—*minus the Tarin incident*— "and it ended just how it was meant to." Larkin shoved into her office and locked the door behind her to eliminate any further Tarin incidents.

"Nonsense. Let me make it up to you."

"No need." She dropped her worldly wares on the top of her desk and didn't look twice at them before heading for her private staircase.

"I want to take you on a proper date. You know, without the thousands of people. Just you and me."

Larkin was the only one in the staircase, and usually, she liked it that way, but tonight, the closer she got to her apartment, the deeper her appetite became. She didn't hunger for food. She didn't care for a friendship turned business fling or finance.

"I don't date friends." She shoved through the apartment-level door and past her own to the mouth of the ladder she'd fallen down more than a week ago.

"Then I'm not your friend," Bronson rebuffed.

A chuckle shook her throat. "You pulled that crap when we were ten. You wanted my Gameboy, and I wouldn't hand it over. It didn't work then, and it won't work now." She ended the call and slipped her phone in her pants pocket. "Good night, Bronson."

THIRTEEN

THE MANWAY COVER CREAKED AS LARKIN HEAVED. Never had she struggled to open the hatch. Tonight, she used every bit of muscle and grit to pry it only a few inches wide. She drew a breath and pressed harder still. A grunt wrestled its way through her teeth. The sound of something scraping the top of the metal doorway. Two thunks followed. From the force of her hands, the door flew wide and smacked against the hinge stops.

Larkin peeked out at the tar top. Steam rose from stacks in the far corner. Behind her, massive water tanks huddled together. Danger wasn't apparent. Then again, it hadn't been last time. Last time, though, she hadn't been looking for it. She hadn't sought it out. Not like she was tonight.

She climbed onto the roof and examined the lid. Two solid cinderblocks lay in a heap. Fresh scrapes marred the manhole's ugly metal cover.

"That shit."

He'd been up here since their encounter, and he'd tried to keep her from her sanctuary.

Larkin scanned the area. Nothing apart from the usual bird poop and cobwebs occupied the space. She walked slowly to the edge of the roof, to the very spot Beckett stood when he yanked her from the ledge. Hope welled with the insane notion that he would appear as he'd done that first night and wrap his arms around her. Only tonight, fear wouldn't consume her. Contentment counterbalanced by unstable desire would.

Atlantic winds battered her face. Cold seeped through her thin layers, chiding her for being up here without a coat. Below, unending lines of cars jockeyed for first place in a race no one could win. The sounds of their horns melded into a symphony with the whooshing gusts of wind, punctuated by the occasional shriek of a car alarm or the roar of an obnoxious engine. While her hope dwindled at seeing Beckett tonight or ever again, she embraced the city, the home she'd known her entire life. It beat within her as much as her heart beat within it.

She spread her fingers on the concrete. Warmth from the day's sun still radiated from the man-formed stone. The large diamond glittered in the lights from the building across the street. Her thumb glided over the smooth top and fierce edges. Throwing the ring would have been a mistake. Inadvertently, it had changed from a reminder of horror to a symbol of strength and kindness to a reminder of him.

"Damn." Larkin had never had a crush. It whipped her insides into a frothy mess. Sticky and sweet. She hugged herself to ward off the cold and propped her elbows on the ledge.

Her gaze found the two rows of windows on the part of the building she saw every day and never really examined. What did the people do there? Did they design great buildings or water filtration systems for rivers to bring fresh drinking water to drought-ravaged villages in Africa? Were they lawyers fighting for the little guy or backing big business? Did they wheel and deal corporate BS for ten hours every day? How many of them were married? Why did she have to be?

Lights flicked on in an office about twenty feet to the right and maybe one story down from the spot where she stood. It was as though someone had heard her questions and wanted to offer answers. It drew her over, despite the sharper bite of the wind in the center of the building's roof.

A man crouched low with his back to her. Three filing cabinet drawers stood open, plus one more that he hunched over. Filing. Larkin couldn't think of anything more boring. It brought starving children food or closed amazing deals. It wasn't exciting in any way, yet it was so necessary. If done properly, it changed the world. He closed the drawers and reached for the light. She blinked to bring him into focus, but then everything plunged back into darkness.

Answers weren't always as exciting as they promised to be. The same was probably true for Beckett. It was time to let go of the idea of him and grasp the reality. She knew nothing about him. He didn't want to be known. End of story.

Several feet back to her left, another light turned on, and her feet moved without thought. The man stood in the doorway, almost assessing the room. He walked into the room, closed the door, and stepped forward. His wide frame and menacingly handsome face came into view.

Half of Larkin's heart jumped up and down and waved frantically. The other smarter half scraped its tiny heart jaw up from the bottom of her stomach and shoved it back into place. Did he work there? Had he been spying on her for the last year and known she'd be on the roof that night? What was he doing?

Beckett removed his jacket, the same one that'd been soaked through the night before, and placed it in front of the door, covering the crack at the threshold. He moved from drawer to drawer, pulling them wide, riffling through, and then closing them. Occasionally he'd read a page or parts of a file, but he never lingered for more than twenty seconds. Finally, he moved to another office. Larkin followed, entranced by the oddity. There, he pulled back the Ferrari of office chairs and sat in front of a computer. The screen lit the familiar scar and dark eyes that had examined every inch of her hours before. Now they were cold and unfeeling. She couldn't really see his eyes, but there was no life in his face, not like she'd witnessed when he'd been inside her.

A light from the opposite end of the building caught her attention. It was about twenty feet past the first office she'd seen him inside. The brightness remained for only a couple of seconds before going off again. A moment later, the light to the office one closer to her turned on for a second, and then off again. Seconds passed and the light to another closer office burned away the dark.

Larkin's gaze jumped back to Beckett. He sat in the chair with his right hand on the mouse, clicking, shifting, clicking. With every passing second, the lights turned off and then on, gaining precious feet on the man she'd let in her bed last night, the man who clearly wasn't meant to be in that pricey office, meddling with who knew what.

She hugged the edge of the building close and yelled his name, but her voice was carried away on a gust of winter air. Her arms flailed, wide and wild. Every cell in her body begged him to look up.

The lights drew closer and closer with the passing of seconds.

Still he clicked and scrolled.

Sweat broke out on Larkin's chest despite the plummeting temperatures. Her heart pounded against her sternum, sounding the alarm. She should go inside. No way in hell did she need to be an accessory to a crime or even a witness. There were enough problems on her doorstep. She pushed away from the ledge but couldn't make herself turn away.

His head lifted from the screen, and she'd swear his gaze zeroed in on her. Maybe it was the lightheadedness from breathing so hard, but he did. He stood, his gaze unwavering. That all-too-familiar mix of excitement and dread whirred within.

She flailed her arms and pointed toward the office, and then motioned for him to get down.

He didn't move. For several beats, he stood and stared.

The light was only two offices away from Beckett.

She started the crazy motions again, but before she could finish, he lunged at the light. Her heart resounded in her ears, a gong. Breaths heaved in and out of her lungs. The cold burned her throat. For minutes that turned into an hour, she waited. And waited more. Her gaze searched floors for him, then the street, which was useless. She could hardly make out the difference between a cab and a cop car at this height. Most useless still, she waited, expecting him to show up on the roof disgruntled but grateful for her help.

When she could no longer feel her toes and her fingers burned, Larkin risked her life shimmying down the ladder and hobbled to her apartment more confused than ever before.

FOURTEEN

THE ONLY THINGS THAT HELP when you're frozen and confused are a hot bath, a fire, and a bottle of wine. She'd managed the first two and was working through the third when she remembered to Google Tarin's pill. Because, by damn, she'd answer the questions she could. Larkin sat on her couch, pulled a blanket over her legs, sipped, and searched … "What was it?" She tapped her lips. "IPO. Nope. That's a different problem." A sigh lifted and dropped her shoulders. They drooped deeper than before. "Focus, Larkin. "PO. APO … something." She started there.

Tarin's condition had nothing to do with the military and diplomatic mail, nor mythical gods or fraternities. She searched APO pill, then scrolled down to WebMD's pill identifier. There were several pills in different shapes and colors. After scrolling down, she found a pill that looked similar to the one she'd found in the bathroom. If only she could remember the other letter on the 5 mg pill, she'd know for sure whether this was the drug. There were more letters on Tarin's. Not quite so many numbers, but this wasn't far off.

Larkin clicked on the description and read, "Benazepril-Hydrochlorothiazide," extremely slowly. "Uses. High blood pressure? Helps prevent stroke, heart attacks, and kidney problems. Huh?" That was far from diabolical.

The woman with a husband, children, and a corporation depending on her had a major medical problem. A twinge of guilt batted around her heart. She'd been such an ass. So the lady was a little off. No wonder. She was juggling swords round the clock. Sure, she was a bit odd. Larkin would be, too, if she had to deal with half the bullshit Tarin did.

She clicked on the side effects tab. The damn pills could cause dizziness, drowsiness, blurred vision, vomiting, and more.

"Good gracious." Larkin closed her laptop and shoved it off her lap in disgust. The machine had done nothing wrong. She had labeled the woman a loon, convinced she was trying to overdose on prescription drugs. She was a damn monster. Three gulps of wine later and she needed a refill.

"Well, hell." The bottle was across the room on the island where she'd opened it. Larkin turned, propped an arm on the back of the sofa, and stared at the bottle, willing it to levitate in her direction. "Please?" The bottle didn't budge. She glared at the red O's that faded across the label. Marlis had brought her the bottle from some winery in Colorado. The woman traveled all over for social media conventions.

"The Olathe Winer ..." Larkin stopped cold, captivated by the uppercase text of the winery's name. "OLA. IPO. OLA 5m." She smacked a hand against her forehead and stared through her still frozen fingers at the letters. "Are you serious?" Of all the bottles she could have chosen—and there were a ton in her wine cooler—she picked that one.

A firm knock sounded on the door. Her entire body flinched for the second time today. The jumping, the fear, and her reactions irritated her more than the kind jerk at the door. Lucas. Would he ever give up? No one else had access or would care to bother her after the week she'd had.

Larkin tossed back the throw and stomped to the door, not that it did any good. Her feet smacked impatiently against the marble floor. She pulled her robe snugger to her chest and tightened the knot. Not that he'd see it. She planned to stay firmly planted behind the—

Her gasp hit the door and fogged the peephole, obscuring her view of Beckett's wide neck and jacket-covered chest. Sweat slicked her palms. Her legs actually freaking wobbled. The hair curtaining her face swayed with each heavy breath.

Common sense demanded she keep the door locked and call the police. After all, she'd witnessed him—doing what—stealing things? No, the worst thing she'd seen him do was break and enter. But really, she hadn't witnessed it. She only knew he ended up in places he shouldn't be.

Common sense demanded she keep the door locked and converse at a safe distance, but Larkin flipped the lock and pulled the door wide.

Beckett strode inside without a greeting.

She closed the door, locked it, and drank him in. His clothes were different from the night before. The jacket was a dark rip-stop material. The jeans were darker but just as lived in. In a lineup, the entire outfit could pass for the ones he'd worn the night before. He had small cuts on the knuckles of his right hand. The first two, anyway.

While she cataloged him, he stared at her face. His dark eyes never gaped at her plunging neckline or the feet of bare legs on display. For too long, they stood and stared. Two stubborn humans in a standoff to end time.

As it passed, her heartbeat slowed but never regulated. It wasn't possible in his presence. Just one look at his hands, one glimpse of a memory of what they'd done to her, and it revved once more. She caved before she started panting and rubbing her thighs together, making a complete fool of herself. She'd done it enough in his company.

"Why are you here, Beckett?"

"You weren't supposed to be on the roof." His expression remained locked. Cold. Completely different from the last time she'd been in the same room with him.

"Try three bricks next time," she snapped. "Why are you here?"

"If I knew the answer to that," he growled, "I wouldn't be." Lines formed around his eyes. A furl divided his brows. "You're not my type."

"Brunette?" She knew that wasn't what he meant, but if it would keep him talking, it was worth the jibe.

"Messy."

Larkin canted her head and glowered.

"Rich. High profile." His feet shifted for the first time since he stopped inside her apartment.

"Are you hiding from something?"

"I don't hide. I hunt."

She swallowed the massive lump in her throat. "That's why you're in the shadows. You're hunting ..."

"I'm good at what I do." Beckett stepped forward, his gaze stalking as he drew near.

"What were you doing in that office?"

"Why were you on the roof?" He stopped less than a foot away from her.

"I wasn't trying to throw myself off," she snapped.

His gaze dropped slowly, caressing her neck, chest, hips, and thighs with a simple look. He didn't speak, only waited.

"I was freezing my ass off," she hedged.

Not a sound, but the almost imperceptible rise of one brow told her what he wanted. She didn't want to give it to him. Every time they met, she gave, and he received information. Now, the physical, that was another story.

Larkin compressed her fingers and formed fists. Why did he have this magnetic power over her? No one else ever wielded anything over her. Except for her father, but they weren't the same.

"Why, Larkin?" He stepped so close his breath tickled her cheek. "Why'd you go to the roof tonight?"

She lifted her chin and challenged his gaze. "I was looking for you."

"After the other night, I said you'd never see me again. You said you wouldn't need to. What the hell happened to that?"

"I don't know." Larkin pulled at her hair and screamed at the ceiling, more than irritated at herself for her honesty. What was it about him that pulled her so incredibly hard?

"Fuck."

One hot hand grabbed her nape while the other landed on her hip. He pulled and pushed at the same time. Her back met the wall, and her lips collided with his. They were insistent and greedy. The hand at her hip rose roughly to grasp her breasts.

Her body responded before her mind caught up with the action. Both her hands grabbed hold, one finding his waistband and the other the front of his jacket.

He touched her body as though he owned it. Any other time, the thought would repulse her, but here, with him, Larkin loved the possession. She wanted the same hold over him. Her hands roved up his chest and under his jacket. Warmth engulfed her fingertips, palms, and arms. Soon, she found a button. With both hands, she unsnapped it. Coarse hair and hot skin rewarded her efforts.

Beckett turned her jaw toward the sky and kissed his way down her neck. He yanked at the secure knot of her robe, and her clit pulsed. She'd scream, "Yes, please," if she had the breath, but they wouldn't stop breezing in and out of her lungs long enough to her to catch one.

A light three knocks on the front door flash-froze them to one another.

"Who is it?" Beckett's voice sounded loud in her ear. In reality, it was only because he was so close. She wanted to keep him close.

"I don't know, but I have a hunch." Fucking Lucas. "Security. Normal people can't get up here."

"Compliment accepted."

Larkin turned them and pinned him to the wall. "Don't leave and don't say anything." She scraped her mouth over his. "That last part shouldn't be hard for you."

His eyes sparked and an almost smile played across his swollen mouth. That tiny win did stupid things to her insides. It made them squishy and warm. In that instant, she knew she was doomed. Addicted. Without hope for survival. Because this man wasn't a forever guy, and she wasn't a forever girl. Yet the only thing she wanted to do with her life was make that almost smile appear again and again, forever.

She shoved away from him, cast the inner demon that corrupted her thoughts to the recesses of her brain, and checked the peephole. Sure enough, Lucas stood with a large bouquet of black roses in a crystal vase. Forehead on the door, she adjusted her robe, drew a deep breath, and then opened the door, sure to keep it between them.

"I was heading out for the night, but these arrived." Lucas shimmied the vase and the stunning display of macabre flowers, assured to boast another colorful card.

"They could have waited until the morning. In fact, all future flowers will be kept in the office," she ordered.

"I never met a girl who didn't like flowers." He flashed a sweet smile.

She was a woman. A woman who didn't like her space breached by evil, and whoever sent these lovely notes was just that. "Is there anything else?"

"I just wanted to check on you. We've been doing maintenance checks all day, and I haven't had a chance to touch … base."

"I'm fine. Thank you." She ignored the innuendo.

"I'm having cameras installed on the roof and the security on the access upgraded."

"No." The word was out before she could recall it. She had no choice but to back it up with a reasonable explanation. "It's my private space. No cameras. No upgrade."

"It's my job to keep you safe, Larkin."

"Miss Ashford," she corrected. "And I'm exceedingly safe." She needed to turn this around before he continued. "I am concerned about Reagan. She vanished before the board meeting without a word. No note. No call. She's not answering my texts. Do you know if anything happened today?"

"I didn't see anyone except for Carl and Dan most of the day. Maintenance." He shrugged. "Maybe she got sick."

"Maybe. She's always called in, though. And she was here this morning." Her mind whirred for a second. "Could you check the security footage for me?"

"I wish I could, but we were down all day. Last night too."

Larkin chewed on her lip, and then remembered how swollen and red they must look. She reached for the flowers. "Thank you. I'm sure I'll hear from her by morning."

"I can bring them in—"

"I have them. Have a good night, Lucas." She grabbed the flowers, pulled them through the small opening, then closed and locked the door.

Every time she found him where she left him, it would be a surprise. The man was a puff of smoke who could vanish or appear in a flash. But there he was, leaning against the wall, a statue built by the gods in honor of women's fertility.

She hugged the vase to her chest and gawked.

"He has feelings for you." It was a statement, uninflected by emotion. A fact.

Larkin nodded.

"Returned?"

Her head shook. "And he knows it."

"Can't blame a man for trying."

"Are you trying?"

"Yeah." He scoffed. "My damnedest not to."

She licked her lips and hurried past him to the island. The vase fit oddly next to the others. When she turned around, he was on her. His hand wrapped around her waist and lifted. Her thighs hit the cold marble countertop. He spread them wide and wedged himself between them. His mouth was on hers in an instant, driving away all thoughts of the day.

Larkin clawed at his jacket. The slick material whined under her fingernails. She pulled him closer, reveling in the heat that radiated from his chest. It warmed her breasts through the thin silk of the robe. His stubble rasped like sandpaper on her cheek. Her knees bent and stroked up and down his legs and full, tight ass.

"Christ, woman," he growled.

She shoved the jacket off his shoulders, down his arms, and tossed it to the floor. His shirt came next. Curses melded against her lips. His. Hers.

Beckett didn't bother with the knot this time. He shoved the robe to the sides, baring her breasts to thighs with the thin strap of material still tied around her middle. She expected an attack, much like their previous encounter. Nearly unhinged strokes and nips, wearing kisses and bruising grips. He stood back. His gaze raked over her top to bottom. He looked at her as though she was a present and untied her bow.

Desire plumped her breasts and slicked her sex.

The foil wrapper crinkled as he pulled it from the back pocket of his jeans and tore it open. Sheathed, he returned with the same fervor. Their bodies collided. She welcomed his invasion into her body. He'd breached her mind a week ago, so there was no keeping him out.

They panted and gasped, shoved and wrestled, fighting for the climax that came too quickly. Larkin shook. Beckett strained. The arm he kept wrapped around her back nearly cut off her oxygen. Then it was over. The shaking ceased. He sagged against her. The one hand he braced on the marble kept them both upright. His head rested on her breasts, so close yet so untouchable.

He pulled from her body and lifted his pants up to his hips without closing them. When he walked away from her, down the hallway, a sense of grief unlike any she'd experienced swept up her bare flesh. She pulled the robe together at the middle. With both hands gripping the ledge, she sought the casual distance that'd guided her through adulthood. Her head sagged between her shoulders.

"Mother fuck." She muffled the words behind swollen lips and gnashing teeth.

"Hey."

Her head popped up to find him standing in front of her; condom gone, pants zipped. Why was he saying hi when goodbye was next in line? She couldn't speak, so she let her brow ask the question.

"Here." He stepped close. The soft terry of a warm cloth grazed her thigh. He moved it across her most intimate parts while his shielded gaze studied. The consummate examiner.

Larkin schooled her features. The last thing she needed was a crying jag with a witness. He'd seen enough of her emotions on the roof. She watched him care for her as though he'd done it a thousand times. As though caring was a part of his genetic structure. She'd have never guessed it.

Beckett finished and disappeared down the hallway again. He returned, grabbed his shirt, and shrugged it on. His boots remained tied and ready on his feet. They turned away. She expected them to march to the door, but he rounded the sofa. He stopped at the wet bar. Her favorite decanter with her favorite whisky caught his attention. The sound of it meeting a crystal glass made her mouth water. He tossed back a finger and then poured two more in the same glass.

His boots faced her. They stared for a minute, more maybe. She loved the way he looked. He was menacing, sexy, and he intrigued the hell out of her, dammit.

"Come here."

She gave orders. She didn't follow them unless he gave them, apparently. Her feet cooled on the floor while she padded his way. For what, she hadn't a clue.

He sat on the sofa and pulled her down next to him.

"Leave it to you to have the best." Beckett gulped more of the amber liquid.

"The best driver. The best whisky. The best friends," she agreed.

"That ain't all." He glared at her mouth.

"No?" The tightness in her chest loosed as she toyed with him.

He offered her the glass. She took it and let a sip swirl

around her mouth before swallowing.

"Creepy flowers."

"What?" She gave back the glass.

His stubbled chin hiked toward the counter. When she looked at it, she saw the place where he'd ruined her, not the three large arrangements.

"Yes, they are."

"Are they all from rent-a-cop Romeo?"

"Not a one."

"Freaky fan club."

Boy, he could say that again, but she didn't want him to. She didn't want to talk about the flowers or the cards they boasted. She didn't want to talk at all. Talking meant feeling.

"Larkin?"

"Huh?" Her gaze had wandered to the collar of his shirt. The hard lines, coarse hair, and the beat of his pulse had her mesmerized.

"Why were you on the ledge that night?" His question was a quiet rumble, but it sounded so loud in her ears.

She stared at the nearly empty crystal glass and his thick fingers. Her mother's glass had been empty. Not a drop of Glenlivet. The carpet had soaked it up. Before that, she managed most of the bottle.

His thumb brushed the wide gold bands on her right ring finger.

"You don't answer my questions," she bit out, "so why do I have to answer yours?"

"You don't." He pulled her hand into his and rubbed the top of her knuckles.

Something about knowing she didn't have to answer him made her want to. Reverse psychology at its best. "I was going to throw them off."

"That thing could finance a gorilla war for months." He toyed with the incredible diamond, then her fingers.

"Why would you toss it?"

Larkin couldn't speak. Her fingers held tightly to his.

"She broke your heart."

Never had she thought about it that way, but it perfectly described what had happened. "Yes."

"So badly that you're not waiting on some knight in Rolls Royce armor to heal it."

"Ha." She found his gaze. "You're too perceptive for my own good. Why are you still here?"

"I've met a lot of people in my life, Larkin, in too many cultures and too many countries to name, but I've never met someone like you."

"So the short answer is curiosity." She offered him a wide pout.

The richest laughter rumbled from his chest. It shook his neck and rattled her insides. "I guess so." He set the glass on the coffee table and threaded their fingers together. "Why'd you open the door?"

"Same reason, I guess." It wasn't the reason at all, and then again, it was the truest reason. They shared the silence together, feeling the interlocking of the puzzle that was their two hands. His giant. Hers small. Both strong.

"You know what curiosity did to the cat, right?" she asked.

"Yep." He placed a kiss on the back of her hand and then stood. "Have lunch with me tomorrow."

A command.

"One condition."

He waited, his eyes once again unreadable.

"What's your name?"

"Calder Beckett."

"No middle name?"

"Only serial killers lead with their middle names. I'll pick you up downstairs at noon." He pointed at her legs. "In pants and comfortable shoes." Before she responded, he turned and headed for the door. "Come lock it behind me."

"Like a lock will stop you." She tossed his words back at him.

"It's not me I'm worried about, sweetheart. This world is full of crazy." He waited until she stood and approached the door, and then he was gone, once again leaving her with more questions than when he'd come.

FIFTEEN

"TWO HOURS TO GO." Larkin closed out her email and stared at her desk. Staying busy was easy with Reagan still MIA. At least it had been. She'd burned through her to-do list and needed her assistant to line out the next things to tackle. The big one—the decision that would change the course of her business and career—was too daunting to deal with today.

The intercom beeped. "Miss Ashford?" Darren, Reagan's assistant and the guy who filled in for her when she needed time off, was almost too chipper for her to handle. Well, on any other day. Today, a smile stretched her face into a cartoonish feature.

"Yes, Darren?"

"There's still no answer at Reagan's apartment."

"Thank you for letting me know. Any word from security?"

"Yes, ma'am. That's why I was calling. Mr. Backstrom is here to see you."

Why the man couldn't pick up a damn phone was beyond her. She didn't want to fire him, but if he insisted on these face-to-face meetings, he'd, in essence, fire himself.

"Send him in. Thank you."

"Right away." The buoyancy in Darren's voice reminded Larkin of her own excitement.

"Calder Beckett," she mused like a schoolgirl. Why'd she have to wear pants? Oh. Make that two hours, one and a half. She had to change clothes.

"Miss Ashford." Lucas bowed upon entrance.

What the hell? He hadn't done that on the first day of the job, but hey, he didn't call her Larkin. It was a start. Weird, though it was.

"I reviewed our tapes from Tuesday—"

"Yesterday," she offered.

"Yes. As I suspected, there was no footage of Reagan leaving."

"How does maintenance of a security system keep it from working? Doesn't that defeat the purpose?"

"All security staff was on duty yesterday to secure the building. If anything untoward happened, we would have been alerted to it and handled the situation immediately." Lucas's shoulders stiffened. "I went by Miss Walstead's apartment. Her car was not there, and there was no answer at the door."

"Now what? It's not like her to blow off anything. She's even remembered my anniversary for the past six years, for goodness sake." Larkin sat back in her seat.

"Anniversary?" Lucas shifted back a step.

"The day I started Duo and Ditto ten years ago." Larkin gestured to the building. "Since she's been with me, she celebrated the day when I would otherwise work through it."

"I'll look through her calendar. Maybe she had a trip that she was so excited about she forgot to tell you." He gestured widely. "Or maybe she told you, and with everything going on, you forgot."

"I thought about that." Larkin shook her head. "I checked this morning. There wasn't anything."

"I'll look." His shiny wingtips headed for the door. "Maybe you missed something."

"If it's on her calendar or her desk, I didn't miss it." Larkin was busy, yes, but not incompetent.

He stopped at the door and looked back. "It won't hurt to have another set of eyes on it. That's all I'm saying."

"I'm going to call her mother and see if she's heard anything. They're close."

"Are you trying to worry the woman?" His tone was almost shrill.

"No. I'm trying to find her daughter." Larkin placed both hands on the cold glass. "If her mother doesn't know where she is, she'd know who to call from there to find her. And she'll call the police, if she needs to."

"The police?"

"Yes, if she's missing ..." She thought about the haunting cards she'd received over the last week. They had nothing to do with Reagan's disappearing act. They couldn't. Because if they did, she'd never forgive herself for not saying something to Lucas or even the police about them sooner.

"She's not missing. You're overreacting. She's a grown woman who took a day and forgot to call in."

"You're right." It was what she wanted to hear even if it came from Lucas's mouth.

"Just give me more time to dig before you upset her mother for no reason." He gave her the sit, stay hands.

"All right." Larkin watched him go and then looked at the clock. "One hour and twenty minutes." She massaged the bridge of her nose and waggled her jaw.

Once she made this major decision, the tension constantly tightening her facial muscles would fade. Once she found Reagan, her nagging mind would stop worrying her with dark thoughts, thoughts too ugly to give credence to. She picked up her phone and messaged Genevieve. Her assistant and Reagan had fostered a working friendship over the years. Maybe she knew what was going on.

Genevieve: No, I asked her about Reagan when you said she didn't show this morning. How are you?

Larkin: Worried about her.

Genevieve: I meant about the news.

A cold chill ran through her arms and seeped into her fingers.

Larkin: What news?

Genevieve: Shit! Reagan's not there to keep you posted. I was waiting for your rage to die down before I asked. You don't know?

Larkin: Tell me already!!!

Genevieve: Do you have a copy of the Times?

Larkin yanked the folded paper from the bottom of a tall stack of mail she'd yet to go through. Reagan usually pared down the pile, tossing anything that wasn't pertinent and seeing to half of the things that were. Gosh, where was she? What was the news? Why was she going to be in a rage about it? The thick pages crinkled under her hands. She straightened the fold and …

Nothing she saw raised red flags except the sweeping tax bill, which she could do nothing about. Well, there was Larry Vincent's name in bold black lettering. The guy was bad news. His daughters, who Bronson had been courting the other night at the same time, had to be too.

Larkin: In my hands. Where?!

Genevieve: Business

Genevieve: Then Fashion & Style, Weddings

Genevieve: I can come over after court.

She ignored the three consecutive bursts from her phone and stared at the business headline. "Multimedia Giant set to go Public if …"

"Please no." Larkin's hands sweated. Her heart dropped, sending waves of bile into her throat. She gagged.

Her phone rang so loudly she dropped the paper and watched the device dance across the glass tabletop. The readout announced the call was Marlis McCain. She pressed answer and placed the phone against her ear.

"Have you read it yet?" Mar asked.

"No."

"You read me the asshole's baby announcement." The asshole being the married guy Mar had been dating but didn't know he was married. "It's only fair that I return the favor."

"Hurry before I throw up." Larkin leaned back in her chair and stared at the ceiling.

"Larkin Ashford, heir of the Ashford fortune—"

"Which her father squandered before she hit puberty," she amended.

"I know," Mar said.

"They don't."

"Screw them. They need to fact check. Okay, let's see. Blah, blah, blah. Successful businesswoman, blah, blah, blah. Gathered a board of seasoned business men and women to aid in the largest decision the business has yet faced; whether or not to go public."

"Have you already read it, Marlis?"

"Yes."

"Then get to the point. I can't take any more bullshit," she pled.

"You just want the bullet with none of the accolades?" Marlis whined.

"Please."

"It's a quite complimentary article."

"Marlis McCain, don't make me order you two shots of tequila at dinner."

"Fine," her friend huffed. "It ends in a cliffhanger that leads to the marriage section that says you're looking for an eligible bachelor to marry to shore up your business before taking it public. It says it nicer than that, but ..."

"Screw nice and screw them," Larkin snapped.

"The story started circulating on the internet last night. Per usual, the papers were late to the party and are citing online sources, who are citing no sources at all."

Larkin tore into the paper, scouring line after line of false claims. Three pictures accompanied the article. One of her, one of Bronson Beauregard, and one of Gregory Evangeline. "Eligible bachelors for one of New York's most eligible bachelorettes?"

"Just throw it away. It doesn't matter. They're just words. The people who know you will know this is a bunch of baloney."

"The problem isn't that people will think I'm looking for a husband. The problem is I have a leak on my board. The information in these articles was privileged, and someone sold it with a slant that makes me and my company a target."

"I'm sorry, sweetie. Do you want me to come over?"

"No." She cradled her head in her hand and exhaled. "I have to start putting out this fire before it engulfs everything."

"Talk to you later?"

"Sure thing." Larkin ended the call and scrolled through her contacts for her publicist.

If only she had Calder's number, she'd call him and postpone their date, if that's what it was. There was so much to do before she was overrun with inquests about her marital status. As a single woman of a certain age, she faced that quite enough already.

Her phone beeped with a text.

Libby: I don't have evidence to back it up, but you know which person on your board is the former media mogul and still has friends in those outlets …

She'd been trying not to jump to the Cornish Gleeson conclusion, but who was she kidding? The man was as old school as they came and in the misogynistic, non-nostalgic way. He wasn't the only one who wanted her saddled, though.

Larkin: Fair point.

After sending her publicist a message to work up a rebuttal to the *Times* articles and find out who was responsible for the pieces, she tossed her phone down and stared at the stack of mail she'd inadvertently strewn across her desk. Ten … no, more like twenty were messages. The thin slip of paper felt like tissue under her finger.

A guy she attended graduate school with online too many years ago had sent her well wishes and would like to get together at her earliest convenience.

She glared at the other messages. "No."

But yes. Note after note were men from her past, begging an audience with her as soon as possible. They spoke of connections felt long ago but never acted upon for some reason or another.

Beside those notes, the damn paper sat mocking her with its black and white letters. As though the simplicity in the color scheme made them true. She flipped the front page facedown and found the extension on the Larry Vincent piece. The man was in custody due to an ongoing investigation by the FBI for his illegal gaming activities and a suspected hit hired on his competitor.

Her fist smacked the intercom. "Darren?"

"Yes, Miss Ashford?"

"I'm going out for lunch."

"Yes, ma'am. Um ..."

"What, Darren? Have you found Reagan?"

"No, ma'am. I wasn't going to bother you until you took your lunch break, but I ..." He squealed. "May I just come and show you?"

"Sure."

Larkin braced both hands on her chair and breathed, trying to prepare herself for Darren's news. She wouldn't be surprised if any number of bridal shows had called with a special offer / show just for her.

"Look." He waltzed into her office. His partner was the largest bouquet of blood-red roses she'd ever seen. They made the ones in her apartment look measly. Darren's wide smile gleamed as did his flawless deep-brown skin. "Four dozen, long-stemmed, thornless, gorgeous roses. And that's just one of probably ten bouquets. They're littering the reception area and making it smell absolutely heavenly."

The large vase clacked into her glass desk. Its large card stared her down, threatening in its gold-trimmed beauty.

"Is it your birthday?" He grasped his chest. Good Lord, he spoke fast. "I mean, if it is, let me say, I'm sorry for not turning up this morning with balloons and a song. How old are you?"

"It's not my birthday." Her fingers shook. She squeezed them into a fist and reached for the card.

"Oh. What's the occasion? Anniversary? New boyfriend? You probably don't know yet. You haven't read the card. I'll be quiet. Read away." He clapped.

The paper tore as though in slow motion. She pulled out the card stock and read. Roses are red. Violets are blue. Sugar is sweet, and so is your mouth. I'd love to kiss it again. Call me any time! Yours, David.

Relief drained the tension clamping her muscles.

"So?" Darren dragged out the word to four syllables.

"Admirers who want to marry me," she groaned, thankful CUNT hadn't been written on the card.

"How romantic." He fanned himself.

"Not at all, Darren. They think I'm looking for a husband to firm up the legs of my business."

"You'd never do that." His thin, dark-chocolate lips pursed.

"Thank you." She lifted a hand to the sky. He gave her an excited high-five. "I wouldn't. So let's null any messages from men looking for a sugar-momma."

"I'm on it." He started sifting through the mess on her desk.

"Then what do you say we donate any arrangements to a local hospital?"

"Ah." His shoulders bobbed and long lashes flapped. "Perfect."

"Not perfect, but it's a start." She grabbed her bag and phone and headed for her staircase. "I'll have my cell if you find Reagan or have an emergency."

"Yes, ma'am. Have a good lunch."

His words drifted off in the cacophony of her heels in the confined space of steel stairs and glass. They echoed off the corridor and into the foyer of her apartment where she came face to face with the flowers she hadn't acknowledged the night before. Now that Calder Beckett wasn't inside her apartment and the feel of his hands on her skin had faded, the black petals and thick metal vase menaced.

She dumped her bag on the sofa and confronted the bouquet. Five minutes ago, she'd read a card. Here, in her home surrounded by silence, she stepped up to the haunting display and grabbed the black envelope. It ripped easily enough. She grabbed the edge and pulled.

"Ugh!" Larkin tossed the card onto the counter. "You're a cunt. Fucking cunt."

Her heels tore down the hallway. The outrageous

stomping couldn't pound out the image of the single offending word written as large as the card would allow.
The top curve of the C nearly dipped off the paper, as did
the lower curve and the side, and each following letter.

Why didn't she have Calder's number? She wasn't
fit for company right now. Especially not with a man she
knew little to nothing about. What, was she asking to get
murdered?

Larkin screamed in the safe confines of her closet. Her
fingers gripped hangers. She tossed them across the small
room and kicked the hamper. Why was all the good mix-
ing with all the bad in her life? Nothing was in her control,
not anymore, it seemed. Maybe it never was in her control.
If it were, her mother would still be alive.

SIXTEEN

SHE HEARD HIM BEFORE SHE SAW HIM. A first. The machine clutched between his legs roared around the corner of the block, drawing the gazes of disconnected and jaded New Yorkers. They looked on as though it were a lion set loose on the city street. Around here, people used bicycles or cocaine if they wanted to toy with their mortality. Calder Beckett didn't toy with his mortality, though; he wielded it like a weapon. The bike dodged agilely through traffic and sped to the front of the herd.

It stopped in front of her. The wind it created made the fur on the edges of her lace-up boots and down-filled coat lay on its side. Her tightly pulled ponytail didn't budge. The engine's rumble vibrated her chest. A blacked-out full-face mask hid him from view, but there was no denying that frame and the command he held over everything, especially her.

He lifted a helmet from a small strip of mesh on an even tinier excuse for a second seat and extended it. Larkin gulped.

Never in her life had she ridden a motorcycle. Never had she dreamed of it until that moment. A sense of pure buoyancy lifted the world of worries from her shoulders and dared her to live more dangerously than she had ever imagined on any rooftop in all her years.

She snatched the helmet from his hand and nearly dropped it on the ground. It weighed more than she expected. With two hands, she opened the strap and wedged her head inside. Suddenly, she wasn't Miss Larkin Ashford, heir to anything, owner of a business, or the woman who had to make hundreds of tough decisions daily. She was a badass embarking on an adventure that those people looking on only dreamed they could grab.

Larkin stepped to the throttled machine, tossed her leg over the back, and sat.

Beckett leaned over, grabbed her left ankle, lifted her foot from the pavement, and placed it on a rung sticking out of the side of the machine. Without having to be told, she moved her right foot onto the peg on the opposite side and waited for takeoff. His big hands reached behind him. She looked for something he might want or need, but there was so little room for anything. It wasn't a car. He filled his hands with her ass and yanked her forward until her thighs fit snug against his backside. His palms hung there, full with her bottom, longer than necessary. He grabbed her wrists and wrapped her arms around his torso. She snuggled into the hold until they took off. Then she held on for dear life.

He maneuvered the bike as though he'd done it a thousand times yet hadn't grown bored of the task. His head swiveled, and his muscles responded as though he still drank in every turn, every shift, every impetus of the gas. An unfamiliar mix of adrenaline and excitement rushed through Larkin's vibrating veins. So much in her life was routine and expected. This was neither. Beckett was neither.

The bike drowned out the noise of passing cars and their yelling drivers. Tall buildings lined their path. Before many blocks had passed, her fingers turned to ice cubes. Wind battered them, but the rest of her, well, he blocked the majority of the onslaught. Luckily, the winter weather had abated overnight, and it was just cold as opposed to freezing and wet.

A few blocks later, the buildings fell away, revealing the tops of trees clinging to their festive fall leaves. Central Park. He pulled into what was certainly an illegal space and killed the engine. The shaking in her chest ceased, but it continued in her ears. He tapped her leg.

Larkin stood and adjusted her skinny jeans, coat, then popped the helmet off her head and breathed deeply. Two teams in boats churned the lake with oars. People jogged. Dog walkers maneuvered their packs. A homeless man shuffled down the sidewalk with a small plastic bag of cans. She looked at Beckett and smiled. He'd removed his helmet and secured his to the handlebar.

"What?" He stood, scratching his stubble.

"This is the best idea I never had."

"Fucking hell." His hands plowed into his thick hair and pulled. The words were gruff, but his tone hedged toward irritated.

"What's wrong?" She looked at his bike. Everything looked beefy and untarnished. Her gaze tracked wide, looking for a meter maid lying in wait to give him a ticket. None appeared.

"You couldn't have complained a little?" He pulled the key from the ignition and stuffed it into his pocket.

"Complain? Why would I?" She shook her head at

him.

"It's cold. It's dangerous. Your hair will get messed up. You want to know where we're going and how long we'll be gone. Is there Wi-Fi?"

"Sorry to disappoint, but this is ..." Lord save her from sounding cheesy, but this was perfect. "This is awesome."

Beckett took off into the park, leaving her laughing at his backside. His very nice backside. She hurried forward and fell into the easy rhythm of his steps. A cyclist weaved around them, calling out, "On the left." Birds flew overhead. Farther down the bank, the water rippled in the tiny wake of a remote control sailboat. Gravel ground under her boots.

"So you date a lot of bitchy women. Sucks for you." She laughed.

"No. I learned from my brother's mistakes."

She stopped walking, and he turned. The WTF expression on his face perfectly mirrored her slacked jaw, bug-eyed mug. His hands shot wide and one shoulder bobbed.

"You mean there are more of you in the world?" Her finger pointed accusatorially.

Beckett batted the air. "Only one of me, sweetheart." He turned and continued walking.

Larkin caught up with him and held her tongue. There was everything to learn about this man if she had the patience to listen. Hints peeked from cover in his ever-scanning gaze and continually shifting orientation, depending on who was around them. He was hyper aware of his surroundings. She was hyper aware of him.

She jerked her head away and stared at a group of moms and toddlers picnicking on a blanket as if it was spring. One made for the tree line. He bobbed and weaved in a single-mindedness to explore that reminded Larkin of an enthusiasm she'd once harbored for her career. A small blanket dragged the ground and hindered his quick getaway, though. Just like meetings and opinions made her second-guess her instincts and lose focus. Maybe that was why Calder Beckett affected her more than usual.

"Luca and Sam."

The names came out of nowhere with no context in her narrative. It took her a minute to reconstruct the conversation, but then a smile tugged at her cheeks. "Two brothers?"

He nodded.

"Wow! Poor Sam."

"Poor Sam? Why poor Sam?"

"You got Calder. Hot. Luca got Luca. Intriguing. He got Sam. Boring Sam."

"That's why he constantly froze my underwear and locked me out of the house?"

"Probably so. Probably that and it's what older brothers are supposed to do. From what I hear."

"Lock you out more than twice a week?" His voice pitched high, playfully and unusually so.

"Naked?" She choked on a laugh.

"Once. Mom tore into him for that one. After that, he always made sure I was clothed. The bad news was Batman pajamas and no shoes counted as clothes, and twelve-year-old girls are brutal."

She loved the way he spoke with his hands. Gesturing with fists when he talked about his mother getting on to his brother and covering his face with both hands. He hadn't used his hands to speak before.

"Never let you live it down, did they?"

"Nope."

"Bitches," Larkin sneered.

"Come on. You made fun of your share of unfortunate boys. Don't lie." He nudged her shoulder.

"I didn't have that luxury." She picked up the pace.

"You have all kinds of luxuries." He matched it easily.

"Now, yes."

"You didn't grow up in squalor. Your dad was heir to a fortune."

Larkin stopped and turned on him, looking with speculative eyes for the first time since that night on the roof. "How do you know that?"

"Who doesn't know that?" He shrugged. "You're a prominent figure in the New York landscape."

"You're not from here," she shot back.

"No. But I'm not an idiot either. The littlest bit of research will tell anyone willing to look about you and your family."

Why had she been so quick to mark him off the list of potential stalkers? Because he was good looking? Because he was easy to talk to? Because he got her in a way most didn't? Because he took care to keep her safe?

"Anyone willing to stalk, maybe." She tossed down the gauntlet and held her breath.

"If you call a quick Google search stalking, then everyone in the country is guilty of it." His finger circled and then landed on her. "Even you."

How had she gotten here in an argument she didn't want with a man she did want more than she should? He wasn't the enemy. She didn't have an enemy. She had a nutso, trying to scare her.

"I've been inside you, Larkin. I won't have you scared of me. You want me to take you back or walk you to hail a cab?"

Tears gathered in her eyes, but she blinked them away. He had planned a lovely date with none of the usual pressures of dating, and she was ruining it. She stepped so close her jacket brushed his. "I want you to kiss me."

His gaze narrowed on her mouth. "Is this a trick? Thanks to Luca, I can tell you I don't like to be kneed in the balls."

"You're the baby."

"I'm not a baby anymore."

Her head shook. She wrapped her fingertips around his neck and pulled him down until they were mouth to mouth.

"Sweetheart, you're full of surprises." He kissed tenderly. Sweetly. The pads of his thumbs grazed her cheekbones and ran the length of her jaw, continuing even after he broke contact with her lips.

"My father inherited money and a name. He also nursed an unhealthy obsession with secret lovers and buying them extravagant homes. The money went fast. The name, the goddamn name, kept us from squalor because I started working. Two jobs. Two jobs plus school while you were trying to find a way to keep your underwear at room temperature."

"I'm sorry." His commanding voice morphed into a whisper.

"I'm sorry about the stalker thing." She buried her head against his chest, took a deep breath, straightened, and motioned between them. "I don't know how to do this. I'm so used to someone wanting something from me and having ulterior motives."

The muscles in his jaw flexed. His animated hands fell to his sides. A part of him that opened to her for the barest of moments closed. She felt the pain as surely as he'd slammed a door on her heart.

"I didn't want this, Larkin. You have to know I did everything in my power to stay away from you."

Why?

"I don't want you to stay away from me. I might have a funny way of showing it, but this has been the best afternoon I've had in as long as I can remember, and I don't want it to be over." Larkin grabbed his hand and tugged him toward a row of food trucks in the distance near a park entrance. "Mexican. Greek. Salads. Pick your poison."

"Anything but a salad." That groan he emitted made her laugh.

"No salad." She pulled him to the back of a small line at the truck, promising the taste of the isles themselves.

"Okay." She nodded and turned to him. "That leaves roasted lamb's head or octopus fried ink sack. Which way are you leaning? I could get the fried sacks and you could get the lamb's head. It's bigger. And I could let you try mine." A smile threatened to crack her serious façade, but she held it together.

His gaze shifted to the menu and back to hers several times. The edges of his lips pursed ever so slightly. A man took his bag of food and exited the line.

"So what'll it be?" Larkin dragged him closer to the order window.

"Don't they have a kabob or gyro or something ... normal?"

"Oh, you can't enter a Greek home around Easter without meeting a lamb's head. It's totally normal." She pulled him forward again.

"We're not in Greece," he whispered, but there was an edge to it.

"Too bad. It's amazing. So laid back. Stunningly gorgeous. And the octopus sack would be fresh out of the ocean. They have urchin salad so delicious it would make you weep."

"Don't worry. I might cry now."

"Oh please. A strong man like you?" She swatted his butt—his very fine, muscular bottom—and tried to maintain focus. "You'll love the brain. The eyeballs are questionable sometimes. It depends on how long they roast the head. Seasoning helps too."

"You're not serious." The bulge of his eyes said he seriously hoped she wasn't, but that she was selling it pretty well.

"What can I get you two?"

Larkin turned to see a young Greek man leaning both his forearms on the high metal counter. Sweat clung to his forehead. Thick brows hiked in question. Beckett squeezed her hand. Not painfully so. The touch was light enough the begging translated.

"We'll take one lamb … gyro, one kabob—"

He smacked her butt.

She yelped and smiled too big at the man taking their order. "One pita motz and two waters."

When the man turned away to help another guy in the back of the truck prepare their food, Beckett grabbed her arm and whirled her around. He stepped close, backing her up until her shoulders met the truck's metal side. His face crowded hers, and she zeroed in on his mouth.

"I'm going to employ some torture tactics to teach you a lesson."

"But I'm innocent." She giggled.

"Not even close, sweetheart." His hand cupped the back of her neck and tilted her face up. Their mouths met in a sultry, smiling kiss. It was fun and playful. A completely new side she enjoyed more than his passionate and slightly domineering one, which she hadn't thought possible until this afternoon.

"That'll be … Oh. Um," the Greek man stuttered.

Beckett pulled back only long enough to give the man a small stack of cash from his front pocket, and then his mouth was back. He didn't kiss her but let his lips hover just above hers. "You had me going for a minute."

Larkin leaned closer. The stingy man kept his mouth just out of reach. "I don't have you going still? A pity." She licked her lips, tasting him. "Mmm."

"Sir? Your change and food …"

Beckett's gaze remained locked on hers. "Sweetheart,

you have me traveling a very dangerous path."

His disregard for their food and location while his sole focus was on her shot a thrill straight to her heart. It beat triple time as though she sprinted through the park in a race with every runner that crossed her path. After years of swearing off the race, here she was, winning without trying. If she trusted him, if she gave this relationship a little effort, what would happen? Hope sprouted in her chest.

"Buckle up, Beckett." Larkin yanked his head to hers and stole a chaste kiss. She bobbed from under his arm, grabbed the change from the food truck's counter, and slipped it in his back pocket. Her hand lingered longer than it should have with an audience. Decorum, nor fear stopped her.

He nipped her earlobe and grinned like a lion about to consume its prey.

To keep from becoming lunch—or the tabloid headline "Couple Jailed for Sex in the Park"—she grabbed theirs. He followed suit, grabbing the drinks and walking with her back to the lake. They chose a bench near the path, overlooking the water. His imposing torso brushed hers. A clear shot of his scent imbued her brain with memories of their bodies tangled together. He sat her drink next to her on the bench and retreated too soon.

She couldn't tear her gaze away from him, and he studied her in return. Her body heated ten degrees, though no kiss was exchanged. Something deeper, more terrifying and meaningful passed between them. Or maybe he just wanted his lunch.

Larkin offered him his choice of paper wrapped food. As expected, he chose the massive gyro. He tore into it. She averted her gaze to her kabob. Embarrassment co-mingled with lust. After years of practice, she knew how to do casual, but meaningful was another beast altogether.

"This place is crazy. An oasis from the madness. The city is mad, you know?" He spoke around a large bite. It endeared him to her more. Every man she knew ate with Emily Post perfection. She had no doubt he could, but she liked that he didn't.

"Where are you from?"

"What makes you think I'm not from here?" He didn't look at her. Instead, his gaze roamed from the water to runners to the squirrels mustering up the courage to approach.

"If you were, you wouldn't question any of it. The park is the park. The city is mad. Has been for centuries. Will be for more to come."

"I'm from all over." He shrugged and took a drink.

Larkin stared at the chunks of onion, bell peppers, and meat. "I'm sorry. I forgot how you are about questions."

Beckett leaned close, pulled a piece of pepper and meat off the skewer, and held it to her lips. She took the offering and licked his index finger clean. "Damn." He cleared his throat. "I wasn't being coy. We lived in nineteen different cities by the time I was fifteen."

"Oh." Larkin chewed and took a bite of her own. "That's … just wow. I can't imagine. I lived in the same house until I moved out. For sixteen years."

"You moved out at sixteen?"

She nodded. "It was the tiniest, most amazing apartment I've ever rented."

"It was your freedom."

"It was." He got it more than she had a right to expect. "Why'd you move so often?" She was afraid of the answer. If it was horrible, she'd want to protect him. Him, a massively capable man who needed protection from no one.

"Navy parents."

The relief was instantaneous. Though moving couldn't have been easy. "Tell me about them?"

"My parents?" His upper lip hiked, along with his brow.

"Yes, your parents. For a while, in my mind, at least, you seemed an island. As though you were so far removed from any other person. I didn't imagine you having a family." Her gaze hit her boots for a second. "I'm sorry." She shrugged.

"I thought of you as the center of a gentry. Insulated by being one in a crush of money and well-to-do friends. Connected."

"Look how wrong we were." A sour smile stretched her mouth.

He wiped it away with his thumb. "My parents retired from the Navy and live in DC, advisors to the Security Council."

"Wow." Her wide eyes matched the word she rarely used. "Are you military?" The question popped out of her mouth before she could catch it and drag it back, kicking and screaming.

Beckett leaned over, grabbed a large chunk from her kabob, and held it out for her. He repeated the process again and again until she'd eaten most of the food. His hand poised in front of her mouth once more.

"If I promise not to ask any more questions, will you eat the rest of it? I'm so full."

He popped the chunks into his mouth and chewed.

"Tell me about your brothers."

His mouth pursed to one side. He grabbed the skewer from her hand and pointed it at her.

"It's not a question." She rolled her eyes.

"Ugh!" He lowered the pointy end and buried his head in the crook of her neck. "You are too much, sweetheart. Too wonderfully much." His lips nibbled a path up to her earlobe.

Their laughs mingled with the bird chirps and carried

off in the wind.

"I'm the smart brother, remember? The handsome one too." He backed up only enough for her to see him waggle his brows.

Her heart melted. This playfulness was an extra treat to an amazing break from the world as she knew it. His mouth was back, tormenting her between fits of laughter.

"Don't forget the humble one." She laughed so hard, her lungs and nasal passages backfired.

"Did you just snort?" He laughed so hard his body shook hers.

Her sides hurt too much to speak. Not that she could for the laughter. Tears blurred her vision. The happiest tears she'd ever known.

"Larkin?"

Her name came loud and questioning from behind them. It didn't belong here in her happy place with her happy man and her happy tears.

They stopped laughing at the same time, but she was drunk on euphoria and couldn't turn. Beckett suffered none of the effects. He whipped around so quickly she felt the need to grab their lunch to keep it from falling to the ground. No need. His hands cradled his trash and her mostly eaten kabob.

Larkin dabbed at the corners of her eyes, drew a deep breath, and turned. Bronson stood on the path. He clutched his phone in his hand and stared at her.

"Hi." She cleared her throat and stood but stayed at Beckett's side. "Bronson."

"Larkin." He stepped off the path and walked toward her.

Beckett set the remnant of their lunch aside and stood.

Bronson stopped abruptly. His gaze rose to meet Beckett's face, and then it jumped to hers.

Why of all times and places did he have to be here in

her tiny sliver of time and space in the park? She was nothing, if not well versed in manners. "Bronson Beauregard, meet—"

"Call me Calder." Beckett thrust out his hand.

Bronson took it, shook it, and then retreated a step.

"Lar, I didn't think you knew where the park was." Her friend eased his gaze from Beckett and centered on hers.

"Hilarious. I've always known where it was. I'd just never had occasion to come until Calder brought me. It's beyond lovely, but then you know. You're here."

"Just grabbing lunch." He used his phone to point toward the row of food trucks in the distance.

"The Greek is delicious," Beckett offered, a hint of condescension in his tone.

"I know. I've had it before." Bronson's expression hinted at a double meaning.

Men. They really were shits.

"You come here often?" Larkin asked, ensuring Beckett knew Bronson had never had her.

"Every once in a while. I like to get away from the crowds." Bronson nodded.

She grabbed Beckett's arm. A stance for all parties involved in the awkward exchange. "Bronson and I were childhood friends. We've recently been reacquainted after his return to the States."

Bronson smoothed the double breast of his suit jacket. "I'm also known as bachelor number one. You must be bachelor number two." At that moment, she hated him and his slicked back blond hair, his too green eyes, and sun-kissed skin.

"Excuse me?" Larkin snapped.

"So, Mr. Beauregard, what was so important it kept you from American soil and this stunning woman's side?" Beckett countered.

"University. And business ventures." Bronson stuffed a hand into his pants pocket.

Beckett shifted ever so slightly to the balls of his feet. Had she not been touching him, she would have never noticed.

"What do you do, Calder?" Bronson said.

Larkin held her breath, awaiting his response. What would he say? Would it be the truth? How would she know?

"You do have a job, don't you?" Bronson snipped, like the spoiled rich brat he was and, apparently, remained.

"That's about enough." Larkin stepped in front of Beckett.

"Enough?" Bronson spat. "It's all over the papers. You're eligible. On the market. Looking for a mister to your missus." His hands plowed through his hair. Red flamed on his cheeks. "Larkin, if you want a ring, come see me. I'll give you one."

He walked away, leaving her in complete shock. It was as though a downpour had caught her without shelter. Here in the park with Calder Beckett, a man she hardly knew and felt too deeply for, she'd forgotten about the mess that was quickly becoming her life.

"You're not looking for a husband." Beckett made the statement in a flat tone that revealed no hint of tumult. The calm ran contrary to her emotions. It helped center her on the here and now. He hadn't asked a question because he knew her better in a few short days than Bronson had in a lifetime.

"No." She swallowed back bile.

"Why does the world think you are?"

He hadn't forced her to face him, but his logical line of inquiry allowed her to turn and find his gaze. "My board wants me to and is apparently a sinking ship with a massive leak." She held her hand over her neck for several heartbeats and then swallowed. "Today was the best day, Beckett. Thank you."

"Reality can wait a little longer." He grabbed her hand and headed for the motorcycle.

SEVENTEEN

NO PHYSICAL INSTRUCTION was needed when she mounted the machine for the second time. Larkin placed her boots on the pegs and scooted so close that not even air could come between them. Still, his hand wrapped around her backside, hugged her closer, and held her there for longer than the first time. She squeezed him tighter still. Her face pressed against the back of his neck. Warmth radiated from his skin. Her eyes closed. The realization that they were hugging shocked her eyes open. This was the most intimate act she'd ever allowed with a man or anyone, for that matter. Even she and her best friends gave weak embraces with air kisses. Those couldn't be construed as anything more than a greeting. This broke barriers. Unorthodox though it was, this meant something. And she never wanted it to end.

A taxi whipped into the loading and unloading zone,

forcing them into motion. Her arms remained around his torso, but she'd broken her death grip. Desperation wasn't a quality she admired, so no way would she offer it to him.

They rumbled back in the direction of her office. Three blocks away, she knew she'd made a grave error by hugging him so openly. The bike purred quietly at a traffic light with two cars in front of them so close to her office. He was taking her back. He'd seen her desperation without even looking. He'd felt it. Was probably still feeling it. Her arms tingled. She hadn't realized she'd been holding her breath until the car behind them honked. Her gaze snapped back to the here and now to see the light green and the first two cars so far in front of them a city bus could wedge itself in the gap.

The car behind them honked again. She felt his heart thrumming inside his chest. Unless he was having a seizure—which she thought would require jerking but wasn't one hundred percent sure—he was in the midst of a decision-making process. Again the car honked, but this time, it added a rev of the engine and hazarded closer with its bumper.

Beckett expelled an audible breath, looked toward the right, and then revved the bike into high gear. He cut across two lanes of traffic, turning them in the opposite direction from her building. Another car honked, or maybe it was the same one. They were too far gone to tell. Two fast blocks later, he turned left into the basement parking of a high-rise. The large metal rolling door lifted, allowing them entrance. He parked in a dark, desolate corner. The kind she'd always been warned to steer clear of. Her head bobbed left and right while she removed and secured her helmet.

"You're safe here." He grabbed the key from the motorcycle and then grabbed her hand.

Of course, she was safe. She was with him.

"This is us." He led her to an elevator, and they rode for what seemed like an eternity. His hand never faltered, even as people crowded them in a corner. On and off, traffic of a uniquely New York sort shifted, carrying on with their day and paying them no attention. Finally, he tugged her off the car behind him.

She weaved around a crush of people and didn't register her surroundings until the elevator doors shut.

White paper crinkled under her boots. Tape fastened the barrier to the walls, completely covering the hallway floor. Massive, clear sheets of plastic hung from the ceiling and covered the walls as far as the eye could see. The only light filtered in from a slim wall of windows far behind her.

Larkin's gaze jumped from the unfeeling plastic to Beckett's back. Her feet refused to move. He didn't stop, moving farther into the unknown. What was this place? Why were they here? She turned back toward the elevator, but the panel which normally held a call button hung upside down. A single screw kept it from falling to the floor, and wires protruded from the wall. They crinkled in every direction, creating a gnarled hand that would not help her escape.

Her breathing slowed, constricted by the tension settling in her neck. She turned toward the window, looking for an exit. A staircase or a fire escape would do. Something to relieve the feeling of being trapped.

"Larkin?"

She turned to find him close. So close that she had to bank the urge to wrap her arms around him and beg once more. For what she didn't know.

"Breathe, Larkin. You're turning colors." He grabbed her face and tilted it up to meet his panicked gaze. "Breathe, dammit."

Hers shifted away to the ceiling and the can lights and

bare conduit hanging from an unfinished ceiling.

"The owner is renovating in hopes rental capacity will rebound."

"Rebound?" Her voice pitched too high. Like the breaths making it through weren't reaching her lungs. "Judging by the length of our elevator ride, there doesn't seem to be a problem with rentals."

"You still don't trust me." His head hung, and then after a moment, it shook. "I don't know why you should. I haven't given you much reason to." He released her. A deep breath, one she needed terribly, expanded his chest. "Those are the commercial floors on long-term lease from the building's owner. All upgrades and cosmetic details are left up to the businesses. The top ten floors are condominiums." He took a step back and braced his hands on his hips. "They were until capacity fell. The old build couldn't compete with the modern marvels and signature loft living popping up all over the skyline.

"He closed and began renovating a year ago. I contacted him and offered more money than he could refuse. In return, he rented me the entire floor, no questions asked."

"Shocking," she stabbed.

His gaze remained on the floor, but his hands balled to massive, dangerous fists. A hint of veins popped at the end of his jacket sleeve.

"Larkin, if I could, I would." He met her face to face. "If I could." His lips pursed, and he nodded. "But this is bigger than me or you."

Her breath came then, deep and full. It stretched her chest and rejuvenated her heart. "I trust you, Beckett. I understand you can't tell me things because there are things I can't share with you." Her heart, for one, which struggled like the devil to leap out of her chest and snatch him up, to hold him close and never let go. "My reaction to this place … Well, it's not you."

"Sure, it is," he countered. "I scared you on the roof the first night we met, and I've given you almost no information about me."

"It's not that really." She closed the gap between them and grabbed his hand. "At every opportunity, you put my safety above your own."

"Then why the reaction?"

"There have been threats."

His eyes narrowed. They turned a terrifying shade darker.

"Through the years, there have been," she added, "but this board leak and bachelorette business have made them more frequent. I'm on edge with no real reason to be." It wasn't the entire truth, but it was as much as she was willing to admit. "Douglas is looking into them."

"I never liked spooks, but I am glad you have one by your side."

"A spook?"

"CIA."

Larkin's mouth fell open before she could grab it and hold it in place. She stared at him dumbstruck. Most people thought Douglas was a mildly sweet, completely forgettable old man. None of them knew what she knew. Except for Beckett.

"How'd you know that?"

"I suspected it. Didn't know until you just confirmed it." The corner of his mouth ticked up. It wasn't a smile, but it broke the tension holding her at bay.

"Okay, smartass." She shoved the side of his abdomen.

He caught her hand and held it against his warm body. "I've crossed paths with my fair share." Like a fish caught on a line, destined to suffer slowly and die, he reeled her in close.

"I have never crossed paths with anyone like you." She didn't fight it. What was the use? She didn't want to.

Beckett's thick arms wrapped around her waist and lifted. Her feet left the floor like that first night. The same amount of unfettered emotions reared inside her, but these were so different. Excitement mingled with despair. Hope shouted over them both, daring her to imagine a life with this man.

The heat of his mouth brushed over hers. Sweetly and softly, they explored the curves and edges she took for granted. His eyes closed for the exquisite contact he offered, and then opened. Each time, he eased back only enough that his face—scars and stunning, chiseled features—came into view. And his eyes. The dark orbs were nimble enough that they peeked in on her soul. His gaze studied her with deep, warm intent before diving back to taste more.

Her right hand toyed with the ridges of the scar on his neck while her left slipped inside the collar of his shirt. The need to experience him was ever present. On occasion, she fended the urges back with a sword sharpened by a lifetime of heart-rending experiences. At this moment, in this unfamiliar setting, Larkin released her defenses and gave herself over to the experience. To Beckett.

He levered one hand under her bottom and hiked her to his waist. She wrapped her legs around him and related the feel of his tongue sliding across the arch of her lip. His head eased back once more.

"Larkin, let me make love to you."

It was a demand, and her mind registered it as such. Her body throbbed in acceptance and anticipation. Her heart removed the shield it had worn for so long that the exposure alone shot waves of angst to her extremities. He offered no comforting words, no kisses to soothe the pain.

"You'd be the first." She swallowed.

"So will you." The man whose stances, expressions, actions, and voice bled confidence sounded as though he stared down the demon who'd taken the skin from his face. It was the only thing she could imagine would scare him, if only a little.

"Yes." Her word hung in the space between their mouths and their heaving chests and racing hearts. He didn't move for a pile of seconds.

Whether he'd sensed the change or followed his own abandon, she wasn't sure, but those words were the last she'd expected from her lips or his.

Finally, he turned and walked them down the long hall. They reached a door with a large, face height security panel. He entered a code with too many numbers for her to begin to commit to memory. Then they were inside. The condominium was modern and sparsely furnished. White floors met white walls, at least the ones that weren't glass. As in her home, one wall boasted floor-to-ceiling windows. Unlike hers, sheer gray curtains were drawn around the living area.

After locking the door, he walked them through the living area and past an open door with a desk, a sleek laptop, and a manila folder overflowing with paper. Beckett grabbed her chin to face him. His lips crashed into hers more forcefully than she'd ever experienced. It stole her breath and reignited the probing of her hands.

His boots continued to tread across the marble floor, but soon, the sound changed. They were in a smaller room that wasn't small by any measure of the word. She glimpsed a white wall that stretched far until it reached the extension of windows and curtains that'd been in the main room.

Larkin shut her eyes tight and nibbled Beckett's arduous mouth. She released her grip on him only long enough to unzip her jacket and cast it aside. The cool air gave instant relief to her fevered skin still constricted in too many clothes.

"Larkin."

Having her name growled against her lips with such urgency beat everything she'd ever thought she'd loved. Fine dining. Beer. Wine. Shoes. A sense of security based on barriers. None of it gave her the nerve-igniting, pulse-pounding euphoria as Beckett did at this moment.

"I'm right here." She grabbed him close.

Good thing she did. The world fell several feet.

Beckett dropped to his knees. It took her a moment to realize what had happened. The pillow softness against her back offered the first clue, and his unfettered gaze gave the second. He laid her in the middle of a thick mattress nestled in the middle of the floor. She didn't try to get her bearings because impatience clawed at her heart. In turn, her hands yanked and tugged at his jacket. No matter how hard she worked, she couldn't manage to get the damn thing off him. One of his hands gripped its fill of her hip, while the other formed a vise on the back of her neck.

They wrestled in a gridlock of desperation. Breaths rasped through her tight throat. His seeped through the cotton of her shirt and warmed her chest.

"Beckett, dammit." Her growl dissipated in fluffy down, thick glass, and yards and yards of white walls.

He laved at her neck, seemingly unaware of her struggle. His fingers worked the tie from her hair and freed her just enough that her attention shifted. The more she focused on his mouth, the less she fought with his sleeves. Her grip, meant for action only moments before, shifted to a needy clutch. She used it to aid his hands and lever her hips off the mattress. The heated cleft of her thighs thrust upward, grazing the bulge of his jeans. Friction and layers drove her toward the brink of madness at an excessive rate of speed.

His hands clamped hers and pried them from his jacket. Heat radiated from his palms. He pressed them to hers, holding them prisoner against the mattress. "Christ, woman."

"What?" Her throat was so dry the word exited as no more than a croak.

"You're so wild I can't get these friggin' clothes off you."

"Me?" she squeaked. "What about you?"

"When I release your hands, they don't move." His face hung just above hers. "You get me?"

She lunged for his lips. They tangled with hers in a manic fit of tongues, flesh, and even teeth.

A growl rumbled against her lips. Then the contact left. "Larkin." His head shook.

Her fingers itched to plow through his hair, to cup his face and yank it back to hers.

Beckett moved so quickly all she could do was watch. He kneeled back and tore the jacket from his back and the shirts from his chest. One long sleeve. One short. She stared in dumbfounded appreciation. If she saw him this way a thousand times, her reaction wouldn't pale. That thought forced a shiver down her spine, rattling it so hard her sides shook.

He leaned forward, yanked her shirt over her head, and pressed his chest to hers. "Sorry, I keep it cold in here."

If only it were the temperature. Her skin was rosy from the heat they created. Sweat kissed her skin. Her heart pounded next to his, racing for tempo, and she loved it so much. Too much.

His hands were back. They roamed the crook of her waist and the swell of her breasts. Bless them. The touch forced her mind to other matters. Like the one pressing insistently against her throbbing clit. She banked the fear and put her hands to work, tracing the ridges of his smooth and scarred skin. Every muscle begot another. Every valley crested to a climax. And hers gathered itself like a neatly forming tornado. Feelings, touch, emotion swirled and whipped inside her, building pressure.

Again, they fought for the lead, gripping and tearing at what remained of their clothes. Words and coherent thought regressed into grunts and washes of ecstasy. It cascaded over her skin, impeding her and bolstering her more than any drug ever could. What would be the effects of Beckett? He wouldn't leave a hole in her brain, but what about her heart? It didn't matter. She helped him fleece the boots, jeans, and undergarments from her body.

They eagerly pulled his from his hips, revealing his spectacular form. Damn the circumstance or the man who hurt him. The scars diminished nothing about him, but oh, the pain must have been great. She'd have taken it away if she could have. She hadn't been there then, but she was here now.

Larkin levered herself up and knelt in front of him. Her lips stole it away one kiss at a time. She started at his shoulder and worked her way over his pecs, down his oblique to his hip, and then back up.

"I'm supposed to be the one making love to you." His arms encompassed her in adoration and safety.

"Who ever said I follow the rules?"

"Sure as hell wasn't me." He pulled her up into his arms and wrapped her legs around his waist.

Beckett filled her completely without pause or reservation. Though, really, he'd had tabs on her body since she realized he would not kill her but save her from herself and destroy her all at once.

Larkin clung to him, used his body as leverage, and worked them to the brink of oblivion, but it was too soon. As though Beckett read her mind, he shifted them, rolling his back onto the bed. Once more, she rode them toward the end, an end that was predestined, and one neither of them wanted to see just yet. His hand played with her bottom, breaking their perfect rhythm. Hot wetness of his mouth encompassed her nipple, further re-charting their course.

He flipped her onto her side and exited her body, leaving her bereft and gasping. His hands roved her skin, molding it to his touch. His kisses eased the tension growing in her throat and shifted it to her belly, winding it there tighter and tighter still. Every time the end was in her sights, they shifted. Time unwound before them in an unending spool of pleasure. They gave and took in equal measure. Both maneuvered the tightrope with steely determination; otherwise, the end would come too swiftly.

Sweat slicked their bodies. Shivers turned to pants. Muscles morphed to Jell-O. Still they toyed, connecting their bodies for as long as they could hold out before one would give and separate.

She was no longer a woman but a billion nerve endings.

He grabbed her hips and flipped her onto her back. His sweat dripped down his cheek, through the ten o'clock shadow, and fell onto her breasts. She bicycled her legs up and down his sides and over his ass, begging for completion and terrified of it.

"I didn't think it could be like this." Beckett's whisper narrowly entered her brain above the pleas of her body.

Her head shook. Rogue tears mixed with her sweat. She pulled him close and hugged him to her chest.

When he entered her, she knew it would be for the last time. Her lungs filled with his scent. Her eyes with his face. Her body with his feel. They came with screams and battle cries, whimpers and gasps. Their muscles quivered. Exhaustion, his arms, and a willingness to ignore reality lulled her to sleep.

It wasn't long before she woke, just a respite to power her through the rest of her life. He still had his arms wrapped protectively around her.

"Come on." He placed a kiss atop her head and pulled her up and toward the door opposite the wall of windows.

A large bathroom greeted them just in time too. The proof of their lovemaking slid down her thighs.

Oh shit!

They hadn't used a condom. Sure, she was on the pill, but this was a first of so many firsts with Beckett. Her heart wedged itself in her throat. She must have stopped walking because he turned and pulled her into his arms.

"We ... um ..." After so many years of facing tough decisions and asking the hard questions, she was a child again. Incapable of broaching the subject.

"It was selfish, but fuck, Larkin, I'm not sorry. I don't want you to hate me, but I'm not sorry."

Her mouth hung open. "I don't hate you." She searched for the words. "I'm on birth control. I just ... I've never ..."

"I've never been bare either."

"Really?"

"Was never willing to risk disease or children."

And now he was? She was so confused. This was goodbye. She'd felt it in the desperation of their lovemaking. In the finality.

"Here." Beckett pulled her toward a massive shower and opened the glass door. He fiddled with the knobs, and soon, steam rose from the water flowing from the massive showerheads. When he turned to her, he held her hair tie between his teeth. His fingers sifted through her hair and pulled it high. He pulled the holder from his mouth and fastened it around a messy bun.

"Not the best, but it'll do for now."

She couldn't form words, but the stupid smile that stretched across her mouth had to communicate something.

He shooed her into the shower and set to work cleaning every part of her. She couldn't remember a time when anyone but her owned the task. Not her mother. Definitely not her father. Never a fuck. Not even in a shower romp.

Beckett took great ceremony in washing himself off her. The first hint of sadness seeped into her chest, cooling the edges of her heart despite the near scalding water. While he cleaned himself, he kept her under the spray, but the insistent warm flow did little to help. This would end up as the best and worst day of her life.

Her clothes helped center her … a little. In the open kitchen, he offered her water. The desire to look for hints in the apartment about his life took hold, but she would find no answers.

"You don't live here."

"No." He grabbed her hand from across the counter and pulled her around it. Their bodies matched up in perfect grooves. Her head on his chest. Her breasts against his abdomen. His cock snuggled against her belly.

She wouldn't ask where he lived. What was the point?

His lips brushed her brow and hung just a little longer than she expected. The goodbye. It stole her breath. A knife to the lungs.

"I'm never going to see you again, am I?" Larkin levered back far enough to see his face.

The heat she'd witnessed in his eyes and gasping mouth only minutes ago hardened. She braced.

"I have to leave. When I get back, I shouldn't see you."

Her feet were still under her. A feat in and of itself. She'd weathered worse in life. Him too. They'd get through this.

"I agree."

"You do?" His eyes softened ever so slightly.

"Yeah." Larkin placed her hand on his. "I like you, Beckett, and that's the last thing I need right now … or ever." She swallowed the what-ifs and could-bes. "I'm sure it's the last thing you need too."

"Give me his name and I'll kill the person who hurt you." His thumb rubbed the underside of her mother's rings.

A derisive laugh caught her unaware. "If it was that easy, I would have had Douglas kill them years ago." Her head shook. "Sometimes, you can't do anything. Life deals you shit, and you make the prettiest shit castle you can."

"I've played around in a fair share of it."

"I'm afraid you have." She kissed his chin and then grabbed his keys. "Time to go." They needed to leave and fast. The longer she was around Beckett, the more she wanted to be around him. The more she wanted to know about him.

His grip held tight, but he said nothing. He was quiet and contemplative, shielding her from the world.

Larkin had no more bullshit nor bravado. Why not lay it out there? She could talk to him about what she could talk to no one else about because this was it.

"My parents' marriage was a fraud. My father was a gay man, faking a straight life, and it broke my mother's heart. I found her with a bottle of Glenlivet and an empty bottle of Valium, and she left me brokenhearted."

"Christ, sweetheart. How old were you?"

"Thirteen." Larkin looked into the layered depths of his eyes. "I'll be damned if I give anyone the chance to break it again, even if I truly want to give them the opportunity."

She hugged him tight and then broke his hold and headed for the door.

He followed behind at a safe distance down the long hallway they'd so passionately crossed hours ago.

The dangling elevator call button clicked under her touch. It responded with a light, and the wait began. She held perfectly still, knowing this would be the hardest part. Who was she kidding? It was all going to be hard.

Beckett's arms wrapped around her. He braced her back against his indomitable front, but he hugged her tightly as though he needed the comfort. She grabbed his arms and held tight as though their lives depended upon it.

Above the door, the readout indicated the approaching elevator car. They released each other in unison. An amicable parting. No one holding on too long. It was how they parted at the creepy side entrance of her building, avoiding the mob of paparazzi crowding the front and back doors. She didn't watch him go, but she listened all the same. The roar would echo in her dreams for years to come.

EIGHTEEN

"WHO IS THAT?" Marlis hugged Larkin but kept an eye on the hot detective leaving her office. Her friend's blonde hair tickled her nose and nearly filled her mouth.

"A detective," Libby interjected from the back of the pack. "What happened?" Her friend's knowing gaze narrowed, and she felt a flash of what perps—or whatever FBI called them—must feel when the pint-size woman turned her steely gaze upon them. Heat clung to Larkin's neck, and she hadn't done anything wrong. With the exception of falling in fucking love.

"Not a chance. He's too fine to be on the right side of the law." Genevieve leaned so far around the corner to look at the man who'd just left her office that Larkin expected her to break a stiletto.

"Into the office. I'll tell you about that before Darren

gets back with our lunch." She hugged Libby, exchanged air kisses with Gen, and ushered them inside.

They sprawled out in her sitting area. Libby took her usual seat, legs hanging over the edge of an oversized chair. Genevieve plopped her briefcase on the glass coffee table and then perched on the edge of the couch. Marlis reclined on the opposite side of the couch with her phone in hand, fingers flying over the screen. "So who was it?" The woman could multitask like no other.

"That was Detective Owen Graham." Larkin closed her office door and headed to her seat opposite Libby in the other single chair, but she didn't sit. She couldn't. There was too much everything zooming through her veins and corrupting her brain.

"Told ya!" Libby fist pumped the air.

"Maybe I need to commit a crime." Genevieve's brows waggled.

"Reagan has been missing since Tuesday." Larkin's statement hit the room like a kamikaze tray of martinis in a crowded bar. Their gazes met hers. Their mouths gaped. "At first, we just thought she'd come down with some-thing and had to leave quickly. When she didn't show up Wednesday or call, I had Lucas go to her house. She wasn't there. I should have called her mom then, but ..." She chewed her lower lip.

"But what?" Libby prodded.

"Lucas convinced me I was overreacting, and then the leak happened. Then ..." Beckett happened. They'd get to that after. "Anyway, I called her last night after I tried Reagan's phone for the tenth time, went by her apartment, and spoke with her neighbor. She hadn't seen Reagan since Monday night."

"She was at work Tuesday, right?" Libby sank deeper into the chair and propped an elbow on the arm.

"Yes." Larkin nodded. "I haven't seen her since she left

to grab coffee after the close of the business day. We were staying late for the board meeting, and she needed a pick-me-up."

"What'd her mom say?" Marlis's voice cut straight to Larkin's tender heart.

"They had a fight Monday evening over a guy she'd been seeing. She hadn't spoken to her since. She just thought Reagan was mad at her." Tears threatened to clog her throat.

"Shit." Genevieve sighed.

"What did the detective say?" Libby's calm, focused tone centered Larkin.

"Besides asking a thousand questions two times over, not much." Her eyes rolled to the ceiling.

"Good," Libby said.

"How is that good?" Larkin's arms flailed for a second before hitting her sides in utter defeat. She'd been shoving off the feeling for about twenty hours now. It was beginning to push back.

"It means he's taking it seriously. He'll question the boyfriend, for sure, friends, family. Who was she dating?" Libby nestled her head on her hand, getting comfortable in the role of expert.

"I don't know." She shrugged. "We talked about meetings and files and tech. Reagan's a professional."

"Good." Libby reclined back, finished with the conversation.

"Again, I ask, how is that good?" Larkin gave up and sat on her chair.

"The less your personal lives are intermingled, the less you'll be looked at as a suspect." Libby's hand seesawed. "And you speak of her in the present tense, meaning you have no knowledge of any ill fate that might have befallen her."

"Christ, Libby." Marlis dropped the phone on which

she'd been texting. "The girl is missing. You can try to show a little empathy."

Larkin's stomach twisted.

"Maybe she ran off to Vegas with the boyfriend to show her mom a lesson. Heaven knows I would." Gen chuckled.

"No, you would not," Libby countered.

"You're right. Prenups first." Genevieve eased her forearm onto the couch's back and tucked her crossed legs under her full bottom.

"Hey—" Libby stalled when the intercom beeped.

They held their breath as though Reagan's voice would fill the speaker and eliminate one of the problems they'd been called here to help her tackle.

"Miss Ashford?" Darren's friendly male voice chimed.

"Yes, Darren?" Larkin hid her disappointment. She tried, at least.

"Your lunch is ready. Would you like me to send it in?" he asked.

The room perked.

"Yes, please." She needed something to take the edge off.

"Right away," he chirped.

"You were saying, Lib?" Larkin asked.

"Trouble will find you or it won't. Don't go looking for it." Libby's brows lifted. "That's our motto, isn't it?"

The collective nodded. All except Larkin. Trouble had found her. It was six-foot-six and weighed in the neighborhood of two hundred and twenty pounds.

"Hi, ladies." Darren shoved through the door with a massive smile and a bag from Sushi Nakazawa. His hips sashayed more than Genevieve's did on a Saturday evening hunt.

"Oh, my goodness," Marlis squealed. "Nakazawa."

"I know, right?" Darren set the bag on the table with a flourish. "Wish I could stay for girl talk and eat sushi, but

I have heaps of chocolates to eat, flowers to redirect, and a pile of emails that won't answer themselves."

"Your boss sounds like a real drag," Gen said loudly behind her hand.

"Yeah, but she wears nice shoes and pays well." Darren blew the girls kisses and turned to her. "If you need anything at all, don't hesitate." He bowed and then left as quickly as he'd entered.

"All right." Gen planted her feet on the floor and straightened. "Libby knows detectives. I know food. You don't order Nakazawa unless someone is getting married—and we know that's not the case here—or you need a major upper. The leak to the paper is shitty, but you've dealt with front page gossip before and at a much younger age. What's going on, Larkin?"

As if sensing a shift in the room, Libby righted herself in the chair. Mar shoved her phone in her purse.

Larkin buried her head in her hands and sobbed. Hot tears seeped between her fingers. Her breaths created moisture that clung to her palms. With each heave, her stomach clenched. Everything she'd banked for the last ten years flowed out her eyes. Small slights and large affronts spread their arms wide, ripping into her flesh in their appeal for release.

"Oh, Larkin." Marlis draped an arm over her back and hugged her to the side.

She continued to fall apart, piece by crumpling piece.

Another hand rubbed her back. More sobs passed. Otherwise, silence filled the room.

Two hands braced atop hers and lifted her head. She blinked Libby's stunning and large green eyes into view. "Tell us, Lar. We can't help until we know the problem."

Her chest heaved, but she reeled in the tears, if for no other reason than she didn't want to ruin Libby's gorgeous emerald blouse.

"That's it," Marlis urged.

"You remember the guy from the roof?" Larkin asked.

Libby's gaze flashed wide and then filled with white-hot rage. "Did he hurt you?"

Her head shook, but her flooding eyes gave her away.

"Oh, Larkin," Marlis cooed. "It's not your fault."

"One in six women and one in six men experience sexual assault in their lifetime," Genevieve announced. As if that statistic was somehow helpful. Then their assumption slapped her in the face.

"No!" Larkin sat straight and looked at each of her friends in turn, hoping she conveyed the honesty of her denial. "He didn't rape me. I fell ..." She growled and slapped the tears from her face. "I feel something for him. Something bigger than I've ever felt for anyone. Ever."

Libby looked at Marlis, who looked at Gen, who braced herself on the arm of the chair as though the ground were shaking. Nine point nine on the Richter scale. Duck. Cover. Hold on. They weren't from California. They weren't married women. None of them had ever been in love as far as she knew.

"Mar?" Libby begged.

"Me?" Marlis reared back. "What do I know about—"

"Does he know?" Genevieve interjected, sending them all for a loop. "Don't look at me like I have answers. I just know how to ask questions." They must have been staring at her like she was an oracle. She wasn't.

Their gazes eventually settled on Larkin.

"No, not exactly." She wiped her nose with the back of her hand. So sexy. So sophisticated.

"Details," Libby demanded.

"We've spent a few nights together after the incident. And then there was a date in Central Park." She wiped her hand on her skirt. Who gave a shit anymore? She didn't. Her assistant was officially a missing person, the entire world thought she was ready to find "Mr. Right," and her heart felt like it'd been ripped from her chest and put on display for everyone to watch beat and bleed.

"Cheesy." Gen dismissed it with a wave of her hand.

"That's what I thought too, but it wasn't like that." Larkin shook her head and wiped under her eyes. "It was … fucking perfect."

"Who is this guy?" Marlis asked. "What does he do?"

"Where does he live, and why was he on your roof that night?" Genevieve pitched in her two questions.

"I don't know." Larkin bobbed one shoulder.

The girls quieted.

"This sounds crazy, but I know in my heart he's a good person," Larkin explained poorly.

"That's what murder victims' friends say they said right before their bodies wash up on the bank of the Hudson." Libby crossed her arms over her big boobs.

"Look, he's had ample opportunity to hurt me, and he hasn't," Larkin retorted.

"You're crying." Marlis raised a finger.

"It's not his fault. This is something neither of us wanted, intended, or need. We made love yesterday and then said our goodbyes." Larkin clamped her teeth on a sob.

"That makes zero sense." Marlis tossed her hands in the air. "If you both like each other, what's the big deal? Why not be together and see where it goes?"

"Everything with him is secretive." For some stupid reason, she suddenly spoke with her hands. The need for them to understand outweighed her self-control. "I think it's for his job. Maybe something military. He's stupid fit, can get places most people can't, and knew Douglas was ex-CIA on sight."

"Douglas is ex-CIA?" Libby blurted.

"That's so hot," Gen purred.

"Yes. But my point is, I don't need anyone in my life

right now. Things are crazy enough as it is, and he is just as vehement as I am about remaining unattached." She blew a breath through her lips and let it fill her cheeks.

They all sat in the fumes of uneaten sushi, a bit dazed. Minutes passed. Their minds wandered, but no one spoke.

Libby was the first to move. She unboxed the food and passed it around their small circle. They each took a side of the coffee table, sat on the floor, and shoved Nakazawa into their mouths.

"At least you felt something." Everyone stopped eating and stared at Genevieve. "I hear love is pure shit on a life and the heart, but I'd like to be given the opportunity to find out for myself."

"Really?" Larkin stared at her in shock at the discovery.

"One day, hell yeah." Gen's red hair swayed. "You can't tell me you guys haven't thought about it."

Gazes jumped from one to the other. Larkin had banished the hint of the thought, but the other girls nodded in turn.

"Not often," Libby qualified.

Marlis's shoulders shook, and a laugh sweetened the stale air. "I think about it every time I have a really awesome conversation with a man. The thoughts usually stop anywhere from five to ten minutes in."

"When he figures out who you are?" Gen asked.

"That or when he suggests we hit the restaurant or bar bathrooms for a quickie." Marlis broke the tension, and Larkin was finally able to swallow a bite.

"I'm not heartless, you know." Gen shoved a hunk of sushi into her mouth and covered it with her hand while she chewed.

"Genevieve Holst." Larkin reached across the table and grabbed her hand. "You are all heart. All heart. That's why you hide it so well. Survival."

Gen's cold hand patted the top of Larkin's. "Don't you dare tell anyone."

"Never." Larkin crossed her heart.

"So this board leak is bullshit, but I don't see why you can't turn it in your favor." Libby pointed toward the doors. "Out there, you have a hundred of New York's most eligible bachelors vying for your time. Ease the pain you're feeling with one of them."

"One?" Gen cackled. "Why not three or four?"

Marlis hopped up, ran across the office, and then out the door.

"Of all the comments you've made, that's the one to push her over the edge?" Larkin stared at the girls.

Genevieve shrugged.

Libby slapped the table. "Remember the time you hit on the waiter, and Mar freaked?"

"You'll have to be more specific?" The hurt throbbed but being with the girls and pretending normalcy helped.

"He was super hot and barely in college." Libby tapped her lips. "Was it in the meatpacking district?"

"Here." Marlis ran through the open doorway with two thick stacks of envelopes; one full-size and one minia-ture. She sat back in her spot and doled out several stacks to the girls. "If nothing else, these have got to be good for a laugh. Let us know when you find a good one."

Larkin stuffed another bite into her mouth while the girls tore into the envelopes as though it was Christmas without the mandatory family gatherings.

"Ooooh." Gen leaned an elbow on the coffee table and waved to get their attention as if her near-orgasmic noise hadn't done the job. "Enrique is a Latin lover ready to show you la vida loca."

"No." Larkin giggled despite herself.

"He didn't really." Libby squawked her signature laugh that was too loud and too genuine not to smile at.

"Sure did." Gen turned the card, and there it was in sloppy script. *La vida loca.*

"I'm living the crazy life. The last thing I need is more crazy."

"I hear you," Libby agreed.

"Oh, my God." Marlis's gasp hooked their attention. Her head shook.

"Read it already. We're dying over here," Gen urged.

"No." Mar covered her mouth.

"Oh, you have to now." Libby wiped her hands and tossed down her napkin as though she was going to pry the words from Marlis if she had to.

"Uh. I hate you girls sometimes." Marlis straightened. "Annalise thinks you're trying the wrong ... things."

"Mar." Genevieve dragged out her name as though it were an admonishment.

"Don't make me say it," Mar begged.

"There's no way you two banged a limo driver together." Larkin threw down her napkin. "She can't even read a dirty card in front of us. There's no way she could do the dirty in front of you." She pointed at Gen.

"Uh." Marlis turned as pink as the card in her hand.

"Sure there is." Gen winked. "It's called tequila, libido, and a bad influence. That'd be me."

"No joke?" Larkin jabbed. "Someone get this girl a tequila sunrise." She motioned for the waiter that wasn't there.

"Read," Libby demanded while ripping into the first card in her own stack.

"Larkin, love, you are a strong, capable businesswoman who needs a vibrant and capable woman in the bedroom. Men serve a purpose, but I can open the world for you. Let me dine of your sweet pussy for breakfast, lunch, dinner, and dessert."

Genevieve and Libby whooped and hollered.

"That's not a terrible offer." Larkin blushed straight to her toes even as she considered the notion for a fraction of a second.

"And dessert." Gen drummed on the table and hit a crescendo. "Hot damn. What's her name?"

"Annalise Giavarrio." Marlis stuck her tongue out at Gen.

"You should really have someone vetting these." Libby's dry tone didn't fit the mood they'd created.

"Yeah, to make her a little black book," Gen agreed.

"I'm being serious." Libby turned a card toward them. In clear, dark letters, the word CUNT punched her in the gut.

"Well, don't show her that." Marlis snatched the offending paper and buried it under her stack. "You're upsetting her."

"I'm trying to keep her safe and aware. The world is full of crazy." Libby's arms spread wide. "Full."

Larkin knew about the crazy. It'd been visiting her for weeks now, but they didn't know about that. She should mention it.

"Well, she has a sexy CIA agent keeping her safe." Gen interjected.

"Old. An ex-CIA," Libby countered.

"Do you really think he's sexy?" Marlis rested her chin on her palm and leaned close, awaiting the answer.

"Hell yes." Gen grinned.

"He's old enough to be your dad. An old dad, at that." Libby's lips crinkled.

"I'd call him daddy." Genevieve popped a piece of sushi into her mouth.

"Gross." Libby rolled her eyes. "That's just—"

A knock sounded on the door. It cracked opened, and Darren poked his head through the tight opening. "I'm so sorry to interrupt." Darren, just as Reagan, always used the intercom. With all that was going on, maybe he didn't want to say it over the phone. Buoyancy fled Larkin's shoulders. She waved him inside and shoved off the floor with her deflated arms. Somehow, they worked. He closed the door behind him and waited near it.

"I'm so sorry." Sweat clung to his forehead.

"It's okay." She hoped her words were true, but from the looks of things, she wasn't so sure. "Just tell me."

His eyes rolled. That simple gesture settled Larkin's fluttering stomach. Reagan's death wouldn't annoy him. She was fine. Everything would be just fine.

"I've tried everything to get her to leave. She says she's not going until she speaks with you. I offered for her to make an appointment or leave a message. Nothing suits her." Darren's shaky hand smoothed down his sleek tie.

"Who?" she inquired.

"Oh." He smacked his forehead. "Tarin Blakely. She says she's your treasurer and friend. But I know your friends are in here." He winked at the ladies, and they waved back.

Larkin tilted her head to the only women in the world whom she considered friends. "I'll be right back."

"If it's Annalise, bring her back with you." Gen held her hand in the air. "I question the validity of her claims. Four times a day is a lot."

Marlis shushed her.

"Let's go." Larkin motioned Darren out the door.

"Thank you," he whispered. "She was on the verge of causing a scene. I guess she's used to getting her way."

Her husband must be a pushover.

The moment Larkin stepped through the threshold, Tarin shoved off Reagan's desk, opposite the seating area for her waiting appointments, and strode her way. Larkin closed her office door and met her in the middle under a large crystal chandelier her decorator thought was perfect for the spot. It was too much, if she had asked Larkin, but she did not.

"Larkin." Tarin opened her arms wide as though she expected a hug.

Larkin waved a sedate hello in front of her body and stopped several feet away, making it impossible for the woman to wrap her arms around her. After the incident at the party, she was more wary of the woman, though she really had no right to be. She hadn't harmed Larkin. She'd scared the shit out of her, sure, but she was no worse for wear. And maybe she couldn't help the effects of her medicine. Maybe that was the first time her body had reacted that way, and maybe she sought help from her doctor. It wasn't any of her business. She still needed to look up the actual medication. APO. Though, how different could one vowel make it?

"There are so many arrangements." Tarin used her wide arms to gesture toward the number of flowers a florist might have in their showroom.

"Yes, there are. How may I help you?" Larkin asked.

Darren weaved around them and practically ran to his desk. Christ, what had Tarin done to him?

"Might we step inside your office?" Tarin pointed at the giant double doors and moved to step around her.

Larkin held her ground. "I'm in the middle of a meeting, which I'm sure Darren explained."

"Oh." The slight woman clutched her chest. "I was certain he was just saying that because you didn't want to be disturbed."

And Tarin thought she overrode that do not disturb status? Or did she not see herself as a disruption?

"I just wanted to make sure you were okay. You are all over the papers." Splayed fingers accentuated her words. "And I know you didn't want this to go public."

"I'm pissed."

Tarin's brown eyes widened. She hooked her muted-blonde hair behind her ears and shoved her hands into her pockets. Her jaw hinged for several beats with no words to make it worth the effort.

Larkin kept perfectly still; a trick she'd learned from her mother. Let the other person give themselves away. Shield your hand.

Slowly, she nodded her head. "Well, if there is anything I can do for you, please let me know."

"I will." Larkin would like to know who she thought broke her confidence, but she didn't want to ask.

Tarin smiled as though she was waiting on something. As though she wanted Larkin to ask her opinion or to confide in her. It was that desire that kept her at bay.

"I have associates waiting for me." Larkin bowed her head, turned, and left Tarin blinking after her.

Larkin was never rude, but it seemed Tarin needed boundaries.

"I hope your day gets better."

She let the door close on the sentiment.

"We've concocted the perfect plan," Libby cheered before she'd taken one step in their direction.

"Tell me," Larkin begged. She needed some perfection to measure against that of Beckett. It would surely be wanting, but at least it would stand a better chance than her every day.

"Girls' trip. Your Hamptons house for a long weekend," Libby announced.

"Wine. A fire on the deck. Good food. Laughs. The beach. Did I mention wine?" Gen pitched.

"Say yes," Marlis begged. "Say yes and I'll even bring tequila."

"Hell yes!" Larkin was ready to get away. "Can we leave now?"

NINETEEN

Genevieve had a client meeting she couldn't postpone, but first thing Friday morning, they were out. Larkin looked at her phone. Only fourteen more hours and packing would take at least three of them. She could stretch out her bath and nighttime routine to two. That'd leave nine to occupy. Perhaps sleep would take a few.

She pressed the call button. "Darren, will you come into my office, please?"

"Right away," he chimed.

Not thirty seconds later, the door opened, and his bright face popped around the corner. "I just want you to know that while I love working for Reagan and hope she returns this very minute, I love, love, love her job. Today alone, I spoke with the mayor. The man himself, not a secretary or associate. The mayor of New York City. And I received two marriage proposals. Though you have me beat on that front by a lot." He swaggered across the room and stopped opposite her desk. "And I think those other two were probably meant for you too, but they were over the phone, and I was on the other line. So I'm claiming them."

Seeming to realize he'd been summoned, he snapped to attention. "What can I do for you?"

"I need to know how many of the other kind of letters I received."

"Oh." His face fell. Thin, long fingers tangled into elegant knots and wound around and around. "I really don't think you should focus on the negativity. It's bad for your skin. Some people are just rotten eggs. You know what I mean?"

"Yes, Darren." She couldn't help but smile. He was so vibrant and full of life. "I know exactly what you mean."

"You received twenty outright proposals and twelve 'if the date goes well' proposals." He beamed. "Plus, the long-term patients of Lenox Hill all have stunning arrangements. And I sent all the chocolates to the battered women's shelter in Brooklyn. Goodness knows they need it. Nothing makes a situation better than chocolate. Well"—he covered his mouth with the back of his hand—"nothing less complicated, anyway."

"I appreciate all your help today."

"No problem at all." He shooed her with both hands but stilled. "Except for that crazy lady. I'm so sorry about that. Nothing I could say was going to make her go away."

"I don't think we'll have that problem with her again."

"Shoot no," Darren snapped. "You put her in her place just like that. It was a beautiful thing to watch."

Larkin hid her smile because sometimes she had to be a professional. "You're free to go home as soon as you tell me the number of other letters."

"The one you found this afternoon and two more." He grimaced.

"Thank you, Darren."

"My pleasure. They're on my desk in a folder labeled *Trifler.*"

"Okay then." Her sides ached from holding back a giggle. Whoever sent those letters was, indeed, and aptly labeled, a trifler.

"Night, Miss Ashford." Darren left as boldly as ever, strutting his stuff as if he were on a runway or surveying the offerings at the club.

"Night."

Larkin toed off her stilettos, propped her feet on her desk, and grabbed the flask from behind her back. She shook it. The liquid sloshed about, hitting high on the half-way mark. Thank goodness it was a small one, and she'd been nursing it for the last hour. Drunk packing was the worst. You never ended up with what you needed. And no one needed salad tongs in their suitcase. She'd had quite the time explaining that one to TSA. It'd been Vegas, though, so they'd seen plenty worse.

The whisky dulled the sharpest edge of her pain. On the flip side, it muddied her thoughts, making them harder to control. Every time she closed her eyes, she saw his face hovering over her. His eyes burning a hole through her heart. Sometimes, she saw the word CUNT admonishing her for a transgression she hadn't known she made. Other times, she saw the paparazzi with their aggressive stances and blinding flashes.

She pressed the metal to her lips and tipped it high. The cold liquid burned its way down her throat.

"Larkin?"

Whisky seared her nose when she jackknifed. The door Darren had exited less than five minutes ago swung open.

Her stupid, traitorous heart gained wings and soared

through her chest, ignoring the fact she choked. He'd come back. Her hand flattened over her sternum. Good thing. It had to catch her heart from plummeting to the ground.

Lucas stepped inside with two armfuls of flower arrangements. "I didn't know if you'd still be here."

Why had she allowed herself to think for one second that it was Beckett, coming to profess his love and beg that they give this thing a go? Because she was a stupid, stupid little girl with stupid little girl dreams—no matter how much she wanted to deny it. She blamed her mother and society at large. Goddamned Disney. Imaginary princesses weren't adequate babysitters.

"If you had knocked, you would have known." She wiped her mouth with the back of her hand and straightened.

"Sorry." He waved the arrangements back and forth as though they were peace offerings. They were the opposite of peace.

"You can leave those on Darren's desk. We're donating them to local hospitals."

"Oh." He stopped at the coffee table and set them down. "That's nice."

"They need them more than I do." She capped the flask and set it on her desk.

"You shouldn't drink alone." He continued toward her desk as though she'd invited him inside.

"Yet it's exactly what I'm doing and will continue to do as soon as you tell me what it is you need?"

When he rounded her desk, she stood. "That's far enough."

"Larkin." His hands raised palms out. "I'm not trying anything. I just ..." He shoved his fists into his pockets.

"Just what, Lucas?" She shoved her feet inside her shoes, not liking the massive height disparity.

"Fuck, Larkin." His blue eyes glared.

Her gaze found her purse, only two feet away on her desk, gun locked and loaded just under the flap.

"You said you weren't looking for the one." He looked toward the ceiling. The veins in his neck plumped with blood. "Apparently, you were just looking for richer. More accomplished."

"Lucas." She forgot the gun and stared him directly in the eyes. "You're a hero. There is no higher accomplishment than saving someone's life. None." Her head shook. "I'm just not looking for any of that."

"Why do the papers say you are?" he snapped.

"Because the papers say whatever they need to in order to sell."

His shoulders slumped. The once proud soldier stood before her defeated by the real world, and she hated it. "If this were a movie, if I were a normal girl without scars so deep you can't see, we would've already set a date." She eased around the end of her desk to catch his eye. "But this isn't a movie, and I'm damaged goods."

"You're perfect," he whispered.

"Not even close." Larkin grabbed her purse, hooked it onto her shoulder, and grabbed the flask. "You know your way out." She headed for her exit.

"You're leaving this weekend?"

Larkin stopped a few feet from the door that led to the stairs to her home, her solemn sanctuary. "How do you know that?"

"The girls were talking about it on their way out."

She turned to look at him.

"They're loud." He shrugged.

That they were.

"Yes. We're leaving in the morning."

"I'll get the house swept and set a parameter before you arrive. I'll get Carl to take lead here."

"That won't be necessary."

His jaw flexed, and nostrils flared. "Women in a house alone isn't wise."

More often than not, she was alone. Sure, there was building security, but as Beckett proved, that was just a superficial comfort. She was born alone and would die that way.

"We won't be alone. We'll be together. We'll be armed. We'll be in The Hamptons. We'll be fine."

"I hope you have a good time." Lucas offered a small bow and turned to leave. He walked past the arrangements and out the door, leaving her irritated and confused and relieved and more alone than she'd been before his interruption.

TWENTY

"I THINK MY NOSE IS BURNED." Genevieve used the camera on her phone to inspect the damage. "What do you think?" She lowered the phone, extended her neck, and presented it to the masses.

"We told you to wear the hat." Marlis threw a piece of ice from her vodka, orange, and cranberry. It shot wide, hit the concrete deck, slid past Genevieve, and stopped on the outdoor bar they'd flipped the shutters open on three days ago.

"But no," Larkin hollered. "The deckhand was so hot." She emphasized the words so and hot as Gen had done the day before when they'd arrived at the Montauk dock for a day of deep sea fishing.

"The captain wasn't bad either." Genevieve shrugged. "His belly was bigger than sister's when she was nine months pregnant." Marlis chucked another cube. It landed in the fire pit at the center of their sprawled circle.

"We're going to have to work on your aim," Libby chided.

"Libby, look." Genevieve leaned over the edge of her hanging basket chair.

"You're getting no sympathy from me." Libby reclined in the chaise next to Gen with her head turned away.

"Does nobody care that my nose is burned?" Gen threw her phone behind her in the woven chair.

"I can't see much for the dark and fire, but it looks just as lovely as it did on Friday," Larkin tried.

"You had fun on the boat, right?" Marlis threw the question out, but Larkin knew it was meant for her. She'd been melancholy since they'd arrived, and eight hours of bobbing on the sea hadn't helped. Neither had their veg day Friday nor their beach day today.

"Sure, I did," Larkin lied. "I caught a ... What was it?"

"He called it a striper," Libby offered.

"Not to be confused with a stripper." Genevieve touched her nose and nodded.

Everyone laughed. Everyone except Larkin.

"You're thinking about him, aren't you?" Marlis's question was quiet, but it ricocheted off the glass doors surrounding them.

"All the time." She pulled another mouthful up her straw, enjoying the chill of the margarita Libby had made for her.

"Let's play never have I ever." Marlis leaned forward and crossed her legs.

"We'll be puking by sunset," Libby announced.

Their gazes all traveled to the horizon where, sure enough, hints of orange, pink, and red still colored the sky. Larkin pulled a blanket over her legs. Why couldn't humans hibernate like bears? Several months of sleep might wipe him from her memory.

"Not the usual scenarios," Mar added. "You know, crazy stuff. Like … Never have I ever seen a dead body."

If Mar was trying to get Larkin in better spirits, this wasn't the way. She and Libby tossed back their drinks.

"Who?" Genevieve asked.

"When?" Marlis's eyes widened until her lashes disappeared in her brows.

"Obvious," Libby huffed. "Good guys. Bad guys. At least one a month."

They all looked at Larkin. "I don't want to talk about it." She tossed back another swallow.

"Okay. Never have I ever streaked." Gen asked the question, and everyone waited for her to drink. Her glass never moved.

Larkin gave a, "Huh."

"Never have I ever prayed." Libby looked around the fire to see which of them moved.

Marlis knocked her glass back.

"Really?" Libby's mouth hung open.

"What? I wanted a pair of Givenchys to be on sale." Mar shrugged. "It didn't work."

"Never have I ever gotten my heart broken." Larkin waited and watched.

Again, Marlis drank. More than the first time around, they stared in awe.

"I only have one more drink in me. Or else someone's going to be holding my hair back," Mar warned. When she realized everyone was looking at her, she stilled.

"You were in love?" Larkin breathed the words as though they were a curse. And weren't they? It'd taken a whole lot of drinks and a crazy game to get her to admit it.

"I don't want to talk about it." Mar sucked on her straw so hard she emptied her cup and peppered the air with the cousin of the most annoying sound on earth.

"Clearly, you bitches don't know how to play the game." Gen planted her feet on the deck. "Never have I ever been in love with someone in high school." No one drank. "Now, narrow the gap."

"What did it feel like?" Larkin ignored Genevieve and locked gazes with Marlis.

"It hurt like a motherfucker." Mar gnawed at her lower lip, still fighting back emotion after all these years.

Larkin wasn't in love, but it was too damn close for comfort.

"Whose idea was it to play this damn game, anyway?" Gen stood and headed for the bar.

"Mine." Mar rolled her eyes, stood, and followed Gen to the bar.

Gen slipped behind the bar, at home in her surroundings. "Who needs a r—"

Marlis's scream shrilled across the deck, threatening to toss Larkin off her feet. She gripped the edge of her chair in an effort to regain her balance.

"Jesus, what?" Gen hollered.

Larkin craned her neck. Her gaze followed the line of Marlis's wide eyes. Every organ in her body slammed into her spine in an effort to run away. Instincts yelled at her to run. Get her friends and run.

Through the wall of glass in the center of her entryway, a dark figure stood in the shadows.

"A man." Marlis's pointed finger trembled.

Libby, the only wise one among them, moved. She jumped to her feet and whirled around with her gun drawn, ready for anything. Larkin wasn't helpless. By all that was right in the world, she wouldn't act that way. She scrambled from her seat and ran toward Marlis. When she reached her friend, Larkin hooked an arm around her and rushed them backward toward the bar.

"Where?" Gen rounded the end of the bar with a knife

made for mayhem clutched in her fist.

"The house." Larkin's voice was shrill and reedy because—contrary to Libby's insistence—her gun wasn't by her side, but on the counter near the man in her house.

"What do we do?" Marlis's shriek rattled her eardrums.

"Stay put," Libby ordered.

Like hell. This was her house. She'd help defend it.

"Stay here," Larkin whispered and sat Marlis on a high stool.

"Don't leave me." Her friend's nails bit into her bare forearms.

"Fine but don't scream." Larkin yanked Mar up and tugged her close to the wall of the bar.

"No promises." Mar's grip on her shirt strangled her a little, especially when she reached over the bar for a knife close in kin to the one Gen wielded.

"Stay behind me then."

"Not a problem."

Larkin eased her face around the corner. The perfect target for a man with a gun. *Idiot.*

Libby and Gen hunkered on the far side of the house and eased slowly toward the sliding glass door. Libby held up her hand in a stay-put motion. Inside the house, a dividing column blocked her view of the intruder.

Her heart beat inside her throat, banging her eardrums like gongs.

"What's going on? Who is it? Why is he here?" Marlis yanked her shirt with each question.

"I don't know."

She needed answers to those questions too. These were her friends. This was her house. They were supposed to be safe here.

Larkin eased around the corner. The noose around her neck tightened.

"No," Mar squeaked.

Nothing would stop her from getting answers. She pushed forward. Mar's grip cinched to the point that, if they survived, she'd have to throw the shirt away. She stepped closer to the wall of glass.

Libby's arm flapped, waving her back. Mar's grip broke.

Larkin ran to the corner, praying the sofa would shield her from the intruder's view. It didn't. The angles didn't line up, and she was completely exposed. Her heaving breaths fogged the glass where she crouched.

"Dammit," Libby growled and raised her gun once more. "Do you see him?"

She angled her head up, over her breaths, and searched the interior. Left and right. High and low. Nothing.

"No." She searched again. "I don't see anyone."

Libby chanced a quick glance. Once, then twice. Her head shook. She slid the glass door open. It was Gen's turn to clutch Libby's shirt. Libby smacked her hand and then stepped into the house.

Larkin slid hers open and crept inside. A hint of cologne clung to the air, proving they weren't all insane.

"You wouldn't shoot an innocent man, would you?" From deep in the house, Douglas's voice filtered into the rear sitting room.

"No." Libby's taut shoulders settled. "But I'd be hard pressed to find one." She flipped the safety on her sidearm and straightened.

"Me too." Larkin fell backward, letting the wall catch her.

Her driver stepped from the kitchen with both hands up. "Me too," he agreed.

Relief turned her knees to gelatin. She leaned an elbow on the wingback chair and took it all in; Libby holstering her gun, Gen collecting a near frantic Marlis, and Douglas at her Hamptons home about sixteen hours too early to collect them.

"Come on." Her heroic friend waved, the least ready for battle inside the house. "It's just Douglas, keeping us on our toes."

"If you want me on my toes, give me ballet shoes." Marlis clutched her chest as though her heart might abandon ship at any moment.

"I'm sorry to startle you. I—"

"Startle?" Marlis plowed over Douglas's apology. "You did a bit more than startle. You stole a good two years off my life." She shoved off Libby and Gen's helpful hands and teetered to the wingback chair across from Larkin.

"That wasn't my intent, but I must say, I'm thankful you responded as you did." He looked at her, Libby, and Genevieve. His gaze traveled back to Marlis. "Well, most of you."

"So I'm not cut out for battle," Mar spat. "I'm great at other things. Plus, I shouldn't have to be good at combat. This isn't the Stone Age, and we live in America."

Larkin shook her head. She and Marlis lived in a veritable bubble but never burrowed in quite like her friend. Douglas stepped forward and placed a hand on Mar's shoulder.

"Why the early call?" Libby asked, a step ahead of her as usual.

"I need to speak with Larkin." His worn blue eyes found hers.

"Reagan." Her name was on a sob Larkin caught behind her hand.

"No. There's been no change on that front." He turned to the girls. "Ladies, if you would …"

What was so bad that the girls couldn't stay? Larkin plopped into the chair before she hit the ground. Everything shook. It couldn't be Beckett. Douglas wouldn't have news from him. She wouldn't have news from him. Not ever again.

Douglas helped Marlis from her chair and handed her over to Gen, who held the knife's blade up close to her forearm.

"Would you like me to take that?" Douglas held out his hand.

"No. I know how to handle long, firm things." Gen hooked her free arm around Marlis and winked at Douglas.

Libby groaned.

"Noted." He stood his ground, expression as rock-solid as ever.

"Huh," Gen purred.

"Out." Libby pointed at the door. "I have an unfinished drink calling my name. And maybe a shot."

"Tequila," Mar announced.

Douglas closed the door behind them and crossed the room, stopping just in front of her.

"You're scaring me."

"You should be scared." His phone screen shined to life, and he handed it over. "This happened between midnight and six a.m."

"Wha ...?" The question died on her lips. Her building filled his screen. The top ten floors. She knew it intimately. She'd fought tooth and nail for the eighty-story structure. Real estate in downtown NYC was rarer than twenty-carat diamonds. Night and day, he'd overseen the three-year renovation until it'd become her dream realized.

"The pictures were taken from a Channel 7 News chopper."

Douglas's words swam in and around the fragments of thoughts and the image that didn't compute.

The top two floors of The Ashford dripped red. Blood red. It was as if her building bled. As though it cried blood.

"What in the world? Is it …?"

"Paint."

"How? Why?"

"It gets worse."

She looked at Douglas. Her mouth opened, but no words escaped. She wasn't ready for worse. He leaned in and swiped the screen. Each picture showed another side of her building disgraced with red. Save for the last.

TNUC.

On the side where her apartment overlooked the city, paint didn't stream full and flowing from the top. Four neatly painted letters clung to the glass.

TNUC.

It didn't make sense for several seconds. Not until she mentally put herself inside her apartment and stared at letters that would graze her floors and reach the top of her ceilings. And for the inside would read CUNT.

Bile sloshed up her throat. The cards. The flowers. Now, the paint.

"The paint has been removed, and I stopped Channel 7 before they ran the story. It's an open investigation of vandalism." Douglas crouched in front of her. "I'm taking it as a major threat. This person was on your roof, right above your home, with the explicit intent to threaten."

Larkin's blood cooled ten degrees as though she sat in an ice bath.

"I have a friend at the FBI who's getting me in touch with a profiler."

"Libby should be in on this conversation." Larkin was glad she could speak. The amount of thought that went into that statement shocked the hell out of her.

"Before she does, Lucas said that a man attacked you on your roof last week."

Douglas didn't stand or perch on the edge of the coffee table. He just stayed in his nimble crouch, demanding answers without a word.

"Nearly two weeks ago," she corrected. "But it wasn't like you're thinking it was. He didn't explain it right." Not that she'd explained it to Lucas after she'd figured it out.

"Explain."

"I went to the roof to blow off steam."

"You said you weren't going up there alone anymore."

"I lied," she snapped. "I need to go up there alone. It's a hell of a lot cheaper than therapy."

"Maybe if you went to therapy, you wouldn't need to go to the roof." He straightened his cuffs.

"You're one to talk, or not. You won't even talk to me, so why would you talk to a stranger? Why would I?" She stood, and he matched her moves, standing toe to toe with her. "We deal with our bullshit in the ways that work for us."

"Do they work?" He broke the stare off and eased back a step.

"Sometimes." Larkin sank back into the chair and slapped hair from her face. She stared into near space, which happened to be the knees of Douglas's pant-legs. "That night was the first night I'd been up in months. Since our talk. I couldn't take it anymore. I got too close to the edge, over the ledge, and he wrapped his arms around me and pulled me back. I thought he would kill me or worse, which was why I called Lucas. By the time I figured out he actually thought I was going to …" She swallowed.

"Were you?"

"No." Her gaze shot to his. She yanked her mother's ring from her finger and smacked it into Douglas's hand. "I was going to throw the damn thing as far as I could."

His knowing gaze dropped to the ring and then found hers once more.

"I dropped it up there. He returned the ring along with my neatly folded jacket."

Douglas closed his hand around the ring and shoved it inside his pants pocket. "Since the vandalism was perpetrated from the roof, we need to talk to this man."

Everything inside her bucked at the thought. Beckett hadn't done this. He wouldn't. He'd protected her and made her feel safe. He cared for her.

"I told you about the creepy flower and card I received nearly two weeks ago," she hedged. "I may have received another bouquet with the same message Tuesday evening."

"A week after the attack."

"I wasn't attacked." She smacked her hands onto her hips. "I received another colorful note at the spa on Friday before Bronson's party, and another couple in the stacks of letters I've received since the board leak."

"All right. I want you to hang out here for a few days until we get a handle on this."

"You can't be serious."

"You know I'm always serious."

"I know you're always joking."

"Not this time, I'm afraid." His head shook, offering one stern negative.

"Now that I know what's going on, I'm not afraid."

"Maybe you should be. Whoever is doing this is escalating. The cards and flowers were for your eyes alone. Now they've defamed you publicly."

"I'm not one to hide from my problems." She pushed to stand, but Douglas didn't back away and give her space. They stood nose to nose.

"You're not the kind to share them with people who can help you, either." In all the years Douglas had worked for her family, he'd never raised his voice. His words rang in her ears.

Douglas stepped back so quickly she almost fell over. He hissed a long, slow breath. A loud clearing of the throat settled the electric aura surrounding him. "Until we have leads, I'd like you to stay here."

"I have work to do." Her rebuttal was more sedate than she liked, but something about this riled Douglas. That more than any ugly word, freaky flower, or bloody paint gave her pause.

"In this day and age, you can conduct business on a cell phone and Wi-Fi. You have more than that here."

"What about my meetings?" He opened his mouth to speak, but she waved him off. "Never mind. I have a cell phone and Wi-Fi, and I don't have to meet with the board for another month." Not until she decided the fate of her company. And her life, for that matter. "What about the girls?"

"I'll take them back with me."

"So I'm just chillin' by myself?"

"You have a gun and know how to use it. Keep it close by. If I'd intended you harm tonight, that knife wouldn't have stopped me."

"Libby's gun would have."

"But Libby won't be here." His gaze narrowed, driving home the point.

"Okay."

"The house is on your list of assets, but only a few people know its location. One of whom is missing. I spoke with the detective this afternoon. There's no way to know if the two are connected yet."

Larkin stared at the gaping, stretched collar of her shirt. She shoved her fingers in the lower hem and twisted them around the hanging silk. Uncertainty wormed its way through her insides. "I should call her mother again."

"You shouldn't talk to anyone right now."

"No one?"

"No one. Not the police. Not her family. Not the press."

Uncertainty blew an arctic gust through the maze of

holes it left behind. Gooseflesh crept over her neck, cascading down her arms and venturing to her fingertips.

Douglas grabbed her forearm and held tight, shocked her with his grip. The strength exceeded her expectation as did the connection it offered. It dug deeper than the witty banter and elbow-in-the-side relationship they'd always maintained.

Larkin felt as though she was missing something. Maybe she was as cut off from real human connection as the people closest to her said. Or maybe Douglas wasn't telling her something.

TWENTY-ONE

LARKIN'S GAZE JUMPED FROM THE LAPTOP resting on her duvet-covered thighs to the pistol on her nightstand and back again. She could shoot the laptop and eliminate the sixty some-odd email proposals clogging her inbox. The bullet would travel through the screen and into her pretty wall, though. She looked at the wall for a long minute, judging the loss.

Her head pounded. Her vision blurred. The clock read 12:10 a.m.

She slammed the lid closed and shoved it to the other side of the bed. Her left fist connected with her pillow two too many times before she plopped her head onto it. The lamplight filled her room with a dim glow. If she turned over and clicked it off, she'd sleep better.

Sleep must have taken her quickly. She didn't remember much after pummeling her pillow.

Her legs kicked at the covers. Her arms knotted in uncontrollable fits. A dream tormented her. Larkin ran and ran but found no way out. She didn't know where she was. No wonder she couldn't get out.

Larkin bolted upright as though she'd been electrocuted.

The covers hung off the corner of her bed, leaving her exposed in the brightly lit room. Her lids blinked and squinted. She tugged at the corner of the covers, but they refused to budge from her numb hand's impotent pull. Lethargy pulled her to the side. She drew two deep breaths, searched for energy, found a tiny bit, and crawled to the edge of the bed. Her computer lay on top of the covers. She must have accidentally kicked it off.

She moaned and pushed from the bed. When she stood, the scent of charred wood slapped her face.

Surely, Douglas had damped the fire before he and the girls left. He'd said he'd do as much, and it wasn't like him to shirk a duty. Even if he hadn't, the logs would have burned themselves out by now. Right?

Niggling urgency forced Larkin to forget about the computer. She rounded the bed to check on the fire pit and stopped cold.

Smoke breathed through the crack under her door; a dragon come calling. Death assured.

"No. No. No. No." Sweat slicked her palms. Fear rattled them. Numbness stabbed needles into her flesh.

Larkin stepped forward and wished like hell she'd listened in school when the fire marshal had come to speak to their class. That was more than twenty years ago, though. Had she listened, she still wouldn't remember.

She looked at the sliding glass door that took up more than half the wall on the far side of the bedroom. The damn thing didn't open. Sometime during her last visit, the latch had broken. She hadn't remembered it breaking but found it inoperable while attempting to use it to access the back deck. It had been so inconsequential that she'd added it to the yearly maintenance list, completed at the end of every summer, and promptly forgotten about it. Only now, as her life was on the line, did she realize what a hazard it was not to have a window that opened in the bedroom.

Her feet quaked as though the ground she stood on shifted from side to side. Slowly, she moved forward. With every step closer to the smoke, the temperature rose until she feared opening the door as much as she feared not opening it.

"You can do this. You have to do this."

Curling her toes against the heat, Larkin pulled her arm inside the sleeve of the robe she'd fallen asleep in and turned the knob. Heat registered cold on her fingertips for a split second before she released her hold.

The door flew open as though she'd tossed it wide.

Larkin snatched her hand to her chest. Flames licked the walls on either side of the hallway. Dark black smoke poured in like an overflowing witch's caldron. It coated the ceiling before she blinked. It strangled her without hands.

Her knees buckled on instinct, pulling her to the floor. Heat slapped her face. She heaved in search of a clear breath. Lips to the floor, she found one.

She scrambled forward on hands and knees and lunged for the door. Black marred the exterior. With all the force she could muster, Larkin shoved the door toward its frame, clicking it in place.

Sweet relief washed over her. Then it died.

The windows in her bedroom and bathroom, while ornate and stunning, didn't open.

Larkin clambered from the floor and sprinted to the bathroom. There had to be a way out. She would find it.

Marble hugged every surface in the room. Glass accentuated its beauty. Those two materials wouldn't burn, but the smoke would kill her. She turned on the shower and the faucet, praying they would do something helpful.

She turned to the tub and screamed.

Orange coated through the frosted glass window, giving the room an ominous hue she hadn't noticed before. The flames were so close. If she broke through the window, could she even make it out safely or would she invite doom as she had by opening the bedroom door?

Larkin stepped into the tub. Icy water froze her feet. She lifted her hand to the window and felt the overbearing heat before she touched the glass.

Her hand caught her cry. She stumbled out of the tub and ran for her phone on the nightstand. The black clouds of smoke gathered into a dense haze. A fit of heaving pulled her down to the floor once more. Through the fog of death, fire shown, stretching long, skinny fingers of flame at the top of the bedroom door. They flickered and lunged for her.

She crawled on her belly to the side of the bed and reached up blindly. Cold metal met her fingertips, stinging them. Larkin grabbed hold, despite the pain. Her gun. It wasn't her phone, but it was more helpful. Glass was no match for a bullet.

Imperfections in the stained concrete floor scraped her knees and snagged her robe. Still, she crawled as quickly as she could. Every second that passed pressed the smoke closer and closer to her back.

Ten feet back from the window, Larkin took aim. Her finger hugged the trigger. Nothing happened. The trigger refused to move. Tears marbled her vision. She screamed, remembered her training. Her thumb smacked off the safety. This time, she didn't bother aiming. She unloaded the magazine in a fit of fury and desperation.

Without ear protection, a high-pitched hum rang between her eyes and flattened to a fine point in both eardrums. She hacked a cough, kissed the floor again for a good breath, and then crawled forward.

Defeat in the form of a solid plate of glass crushed all hope.

Her bullets pierced the glass in a wide spray, but she couldn't fit through the hole made by a round. If she had more bullets, she could carve out a rectangle, but too fucking bad they were in her closet at The Ashford.

Larkin pushed close to the window and pressed her nose as close as she dared to a low hole. Sweet fresh air filled her lungs. She dragged several breaths until the gears loosened in her brain. Desperation crept in from every angle. Its clouds were dark and heavy. Her usually agile mind ground and jerked.

A siren's wail called in the distance. Or had it?

The fire popped and crackled outside the door. Wood groaned and snapped. Dishes crashed to the ground.

She grabbed the business end of her gun and reared back. The metal connected with the glass and cracked wildly in her ears. Again and again, she hit it, but the pane remained sturdy and upright. She'd managed to widen the tiny hole to small, but it wasn't enough.

Maybe if she'd gone for the stool in her bathroom, but the black smoke now filling the room wouldn't let her move. Her limbs weighed a hundred pounds apiece. She pressed closer to the glass, not caring if it cut her face. A cut wouldn't matter to her corpse.

Her eyes watered so much. Tears free flowed. She blinked. Red swam in her vision. Fire. Flames. What a shitty way to go.

The red danced again. This time, though, she discerned a rhythm. It was fast and insistent. Overbearing even.

Larkin cupped her hands around her face and pressed

it to the glass. She couldn't see a fire truck, but she recognized the rhythmic whirl of light as it danced through her yard. Reinvigorated, she gripped the gun and slammed it into the glass time and again. Her strikes were sloppy. Her timing faltered. Her lungs burned.

She choked on noxious fumes, but she didn't let up … until her arms gave out.

TWENTY-TWO

IT WAS HEAVEN OR HELL. The lights were too blinding to discern, causing Larkin to clamp her eyes closed.

"Hey," a soothing familiar male voice cooed.

Something brushed her forehead. Hands? Lips?

"I'm here, Larkin."

Who? It wasn't Beckett. She'd recognize his voice in the pits of hell. The fire. Memories swarmed her in the darkness. Her body shook.

"You're safe now. I'm here with you."

A hand stopped hers from trembling. It snuggled her palm to his palm.

Douglas? No, it wasn't Douglas. He was in the city. The girls? They didn't possess quite the timbre.

"Sleep now. The doctor said you suffered smoke inhalation. You'll be fine. He promised. He said you'd be tired and weak for a while, but you're safe." Lips trailed over her brow and then jumped to her hand.

Had she the strength to open her eye, she'd glare the zealot into submission. But she couldn't defend herself. How dare he take advantage of her?

"It's my job to take care of you. I know you'll let me do it now."

Lucas.

Where were they? What time was it? Why was he here and not her friends? Not Douglas?

Exhaustion pulled her under.

When she came to, the tempo of things had changed. The background noise had died down, and the light didn't press on her sockets even with her lids closed. Her head pounded, but the drum had gotten smaller. Incrementally so.

Larkin dared to open her lids, but it felt as though they were made of sandpaper. Her eyes watered, so she tried not to blink. Blinking hurt.

A blinking green light and white, shining numbers gave her something to focus on. They didn't make sense for several heartbeats. Heartbeats that elevated and read out of the monitor. She looked past the monitor to an IV drip.

She was in a hospital. Lucas had told her as much.

Where was he?

She shifted her face, but the pounding intensified, shaking the clock on the wall. The hands danced with each pump of her heart.

Two fifty a.m.

She'd closed her eyes for the night not much more than two hours ago. How had all that transpired in such a short amount of time?

Larkin turned her head farther.

Lucas sat in a chair beside the bed. Her bed. Her hospital bed. He sat and watched her without a word. Without an expression. Vacant eyes stared at her. For an instant, she thought he was dead, but then he blinked. Slowly, a hint of warmth returned to his features.

"How'd you get here so fast?" Larkin sank deeper into the bed. It'd taken so much effort to speak, and her voice sounded like a fifty-year-old career drunk.

He leaned forward and grabbed her hand and brought it to his cheek. His stubble poked the back of it. She felt his jaw hinge before he spoke. "I was on my way up when I got the call. I wouldn't let Douglas leave you alone." His head shook. The hair on his chin scraped her sore fingers. "I should have left sooner. If I had, you wouldn't be here."

Here in the hospital or here on earth?

At this point, she didn't trust Lucas. Her in case of emergency people were Libby and Douglas, and neither of them was here. Her alarm system should have dialed them right away when the first beep sounded.

Wait. She hadn't heard an alarm, and she had one of the most intricate ones on the market in each of her homes.

Weakness weighed her down. Fear smothered her.

She fought against them with all she possessed. "My phone?" If she had it, who would she call?

Beckett.

But she didn't have his number.

"You need to sleep. The world doesn't matter right now. Getting you better does."

Larkin couldn't fight. Weakness and vulnerability shrouded her. She despised it.

TWENTY-THREE

HOSPITAL FOOD SUCKED. It sucked even worse under the watchful gaze of the head of your security detail, who you also happened to have boned twice and who then had an unrelenting thing for you that you didn't understand. It sucked more still when you felt like wrung-out laundry and all you wanted to do was leave, but you couldn't until the doctor you didn't remember evaluating you evaluated you again. And it sucked a bit more still when you didn't have a phone or computer, and you didn't remember the phone number of anyone who could get you out of this predicament.

"Miss Ashford?" A firm and decisive double knock filled the room after the sure feminine voice.

"Yes." Larkin answered with a gust that was honest, only in the fact that she wanted out of this place. The doc was her ticket home. "Come in."

A woman dressed in sleek black slacks and a leather jacket pushed inside. Her near-black hair was pulled into a tight bun at the base of her neck. The jut of her jaw spoke business.

Maybe the doc was heading out and wanted to sign her discharge papers. Larkin held out hope until the black gun on her hip holster shot it from the sky. The woman surveyed the room in a quick glance and stopped less than a foot from Larkin's bed.

"Larkin Ashford?" she demanded.

"Yes." Larkin sat as straight as she could with the persistent cramp in her side.

"I'm Detective Fitzgerald with the East Hampton PD. I'd like to ask you some questions."

"Okay." Larkin couldn't figure out why a detective would ask questions about a fire, but she'd answer them all the same, despite Douglas's warning. She had nothing to hide.

"Ideally, we'd have done this right after the incident, but you were unconscious," the detective said.

"She came to once during the night but didn't say much," Lucas offered.

The detective's gaze remained on Larkin. "This will be your first formal statement about the incident. You are permitted to have counsel present, should you choose to do so."

"No. I don't need my lawyer." The moment the words were out, Larkin wished she'd taken the opportunity to request Genevieve's presence. Not for legal counsel, but for support.

"You may also request to do this in private or at the station upon your release from the hospital," the detective added.

"I'm ready." Larkin grabbed her water from the tray

and sucked down several gulps.

"All right. To the best of your ability, please recall the events of last night." Detective Fitzgerald stood with her hands at her side without a notepad or recorder. Her keen eyes watched Larkin's every move.

Larkin gave up the pretense of whole health, slumping back on the bed, and told the detective about the day and evening from fishing, the bonfire, all the way until she passed out. To Lucas's credit, he didn't say a word.

"So, to your knowledge, no one was with you inside the house last night?" the detective asked.

"No. Douglas and the girls left at about eight thirty. My driver would be able to give you the precise time. I was showered and in bed by nine ten; I know that because I worked on my laptop until ten after midnight." Why did she feel the need to explain what'd she'd already plainly said? Because the detective asked questions that Larkin had already answered. It made her squirm, and she had no reason to.

"And the women in your company until your driver showed to escort them home were?"

"Libby Irish, Genevieve Holst, and Marlis McCain."

"Do you have any enemies, Miss Ashford?"

"No."

"None?"

Larkin took another drink and thought. "Not that I know of. I run a large company that has been in the media as of late. Only local news and it's not news at all."

"And that news, not news is?"

"I'm trying to decide whether or not to go public. My board thinks I need to marry to firm up the company's place in the market, but I disagree. There was a leak to the media, saying that I was on the hunt for Mr. Ashford."

The detective's upper lip curled.

"Exactly. Thank you." Larkin smiled.

The woman was about business and schooled her features. "Any disgruntled lovers?"

"She's been receiving threats." Lucas stood like he was a jack-in-the-box, waiting for someone to turn his lever.

"Who are you?" Fitzgerald assessed Lucas full on for the first time.

My disgruntled lover. Larkin gnawed on her lips.

"Lucas Backstrom. Head of security for Miss Ashford." Lucas answered the question with his hands behind his back, his shoulders back, and chin up as though he was back in his uniform.

"And where were you last night?" The detective struck so swiftly Lucas's mouth dropped wide and hung slack for a second too long.

"Miss Ashford requested that no security escort her to or stay at her Hamptons house." Lucas hadn't exactly answered the question, but Fitzgerald's gaze rested on Larkin, which likely had its desired effect.

"Why not?" the detective demanded.

"Very few people know about my Hamptons house. I was bringing three guests, which met the house's capacity. And I wanted to get away." Larkin shrugged.

"From the head of your security." Fitzgerald didn't blink at her blunt statement or wait for a rebuttal. She turned to Lucas. "What kind of threats?"

His gaze shifted this way and that, trying to find steady ground. The detective's questions were quick and precise.

"Foul words on the greeting cards of freaky flower arrangements." Lucas was back to his ma'am-yes-ma'am stance.

"Freaky flowers?" The woman's brow hiked.

"Dolls eyes, black roses, flesh-colored calla lilies." He listed them off as though it were natural for him to know flowers on sight. As though he'd known about them all along. Because she hadn't said anything to him about the flowers or the cards.

"Doll's eyes?" Fitzgerald asked.

"It's a plant with thick red stems. They have white berries with black dots on the tip that look like eyes. If ingested, the berries can cause cardiac arrest and death."

"Death?" Larkin gasped. Someone sent her death flowers. She set the cup to the side and drew a deep breath, then another to keep from being sick.

"Black roses represent mortality and the pink calla lilies pair too well with the cards' messages," Lucas continued. His voice was a distant muddle of sounds.

"Which was?" The detective braced both hands on her hips.

"Cunt," Larkin offered.

Fitzgerald nodded. Her gaze slipped from Lucas to Larkin and back. "Mr. Backstrom, you seem to know an awful lot about flowers and their meanings."

"I researched them after Douglas told me about them." Lucas stepped closer to the bed. "You should have told me about them as soon as they arrived."

"It was nothing," Larkin snapped.

"It's not nothing anymore," he bit back. His gaze jumped to the detective. "They poured paint over her building downtown, The Ashford."

"They?" Fitzgerald was quick. The detective picked up on things faster than she did. Larkin was pretty sure she knew that they'd slept together at some point.

"The culprit." His hands flapped. "Whoever did it." Lucas focused on her again. The crests of his cheeks were pink, and a line of sweat broke out in a crease on his forehead. "You should have let me put cameras up there and lock it up tight," he bellowed. "No one saw anything."

"Why would I let you invade my space?" Larkin hated being anchored to the bed. She hated being questioned by a man whose paycheck she signed.

"Because of the man on the roof." He grabbed the bedrail, jostling the mattress.

"That was a fluke thing. A one-off. A misunderstanding."

"What's to misunderstand about a man who's not supposed to be on your roof, being on your roof? What's to misunderstand about him putting his hands on you?" He openly shook the bedrail.

"Miss Ashford needs more water." Fitzgerald shoved the Styrofoam pitcher against Lucas's chest.

The slosh of ice and contact broke Lucas's single-minded concentration on her. He released the bedrail from his forceful grip and staggered back a step, catching the wayward pitcher in the process.

"I'll let you back in when we're finished." The detective rivaled Lucas in height. He had her in width by a mile, but the authority in her voice brooked no contest.

He let loose a long breath and headed for the door.

When the door closed, Fitzgerald propped a hip on the side of the bed. "Is he always that intense?"

"No, not always. It's never been that bad. It's gotten worse each time I refuse a relationship with him."

"How many times did you two screw?"

Larkin smiled in spite of herself. "I figured you picked up on that. It should have been zero." She groaned. "Twice."

"How long ago?"

"A month. Six weeks. When I get back to my computer, I can tell you for certain."

"You haven't faltered once since the time of the severing?"

"No. And I was clear from the beginning, as I am with every man I fuck, that the interaction is all there is and will ever be between us."

"Ever faltered on that?"

"No." To the detriment of her heart.

Detective Fitzgerald's phone beeped once. Then twice in a row.

She ignored it. "Tell me about the man on the roof."

Christ, she'd walked right into that trap. Had Fitzgerald set it intentionally? Her story remained the same, regardless. She told her about the night on the roof and explained the misunderstanding.

"Have you seen him since?"

"No." How the hell could she lie so easily? Because everything inside her said, 'Protect Beckett.' "I think I scared him as much as he scared me."

"What do you think he was doing on the roof?"

"I don't know." She still didn't know. Not exactly.

"You said the roof is your haven. Who knows that?"

"My girlfriends. Douglas. Lucas."

Her phone beeped once more. She wasn't taken off course. "Does your assistant know about it?"

"I don't think so, but I can't be sure. She was in and out of the occasional lunch I had with the girls. Why?"

"Did she know about your house in The Hamptons?"

Larkin hated the detective's evasion, but she was doing her job. "Yes. She wouldn't have, normally, because I only use the house for personal retreats, but over the summer, I hosted a party there for potential board members. It was a small affair with only twelve people, but Reagan helped me coordinate the caterer, rentals, and the one-man band."

"So you could make me a list of all the people you've invited into the house?"

"I think so. It would only be those people, my girl-friends, my security, and the cleaning company I have come in at the end of every summer." Larkin rubbed her gently throbbing head. Thinking hurt.

"What do they clean?"

"Everything. Rafters to baseboards. I leave the doors open when I'm there in the summer, and the sand is everywhere by the end of season."

"How often are you at your house in The Hamptons?"

"Last summer only twice. Once with the girls and once for the board candidate party." She rubbed her head, trying to remember dates. "June. The party was June third. I haven't had anyone there except the girls since the cleaning."

"I'll need that list as soon as you're released and back in the city."

"Okay." She pinched the bridge of her nose.

"And we need to find out who this mystery man is from the roof."

"Why?" Larkin's hand dropped. She hoped she didn't sound too desperate.

"Because someone is trying to kill you."

Larkin scanned the room, looking for the threat. Antiseptic white surrounded her from the linoleum floors to the privacy curtain that hung in a clump at the far corner of the room.

"I don't understand." Larkin's tongue stuck to the roof of her mouth. She tried to swallow, but nothing moved.

"The fire was intentional." The detective might as well have flipped her mattress and toppled her to the floor. She'd have socked her less.

"Are you sure? We had a bonfire on the deck last night. Maybe it didn't get banked adequately."

"I'd hardly call that fire pit a campfire. It's nowhere near a bonfire."

"Still, it could have been it. Right?" Larkin needed something to make more sense than the bullshit this lady was peddling.

"It originated from the kitchen—"

"Electrical? They happen all the time. I hear." She

chewed the edge of a fingernail. A nervous tic when someone was trying to kill her ... apparently.

"From the kitchen and guest room, closest to yours, almost simultaneously. A third origin point was found in the garage."

Tears slipped down Larkin's cheek. She blinked furiously, but it was too late. Fitzgerald's gaze locked on the streaming emotion.

"Why are you crying?"

Her teeth ground together to staunch the flow, but it didn't help. Nothing helped. "I don't understand this. Libby and Douglas made certain I was trained for an attack, but how do you fight someone who won't face you?"

"You've seen them. Talked to them."

"I've talked to them?" She wiped her nose and ignored the tremors in her hands.

"Yes. They're not stepping out in plain sight yet, but they're leaving tracks."

"What kind of tracks?"

"A body."

Larkin stared at her as if she'd spoken in an alien language. She replayed the words, but they made no better sense by the fourth repeat. "I don't ..." Nausea flopped her belly this way and that. "What do you mean?"

This was one of those turning points. A thing you couldn't wipe from your memory. A thing that would change everything. The image of her mother's body hunched inhumanly on the sofa in their living room stamped itself on the back of her lids.

"There was a body in your garage."

A body in the house with her ...

"No." Her head shook. "No. That's not possible. I was there alone. No." She cupped a scream in her hands. Her skin crawled as though it'd never been cleaned, not in her entire life. Bugs. Viruses. Dirt. They clung to her like six feet of earth burdened the dead.

There were signs of forced entry fresh on the garage door.

Larkin heaved.

Fitzgerald jumped from the bed, grabbed an ugly pink bucket from under it, and held it out.

There was so much Larkin had handled over the course of her years. A creep in her house, killing while she was there, and intending her harm weren't on the list. She couldn't take it. If her hands moved from her mouth, she'd surely explode. Or implode.

"At first, it read murder cover-up with you as our number one suspect."

Larkin couldn't react. All her focus was on not puking all over herself.

"But after the arson investigator studied the scene and now after questioning you, I realize there's no way. You should've been dead. Would have been, if your alarm hadn't dialed the station directly."

"It didn't go off. The alarm." She spoke into her palm.

"Nope. You have a central unit. Whoever did it thought they'd disabled the alarm, but they only paralyzed the bells, not the call."

"The body. Who is it?" Her breaths came slowly through her fingertips.

"Best the medical examiner can tell at the scene, a Caucasian female between twenty-five and fifty years of age. He's already sent off the DNA."

The thudding in her head increased to the point of shattering her skull. The girls. Larkin used the bedrails and leaned forward as best as she could. "I know they left because I watched the car pull away, but can you please call my girlfriends? I don't have my phone, and goddammit, I don't remember their numbers. Please," she begged. "I need to know they're okay."

"All right." She nodded. "I'll look them up as soon as I get back to the station."

"No. Now. Please." She shoved the hospital phone toward the woman. "I'm sure you have someone at the station who can look that up for you. Please call them."

TWENTY-FOUR

"LARKIN?" LUCAS'S THICK VOICE held a singsong edge.

Larkin's eyes remained loosely closed as though she was in a deep, restful slumber. The opposite was true. Being locked in the suffocating confines of his two-seater sports car had her nerves clamoring for freedom. From the moment they'd hit the interstate, she'd feigned sleep to keep from having to deal with his multitude of questions and prodding gaze.

They'd exited the smooth, relative straightness of the highway several minutes ago, but his car continued its aggressive rumble through stop-and-go traffic. She'd deal with Lucas when she had all her strength and wits about her, but right now, even faking sleep was nearly too much for her to handle. Smoke had her throat a raw mess. Death and destruction did the same to her brain. Raw and scrambled.

His big hand rubbed a line up her arm. She jerked as though he'd poked her with the end of a stiletto. Her back twinged, and she cried out. There was no escaping the reaction. She was wide-awake, and he knew it.

"Whoa." The offending hand smoothed over her shoulder in an irritating rhythm. "You're safe. I've got you."

Yeah, that was the problem. She needed away from him. She needed away from the prodding doctors. She needed away from inquisitive and bomb detonating detectives.

Larkin dragged a hand over her face. Everything felt swollen and puffy to the touch. Her eyes. Her cheeks. Everything hurt. Even her palms. Red, jagged scrapes crisscrossed the skin. She straightened as much as she could and surveyed the landscape. Relief, the first she'd felt in what seemed like days, tamed her wild edges. They were only two blocks from her Upper East home.

"Larkin?" he asked again.

"Huh?" Larkin grabbed her throat and pretended talking hurt. Well, she didn't exactly pretend. It hurt, but not so much that she couldn't do it.

"We need to talk." He whipped the car into her reserved parking space in front of her home, killed the engine, and turned toward her.

"Can't." She squeezed her throat. "Not now."

"I really—"

"Lar!"

"Oh, my God!"

"Larkin!"

Larkin turned in time to see Libby, Genevieve, and Marlis racing down her stairs. The front door hung wide open behind them. Libby beat the other two by several steps. Practical footwear and on-the-job training helped. She stopped at the passenger door and yanked on the handle. It didn't give. Lib pounded on the window.

"Christ. Give me a second." Lucas pressed a button on the control panel between them, unlocking the doors.

"Jesus fucking Christ." Libby yanked the door wide, crouched beside Larkin, and tossed her arms around her.

A hiss seeped between her teeth, but she clamped it back. The comfort overrode the pain.

Gen and Mar added their arms, and they were a tangled knot of emotion on the New York City street. The heap didn't last long. They had her up and walking toward the house in no time.

"Wait." Lucas slammed his car door.

Marlis looked back. Lib and Gen continued their gentle carry of her up the steps.

Lucas ran past them and placed himself in the doorway. "You all need to wait. I have to clear the interior."

Libby snorted.

"We've been here for thirty minutes." Genevieve shooed him out of the way with a well-manicured hand.

"Someone could be lying in wait, and you'd never know." He held out his hand.

"I've been through the house but knock yourself out," Libby announced.

Lucas nodded. "Thank you." He turned to go inside.

The girls followed suit.

"What are you doing?" Lucas snapped.

"We're not waiting." Libby maneuvered them past him. Gen followed. "Will you get that door? Thanks."

"Where to?" Marlis asked.

"My bedroom," Larkin croaked.

"Let me carry her up the stairs." Lucas's voice carried from the foyer. The door closed with a thud.

Larkin doubled her grip on Genevieve's and Libby's shoulders, conveying her wishes without a word.

"Here." Libby nodded to Gen, who released her hold.

Panic clawed at Larkin for a split second before Libby scooped an arm under her thighs and hoisted Larkin to her chest.

"I've got her." Libby hustled up the stairs before he could say a word.

"My bad muscles," Genevieve hooted from behind them.

"I'm sorry." Larkin had never felt so heavy as she did with her girlfriend hoofing her up the various levels. When Beckett had done it, she'd felt beautiful. Today, she felt like a burden.

"Shut your mouth," Lib snarled. "I've toted men twice your size out of burning buildings."

"Really?" Man, her friend was a total badass.

"No, but it sounded cool, huh?" Lib winked.

"Yeah." Larkin nodded and regretted the move.

"The building wasn't on fire." Libby moved double time up the last flight and set her on her feet on the landing.

"Here. Let me help." Marlis took her arm from Libby.

"I'm here." Genevieve took her other.

Libby huffed a deep breath and stripped the sweatshirt from her muscular curves. "I'm warm now." She used the fabric to dab at her neck and the valley of her breasts, peeking out from her plunging tank top.

The girls ushered her into the bedroom and headed for her bed, but she redirected them to the bathroom. Libby hung back.

"No," Larkin corrected. "Everyone in."

They propped her on the chair at her vanity. She turned to the mirror before thinking and reeled at her reflection. The lines hugging her mouth and separating her brows seemed twice as deep. Dark, baggy circles settled under her lower lashes as though they'd never leave. The whites of her eyes were red with so many squiggly lines they formed a solid unit.

"I look like …" What? A victim? She touched her chin where a small crack split her skin.

"Like you just survived a house fire." Marlis's hand settled gently on her head. "Jesus, Larkin, you could have died. You look gorgeous."

"Can we not talk about death?" Genevieve begged.

"We have to." Larkin forgot her reflection and turned to face her friends.

"What happened?" Libby sat on the edge of the massive tub.

"Turn that on, please." Larkin pointed at the waterfall spout. "Might as well turn the plug while you're at it."

Libby's knowing gaze flew to the open door. "Gen, close that, would you?"

The two women completed their tasks while Marlis gave her a "WTF is going on" expression.

The thunder of rolling water filled the space, and all six eyes focused on her. Not one of their mouths moved. A first.

"I'm going to have to say this fast, or I won't get through it." If she thought too much, she'd end up a blubbering heap like she'd been when the detective had left her hospital room. Turned out the beeps on her phone conveyed more explosive information than the quiet chirps let on.

"You have this," Marlis urged.

She started with the easy stuff. The flowers and their cards. The fire that destroyed her house. The detective's visit. Then it was time. Larkin drew a breath.

"The fire was arson, intentionally set to destroy evidence and kill me." So not the hard part yet. She hugged her arms to herself.

"Holy shit, Larkin." Genevieve straightened from her prop on the edge of the counter.

"What?" Mar cried and grabbed her hand.

"That's not the awful part," Larkin warned. Tears gathered in the back of her throat. She tried to choke them down, but they refused to budge.

"What evidence?" Libby dropped her elbows to her knees, leaning in for the coup de grâce.

"Reagan's body was found in the garage." It was a knife to the heart all over again.

"Reagan, your assistant? Sweet Reagan, who is young and vibrant and has her whole life ahead of her?" Marlis's hands sliced the air with each descriptor.

Larkin nodded, unable to speak.

"Had her whole life ahead of her. Fuck." Genevieve slapped the counter. "Just what the fuck?"

"Details," Libby demanded.

"They don't have DNA results and haven't confirmed it." Larkin rocked slowly back and forth. "I wasn't supposed to know, but I overhead the detective's conversation. Her purse and identification were found under that guest room bed. They believe that's where the first fire originated." She shuddered in a breath. "The medical examiner said that she'd been dead for some time."

"So the fire didn't kill her?" Mar asked.

"No." It was impossible to think that Reagan would never again pop her head into Larkin's office and tell her some crazy story about her weekend. It was devastating to think about the young woman's mother and how much she would miss her child. The tears started again. How was it possible she had any left? "Have any of you heard from Douglas?"

"He gathered us this morning, told us about the fire, and brought us to the house so we'd be here when you arrived," Libby explained. "I thought he would stay, but he'd gone to talk to some friends." Her brows hiked. "Now I know he suspected arson. I think he's mounting a hunting party."

"Probably." Larkin felt for the SOB who targeted her.

"Do they have a cause of death?" Libby asked quietly.

Larkin shook her head. The side to side movement increased the pounding behind her eyes.

"I'm spending the night," Libby announced.

"Me too," Gen agreed.

"Me too, if I can bring my security detail." Marlis pointed at the bathroom door. "Lucas is here to protect you. I don't want us left out in the cold if something happens."

"Is he?" Libby asked. Marlis looked at Libby as if she had two heads. "She's not acting like he is here to protect her," she explained.

"I don't know." Larkin pointed at the near overflowing water. She stood and crossed to the inviting tub. "He's being weird," she breathed. "He was at the hospital so soon after they pulled me from the fire, and he's acting possessive and overbearing. It just creeps me out."

"I'm less worried about him and more worried about your rooftop lover boy." Libby grabbed both her hands and sat her on the edge of the tub.

"You read people well, but now's not the time to take chances," Marlis urged. "Let them figure things out before you see him again, at least."

"That's just it." She shook her head. "I won't see him again. We left it at fond memories."

"Because he was going to kill you." Genevieve's forceful voice ricocheted off the marble walls.

"No." Larkin turned toward Gen to find her rock-solid friend leaky eyed and red faced. "Because things were getting too serious."

"If he had nothing to hide, there's nothing to worry about in giving me his name," Libby said.

"Oh," Larkin said, "I know he has things to hide."

TWENTY-FIVE

"I'M FINE. REALLY." Larkin patted Genevieve's back for the third time to get her friend to release her gridlocked hug.

"Are you sure Douglas shouldn't come with you into the office today?" Gen finally levered back. Tears hugged the edges of the strong, wild redhead's eyes.

"No tears," Larkin demanded. "And yes, I'm sure. I'm perfectly safe inside my building with Charlotte at my side." She patted the gun that hung in the swanky purse crossing her body. "Besides, he's meeting with Libby's FBI friend today."

Genevieve sighed and relented after an internal battle Larkin could only discern from her friend's rapidly moving eyes. "I love you, stupid ass. You know that? I don't know what I'd do if something happened to you or one of the girls."

"I love you too, you crazy ass. Nothing is going to happen to me or any of the girls." If she said it enough, maybe she'd believe it. If she said it enough, maybe it would be true. Only one way to find out. Time to live life. She kissed Gen's cheek and then slipped out the open car door.

"You are more stubborn than I remember." Douglas closed the car door behind her. He stepped so close he could kiss her cheek, if he puckered his lips, but he didn't. Good thing they were in the underground entrance. Otherwise, he'd be a popsicle by now. His warm arms wrapped around her back and pulled her close. "That gun doesn't leave your side. Not to go to the bathroom. Not for a dear friend in for a visit. Never."

"I'll be fine." Larkin hugged him back more aggressively than she ever had, proving her words false. She was anything but fine. Her heart ached. Her insides quaked. And someone wanted her dead. She kissed Douglas's cheek and moved to step back. His hold didn't budge. "Not you too."

He squeezed her tighter, as though daring her to make something of it.

"I expect this much from Mar, but you and Gen are better than this."

"We play things close to the vest, but we're not better than caring for our ..."

Her breath caught. What was Douglas to her? Gen was her friend. Douglas was her driver, but he was more. Had the years done that, or was it something else?

"Well," he huffed, gave her one last squeeze, and then released her. "Is it so awful to have people who care about you?"

"Not at all." She held his hand for a second, struggling to read the expression on his face. There was so much in those old blue eyes and the deep creases framing his features.

He patted her hand and turned away as though he'd known she sought answers and refused to give any.

Larkin pressed the elevator call and was surprised to find it on the underground level. She waved goodbye, stepped onto the car, and pressed the button for her office. Her back snugged up to the car's back corner. The leather of her purse warmed under her fierce grip. She watched the floors pass one blinking set of figures at a time. When she reached the third floor, her breath held without the command.

The lights didn't flicker past. They held the offending number. Her shoulders shook, and she hated it.

"Don't be stupid."

The doors opened on the third floor, which was the security headquarters, but no one was there. The place where someone should be waiting impatiently for the elevator car to carry them higher into the sky was eerily, irritatingly devoid of the person who'd pressed the call button.

It was nothing. Really. They'd just decided three flights of stairs wasn't too much to descend. Then again, her car had been moving up and shouldn't have stopped for a down call.

Larkin slid up the side wall. Her gaze never left the gray carpet and blank white walls. She reached out and pressed the button to close the doors. Her sweaty fingers slipped off the slick button without making it light. Teeth ground to nubs, she tried again.

The button lit from the inside and warmed hers, just a little.

Slowly, too slowly the two sides of the door slid toward one another. Five inches remained. Three. Then one. In her mind, a hand reached through the thin opening and grabbed at her. Thank fuck it was just her twisted brain. The door closed, and the car jerked into motion.

It stopped on the twentieth floor. Larkin's grip hadn't moved from her purse, so close to her gun. Two men she'd never seen before stepped onto the car.

The first eyed her as though she was a turkey dinner. Larkin glared. She had no time for pleasantries. There were no fucks to give on politeness. They were spread out elsewhere. Like trying to keep her alive. His buddy pressed the button for the thirty-second floor and accidentally on purpose jabbed his too friendly friend in the side. They whispered some exchange that pulled the friend's gaze back to the front of the elevator.

She didn't draw a deep breath until they exited. The car arrived on her floor, and she sighed. Yelling filtered through the open door. She choked on the breath.

"You cannot dictate to me, little piss-ant. Step aside."

Rage bubbled in Larkin's veins. She'd recognize that voice anywhere.

"Sir, please don't do that," Darren pleaded. "If I have to tell you again, I'll be forced to call security."

"Security?" her father bellowed.

Larkin drew herself to her fullest height and marched out of the elevator and straight into the middle of the tussle for her office doorknob.

"Miss Ashford." Darren released his hold and sagged against the wall. "Thank goodness."

"It's about time you showed up." Her dad's index finger stabbed at Darren. "This little piss—"

"Felix Ashford," Larkin growled. "Don't you dare say another disparaging word about my assistant. You are not allowed in my office without my presence and consent. I've given you neither, and Darren knows it." She turned her back on her father and grabbed Darren's hand. More than anything, she wanted to tell him about Reagan. The two had worked closely together, but she couldn't. "I apologize for my father. There is no excuse for his behavior.

None at all. You did the right thing. Thank you."

"The right thing?" her father shrieked.

"The next time he shows up without me being present, call Carl or Dan in security right away." Larkin patted Darren's hand, then released it and turned on her father. "You want in my office so badly? Go. Now." She pointed toward the double doors. Her father removed his hand from the knob, shoved it inside his pockets, and stood his ground. He hated being told what to do, even if it was his exact goal.

After a long glare, he relented. He wrenched the handle, tossed the door wide, and stomped into her office. The lights greeted him with a flicker before burning bright. Larkin offered Darren an overly bright smile and strode after the man who'd raised her, if only a little. He paced a tight circle around her desk. His gaze studied the clean top and the wall of hidden, modern drawers behind it too closely for her comfort.

"What is so important you had to get inside my office this morning without me inside it?" She closed the door. It echoed inside the fresh confines.

"It wasn't that you weren't here. I just needed ..." He stopped pacing and turned to face her. "Your attorney won't tell me whether you have a will drawn or its contents, if it does exist." One of his palms slapped onto the back of her desk chair. His face drew tight with indignation.

Heat burned her cheeks so intensely, she expected to see steam rise from them any second. He had no business contacting Genevieve. Why hadn't her friend said anything about her father's antics? Gen had most likely told him to fuck off, and she probably hadn't mentioned it because she didn't want to add to Larkin's worry.

"Damn right, she didn't." Larkin continued to her chair and shoved it back.

Felix gasped and stumbled back as though she'd struck him. It wasn't outside the realm of possibilities. Her fists were ready for a task. They were clenched so tightly they vibrated at her sides.

"You don't understand." Her father smoothed back his perfectly combed hair. "We must have a contingency in place. If you die, you don't want your business to collapse. You don't want your money to go to the state, do you?"

Larkin reached deep inside, to the core of her being, and grabbed hold of the strength that kept the world at bay. To the strength that kept her alive when she'd wanted nothing more than to meet her mother in the land of not. She drew a deep breath, let it out slowly, and then repeated the process. Her hands loosened at her sides.

"No. I don't, which is why my will states that the company will be sold and all my assets will be distributed equally among the charities I've named." Larkin offered a salty smile. "You are not one of them. So I hope you're not trying to kill me for my money."

His face blanched. No way to know it if was from knowing he'd get nothing from her or from the accusation she'd made. It made a sick sort of sense. Had he killed her mother and made it look like suicide? Who was there to question him or his intentions? She was older, a little wiser, and a hell of a lot more wary.

"I'd never hurt you," he snarled. "How can you think that of me?"

"Really?" She offered an eye roll that contradicted her mature stature and powerful position. "Because I was in the hospital. Someone burned my house down with me inside it, and the first thing you say when you see me is what's in your will."

"Larkin, you don't make it easy, but I do love you."

"And you make it easy?" Her head shook. "You order me a Glenlivet every time we share a meal. It's the same bottle I found in my mother's arms, her dead arms, when I was thirteen." She braced both hands on the back of the chair and breathed deeply. When had she started yelling?

"I'm sorry," he gasped. His hand covered his mouth. "I didn't know. I only saw her in the … in the morgue."

No, he hadn't been at the house when she'd needed him or anyone for that matter. He'd been at his lover's hideaway. She'd been home alone with her mother's corpse.

"You won't let me come by the house." Larkin swallowed the emotions welling inside her. "Every time, you want to meet at a restaurant or at my office."

"Oh, Larkin, it's not you."

"It's not you, it's me?" She let her brows hike.

"Franklin is at the house."

Relief, the first she'd felt in a while, washed over her. Felix sat across from her in one of the two chairs on offer. She collapsed into her chair and stared at him. "You should stop hiding Franklin. Stop hiding who you are."

"You don't understand. The world will judge me. They'll look at me differently."

"Fuck them."

Her father blinked widely.

"The world judges, period. Let them, at least, judge the real you, not some affable concoction of bullshit."

"You wouldn't be ashamed of me?" A side of her father she'd never seen flashed in his slacked jaw and wondrous eyes.

"Only when you treat my assistant like shit. Not for loving who you love, or hell, screwing who you screw. Love isn't a requirement."

"I don't know what came over me. He is just so … out and proud. It made me insane with hatred because I'm not brave enough to do it."

"Yes, you are. We're stronger than we know." She

slipped the purse from around her shoulder and set it on top of her desk.

"You are." He offered her a smile, a genuine smile that warmed the blood flowing through her veins. "You always have been strong, determined, the best of us."

She couldn't speak without crying.

"When I heard you'd been in a fire, I freaked. I'd never expected that I could outlive you. I'd never want to, but if I did, I didn't want your legacy to be ripped apart and auctioned to the highest bidder."

Larkin wanted to believe that. The thought snuggled up to her jaded, jagged edges. They spurred it away. "Why did you and my mother get married in the first place?"

"Ha." He smiled and drummed the edge of his shoes with two fingers. His gaze drifted as though off to the past. "She wanted money. I wanted a cover. It was as simple and as complicated as that."

"Did she know right away?"

"Perhaps she thought I was a supreme gentleman. From her stories, she'd never met one of those." He shrugged and quit drumming. "She figured it out pretty quickly."

"Am I even your daughter?" She hadn't meant to ask, but it flew from her lips before she could call it back. She'd thought about it a thousand times, so it was bound to come out.

Felix Ashford shrank back against the chair. His shoulders hunched. If he gave her nothing more, it was an answer in itself.

He sat forward and found her gaze. "I raised you. You are my daughter, whether we share blood or not."

The good memories washed over her. Him reading her favorite books over and over again. Them playing dress-up and tea party. The balloons he brought her for every birthday. The memories doused her fear and rage in contentment. It had been good … before her mother died.

"Do you know?" Larkin asked.

"She never said. I never asked because it didn't matter. She gave me you and let me be your father. I used to be a good one. I can be again."

TWENTY-SIX

LARKIN READ THROUGH THE FINANCIALS for the third quarter, compared them to the second and first, and was shocked to find that she was able to make sense of all the figures. Even with so much tumult in her mind and heart, the numbers pushed everything to the side. They were mundane. They were predictable. They provided her a focus and offered a sense of accomplishment. The run-in with her father had been long overdue. Though it left more questions atop the ever-mounting pile, they'd narrowed the chasm between them.

She tapped the mouse and focused on the projections for the fourth quarter. No matter her decision on the future of her business, Duo and Ditto were growing. They would continue to do so.

The trill of her cell phone yanked her from the narrow

window of peace she'd carved for herself. Her gaze slid to the bright screen, expecting to see either the detective's phone number or Lucas demanding she allow him to stay by her side every second of every day until, well, probably ever, if she'd let him.

Her hand leaped for the phone to take the call. Of all the people wanting things from her, Bronson Beauregard's eager cock was something she could easily fend off.

"Hello?"

"Larkin, have lunch with me." His tone was breathless and frantic more than demanding. It shoved her off the small space of even footing she'd thought she'd found.

"I would love to, Bronson, but it's not a good time." Not at all.

"You have to meet me. This sounds dramatic and stupid, but it's life and death, Lar. I need your help."

An image of Larry Vincent appeared front and center of her brain. Ice formed crystal daggers along her spine. They infiltrated her blood stream, forcing a bone-deep chill through her entire body.

No. Better judgment and common sense begged her not to get involved in Bronson's misdeeds. She had more than enough on her plate.

"Please, Lar. You know I wouldn't ask if I didn't really need you."

"When? Where?" Larkin heard her voice but didn't remember okaying the response.

"Now, please." His voice pitched. "In front of your building. I'll be there."

"I'm on my way."

"Hurry, please."

Larkin ended the call and tossed her phone onto the desk. She stood and stared at it. What had she just agreed to? Nothing more than to meet her friend in his time of need. He'd always been a little dramatic, so she was sure this was an overreaction and nothing more.

"It's nothing." She shoved her phone inside the pocket of her red slacks and slung her purse across her body, in case it was something.

Instead of going out the front entrance, she left through her private exit and hustled through the maze to the service elevators. Just about the time she reached the quiet, dark hallway, she remembered swearing these things off for the rest of her days. They radiated bad vibes and exacerbated her unease.

She pushed on, and after two long minutes, she was on the street in front of her building. Her gaze swung left and right for Bronson's car or his driver. Plenty of black Town Cars dotted the landscape.

A hand, large and cold, grabbed her upper arm.

"No." Larkin jerked her elbow high and across her body, breaking the hold. At the same time, she turned with her knee cocked and ready to inflict maximum damage.

"Jesus, Larkin." Bronson shrank back. "It's me."

"Bronson. Shit, don't grab me."

"I didn't expect you to act like I was trying to abduct you." His gaze slid left and right. "Christ, people are looking." He scrubbed his palm down his pants and jerked his suit jacket back into place. "Let's go, please."

"Where's your car?"

He took off on foot. His pace was that of a lunchtime workout walker, not a playboy turned businessman. If Vincent was involved, anyone would speed their gait to keep from getting gunned down in the street.

"Don't need one." He waved her along.

Larkin put her spiked boots to the test and reached him in time to stop at the street for a split second. He grabbed her hand and pulled her into the road, through a pedestrian stop sign.

"I didn't realize the death part would come in the form

of a cab." Larkin yanked her hand away and ran across the street to miss becoming roadkill. When she reached safety, she placed both hands on her hips, looked toward the sky, and filled her lungs with exhaust and a hit of actual oxygen. The building directly across from her office loomed like a sleek beast.

"Let's go." Bronson grabbed her above the elbow and ushered her forward.

She yanked loose from his grip again. "Do not grab me." Her feet stuck to the concrete, and her gaze bore into his. "Do not. How else do I have to say it for you to understand?"

"Christ." His hands shot up. "I'm sorry. Please, I just need to talk to you, and I need to hurry. Not again. I promise."

"If you were in such a hurry to talk to me, why didn't you just come to my office? You didn't have to buy me lunch."

He motioned her forward. "Can we walk and talk?"

"Fine." She shooed him ahead since she had no clue where they were going.

"I don't know what kind of security cameras you have in your office. I don't want anyone eavesdropping on us." He headed for the front door of the building that towered above them and her building.

If there was a new restaurant in the building, she hadn't heard of it.

"No one is listening to my conversations." The second the words were out of her mouth, she wondered if they were true. What if Lucas in all his upgrading had placed surveillance cameras with microphones in her office? In her boardroom? In her home?

No. He couldn't have without her knowing. Right?

They weaved through a maze of people in the ultra-mod lobby, then crammed onto an elevator car that flirted with capacity. Neither said a word as they slowly, irritatingly worked their way up the floors.

"This is me." Bronson nodded toward the door and stepped out of the way for her to exit.

Her gaze locked on the floor. Eighty-one.

Someone behind her cleared their throat. Another muttered, "Come on."

She shuffled forward on numb feet, praying he turned right, the opposite direction from her building. He dipped left and hustled down the corridor.

Her stomach cramped.

"Here." Bronson slipped inside an office.

She followed him into the benign room with a desk, filing cabinets, a computer, and a rolling leather chair. He slipped inside an office she'd seen before on a cold, dark night. It was the same office she'd watched Calder Beckett close the door to and rummage through its cabinets and search on its computer.

Her legs wobbled beneath her. She teetered toward the ground but caught herself on the cabinet Beckett had rifled through.

"Whoa. Are you okay?" Bronson pulled out a chair opposite his and offered his hand, careful not to grab her.

"I ..." She reeled. What the fuck was going on?

"I heard about the fire." His head shook. "I can't believe your house went up with you inside it."

Her cheeks cooled. Her stomach dropped. "How'd you hear about it?"

"A mansion in The Hamptons went up in flames. How would I have not heard about it?" He scoffed and stared at her like she was crazy. He had a point.

"I'm dizzy. The doctor said it could hit on and off for the next few days," she lied.

"I'm glad you're okay." He knelt in front of her.

"Me too." She hoped she would be at the end of all this

cloak and dagger bullshit. Her gaze lifted to the familiar and unrecognizable surroundings. "Whose office is this?"

"Mine." He smiled wanly. "I didn't want to be under my father's thumb. This was close but my own."

"For how long?"

"A few weeks." Bronson bobbed one shoulder. "He was pissed, of course."

"Of course." A man like Brice Beauregard liked things under his watchful eye and willful hand. "So what's the problem, Bronson?"

He grabbed her hand and held it between his. "How do you know your friend?"

Bronson didn't help her anti-aging regimen. Not to mention how the past two weeks had worked against it as fiercely as it could. Her brow furled so much she added several years to her appearance. "My friend?"

"The guy from the park?"

She was going to vomit all over Bronson Beauregard. It probably wouldn't be a first for him. His pupils shrank as they stared at her face, willing her to profess the answer.

Again, her protective instincts roared. They bolstered her body temperature and shaky legs and fortified her enough to answer.

"I don't know him. I fucked him. There's a difference." Larkin smiled at him as though hinting to Bronson's romantic overtures that had yet to present themselves today. She used the opportunity to turn the conversation away from Beckett. "Which is why we couldn't."

"But you were in the park with him." Bronson's grip tightened, encasing her hands.

"I was hungry. He was too. We worked up an appetite." She shrugged.

"I've seen him around a few times." His grip broke. He scrubbed both palms down his pants, stood, and then collapsed onto the edge of his desk. "With you and before that once."

"Twice. You've seen him twice. That's hardly cause for concern." She pointed at the window. "Do you know how many of the same people we pass on a daily basis? You don't notice them until you do. Then you see them everywhere."

"There are other things." He scrubbed an invisible stain on the knee of his pants. "Little things are moved in my house. In my office. Here! Nothing big but enough to freak me the hell out."

"Have you called the cops?"

His head shook and hung low. "No evidence."

"Security system?" she tried.

"Nothing. He's not on any camera. It's like he's a goddamned ghost."

Yep, that about summed up the man she knew. A ghost who'd reached inside her chest, forced her heart to beat, and then made off with a piece.

"Do you think he works for Larry Vincent?"

"No."

He answered so quickly she wanted to know how he knew, but if she asked too many questions, she'd tip her hand.

"I need you to contact him. Get him to meet you somewhere." His eyes were wide. He shifted his head several times in a crazy staccato. "The park. Yes, the park again. I'll be there instead." He sneered. "I don't want you around this creep."

"I don't have a way to contact him." That was honest as honest got. She couldn't if she wanted to, and she suddenly needed answers more than she'd ever needed them before.

"When will you see him again?"

"I won't." Larkin stood and walked to the window. Her gaze found the roof instantly. "I told you it was a fuck and nothing more." Lies. "I don't understand why you're fixated on this guy. Why do you think he's tormenting you?" She turned away from the roof and the memories and found Bronson on his feet only a couple of feet from her. "Someone's tormenting me, and I don't think it's him."

"Was his cock really that good?" he spat.

"Yeah." She nodded with no compunction or sarcasm. "Besides that, there's nothing for him to gain by targeting me or you."

"I can't believe you're not going to help me." Bronson's cheeks flushed. His foot lifted in a flash, connecting to his office chair. The thing rolled to the edge of the plastic pad and slammed into the wall, leaving an ugly scuff as evidence.

"I don't know anything." She could rebuild her house using the things she didn't know.

"You know the way out."

"So no lunch?"

"I needed to get you here. That was the fastest way I knew how, but it didn't work."

"What about Larry Vincent?" She leaned over his desk and planted both hands in front of him. "If you're involved with him, that could explain why you and I are both being targeted. Think about it. Your welcome home party. I was your plus one."

"It's not Larry Vincent. I'm one of ten guys who's fucked his daughters this month. He has no reason to target me."

"Both at once?"

"Shut up, Larkin."

"I'm just trying to figure this out," she explained.

He slumped into his chair. "Just go. You can't help."

That was a knife to the heart. Bronson had once been her good friend. She wanted to help him, but they were both hiding something they weren't willing to admit.

"Goodbye, Bronson."

TWENTY-SEVEN

EVERYONE HAD MADE THEIR CALLS, either in person or by phone, to check in on her. The night grew dark. Not even a shimmer of moonlight filtered in through her windows. No lights shined inside. She sat on a stool with her wine in hand and stared at the cloudy skyline. An hour ago, her butt had numbed, and then the rest of her body followed suit. If only her brain would. That rat fucker kept on and kept on, poking and prodding the layers of mystery shrouding her life.

There was no way around it. All the evidence stacked against him, reinforcing an insurmountable wall.

Calder Beckett was a stalker.

He just wasn't stalking her.

Bronson was the reason Beckett had been up on the rooftop that first night. She'd just crashed his stalker party.

Then she'd found him again outside Bronson's apartment, and he'd eluded her grasp. The last time, she'd caught him snooping in her friend's office.

No, the office hadn't been the last place she'd seen Beckett near Bronson. The park had been. On their date. On the magical day that was less real than a man pulling a rabbit out of his hat.

The temptation to go to the roof, find him, and shove him off to his death taunted her, but she'd only find unforgiving wind and a chill she couldn't shake. Well, the wind would be new. The chills had hung with her all afternoon, evening, and crept into the early morning hours. She clutched the blanket tighter around her shoulders and wiped at the tears wetting her chest.

A soft, firm knock sounded at the door.

Larkin turned and stared at the smoothly painted wood as though the inanimate object had called her name. No one should be here at this hour. The girls, all except Libby, had come and gone. Douglas and Lucas too, together. She'd made sure of it. No one had called from the front desk, so no one should be past security and at her door. Then again, no one should have defiled her building. No one should have burned her house to the ground.

She threw off the blanket, leaped from the chair, and ran to the island. Her purse sat in the center of the granite slab where she'd left it earlier. The metal clasp slipped under her frantic grasp. She grabbed the purse and wrestled with it, struggling to free her pistol. Finally, her hand found the metal stock, and she yanked. The purse clattered to the floor.

Another, more aggressive knock came, and then his voice filtered through the door. To keep from collapsing, one hand latched on to the edge of the bar top. The gun shook in her other hand. Tears blurred her vision.

"Larkin, open the door."

Calder Beckett's voice sounded too sweet to her ears. Her heart rammed against her sternum to get closer to him. Her brain jerked away from the plea. She turned the pistol around. It weighed her down as though it was a boulder. At the range or on Douglas's farm, she whipped the thing up with no effort at all, but this was the first time she intended to use it for self-defense ... or cold-blooded murder.

She shuffled forward, using the bar for support. The gap between her and the door loomed so wide, dark, and deep, it might have been a trench.

"Larkin. I'm coming in."

Her head shook, but her mouth refused to move.

Douglas had locked the deadbolt on his way out. She'd watched the lever flip into place. Despite it, the knob twisted, and the door opened slowly. Beckett's hulking frame blotted the light from the hallway. It emphasized his sheer size and strength. If he intended her harm, would her rounds even penetrate him? Her entire wobbly frame shook at the thought of hurting him.

He stepped inside, closed the door, and drew up short. His gaze locked on her pistol.

"God, Larkin, I'm sorry."

What did he have to be sorry about? Breaking in? Breaking her heart? Stalking her friend? Lighting her house on fire?

His steps were slow but insistent. Each one brought him closer. Each one closed the chasm between her and sanity. She knew nothing about this man except that he used her to get close to Bronson.

"Stop. Don't you come near me." The shrillness in her tone scraped across her eardrums.

He stopped on the other side of the sofa. Too close. The first scent of him hit her like a tranquilizer. Her grip doubled on the pistol.

"I came as soon as I heard about the fire. It took me …
for-fucking-ever to get here." He tugged on the short beard
he'd grown since she'd last seen him. "Are you okay?"

"Am I okay?" She shook the gun. "No. No, I'm not
okay. Someone tried to kill me." Tears slid down her cheek
in earnest. "I argued with people that it wasn't you and
now …" Her teeth ground together.

"Now what?" His eyes were shiny, black orbs in the
dim light.

"I know you're stalking Bronson Beauregard."

His nose wrinkled. The massive man looked as though
he'd smelled a dubious odor. "Hunting. Not stalking."

"I put all the pieces together, and now you have to kill
me." If she didn't kill him first.

Beckett's head shook gently, just once. As denials went,
it was a shit effort on his part.

He moved so quickly, she had zero time to react. His
hand was hot over hers, twisting the cold metal from her
hand and burning her fingertips from the friction. Before
she could register it, his face was too close. His arms too
tight around her.

Beckett pressed his mouth to hers. Their mouths tangled in fury and sorrow. It was the best relief and worst
betrayal. It cut so deep she could see moonlight shining
through her soul.

Sobs wracked her. She shoved him back.

"I wasn't even in the country when it all went down.
I can prove it." He reached for her. His big hand offering
warmth and protection. But he was the one she needed
protecting from.

"Bronson?" Her lips trembled. She bit them together.

"I didn't know you two were friends until the welcome home party. I saw you drop him off. Then you ran
after me." He stepped forward.

She drew back from his reach. "Why did you ask me to

lunch in the park?"

"I needed an introduction to Beauregard."

He should have raised the gun and shot her. It would have been quicker. Cleaner. She slapped at the tears. Too soon, they multiplied, soaking the top of her camisole.

"There's so much—"

"You're using me. I get it." She hated it, and she didn't understand it at all, but she wouldn't get real answers from him. Not now. Not ever. "Why are you here? What do you need now?"

"I needed to know you were okay."

Her swollen eyes closed. "I don't believe you."

"I don't believe me either."

Her eyes popped open.

He set the pistol on the counter and gestured back and forth between them. "I don't do this kind of shit."

"You're not the only one. So problem solved." Larkin walked on shaky, bare feet around him and to the door. Before she could open the damn thing, she wiped the tears off her hand onto her lounge pants. "We're done with each other."

"No, we're not." His voice rumbled, and his breaths hit the back of her neck. The warmth from his body radiated against her back.

Larkin closed her eyes and dug deep, so deep she ripped part of her heart out with the inner strength. "You used me." She opened the door.

Beckett's hand flattened against the wood and closed it. She tried to hold it open, but there was no fighting his strength. He pressed his cheek to hers. A connection more profound than any she'd experienced passed between their connected skin, and sobs shook her.

His arms encircled her shoulder. His body shielded her back.

The need to sink into him, to lose every part of herself

in this man, tempted her like an illicit drug. Just one more time. Just one more hit. What would it hurt? Everything.

He was dangerous in so many ways.

"No." Larkin shoved off his hold and wrenched the door wide. "Leave." She looked him directly in the eyes without blinking.

His head shook.

"Now," she growled … and sobbed.

"Bronson isn't who you think he is."

"Neither are you."

He opened his mouth to speak.

Larkin wanted all the answers. She wanted him, and everything he could give her, if he would share. There had to be a logical explanation for his behavior.

The muscles in his jaw stretched, then flexed. His mouth closed.

"Goodbye, Beckett."

He gripped the hem of his leather jacket and strained the material. His head dropped, and he walked through the doorway and out of her life.

TWENTY-EIGHT

IT IS IN YOUR DARKEST HOURS that you find light.

"I'm going to join the eager masses." Marlis grinned wider than wide and kissed Larkin's cheek. "Knock 'em dead." Her friend winked before slipping out the door.

Larkin stood in the waiting room at the bottom of The Ashford. Chatter from the small crowd gathered in the opulent lobby seeped inside for a split second. Shutters clicked. Camera flashes glared. Test shots. She checked her watch. Nine fifty-five. Five more minutes.

She hadn't given people much warning, so Libby and Genevieve couldn't attend. A criminal to catch and court. Libby cheered her on with over-the-top GIFs, and Gen sent a case of the cheapest beer ever made. Her friends were the best. With their help and the backbone she'd fortified over a lifetime, she would make it through.

The door swung wide and hard, coming directly for her face. Larkin jumped back, teetering on her heels. She used the arm of a chair to catch herself.

"What the hell is going on?" Lucas stormed through the door.

"Besides you almost clocking me with the door?" She assessed both heels for a crack. The last thing she wanted to do was make headlines for falling on her entrance. Then the headlines would read, "Duo and Ditto CEO is a Fall-down Drunk."

"Why is every member of the media in the lobby?"

Lucas's hair was ruffled. His chin boasted never-be-fore-seen stubble. The tail of his blue tie hung out of his jacket.

"If you'd bothered to show up to work on time, you would have been informed." Larkin straightened her skirt, blouse, and jacket. "I'm fine, by the way." She smoothed the top of her low ponytail.

"What's going on out there, Larkin? Why are all those people out there? Reporters and their greasy-fingered photographers are crowding the lobby." He slammed the door and stood between her and the only exit.

The tiny hairs on the back of Larkin's neck rose.

"I'm the head of security for The Ashford. How can I secure the location if I'm not informed of events taking place?" He slung a hand toward the closed door. "I need to vet those people. Any one of them could mean you harm." His voice rattled the walls.

"Larkin, they're ready for you." Douglas's calm voice filled the room.

"What's going on?" Lucas bellowed.

Bolstered by Douglas's presence, Larkin stepped for-ward. "Yell at me one more time, and it'll be your resig-nation." She maneuvered around him and walked toward

Douglas. "As for the crowd, you'll see soon enough."

Douglas's hand slipped from inside his jacket. His gaze fixed on Lucas until he shut the door, closing Lucas inside. "He's got to go." Douglas placed his hand on the small of her back and led her down a short maze of corridors toward the lobby. The rumble of the crowd grew with their every step. "I know a guy, overqualified and in need of a new mission. He can fill Lucas's role tomorrow."

"Were you going to shoot him?"

"Let me fire him before it comes to that. I don't trust the guy."

Larkin hated letting anyone go. In the current economic climate, job stability was everything. "I don't trust him either."

"Good." His steps slowed before they rounded the last corner. She matched his pace. "I'll do it while you give your speech. He'll be out of here before the applause dies."

"Oh, no." A sudden inexplicable sadness deflated the buoyancy keeping her afloat. "You'll miss my big to-do?"

"Larkin, I already know what you're going to say." He placed his hand on her shoulder and squeezed.

"How? I haven't told anyone."

"I've known you since you were a crying, chubby-cheeked baby." His eyes glistened for a fraction of a second. Maybe it was the light. His hand fell away. "Your teenage years were trial and error, but I know the way you think."

Douglas had been in her family's employ before hers, but only after her mother passed away. Her mind tried to calculate the angles. So many sides were misshapen or blurred. "You knew my mother?"

His shoulders didn't budge. The stern line of his chin locked in place. If she hadn't known him for most of her life, she never would have caught the sudden gleam in his eye. It was subtle. Like the shift from twelve p.m. to noon.

It was so miniscule she might have imagined it.

"Your mother and I grew up together."

"Really?" How had she not known this? Her mother never mentioned him. He never mentioned her, other than in passing conversation.

"Yep." They'd stopped walking altogether.

Come to think of it, her mother never mentioned anything about her childhood. Her parents had been killed when she was a little girl. That was all she'd ever said about her past.

"Where? When? How did you know each other?" She grabbed his arm as though it were a life raft. "Why are you just telling me this now?"

He hugged her close. Really hugged her. "Because I almost lost you, and I realized I've never really had you."

"What does that mean?" Did it mean what she stupidly hoped it meant?

Douglas leaned her back. His arms still held tightly to hers. "After your big to-do, let me take you to lunch." The request was so quiet she might have missed it with the impatient crowd that grew louder by the second had she not been staring at his face.

"Yes." Her smile stretched her cheeks so wide they hurt from lack of use of her smile muscles. "Of course."

"I'll kick Lucas to the curb and have the car waiting out front. Whenever you're ready."

"Okay."

Douglas kissed her cheek and turned her toward the lobby. "I'm proud of you, Larkin." When she stood there stunned, he gave her the nudge she needed to move forward. Her mind was in a thousand places at once. But the moment the elbow-to-elbow full lobby came into view, her mission boomeranged back into focus.

Larkin was tired of the world dictating her truth. This was her time to set the record straight.

Shoulders back and chin high, she stepped onto the low stage and took hold of the podium. She didn't say a word. Instead, she eyed each of the screaming reporters in turn and waited for the room to hear what she had to say. That was why they'd come. One by one, they quieted until the room breathed in time with her inhales and exhales.

Everyone breathed with her except the members of her board. With the exception of Genevieve, the rest had jumped at the opportunity for camera time. Tarin sat front and center with an ugly cream-colored purse in her lap atop terrible brown slacks. Worst thing she wore was a clown-like smile and eager eyes. The eyes wormed their way under Larkin's skin. They were too wide. Too crazy. Too ready for an explosion. Cornish sat next to her on his phone oblivious to everything. Brice and Bitsy sat together at the end of the second row, looking poised to make a break for it if things went sideways. Smart. Benjamin Daily sat on the opposite end of the row from the two old lovebirds, an island unto himself.

"Thank you all for coming on such short notice. I know your time is valuable, so I'll keep this brief."

Again, the room erupted in questions. Again, she quieted.

It took a bit longer, but they came to heel.

"As of late, the media has been abuzz with false information. False information leaked by a member of my board of directors." Each member reacted to the jab. Tarin's crazy eyes focused. Brice's shoulders straightened even more, though it didn't seem possible. Cornish dropped his phone. Benjamin slouched in his chair. Marlis, who leaned against the wall, smiled.

"By some members of my board, I was very strongly urged to marry. They didn't want me to marry out of love or tradition, but they begged me to marry so that I might more successfully launch my company onto the public market."

The room lit with flashes and questions. She bided her time until they were ready.

"We live in a time and country where women marry because they want to, not because they have to. Where women are waiting later and later to marry. Where some choose to never marry. Where they create families through single adoption or artificial insemination. I live in a time and a country where I don't have to mold my life choices to fit any preconceived path and neither do you."

One female reporter, in particular, whooped in the back of the room. Her hands lifted into the air and another joined her. A small murmur started and grew to a conservative cheer.

Larkin spoke over the cheers. "Duo and Ditto offer a platform to help make marriage and bringing a baby into the world easier, but, by no means, are either of those things necessary for happiness. Find your passions and pursue them wholeheartedly. Above all, don't let anyone dictate your truth except you."

The room burst into cheers and whoops. The women grew bolder with each passing second. Her message would find its audience. She hoped the next one would too.

She looked at the side of the room where Darren and Marlis stood apart from the crowd. Darren offered her a large smile and shook the large stack of manila envelopes filling his arms. Mar held a load as well.

Larkin held up her hand and waited for quiet. "Now, to the real reason we are all here today."

Tarin Blakely crouched low and crept her way down the aisle. The front half of the room stared at the woman and the awkward way she crawled over laps and out to the aisle. Once there, she booked it toward the exit with her head down and hideous purse shrouding her face.

Several reporters whispered among themselves.

Screw Tarin and her weird ass ways. They had more important things to handle.

"My assistant and friend, Reagan Walstead, was found murdered early Sunday morning. She first went missing Tuesday, the tenth, between the hours of five and seven p.m."

The quiet hardened into something else. Layers of surprise contorted the reporters' faces. She was telling them something they didn't know. They were accustomed to knowing everything and assuming more.

Larkin turned her head to motion Darren and Marlis ahead. The sexy detective, Owen Graham, stood next to them, giving her a surprise of her own. She swallowed it back and gave the nod.

"My colleagues are passing around a packet with digital and print images of Reagan Walstead as well as her last known whereabouts, the clothes she was wearing, and other important information." Whispers started up as Darren and Marlis moved through the crowd, dispensing the information. "If you care enough to run an article about my love life, I ask you to care enough to put my murdered friend's face on the front pages of your outlets. Please help us garner credible leads and catch her killer."

The crowd lobbed hundreds of questions in her direction at once. "Please, I'd love the opportunity to answer your questions, but I have to hear them, and you need to hear my response. Know there are some things I'm not at liberty to discuss. There are other things I will not discuss in regards to my personal life. So with a show of hands, who has a question?"

She stared into a sea of arms and flapping hands.

As her teacher had when she was young, Larkin picked the quietest reporters first. Soon, the masses caught on and followed their colleagues' examples. The more questions she answered, the more members of her esteemed board bowed out. An hour was eaten up in a blink. A blink and a sore throat.

"Again, thank you all for attending. Any help you can give in bringing my friend's killer to justice is greatly appreciated."

Larkin walked off the stage toward the corridor. Marlis and Darren rushed to her side. She motioned the detective along. The small group walked through the cordoned-off path past Carl and Dan, who stood sentinel. They rounded the corner out of camera shot, and Larkin exhaled so deeply her bra strap slipped off the edge of her shoulder under her shirt.

"I'm so proud of you." Marlis tackled her in a hug.

"That was pretty ballsy, if I do say so myself." Darren preened, accentuating a waist most women would die for.

Larkin smiled until her gaze reached the detective's. His jaw worked in a circle as though he'd been chewing on words for forty minutes and they'd turned to gum in his mouth. "I didn't deviate from the speech you okayed. I stuck to the issue without giving anything away."

Why was she defending herself? She'd done nothing wrong.

"We need to talk now." His gaze scanned the area as though looking for a place to speak in private.

Mar kissed her cheek. "I'm gone. Dinner with the girls, my place?"

"Sounds great." Larkin waved her off.

Darren stepped out of the small circle. "I'm sure I have a thousand messages to tend to. Amazing speech, really." He waved and headed for the elevator.

"This way." Larkin led the way to the waiting room. She needed to grab her purse and phone out of there anyway.

The stony man didn't say a word. They speed-walked

their way to the windowless room … the windowless room she was about to close herself inside with a man she hardly knew. Huh, familiar situations. Beckett. None of the familiar feelings boiled to the surface. Not fear. Not intrigue. Nothing. The high of the press conference died a swift death, leaving her devoid. Leaving her a void.

Hearing Douglas's voice in her mind, Larkin crossed to her purse and looped the long leather strap over her head and around one arm. Behind her, the click of the door latch catching in its frame pinged off her spine. Maybe not nothing. She turned quickly. The detective stood near the door. Both his arms crossed over a wide chest. He was too wide and his clothes too wrinkled at the edges to be automatically pegged for a lawman. Actually, take away the badge and he looked more like a vagabond.

"Miss Ashford—"

"Detective Graham, was anything wrong with my speech?" He hadn't wanted her to speak about Reagan at all. She'd had no qualms about arguing with him over the phone. In person, however, she wanted to stay on his good side.

"No. Would Tarin Blakely have ever had cause to be in your garage at your house in The Hamptons?"

The question caught her sideways, taking her for quite the ride. Tarin? Why was he asking about her? Had he answered her question? Minimally. Concisely. The detective was a wanderer who had nothing tying him to a home. A detective with nothing to lose but the case. His single-mindedness offered an unexpected level of comfort.

"No." Her head shook. It helped with the disorientation.

"But she was at your house?" His gaze narrowed.

"Yes, once, for a party I threw for the pool of board members I was considering."

"June third?"

"Yes." Larkin blinked. How had he known the date?

"I spoke with Fitzgerald. East Hampton PD sent over the transcript from your conversation."

"I didn't know I was being recorded."

"Do you have anything to hide?"

"Everyone does, I suppose, but no, not where finding Reagan's killer is concerned." Was that the whole truth? What if Beckett was involved? He wasn't. Even though he tore a hole in her heart, he wasn't capable of hurting an innocent woman. She didn't question whether he was capable of killing someone. It read in the way he moved. He could, if he hadn't already.

"What areas did she have access to at the party?"

"The living room, first bathroom off the main hallway. Foyer. Back deck and bar. The patio bathroom." Larkin shrugged. "I suppose she could have wandered into any of the rooms except my bedroom, which was locked. The caterers were set up in the kitchen and had their supplies and van in the garage. She couldn't have gone in there without being seen, but what reason would she have had for going in there in the first place?"

"No good reason."

"Why are you asking me about Tarin?" Then her brain snapped the pieces together. Reagan's body was found in the garage. "Why?"

"Evidence found in the garage links Tarin Blakely to Reagan's murder."

"No." Larkin's head shook hard. So hard it rattled her brain against her skull. "No way. What reason would she have? They had next to no interaction. And her family. Tarin wouldn't do that to her family. She wouldn't put her children through this."

"Family?" The detective's crossed arms dropped to his sides. He stepped forward. "They were all killed in a car accident when she was a teenager."

That was awful, but not what she was talking about. "No, her children and her husband."

"Tarin Blakely isn't married and has no children."

Larkin stared at him as though he'd slapped on a leotard and started dancing *Swan Lake.*

The corners of his mouth twitched. "She's spun you quite the story, hasn't she?"

"I don't understand." Larkin was shocked her lips moved.

"Where do you think she lives?" A light sparked in Detective Graham's eyes.

"A colonial two story in Connecticut. She also has a townhouse on the Lower East Side where she stays if she needs to be in town for work." Larkin grabbed her phone and scrolled to Tarin's contact information. "Here. I have the addresses right here." She held up the phone.

Graham stepped closer, grabbed his own phone, and took a picture of her screen. "She's been living in a shit apartment near Chinatown for two years. It's littered with takeout boxes and rats. All except for one room." The detective swiped his screen several times and then held the phone up for Larkin.

Her entire body shook.

"Shit." He drew the phone away and grabbed her shoulders. "Sit down." He maneuvered her to a chair.

She couldn't look anywhere but the picture that was seared into her mind.

"They gave us sensitivity training. It didn't take. Sorry." He swiped on his phone once more. "I need to know if you've seen this writing anywhere before?"

Larkin shrank away from the screen. She managed to keep her eyes open. Gone were the millions of black marks on the wall that looked like bugs infesting the tidy room. Gone was the rack of ugly brown suits, shoes, and purses set in the center of the room like a monument. Gone was the collage of pictures taped to every surface of the en-suite bathroom mirror and vanity top lit by naked bulbs that accentuated the eyes cut out of each image ... of her.

Just one of the tiny black bugs centered the detective's phone. Only, it wasn't a bug at all. The word she'd seen scratched on each threatening card stared back at her. CUNT.

Her head nodded.

"Where?"

"Oh God!" Larkin covered her mouth. Bile rose high-er and higher. She'd gotten Reagan killed. "This is all my fault." Her voice quaked.

"How?" Graham crouched in front of her.

"The cards. The flowers. I'd been receiving the threats for weeks and never brought them to the police."

"Where are they?"

"The cards are in my apartment upstairs. A few are at the office."

"I need them."

"We can go get them now." She wanted them out of her house anyway.

"Who all's touched them?"

"Me. My driver touched one, the first one. I had him try to track their origin."

"Your driver?" Graham's gaze narrowed.

"He wasn't always a driver," she hedged. Why hadn't she agreed to call in the police when he'd first suggested?

"Anyone else?"

"Darren, my new assistant, touched the ones at my of-fice, and the girls."

"Look, it's not your fault. This woman has been in a psychiatric ward three times. She should have been locked up years ago. They thought she caused the accident that killed her parents and brother but couldn't prove it. She's a schizophrenic off her meds."

Off her meds. Had that been what she'd seen in the bathroom at Bronson's party? Her skin crawled. If she'd remembered what was on that fucking pill and looked it up instead of blowing it off, Reagan would still be alive. "If I had reported the threats—"

"She might have escalated sooner and maybe bigger."

"Reagan is dead," she whispered. It couldn't escalate much more.

"With the incendiary devices in her apartment, she could have taken out several floors of your building. And let's remember, she'd fixated upon you. Reagan just got in her way."

"Who's to say she won't escalate now?" Larkin's voice pitched. "She's free."

"Only because we haven't located her. I have a car at her house. Have had since midnight."

"She was here for the speech."

"Here?" Graham stood.

The door opened, and Lucas stood in the gap. Layers caked upon layers of confusion.

Graham looked at Lucas, then back at her. "Where was she?"

"She was in the front row for the speech, and she left when I started talking about Reagan. I didn't realize it at the time. I just figured she was pissed about the first part." Larkin jumped up and wobbled. She caught herself on the chair back. Her stomach cramped.

"I've got you." Lucas grabbed her elbow and steadied her.

Somehow, the two men changed places seamlessly. Lucas was inside, and Graham stood at the exit, his quads firing in place. "I need to check your security footage."

"Talk to Carl, he's behind the desk. I'll let him know you're coming."

Graham pointed at Larkin. "She shouldn't be alone."

"I've got her." Lucas draped an arm around her and pulled her close.

TWENTY-NINE

The boom it circulated in the room snapped Larkin out of her stupor. She shoved out of Lucas's arm and faced him. "Where's Douglas?"

His nose crinkled. "How should I know?"

"Because he was coming to speak to you." And she was supposed to meet him out front for their lunch date.

"I never saw him."

It wasn't like him to miss his man. Larkin grabbed her phone to text Douglas. At least, he needed to know she was running later than expected. Though he probably thought she was still entertaining the reporters' questions. From the roar in the lobby, they'd yet to leave.

Lucas held her free hand, yanking her attention from the screen. His eyes were wet. Not from tears, but from what she didn't know. "Larkin, after you left, I went outside to blow off steam. When I came back in, I heard your speech."

"Oh." She was surprised he'd cared to listen. Of course, Douglas hadn't told him he was fired yet. The thought crossed her mind to tell him, but the instinctual part of her brain rebelled.

His hand closed around hers. "You're right. I needed to hear it. You deserve to dictate your future. If your future is not with me, I realize, now, that it has nothing to do with me. It's you."

Larkin pressed her lips together to keep from saying something ugly. So many things came to mind, all in self-defense. There was nothing wrong with her. Well, maybe there was. Maybe she needed therapy. Regardless, it was hardly his place to say so. They weren't friends. They weren't lovers. But this was his attempt at an apology. A piss-poor one.

"I'm glad you understand." She couldn't muster more. Right now, none of the history between them mattered. Not even that he was fired. "We need to find Tarin."

"Tarin?" The woman's name was a bark from his lips.

He didn't know what she knew. If he did, he wouldn't be upset that she was bringing up someone seemingly unrelated to their conversation. She huffed. Despite his we're all good speech, they weren't all good. He still monopolized her attention for himself.

"Yes, Tarin." She shoved her phone in the pocket of her suit and used both hands to speak. "That woman murdered Reagan."

"What?" His eyes widened. The hinge of his jaw screwed tight.

"The detective said evidence in the burned garage linked her to the crime, and her apartment …" Larkin covered her mouth just imagining all those tiny cunts written across the walls. "She's the one behind the threatening notes and flowers too. She's sick. She's crazy beyond anything you've ever imagined. Crazy." Her mind drifted to the notes in her office and in her house. "I need to get the notes to Detective Graham. He'll need my fingerprints, Douglas's, Darren's, and the girls' for cross reference."

"What?" Lucas growled.

She'd fallen into the trap of her own mind and forgotten she'd been talking to him. There were so many things to do. "First, we need to find Tarin."

"She's a crazy killer, and you want to find her?"

"The reporters are still out there. I can use them to get her image out there." She headed for the door. "You have a picture of her in the security database, right?"

"Sure, but Larkin, stop a minute and think." He stepped into her path with both hands wide.

Larkin had no choice but to stop. "What?" she bit out.

"If you go out there, you're making yourself an easy target for her."

"An easy target." Her hands balled to fists. She fought the tears welling in her eyes. "Tarin was in the front row at the conference. If she was going to kill me, I gave her the perfect opportunity."

"Then, no one knew Tarin was guilty. She was playing her part of trusted board member."

"I waited to report Reagan missing because of you. I'm done waiting. Maybe I couldn't have saved her, even by reporting it sooner, but I will help catch her killer." Larkin bobbed under Lucas's arm and grabbed the door handle.

The loudest boom she'd ever heard radiated from within her. It was as though she'd exploded. Not her heart this time, but her head.

In slow motion, the room tilted. The door handle moved farther and farther away until she stared at it from the floor. She reached for it. Nothing moved. Then the shutters closed, leaving only darkness.

THIRTY

HER FACE WAS COLD. Too cold. Every thought hurt. Pain radiated through her skull, threatening to crack it like fine china. A high frequency of sound would leave her in pieces.

A loud rumble churned deep and consistently. She wanted to scream at it to shut up, but nothing responded.

Each wave of the rhythmic noise punched her in the head, pressing her face flatter against the floor. It had to be a floor. The thing was hard as a rock and freezing. She tried her best not to move. Any shift would bring unrelenting agony. Breathing aggravated the demons banging against her brain.

Stress. Stress caused catastrophic damage to the body. Did she have an aneurysm?

"You fucking thing. Work, goddammit," Lucas

screamed. Panic laced his words.

Dread filled her belly. If he was freaking out, something bad had happened to her. She needed to assure him that she was okay. Everything would be fine if she could just open her eyes and tell him so.

A sliver of light struck the back of her retina like lightning. Nausea rolled through her stomach like back-to-back storm surges. Sound the alarms. Run for your lives. This was bad.

Light formed swirls of gray. The loops and curves refused to form a coherent picture.

"No. No. No," Lucas bellowed.

Larkin hated the despair in his tone. If a battle-seasoned man like him panicked, the situation was dire. She focused on the stabbing light and looping lines. Why wouldn't her right eye cooperate and open? The left was smashed against the cold ... tile? No. Concrete. That didn't make sense. Short, scratchy carpet covered the floor in the waiting room.

The need to see and assess her condition overrode everything. Bit by hazy bit, the whips and mixes of color formed an image, an image she wished she could erase.

Gray concrete walls, floor, and ceiling framed the sole of black wingtips. The shoes were attached to feet that lay unmoving on the chilling, unforgiving floor. Ruffled pant cuffs revealed a hint of socks. Black with fine white pinstripes. The same pattern Douglas wore every single day.

They both lay on the floor.

She closed her eye and willed away reality.

Neither she nor Douglas would have lain on a floor unless they were injured or under attack. Fear turned her saliva to sludge. They were both injured and attacked, if Douglas wasn't ...

Her mind refused to allow the possibility. Reagan was too much. Losing Douglas wasn't an option.

"Dammit," Lucas hissed. The sound of metal on metal squeaked.

Larkin exhaled long and slow and waited for a bullet's impact. A loud boom filled the room. Pain shimmied through her skull but not more than before. She mentally checked her limbs and torso. Nothing new.

Lucas's irritation turned to a mumble that faded quickly in the rumble of whatever it was.

She blinked in the room with one eye. The other made a fair effort, giving her a half-lidded view. It didn't improve the fear clouding her already muddled judgment. Thick pipes and skinny ones ran across the ceiling in a tight line through the room. The image of her being hung by them corrupted what little faculties she possessed.

"Douglas?" His name was a quaking mess on her lips. "Douglas?"

His feet remained perfectly still. Too damn still.

Larkin shoved off the floor. Her wrists twisted. The skin around them pinched as though tension would sheer them off. Her thin purse strap was wound around her wrists and tied in a fat knot between her arms and her body. She pressed her elbow to the ground and pushed to sit. A small pool of blood marked where her head and face had been. Her stomach clenched.

The room spun like a fair ride. Lights whirred and blurred past her eyes.

She spread her legs wide and braced her knuckles on the ground. The ride came to a gradual stop until she tried to stand. Her knees hit the ground. Nothing bound her ankles, but it didn't help her crooked steps.

"Douglas?" Larkin stumbled to the wall and leaned against it for stability. Her head pounded as though it might pop right off. She shimmied down, trying to get a better look at his face.

Her gaze lifted to the bleak horizon. The throbbing

minimized. Her fear, though … There were no shrines of her taped to the walls. There were no ugly expletives. There was nothing. The room scared her more than Tarin's apartment.

It was as though the room had been cleared of all furniture or equipment. This room had a purpose. And it frightened her. She imagined Reagan huddled in the corner, tears streaking her cheeks.

"Douglas?" She peered down. His face was pale. Lips chalky. Blood seeped from a gash above his eye. "No!" The shriek fled her lips without permission. Her knees hit the floor. She grabbed his collar, yanked it back, and felt for a pulse. Cold, clammy skin met her fingertips, and nothing. She repositioned. It was so light as to be imagined.

"No!" She jerked his shoulder. "Douglas, wake up."

Larkin jerked upright and reached for her pocket. He needed an ambulance. Her head boomed from the movement. She needed an ambulance. They needed the fucking police.

The leather tightened and pinched. She strained. Her fingers smoothed over the stitched fabric. "No." The sob leaked from her lips. Her pocket was empty.

Lucas had seen Douglas before coming to the waiting room. Lucas had thrown him in this room. Lucas had taken her phone. Lucas had knocked her so hard over the head that she might never see without the shimmy of the image again.

"Why would Lucas do this? Why?" She didn't ask in self-pity. If she knew his reasoning, she could calculate a way to get her and Douglas out alive. Her unconscious friend didn't offer an explanation.

She shoved off the wall and stumbled toward the door on rubbery legs. Her hands clasped the knob, twisted, and heaved. The door didn't budge.

It didn't compute. The knob wasn't even equipped

with a lock.

Larkin repositioned her hands, twisted, and pushed. Again, it didn't move.

"No." She yanked and jerked.

Thump. Thump. Thump. Her head drummed. Defeat left her weak. Nausea scaled her esophagus.

She stumbled to the far side of the room, braced her elbows on her thighs, and retched. Nothing came out. There was nothing in there to lose. Food wasn't high on her list of priorities last night. Reclaiming herself and shielding her heart from Beckett had been.

"Beckett." Why had she sent him away? Pride? Self-preservation?

If she died today, he'd never know how she felt about him. If she died today, she'd die without ever loving someone and having been loved by them in return. What was heartbreak compared to death? Worth the risk.

She had to live past this day.

Larkin sank to the floor and grabbed the back of her head. A sharp and acute pain stabbed at the crown. She winced but forced herself to explore the broken lump. Sticky wetness coated her fingers. By God, if she died today, she'd leave a clue or ten as to her killer. She scrawled *Lucas B. killed me* on the floor. That was more of a declaration and less of a clue. A declaration she hoped was wrong, but just in case …

Why did the detectives think it was Tarin? Had he set her up?

Metal squeaked on metal. Her gaze whipped to the door. The knob twisted, and the door opened.

Lucas stepped into the room. When his gaze found her, his face scrunched into an unfamiliar mask of rage.

He stepped inside and slammed the door.

She hated that he didn't care about making noise. It didn't bode well for her chances of survival.

Larkin expected him to charge, head down, and crush her with a single blow. Instead, he hung his head, breathed hard, and paced a line from one side of the room to the other in front of the door. She breathed through her mouth to keep from retching, and she watched him pace back and forth. He tugged his hair. Sweat trickled down his chin. He'd lost his tie somewhere, and the top two buttons of his shirt hung wide.

He didn't lock the door.

"Lucas, it's okay." Her voice quaked, maligning her. She swallowed. "Just talk to me. I know there's a reasonable explanation for all this."

"Yeah." His head snapped up. "There is. You're a spoiled, rich bitch." The crest of his lip curled on the angry words.

"You know that's not true." She was anything but a bitch to him. "I gave you a job when how many people had turned you down?" What had they seen that she'd missed?

"Sure, you gave me a job, but what about your heart? You never gave me a chance at that." He paced, a predator preparing to strike.

"I've never given anyone a chance at it. I'm damaged goods, Lu—"

"Shut up!" His chest heaved. The blood vessels in his face bulged. "You don't know anything about damaged goods. This is all your fault. You and that crazy fucking bitch."

"Tarin?" She couldn't make herself shut up. If she was going to die, she'd go down with as many answers as she could. Answers and a fight.

He turned away from her and paced.

"I never told you about the flowers or the threatening notes." The more she spoke, the more solid her voice became. "Douglas didn't either, did he?"

"You were supposed to be scared, damn you." He scraped a hand down his face. Pellets of sweat littered the ground.

"Scared?"

"Tarin was just supposed to scare you, but you wouldn't react." He looked at her sideways but continued pacing the uneven, agitated line. "You wouldn't let me ..."

A gasp caught in Larkin's throat. "You knew she was sending the threats."

"I caught her trying to break into your apartment two months ago. The woman has a sick fucking fetish with you." His head shook. "I thought she was harmless. I thought the whole thing was harmless." He pulled his hair so hard she expected to see chunks come out. "No one was supposed to get hurt. You were supposed to let me protect you and ..."

And she was supposed to fall in love with Lucas. Her hands shook. He wasn't as insane as Tarin was, but a number of delusions were at play in this once upon a hero's mind. Tears slipped down Larkin's cheek. He would kill her to protect himself.

His sigh filled the room.

Larkin looked at her white hands and the leather binding them. She looked at the ceiling again and remembered the same piping in the bowels of her building. They'd been overhead when she'd taken the back entrance Beckett had shown her the day he'd left. Hope bloomed in her chest. The roar of the machinery had been there too. She closed her eyes trying to remember the steps she'd taken under his guidance. In the side door, turn right, past two doors, then left to the underground level of service elevators.

This was her building. This room was one of those two doors.

"They weren't supposed to stick their noses where they didn't belong." He looked at Douglas on the floor.

They?

Lucas had killed Reagan.

Ice raced through her veins. Had Reagan been in here when she'd jogged through that fateful day?

Douglas wasn't dead. She'd found his pulse, and she wouldn't let him die, dammit. When Lucas turned away on his unsettling back and forth, Larkin lifted her hands to her mouth. Her teeth sank into the leather and tugged. The tempo of her heartbeat soared. It thundered in her ears.

She dropped her hands to her lap and hung her head before he turned and paced in her direction.

"They think Tarin did everything. She's a lunatic. You just got caught up in her crazy scheme."

His gaze lifted to her, then drifted back to Douglas. He snarled, turned, and walked away.

Larkin yanked the loose strip of leather, pulled it through the loop, and then yanked another and another. She dropped her hand just in time. Her heart pounded in her throat.

"It won't work."

"It will," she countered. She'd wait until he turned his back to stand. If she ran as hard and as fast as she ever had, she could get out the door in time to jet right down a short hallway, and then left through the door to the outside world.

His head shook. He turned.

Larkin shrugged the leather and stood. Her legs felt like cement pillars. A taxi rolled over her chest. Her gaze slid to Douglas. This was it.

She ran.

THIRTY-ONE

LARKIN STAYED ON THE BALLS of her feet, eliminating the clack of the slim stilettos she'd worn to give her confidence in front of the crowd. The obnoxious shoes weren't crafted for stealthy moves or traction. Her gaze remained fixed on Lucas's back. Anticipation of his reaction to her escape attempt knotted her intestines. Fear cycled through her limbs. They jerked and stuttered in response to her demands, slicing her effort in half.

No. If she focused on him, she was defeated before she began. Larkin drove her knees high. Her arms pumped. The knob. She focused every cell in her body on the small round metal piece. Adrenaline streamed through her veins. It went head to head with fear. The knob. The knob. Get there.

Four long strides toward the door and adrenaline

took the lead. The knob was three strides away. His back was still toward her. She hinged her arms, pumping them harder. Her legs stretched farther, eating the concrete.

The back of her shoe slipped off her right heel. Lose the shoe or let the spiky stiletto hit the floor. Larkin's legs churned so quickly she didn't have time to make the decision.

Clack. It rattled above the low mechanical rumble.

The knob. The knob.

Her right hand wrapped around the cold metal. The left hit the concrete wall, breaking her crash into it. She twisted the knob and wrenched, pushing off the wall to help open the heavy door. It opened. The double paneled metal door flung wide. Freedom. It smelled like oil and sounded like machines. She loved it.

"No!" Lucas's voice boomed behind her.

Fuck him.

Larkin crouched low to maintain her balance. Her legs powered forward. Both feet chopped at the floor, propelling her through the opening.

The hallway was deserted. A coffin of concrete. Fear fought for top billing. She looked to the right. At the end was one turn to light and help. Her feet paddled toward freedom. The sole of her left shoe slipped out from under her. She reached for the doorframe to steady herself. It was too far away. The right sole followed suit.

Her world tilted once more.

Lucas's frame blotted the light. His hand came at her, big and grabbing.

She scrambled away on knees and elbows.

His hand sank into her hair. Moisture filled her eyes. Not tears. He pulled so hard hairs ripped from her skin. The entire thing stretched to its limits. She reached for his hand. Both hers bracketed it.

Larkin pulled herself to him to keep from losing her

scalp. The fabric of her suit whined and ripped against the uneven floor. They switched direction without her permission.

"No!" Larkin bellowed with everything she had. "Lucas, no!"

The doorframe she'd worked so hard to get past entered her periphery.

"Help! Please! No!" She hooked a leg around the frame and yanked against Lucas's grip.

His boot connected with her ribs. Pain blinded her, stealing her breath. Fuck, it stole her lungs. The damn things refused to operate. They convulsed. Her body spasmed. A shoe fell off in the mayhem.

Larkin rolled onto her side and cocooned, shielding her sides with her elbows. He latched onto the collar of her suit and hauled her farther into the room.

If he closed the door with her inside, she was dead.

She rolled onto her belly and shoved to her hands and knees, still fighting for a single molecule of oxygen. Just one would do.

Douglas was a few feet away. He carried a gun. Why hadn't she thought to look for it earlier? Before she could use it, she had to get to him.

"Why did you do that? You ruined everything," Lucas bellowed. It sounded like he was at the far end of an echo chamber, but he was so close. She saw a tiny scuff on the side of his shoe.

Larkin lunged at his leg. Both arms wrapped around it. She held it tight. Her mouth opened wide. She sank teeth onto his inner thigh and bit with everything she had.

"Fuc …"

He struck her head. Once. Twice. The hits were hollow. Maybe it was adrenaline. Maybe oxygen was a bigger priority. Maybe her head was numb. She shook from side to side like a rabid animal.

Blood warmed her cheeks. Hers or his? She didn't know until the metallic tang hit her tongue. A gag caught her unaware. Oxygen returned in wicked, wet gulps. She choked but held tight and shook again.

His bellow turned into a whimper.

It fueled her drive. She released the bite and lunged for another. Blood spread wide on his pant leg, creating a soggy palette. Her teeth sank deep again.

Lucas whined and jerked back.

Her jaw shook with fatigue. Blood made her fingers slip.

His finger hooked around her nose and lifted. Flesh tore from her gums. He flipped her backward into the doorway.

Blood pooled at his foot and clung to her face. Rage contorted his into an ugly snarl. Gone was the kind, handsome hero she'd known and in his place was a monster.

She gasped and spat blood from her mouth. It created a hideous masterpiece. With the back of her arm, she swiped her face.

Indecision tormented her. Gun or run?

Lucas barreled at her before she could make up her mind. She shuffled back on her hands and feet, scraping her bare heel against the floor. The stiletto slipped. He was on top of her before she could blink. His hands wrapped around her neck and lifted.

In an instant, the floor seemed so far away. Her toes reached for it and found nothing. Her hands instinctually grabbed at his. She pinched and clawed at his thumbs.

His smug grin filled Larkin's view. Oxygen once again abandoned her.

"You'll die like your pretty friend."

Larkin tried to say Reagan as though they were having a civilized conversation. It didn't matter. The word came out as a wheeze.

"She poked her nose where it didn't belong." Red stained his cheeks. He snarled. A monster. Not a man.

Black clouded the edges of her periphery. Her slashing nails made no difference to the madman's skin. Larkin spat with the last of the air in her lungs. Blood and spit speckled his angry face. His grip doubled.

Darkness cut in and out like a strobe.

Larkin lifted her heel and rammed the point at his inner thigh.

"Ahhhhh!" His grip released.

She fell to the floor, landing hard on her bottom. The heel stuck out of his flesh, still attached. Using her hands, she shuffled back as far as she could before her lungs took priority, demanding filling.

Her body heaved and hacked. Everything shook.

So she'd staved off that attack. There was no way she could win against him, but she'd die trying.

Lucas bent over and yanked the stiletto from his leg.

A roar, brittle and gruff, lit her ears. It wasn't Lucas. It wasn't her.

Douglas jumped onto Lucas's back. His bent arm hooked around Lucas's neck, wrenching him back. Douglas's elbow formed a V around Lucas's throat.

A cry of relief lodged in her throat. He was alive. He was taking this fucker down.

Lucas's hand slipped from inside his coat. The gun glinted silver in the light.

"No!" Her scream was drowned out by two shots.

Douglas slid from Lucas's back and fell to the floor. His hands flew to his right side where red seeped from two holes.

Lucas turned on the older man.

Larkin moved without thought. She launched herself onto Lucas's back. The thing that just got Douglas shot.

Lucas's hands were up, the gun clutched tight, the barrel aimed toward Douglas.

She wrapped both legs around his middle. Her fingers found his eye sockets and dug. The gun flew across the room and clattered to the floor. Lucas's scream filled her ears. A maniac's yell ricocheted around the room, and she realized it poured from her raw throat.

He yanked her left hand. It slipped from the warm, meaty hole. She couldn't lose hold of the other one. If he got her off his back, all was lost.

Larkin twisted and pulled her hand time and again in a desperate fight for life. The blood on their hands made his hold slip but not free.

His feet moved, spinning the room.

Her back slammed into the concrete. "Uh." He stepped out and rammed backward again. It forced the air from her lungs again and again.

No. No.

Her fingers slipped from his face and latched onto his shoulder, trying to hold with her legs. He turned and battered her knee into the wall. It cracked her hold. She slid down his body and landed on her hip.

"No!" Larkin bellowed.

Lucas dropped to his hands and knees and scrambled toward the gun.

"No!" She shoved to her feet, but her knee gave out, slamming her back to the ground.

Everything hurt. Blood covered her head to toe. But this was it. This race would mean life or death.

Larkin rolled to her belly and army crawled.

"Larkin!" The voice was the only one she wanted to hear in that moment. Beckett's deep rumbling base gave her the burst of energy she needed to crawl harder, faster for the gun. She reached it at the same time as Lucas and slung the barrel out of his reach just in time.

Lucas growled and grabbed the back of her neck,

pinching tight. Instantly, stars danced in her field of vision.

A roar rippled through the room unlike any she'd ever heard.

The grip at her neck slipped, setting her free. She crawled away, desperate for any distance between them.

Sickening sounds of flesh meeting flesh filled the room. The impacts didn't find her, though. It didn't make sense unless she was parting with her body. She rolled onto her bruised bottom.

"Beckett." He stood toe to toe with the man who wanted to kill her, who was moments away from killing her. "No." She didn't want him hurt. So many people had already paid the price for her.

Larkin used the wall and pushed to her feet. Well, foot. Her right leg refused to function. She shuffled forward toward the gun. What would she do with it when she got it? No way could she chance hitting Beckett.

She reached for it and fell to the floor, trying to pick up the blood-covered weapon. The room tilted and wobbled with every move she made.

In the center of the room, the two men tangled. Too close. She hated Beckett being so close to danger. Lucas swung an angry fist. Beckett bobbed easily out of reach. His dark gaze jumped side to side, calculating everything.

Then she realized Beckett was danger.

He didn't blink. He didn't sweat. He stepped in, grabbed Lucas's head, and jerked it in an unnatural angle.

The monster that used to be a man, the one who'd tormented her and killed her friend, dropped as though his skeleton had dissolved.

Without a second glance, Beckett rushed to Douglas's side. "Larkin, talk to me. Tell me you're okay." He moved Douglas's weak hands to the side and ripped the old man's shirt wide.

Douglas's groan hit her between the eyes.

"Larkin!" Beckett barked.

"Yes." Her head shook in contraction. "I'm fine."

"Good girl." Beckett's fingers moved skillfully over Douglas's bloody belly. "Can you come over here and help me?"

"Yes." She left the gun and levered herself up the wall slowly. One inch at a time. "Is he …?"

"Hear all his whining? He's going to be just fine." Beckett slipped from his jacket and pulled the long sleeve over his head with one hand. Blood from his hands stained the edge of the short sleeve clinging to his torso. He used his teeth and ripped the long sleeve into two strips.

The closer she got to Lucas's body, the slower her steps became.

"Don't look. He's never going to hurt you again." His gaze found hers. "Do you hear me?"

She nodded, locking on his steady gaze, and shuffled to him. He stood, offered his hands, and helped her to the floor.

"What do I do?" Her voice quaked.

Douglas looked so … pale. Blood covered the floor under him.

"When I get these in place, you'll hold them there. Front and back, okay?"

"Okay." She used the back of her only clean sleeve and wiped the blood from her face.

Beckett placed the square strips over the two holes that were so damn close they seemed to make one big hole. "Here." He moved his hands and guided hers to the cloths. His hands pressed hard against hers. "Hold as tight as you can. I'll be back."

"Back?" Panic filled her.

He sighed. His forehead pressed to hers. He held both her shoulders and hugged her close. "You're so fucking brave, Larkin. You can do this. I'm going to get an ambulance. I will be back with help."

"Promise?" She hated how pathetic she sounded. Lucas syphoned all the strength from her.

"I've never promised anything more, sweetheart."

He stood and ran, leaving her alone with her dying friend and the man who tried his best to kill her.

THIRTY-TWO

LARKIN STARED AT A BLANK white arch six inches in front of her face. After the paramedics immobilized her on the stretcher and forbid Beckett entry into the ambulance, numbness set in. Hysterics weren't an option. The longer she stared at nothingness and the louder the machine whirred around her, the more it looked like the route to go. She wanted answers, and no one was giving them to her.

They'd taken Douglas first. His blood still stained her hands. Along with Lucas's and her own.

Slowly, the whoop whoops of the CT stretched their tempo. The technician's voice came over the speaker by her head. "Great job, Miss Ashford. Just a minute more and we'll have you out of there."

She waited and waited. The minute stretched to two. Then three. Panic bubbled to the surface, but she breathed through her nose and released it out her mouth. Once. Twice.

The table shimmied to life, mechanically shifting her toward the light at the end of the literal tunnel. A large, warm hand wrapped around hers. It contrasted the petite tech's one hundred percent.

"Miss Ashford." Beckett's steady gaze calmed the rattle of her frayed nerve endings.

"How ...?"

He wore a white coat. A stethoscope hooked around his neck and a badge with his picture and someone else's name was clipped to the coat pocket.

"I have friends in strategic places." His lips crooked up on one end. It was the best medicine they could give her.

"Of course, you do."

"Speaking of friends, yours are about to break down the door to get to you." He unclipped some straps as though he'd done it a thousand times before.

"I bet they are." She hated causing them stress. When he unfastened the strap that freed her head, she blinked. "Are you a doctor?"

"Hell no," he scoffed. "But I have extensive field training and good news."

"I could use some of that about now."

Beckett's stunning face levered over hers. His gaze drank her in, and she did the same. It'd been too long since she'd seen him, really seen him. "You have no cranial bleeding."

"Okay." Her heart stuttered. At that moment, whether he felt anywhere near the same way or not, she knew without a doubt that she loved this man.

"Just okay? I expected you to be a little happier than okay." He ran his thumb over her swollen lip.

"You're here. Nothing else matters."

"Fuck, Larkin." His gaze warmed.

"What?"

His head shook. He stepped out of her line of sight. Was he

scared away by her declaration? It was nothing near the declaration stamped on her heart and swimming in her mind. She stared at the blinding florescent light above and thought about how she'd shunned Lucas. If Beckett denied her, would she become a maniac like Lucas had?

No.

But she'd hurt like hell for a long time, and that was okay.

Wheels squeaked across the floor, stopping close to the CT machine. "Here." Beckett's arms looped around her back. "We're going to go slow." True to his word, he eased her to sit. A gurney waited next to the bed. The top of it was folded into a reclined sitting position. He sat on the flat part of it, his body cuddled up next to hers. He held her to his chest for a long minute. They didn't rock. They became the rock, a solid coupling of two minerals.

Too soon, he eased back. His hand braced her face.

"You make me want to forget everything else." He smoothed a thumb over her brow. His gaze danced from her aching brow to her mouth and back. "And I can't do that." He sighed. "Too many people are counting on me."

"I don't want you to forget anything for me."

His brow hiked. "What about your friend Bronson?"

She reached a hand up to tell him exactly how she felt about him. Knowing there was other people's blood on your hands was vastly different than seeing broken skin, swollen cuts, and crusted red on every inch of what had been well-manicured hands. Her mind stalled.

"Shit." Beckett covered the evidence with his hand. "I should have waited."

"No." She latched onto his hand. "No, you shouldn't have. I … I …"

"You just went through hell." He eased her onto the gurney and straightened the blankets covering the hospital gown they'd slipped her into before shoving her into the machine. The rolling bed shifted beneath her. "We'll get you cleaned up. You'll need

some sutures and more IV fluids. They'll keep you overnight."
He grabbed the rail next to her and prepared to move them out
of the small sanctuary he'd found for them.

"Beckett?"

"It's okay, Larkin." He rolled them forward.

She rested her horrific hand atop his. Their progress stopped.
"You looked a little too comfortable in hell."

He'd entered the battle without pause. He'd controlled the
most horrifying situation she'd ever experienced without blinking.

"I am." He laughed. "Too comfortable in hell." His head
hung. "I didn't mean to scare you."

"You didn't. Not after that first night."

"I killed a man in front of you." His lips pressed together. The
beard he'd grown since he'd left her at the side of her building
shifted with his working jaw.

He was so warm. So strong. So haunted.

"If you say Bronson is not what he seems, I know he's bad. I
trust you."

"You met me less than three weeks ago and know nothing
about me." His eyes closed on a growl.

"I know the important things. You're good. You're who I
want when I've never wanted anyone. You're good to me. And
you like me even though you don't want to."

"Like you?"

"Yeah." She smiled.

"You need to work on your terminology." He rolled her toward the double doors.

"Why?" Larkin pulled the blanket closer to her chin, sure
a thousand people were going to be on the other side of it with
cameras flashing.

"Like is too tame a word."

Her toes curled, sending fresh pain to the abrasions on her
heels. They entered a bustling hallway. The media didn't bombard
them, but a lane of fast moving gurneys did. Beckett wheeled her

around, masterfully avoiding corners and patients.

"Douglas?" Why hadn't she asked sooner? She had asked the CT tech and the nurse, but no one had been able to tell her shit.

"He's next on my list." He stopped in front of a cloth curtain. "First things, first." His knuckles brushed her hair back, and then he stepped to the end of the gurney. His head disappeared behind the curtain. "Promises, remember them," he demanded.

Who was he—

"We promise," Libby's strong voice carried above the rest.

Tears filled Larkin's eyes.

Beckett slipped from behind the curtain and looked at her. "Are you ready for them?"

"Yes." Her tears came in earnest. "Thank you."

He shoved the curtain wide. Her three best friends stood in the small, impersonal space, clinging to one another. Marlis's makeup created tracks of black and milk white down her cheeks, and she had her hand clamped over her mouth. Genevieve hugged Mar close, lifted her free hand, and waved Larkin into the room. Libby stepped forward and helped Beckett maneuver her behind the curtain.

"I hear you put up one hell of a fight." Libby smiled so big. She blinked back tears. "That's my girl."

"Of course, she did. She looks like hell," Gen quipped.

Marlis's sobs slipped through her fingers.

"Jesus, I've never trusted a woman. How'd I think I could trust four at once." Beckett's stern gaze slid from Mar to Gen to Libby and finally landed on hers. "Your tears kill me, you know?"

"They kill me too," she agreed.

"I know." Beckett pressed his hand to her collarbone. His fingers grazed across her sore neck. "The nurse will be in shortly to stitch you up."

He shifted to leave.

Larkin grabbed his arm. "You can't do that?" She didn't want him out of her sight, but she didn't want to say it.

"Not on your precious skin." He leaned close and pressed his cheek to the top of her forehead. "I'll be back after I check on Douglas."

"Thank you." She squeezed him and then released her hold.

They watched him leave without a word.

Her heart burst in a fountain of confetti and gushy-mushy warmth. It coursed through her body, easing the pounding of her head and the aches and pains that dogged her heels. She'd always thought love hurt, but love overrode everything. Even hell.

"Holy shit." Libby rounded on Larkin. "That's the guy from the roof?"

She grinned like a lunatic. Surely, she looked like one.

"No wonder you didn't want to give him up," Libby said.

Genevieve fanned herself, and Marlis, by default. "He's scary. Sexy scary."

"Gen." Mar shoved her shoulder. "He's nice."

Nice? He was all those things and so much more.

"They wouldn't let us see you because we weren't family," Genevieve scoffed. "Like they know what family is." She scooted herself and Mar closer.

"I'm so sorry," Marlis simpered.

"I look like hell, but I'll be okay." Larkin believed it with all her heart … just as long as Douglas pulled through.

"If I hadn't left you …" Marlis's eyes clamped shut. Her petite chest heaved.

Guilt was an unrelenting bitch. Larkin knew from experience.

"Marlis McCain, it's not your fault." Her head pounded with each word. "Tarin and Lucas are to blame." She wanted Beckett back. He dulled the edges of the pain.

"One is in custody and the other is dead," Libby announced.

Did they know how Lucas died? Did they know what she'd been through? What Douglas had endured?

"If you'd been there, who knows what he'd have done to you." Her head shook. Once was enough to teach her better. "I don't want to think about it." She reached for Mar and realized again that her hands were repulsive.

Marlis, like Beckett, didn't seem to care. She stepped forward and took hold. "I'm so glad you're okay. You're so strong, Larkin."

The other girls gathered in close. Their arms, their love surrounded her. The pounding in her head eased. Love was everything. "I love you crazy ladies."

Each said the thing they'd never said to one another for the life of their friendship. Each meant it. They stood or sat around her small gurney. She was lucky. Despite her mother's death and her father's life, she had amazing friends. Why had it taken a mysterious man and a near-death experience for her to truly embrace it?

Douglas wouldn't have any of this when he woke up. If he woke.

Her heart beat inside her chest stronger and more sure than ever before. Yes, he would. He had her.

"Let's get you cleaned up a little before the nurse gets here." Libby grabbed a rag and an ugly pink bucket of water as though it were just another day at the office. It might have been for her Bureau babe of a friend.

"Sounds good," Larkin agreed.

THIRTY-THREE

"WHY AREN'T YOU ASLEEP?"

Larkin's gaze slid from the plastic tube sticking out of the top of her hand to the doorway of her hospital room. Beckett's thick shoulder leaned against the frame as though he'd been there a while. She hadn't noticed him, and she was on high alert. Well, her mind was. The rest of her could fall off the cliff of consciousness at any moment. Hence, the mind.

The corner of Beckett's mouth kicked upward, and a hint of a smile played in his eyes.

"I have a concussion. I'm not supposed to go to sleep."

"That's a myth." Beckett stepped into the room, his swagger confident. Why shouldn't it be? He feared nothing and no one. He closed the door behind him and rounded the bed to the side without all the hoses and leaders stringing from her body. His thighs brushed the mattress. Gone was the white coat and stethoscope and in its place was well-worn jeans and a T-shirt that hugged him as tightly as she wanted to. "Did the nurses tell you to stay awake?"

"Not exactly." She bobbed one shoulder.

"What did they say?" He leaned close. His eyes leveled hers.

"Get some rest." She'd look away if she could, but his dark gaze filled her up.

"That's what I thought." His lips brushed her nose.

"You just know everything, don't you?"

"Not hardly." He winked and straightened.

Panic rose in her chest. She didn't want him to leave. Not tonight. Not ever.

Beckett's weighty muscles pressed into the bed. He lifted her gently and scooted her toward the edge to make room for his width. The heat of his arm draped over her shoulders. Larkin's legs curled into his lap. For shame or not, she burrowed into his side and wedged her swooning head between his shoulder and chin. His beard was long enough that the hairs tickled over her forehead.

"Christ, you feel good right here." His hold constricted but not too tight. He couldn't hold her too close. If he wanted, he could smother her, and she wouldn't fight. He wouldn't. And that certainty, this comfort, felt better than any drug the doctors could offer.

If Larkin said anything about how she felt, she'd spill the whole damn pot and send him scrambling for the door. She wrapped her free hand around his and squeezed, ignoring the pain it caused in her split knuckles. "How's Douglas?"

"As worried about you as you are about him. Maybe more."

His throat rumbled against her forehead. Larkin was

so focused on the calming sensation it took the words a second to sink in.

"He's awake?"

"Boy is he." His chuckle shook them. "That man was screaming down the hospital to find out about you. When Dr. Crenshaw stepped in and calmed the patient, the nurses were so relieved to have him reeled in, they didn't ask who the hell I was or why I was there."

"Dr. Crenshaw, huh?"

"At your service." He relaxed back into the upright mattress and took her with him. His fingers played over her forearm and the tops of her fingers, carefully avoiding the cuts and bruises.

"Who is he?" Her gaze slid to his. She waited for the sidestep.

"No one. A tool to help me hunt. A false lead made up by the people I work for."

"Is your name really Beckett?"

"Calder Wayne Beckett, only true born son of Zachary and Becky Beckett."

She couldn't fight the smile on her lips.

"She didn't go by Becky." Beckett's smile matched hers. "Since I can remember, everyone has called her Bolt."

"Bolt?"

"She earned it in basic, beating everyone in speed, be it running, repelling, shooting. Hell, she can still get the drop on me at the range." His head shook. "It's amazing, really."

"The woman who raised you. Gah. She'd have to be amazing."

"In a lot of ways, the Navy raised Luca, Sam, and me. They taught my parents structure, dedication, and the inability to fail, and they filtered that to us." His fingers intertwined gently with hers.

She wanted to ask a thousand questions, but what he

volunteered was better than an inquest.

"I wasn't intended. Bolt was, and still is, career driven. She's one of the highest-ranking women in the Navy."

That sucked for him.

"After she had me, she closed up shop."

"You are a lot to handle." She sighed.

"You have no idea. I was an obstinate shit until they brought Sam home." He lifted her palm to his lips and slid them over skin that hadn't ever been so sensitive. "That kid was so puny and beat down he made me realize how good I had it. My parents were always busy and away, but they never tortured me." His groan heated her collarbone. "They saved Sam, and he saved me."

"Luca was the goofy glue that held us all together. His dad and mine were in DEVGRU together."

"DEVGRU?" She hated admitting her ignorance to this man.

"It's fine. You weren't raised by people who bleed blue and gold."

"No, my mom bled Glenlevit and self-pity. And my father, he'd never bled in his life."

"She killed herself?" His voice was a firm whisper.

"Yep." Larkin waited for the familiar stab of sorrow. Her breaths came slowly, steadily without a hiccup.

"She didn't have your strength."

Her head shook.

"You are the most indomitable woman I've ever met, Larkin. And that's saying something."

A tear slipped onto her cheek. She didn't think she had any more tears to give. "Yeah, so strong."

"Strength is only evident in the face of unimaginable fear." His thumb dabbed the drop and slipped it inside his mouth.

Larkin rested her cheek against Beckett's. They breathed together quietly for several moments.

"So DEVGRU?"

"SEAL Team 6?" he asked.

"Oh, yeah." She wasn't that out of touch with the world. "Your dad was …?"

"Yep."

Shit, no wonder Beckett was a beast. It was engrained in his DNA.

"A mission went sideways. Three team members didn't come home. Luca's father was one of them. His mother gave up rights at his birth and was never in the picture. Taking him in was the least my dad could do. He felt responsible for his father's death."

"He may have been something," Larkin conceded, "but no one can control the hand of fate."

"I told him that too. I believed it until it's one of your own you let down."

"No," she breathed.

Beckett pointed at his gnarled face. She didn't see it anymore. It was a part of him, and she loved every single one harder and harder the more she knew about him.

"We were on a peace-keeping mission near a diamond mine in Botswana. Missiles. Two. They whistled in from above. Hard and fast. They incinerated half a village. Men. Women. Children."

Larkin covered her mouth. She knew where this was going and hated the points it would take to get there.

"They took out my team. Years. I spent two recovering, remembering everything. It took no time to track down the parties responsible. Money only covers tracks so well. It's nothing against the well-placed point of a knife. Then I mounted my offensive against them. Disavowed, if I get caught."

"Bronson." Larkin's teeth clenched, shooting pain into her skull.

"His family financed the mission, whether knowingly

or not. Bronson gave the okay to wipe thirty people off the map to maintain control of his family's teetering empire."

Words wouldn't form in the vacuums of her lungs. Anger and sorrow created a potent mix that wailed her in the gut.

"Larkin." He grabbed her hand and pulled it from her face. "Look at me."

"I can't." She averted her gaze. "I … I'm sorry." Her head shook back and forth. It pounded but not enough to blur the truth. Her friend was a mass murderer. He was the worst criminal she'd ever known, yet she'd been oblivious. Completely oblivious.

No wonder he hated her.

"I used you to get to him."

"You should have." She needed to get up. She needed air. Everything crowded in on her. The fear returned, washing over her like a torrent of water drowning her. "Sorry. I'm sorry."

"Larkin, it's not your fault." His hand braced on either side of her face and turned her gently to face him. "I never blamed you. Never." He pulled her into his side and held her tight as her frantic breaths calmed one at a time.

She shivered and clung to him. His pain became hers. It seeped into her bones and sank its teeth deep.

Beckett stroked the length of her back. His chest moved hers, coaxing her to breathe in time with him.

"I'm sorry."

"The only thing you should apologize for is making me love you."

Her eyes blinked open and found his gaze warm and insistent. Some-stupid-how, those words diffused the sorrow and agony. Love. The word had always aggravated her gag reflex, but when Beckett used it, joy and an unfamiliar sense of contentment settled between her heart and sternum. It gave her an added layer of protection from life and all its trials.

"Why would I apologize for that?" she quipped.

"Because you don't do love."

"Nope," she agreed. A silly smile stretched her busted lip. "Not until you."

"Should I apologize?" He grinned.

"You most certainly should." Larkin grabbed his hand and held it between hers. "Loving you is the most terrifying thing I've ever done."

He lifted her fingers to his mouth and kissed each busted one. "Shit, I've been through hell, and I have to agree."

His lips brushed her forehead. They held each other and stared at the bulletin board that asked her scale of pain from smiley face to red frowning face and announced her nurse's name as Pam.

"So what now?" Her feet twitched unrelentingly under the covers.

"Now, you sleep. Tomorrow, we get you to Douglas. The next day?" He shrugged. "We'll deal with it when it comes."

The spiking heart rate monitor told her sleep was a ways off. "Do you work for the Navy?"

"No." He turned toward her. "Just to be clear, you love me?"

"Yes." She giggled. "I love you, Beckett."

"Okay." His mouth lined into a smirk. "And you want to try to make this work?" He gestured back and forth between them.

"Oh, my goodness." She shoved his chest. "Yes."

"It's not going to be easy."

"Then we should give up now." She nodded. "We only do easy."

"Sweetheart, sweetheart." Beckett licked his lips and stared at her mouth. "Once I get you healthy, you're not going to get away with smart mouth comments like that without consequences.

"I'm healthy."

"You're stubborn."

"No more than you, with your super-secret secrets."

"True." His smile faltered. "There will be a lot I can't tell you, but I'll share what I can."

"All right."

Beckett pressed his lips to her earlobe. Desire crested and overflowed the edges of her restraint with the simple touch.

"I'm an operative for the Base Branch."

Larkin pressed her lips to his earlobe and sucked the edge of it into her mouth. He tasted as good as she remembered. "I know this will shock you," she breathed, "but I've never heard of it."

"Not many have." He lifted her hair back from her ear and moved close once more. "We're a covert operations branch of the UN with bases and special operations all over the world."

Calder Beckett was the real deal James Bond minus the accent and adding several feet of muscles and a heap of attitude. She swallowed. "I couldn't have fallen for a nice Wall Street banker?"

"I don't guess so." He winked. "You know a lot of them, huh?"

"Too many." She snuggled into his side, pulled his arm around her front, and fastened it across her chest.

More than anything, she wanted to stay awake and talk to him all night, but her eyelids scheduled other plans for the evening. They dragged down. Once. Twice. She fought hard. "Where do you live now?"

"I have an apartment in DC and a house in the mountains."

She envisioned an off-the-grid, hand-built cabin in the middle of dense forest.

"Where are your parents?"

"Why are you dodging sleep?"

She opened her mouth to respond.

"The truth," he demanded.

Larkin pressed his palm to her cheek. "Every time I close my eyes, I see his face. The anger. His intent to kill me."

Beckett eased the bed back to lay flat and levered over her. "Look in my eyes, Larkin. Can you see my intent?" His strong, indomitable body shielded her from the world and her demons.

She nodded.

"Sleep. I'll be here right by your side when you wake."

"Promise?" Why did she need reassurance when his words and his eyes were enough?

He pressed his lips to hers, too sweetly. "With my whole heart. It's yours anyway, so I might as well stay with you."

They snuggled into a tight ball on the small bed. Before the clock's hand had passed the next quarter of an hour, she slept.

"No, it's okay. I'll find it."

Larkin jerked awake. Agony masterfully beat a rhythm, using her frontal lobe as the instrument. It should hurt in the back. That's where Lucas had hit her … repeatedly. She thought past the pain to the thing that woke her.

The voice. It was loud. It was close. It was familiar. The voice terrified her.

Was it a dream?

Her vision swam in a murky mix of red, orange, and white. She blinked frantically. A heavy, warm weight settled the frantic pace of her heart. Beckett's scent filled her nose. His body molded around the back of hers.

The open hospital room door focused in her view. Orange and red clung to the walls as though they'd been painted the rich colors. Last night, they'd been stark and white.

"Thank you. I'm sure."

The voice ricocheted into the open hospital room door, proving it to be a nightmare.

Larkin turned in Beckett's arms to see his stunning, sleep-slacked expression and the morning's sunrise pouring into the room. She placed her palm over his mouth and whispered.

"Bronson is here."

Beckett's muscles tensed at the name alone. It skyrocketed her pulse, pinging the machine attached to her finger. Shit. His eyes opened, revealing the devastating gaze she'd come to love. The need to protect him reared its head like a wild stallion in a cowboy's rope. It wasn't the first time she'd reacted that way, but it might be the most important. If Beckett got caught, he'd be pegged as a common criminal. If Bronson shot Beckett, she'd go to jail as a common criminal for murdering her former friend.

"Get in the chair." Larkin shoved him from the bed. She tried. He didn't budge. The look on his face said hell, heaven, nor earth could make him move. "Trust me."

He huffed and moved, lightning without the thunder and just as deadly.

"If he hurts you—"

"He won't." Larkin pressed the up button on the bed. "Now smile." She drew a deep breath, held it for three seconds, and then let it out slowly. Necessity forced her mind to Beckett and the most comforting night of sleep she'd had, maybe ever. His arms made all the difference. They bunched, ready to attack, but last night, they'd been tender and adoring.

"You really should take that story to the police." Her voice filled the room. She flashed Beckett an extreme smile. He schooled his features, must have completely forgotten about her edict, and missed the hint she offered.

A knock sounded on the hospital door.

"I'm sure they need to know." Larkin winked at Beckett, then turned. She moved slowly to keep her heart rate and headache in check. Bronson's primly suited frame stood just inside the doorway, giving himself entry before her invitation. A hefty bunch of flowers hung loosely in his hand. "Bronson, come in."

"Larkin, I …" His gaze slid past her, the injured friend, to Beckett sitting in the closest chair to the head of the bed. "I'm interrupting, clearly."

"Nonsense." She waved Bronson in and pointed at Beckett. "Billy was just telling me about what he saw."

Bronson's Adam's apple bobbed. His wingtip scuffed the floor, creating a high-pitched squeak. The light blue gaze she'd known since she was a child narrowed and hopped back and forth from her to Beckett.

"I can hardly believe it, and I lived it." Larkin lifted a hand to her head and tested the amount of swelling above her eye. Not nearly as bad as it was last night, but the bruising probably matched the deep purple and blue on her fingers.

She let her gaze slide to Beckett. He leaned forward, bracing his elbows against his powerful thighs. His shoulders were set a little off center, giving him an air of relaxation, but his gaze didn't lie. It studied every nuance. Ones she surely missed.

"I just can't believe it." Her gaze shifted back to Bronson. "Do you remember the day we saw you in Central Park?"

"I just wanted to bring these by and make sure you were okay." Bronson stepped toward her and held out the flowers.

"That day, when he dropped me off at The Ashford, he saw Lucas and Tarin arguing behind the building." She let her eyes bulge wide; playing the part of shocked victim wasn't difficult. It still didn't seem real, and she was forced into another drama before the blood had dried from the first.

"I'm sorry." Bronson's head shook. He pointed at Beckett with the flowers she still hadn't taken. "Who is he?"

"Billy Crete." Beckett's calm, nearing voice threw her off balance. Not difficult with a splitting skull. His thick hand extended to Bronson. The point of his beard jutted at the man who used to be her friend, the man who was an enemy to her as much as Lucas.

Over the foot of her hospital bed, the two men exchanged a handshake that could crack nuts.

"And how do you know Larkin?" Bronson wiped the palm of his hand on his pant leg.

"Bronson," she snapped.

"Intimately," Beckett offered.

Despite the situation and her physical state, her core heated.

Having delivered his blow, Beckett sat. He reclined, draped his arms across the back of the large chair, and propped a foot on his knee. "Yeah, I didn't know it was important until I saw the late news last night. Their faces were on the screen big as day in connection with Larkin's attack."

"Is it true?" Bronson looked at her, and she didn't have a clue to which part he referred. "Lucas tried to kill you?"

She nodded and embraced the pain it caused. "And now he's dead."

"Dead?" Bronson choked.

"The rat fuck deserved to die." Beckett slid his foot off his knee and let it hit the floor with a stomp.

The guy she'd known for years and years stared at Beckett as though he'd pulled a gun on him. Bronson, the delicate and refined man who'd traveled the globe and destroyed parts of it with a word and several hundreds, thousands of dollars, had never gotten his hands dirty. And Beckett was the mud. He was the blood. He was the hunter who always got his man.

"Well, I need to get to the office." Bronson turned to her. "I'll drop by The Ashford after you've had some time to recover." He headed for the door.

"Beauregard?" Beckett's voice boomed across the room.

Bronson stopped in the doorway and turned slowly. His eyes brimmed with apprehension. "How do you know my name?"

"It's New York. Everyone knows your name." Beckett's expression didn't budge.

"What do you want?" A hint of desperation laced Bronson's tone.

"The flowers?" Beckett's full beard jutted toward the bouquet still in Bronson's hand.

Bronson shuffled forward and set them on the meal tray near her bed. "Here." He bolted as though Beckett was hot on his heels.

Larkin sank back against the bed. Her limbs shook from the adrenaline dump.

Beckett stood and walked to the doorway. He stood there, filling the space for a long minute, and then he turned. A smile unlike any she'd witnessed on his features filled his face and danced in his eyes. "You are amazing."

"Puh." She lifted her hand and let the quivering thing do the talking for her.

He stalked forward, grabbed her face, and stared deep into her soul. "I fucking love you, sweetheart."

A giggle tickled the back of her throat. "Calder Beckett,

I fucking love you."

Beckett sat on the edge of the bed, held her hand, and stroked it. His gaze turned speculative.

"What?"

"Could you get to his phone?"

"I know just the way."

"How? I don't want you alone with him."

"Knowing what I know, he doesn't want me to be alone with him." She smiled. "No one loves a party more than the Beauregard's. And I know just the girl who'll need an I'm-Not-Dead party. How's next Saturday?"

His lips sealed over her mouth, giving her all the answer she needed.

THIRTY-FOUR

"WHEN I ASKED YOU TO LUNCH, I intended to take you to Per Se or somewhere nicer than this." Douglas's blue eyes rolled toward the hospital ceiling. He bit off a healthy chunk of roll.

"What's wrong with this?" Larkin patted the white sheet covering his legs. "We have white linens, and the most important things." She leaned forward and placed the opened packet of applesauce on the tray between them. It smelled like medicine, not fruit. No doubt, she should've ordered in their lunch. "You and me."

His gaze cast down toward his belly, but he wasn't looking at the hospital gown or the drain tubes poking from it. He was a thousand miles and a million years away.

"I said me and you," she dragged out the conjunction. He blinked her into view and swallowed his roll.

"Where were you?"

Douglas huffed. He looked older than his fifty-eight years. Once, he'd told her it wasn't the age but the mileage. He gained a hefty chunk of miles a few short days ago.

"Before your mother died, she contacted me."

Larkin set down her spoon.

"I thought she was being melancholy. Selfishly, I hoped she'd regretted the decisions she'd made."

A hundred questions swarmed her like angry bees. She clamped her lips shut and listened.

"We grew up together, your mother and me. On the wrong side of town, on the wrong side of the tracks. She and her mother lived in a one-room apartment above my family's one-room apartment. My mother, father, three siblings, and me." He grabbed the tray and slowly shoved it to the side.

Her palms itched to help him, but she had a feeling it would hurt him more than shifting the rolling buffet would.

"You could hear everything. Above. Below. To the left and right. We were loud and boisterous, but at our core was love and a yearning for better things. Her mother ..." Douglas drew a deep breath. "Cruel fit the woman too well. She beat Gwen with sharp words at first, but later, she and her many boyfriends used their fists." He wiped at a tear that'd collected in the corner of an eye.

Larkin imagined a dingy apartment with faces like Lucas's staring angrily at her mother. For the first time in a long time, a pang of sympathy struck her between the boobs. She'd been a woman when dealing with Lucas. Her mother had been a girl, alone and betrayed by her own blood.

"I did well in school. Had a full ride to Columbia. Your mom didn't do too well. How could she? I tried to get her to come with me. It would have been another tiny apartment, and it would have been full of love, but she wanted out. After high school, she used one of her mom's old boyfriends as a stepping-stone to a wealthier one."

"And somehow, she ended up with my dad." She could see the probable chain of possession in her mind. Any of them could be her father. The thought knotted her stomach, slamming it against her spine.

Douglas nodded. "I was glad she got out. Glad she found a man who treated her with respect. My life went a different route, and I left the past where it belonged until my mother's funeral. I made my way to Brooklyn from Marrakesh and was floored to see Gwen." His eyes closed. "Everyone wore black, and she strutted into the church in a violet number that wrapped around her body. She'd always been beautiful, but for a man who'd seen dusty desert for five years to see the woman he loved in that rich purple." He placed his hand over his heart. "When she asked me up for a drink, I didn't question anything. Not the state of her relationship. Not about birth control. Nothing."

Larkin's heart slowed. "When was the funeral?"

"Thirty years ago." He stared at her, a smile curved his lips. "It was wrong. She was married, but I wouldn't have changed it. Not then. Not now. Not ever." His hand wrapped around hers.

"She refused my calls. Didn't return my letters. So after six months, I let her go again. I would change that if I could. If I'd known …"

"You didn't know?" Tears filled her eyes. Sad ones. Happy ones too.

"Gwen called me the day before she took her life. I'd retired from the CIA. Contrary to popular belief, you can retire without being whacked. She begged me to take this job. 'Drive my daughter around. Keep her safe. You can do it better than anyone else. I need you, Doug.' I didn't know how old you were until after her funeral." He sighed. "Then it was too late for me to confront her. You were your father's daughter. You'd just lost your mother. I wasn't about to take him away from you too. So I protected you just as she'd asked me to until Lucas Backstrom." His head hung low.

"Hey." Larkin grabbed his hand with both of hers. "He tricked us all. And he had help."

"It was my job to sniff him out. It was my job to keep you safe." He buried his face in his hands.

"Look at me," Larkin ordered. "I'm not going to waste a minute more on Lucas or Tarin—until her court date. I'm not going to piss my precious time away with the people I love worrying about things we can't change. Do you hear me?"

She held his brittle fingers and cried and laughed.

"I'm here. I'm safe and alive because of you and me and Beckett. I'm here with my dad."

His laugh, as full and rich as she'd ever heard it, surrounded her. It wrapped around her and pulled her in close. "I love you, Larkin."

"I love you, Dad."

"Ma'am, I'm sorry, but if you cause my patient distre—" The nurse stopped halfway into the room. "Oh, sorry." She slowly backed out.

Larkin straightened and squeezed her dad's shoulders. "So you want to help me and Beckett?"

"Beckett, huh?" His wet eyes waggled with mischief.

Her grin was too wide.

"Wow. That's a new look."

"It's a new feeling too."

"You know ... ah." Douglas—her dad—reclined onto the bed, covering his side with his hand.

She schooled her features, careful not to show too

much concern. He was on the mend, and she knew there would be pain, but he'd already shown such progress in just a few days. "I know …"

"I was loopy and close to passing out, but I saw the way he moved. I don't know exactly what he is, but I have an idea. There's not going to be anything easy about a relationship with him."

"Dou—Dad." She winked. "I know what he is. Better than that, I know who he is. It's not going to be easy, but when it comes to men, I've had easy. I'm ready for a challenge."

"I read your speech in the paper. Now, Beckett." He cupped her cheek and smiled. "You've gone and grown up before my eyes."

"It was bound to happen." Larkin held his hand to her face until he let it fall away.

"What do you lovebirds need my help with?" He gestured to the hospital bed.

"The doctor plans to release you tomorrow. We need your brain, not your brawn to catch a bad guy."

Her dad's gaze narrowed to an angry slit. "Another one?"

"Bronson Beauregard."

"I knew that kid was bad news," he growled.

"Could've told me." She smacked his foot, knowing it wouldn't hurt through the sheets.

"Pfft, you wouldn't have listened."

"True." Larkin rolled her eyes at herself.

A knock sounded on the door. Douglas's gaze slid to the nightstand beside his bed instead of the door.

"Don't tell me you have a gun in there," she whisper-screamed.

"Okay, I won't tell you Beckett put my gun in there."

"You two." Her heart pounded. They were going to be the end of her. She shifted toward the door. "Come in."

Speak of the devil and he shall appear.

"Room service." Beckett opened the door with a sack in one hand and a tray of drinks in the other.

"Hot damn." Douglas clapped his hands and waved the man she loved inside. "Tell me about Beauregard and what you need from me. Oh, and give me one of whatever's in that bag. It smells like real food."

"Yes, sir." Beckett strolled in, closing the door firmly behind him. He planted a kiss square on Larkin's lips, handed Douglas the bag, dragged a chair close to the bed and sat with a smile on his face and a devilish glint in his eyes.

THIRTY-FIVE

"EEEEEEEEEEEEEK!" Marlis jumped up and down like a toddler on a sugar high. She clapped too. Larkin was surprised she could hear the frantic applause after the intense shriek.

"God is a woman. Bet on it." Behind Mar, Genevieve lifted her hands to the sky in praise.

Libby stood in the circle of friends in the bedroom where she and Beckett had first acted upon their desire for one another. Her friend didn't yell or thank a deity. She just shook her head.

"What?" Dread gathered in Larkin's belly. If Libby didn't like him … Well, she'd hate losing touch with one of her dearest friends. The last thing she intended to do was lose touch with Beckett. Why would she, when they were so mind-meltingly good?

"I just can't believe it." Libby draped the dress she intended to wear for the party on the bed. She spread her arms wide and tackled Larkin.

"Oh!" Larkin's laughter bubbled full and frothy through her chest like it hadn't all day.

"Love. Jesus. Who'd have thought you'd be the first of us to fall?" Genevieve hooked an arm around Marlis and pulled her close. "No offense, muffin, but I always thought it'd be you."

"She has to stop boning married men first," Libby jabbed.

"One time. It was one time." Marlis threw a shoe at Libby, and her, by default.

"All right. All right." Larkin waved around the black dress she'd yet to put on. "We only have five more minutes before people will begin arriving. Do we need to go over the plan again?"

"I think I'm going to be sick." Marlis held the other shoe to her bare stomach.

"No, muffin, you're with me. We'll be fine." Genevieve hugged her close. "How many drinks is the limit again?" She held up a manicured hand.

"Half of that," Larkin corrected.

"Party pooper." Gen shooed her words away. "We have reason to celebrate. Love is in the air," she crooned.

"Save it for the after-party." Libby kissed Larkin's cheek and released her hold. "Get ready." Her friend grabbed the pink cocktail dress she'd chosen from Larkin's overstuffed closet, unzipped the side, and slipped it over her head. "Now we know what to do. Don't we, ladies?"

"Damn skippy." Gen smoothed a hand down the red beads clinging to her body that in total made a dress.

"I'm with her." Mar slipped the shoe on her foot. "Will one of you pass me the other shoe?"

"Can you catch?" Libby asked.

"No." Marlis crinkled her nose. "It's not a skill I need to run my business."

"It's a life skill, Mar. A life skill." Libby crossed the distance with the stiletto.

"Thanks, Mom." Marlis puckered her lips.

"Call me mom again and you'll be kissing something, and it won't be my ass." Libby walked back to the shoes on the bed, zipped the dress as she went, and swished her bottom side to side for emphasis.

Gen hooted. Larkin laughed and stepped into the high-neck, low-back number she'd chosen.

"Zip me?" Larkin turned her back to Genevieve.

"It's not my specialty, but I'll see what I can do." Gen shrugged.

Her friend did a great job.

"Thanks." Larkin breathed deeply. The material gave enough for her to move quickly, if the need arose.

"I'm going down," Libby called.

"You're so ready for this." Mar huffed.

"Just another day at the office, babe." Libby's voice faded down the staircase.

"Let's go get you a drink." Gen grabbed Marlis's hand and dragged her toward the staircase.

"You'll do great. I know it." Larkin smiled at Mar until they disappeared. "Not a big drink," she yelled.

"What, Mom? I couldn't hear you." At least Marlis was joking. It was a step in the right direction.

Larkin walked to the vanity and opened the top drawer. The small flesh-colored earpiece lay where Beckett had placed it not thirty minutes ago. She ignored the quiver in her hand, reached for it, and stuffed it into her ear behind her long, loose hair.

"Beckett?" she whispered.

"Larkin, you just made a fatal mistake." His rich voice rumbled in her ear.

"Mistake?"

"I'm inside you, sweetheart."

Her cheeks flushed in the reflection. "It's not the first time."

"Oh, but it is. No one has been in you like I am."

"That was true before I put this thing in my ear, Beckett."

"Hot damn, I love it when you talk dirty to me."

A laugh shook her shoulders. Voices filtered up from downstairs. "Will you focus?"

"I am focused. One hundred percent. Come to the window by your frilly flower painting."

She chuckled. The artist was famous. The painting cost more than her car. She'd bought it as a hurray for turning a profit in her first year of business. And he called it her frilly flower painting as though she'd smeared her fingers in paint and swirled them around the canvas.

"What's fu ... Holy shit."

"What's wrong?" Larkin's heartbeat spiked. Her neck warmed. She looked down to the road below. A short string of limos and Town Cars rolled slowly in front of her pre-war home. "Is Bronson here?"

"Forget Bronson. You look good enough to eat."

"You can see me?" Her gaze darted around the rooftops, looking for him.

"Don't waste your time looking, sweetheart. You won't find me."

"Where are you?"

"Touch your lips."

Larkin did as he commanded.

"I'm right here."

Her lips spread under her touch.

"Now, your neck." His voice was husky, gravelly with hunger.

She swallowed, and her neck moved under her fingers.

"I'm here." He waited a beat. "The clasp of your zipper. Now lower. Yes, Larkin, over that sweet ass. I'm here."

He was in her. All over her. Every touch raced a thoroughbred herd of want through her veins. She licked her lips, closed her eyes, and sighed. "Beckett."

"Touch your delicious clit."

Her eyes shot wide. Heat filled her cheeks. "People can see me."

"Show them where I am."

Inside her chest, her heart beat its fists against her sternum demanding obedience or sanity, she wasn't sure.

Larkin's hand slid across her hips, down her thigh, and to the sweet center of her need.

"I'm here."

Before he could ask, her hand slid up to her breasts. Both her nipples fought against the confines of her dress and thin bra. "You're here."

"Larkin," he growled.

Her hand slid over her belly and up her side. At her neck, her hand spread wide, encompassing her throat.

"The valley between your breasts now." She obeyed. The snap in his voice made her move faster than she had been. "I'm here."

"You're here." Euphoria lifted her to stand ten feet tall. It strengthened her determination and reinforced her nerves. "We're going to get him, Beckett."

"I know we will, sweetheart."

She blew him a kiss.

"Are you ready?"

"As I'll ever be."

"His car just rounded the corner."

"Here we go." She turned away from the window.

"Sweet Jesus," Beckett barked.

"What?" She headed for the stairs.

"That's a dress, but the body inside it. Fuck. I can't

wait to get it off you."

"Work first." Larkin cleared the one flight. "I'm nearing the main."

"Going quiet. I'm here. If you need me, I'm there in less than twenty seconds."

"I know. Prepare to be lulled to sleep by elite NYC socialization."

"The sound of your sexy voice will keep me awake and ready."

Larkin hit the middle of the last flight of stairs and cheers erupted. Her gaze flew around the room in search of the cause of the commotion.

"Let's hear it for Larkin Ashford." The owner of the bank she used clapped and whooped above the crowd. Of course, he was glad she hadn't kicked it. More digital dollars behind his thick walls.

She smiled sweetly and waved to the room brimming with people she knew from one venture or another. They hugged her. They patted her hands. They kissed her cheeks. Ten times over, she told the same story.

"Larkin." Cornish Gleeson offered his hand and gave a heavy shake that threatened to jerk her off her heels.

"Cornish, I hope you're enjoying yourself," she lied. If he choked on a shrimp canapé, she wouldn't use her earpiece to get him an ambulance. She lied to herself too. So it was okay.

"Something was off about that boy. I knew it the first time he scanned me into your building. I knew it." The balls of his cheeks scrunched into even tighter circles. The broken blood vessels shined purple against the high red of his general complexion.

Larkin gritted her teeth. Cornish wasn't the first to say as much.

Lucas Backstrom had been a grown-ass man. A man who had problems, and if any one of them had known how deeply they ran, he'd have gotten the help he needed. If she had known, she would have tried to get him help.

"Have you tried the canapés?" Larkin waved in a server. "Enjoy." She smiled, snagged one of her own, and headed for the back of the room in need of distance from such stupidity.

More people than she'd expected had turned out for what was supposed to be an intimate event. In fact, she had yet to get close to Bronson, the entire reason they were having this party.

She shoved the hors d'oeuvre toward her mouth but didn't bite. "Beckett?"

"I'm here."

"When you get the evidence, please tell me if Cornish Gleeson is in on it."

"You think he's in on it?"

"I have no idea. Is it bad that I want him to be?"

His laughter filtered into her ear.

"He's such an asshole." Larkin shrugged as though Beckett were there, right by her side.

"Larkin!" Another group of NYC businesswomen sauntered toward her for another round of much the same. When they left, Lucas's ghost stayed behind. He prodded the sore spots on her head and tormented her resolve.

She stood, staring at the floor and wondering if she could have done anything to help Lucas. If she'd committed to him, like she longed to commit to Beckett, would things have turned out differently? Differently, better or worse?

"You holding up?" Libby's knowing smile and pale-pink dress pulled her from beneath the depth of her what-ifs.

"Glad to see a face I trust." Larkin whispered the last. "I didn't expect so many people to turn out."

"People love a good tragedy as long as it doesn't touch

them." Libby rolled her eyes, plucked a flute of champagne from a server's tray, and handed it to her.

"Thank you." She drank deeply.

"Larkin, my goodness." Bronson's voice curled around her spine and constricted, winding fast and hard.

Bubbles fizzed up the back of her throat. She coughed up the ones that breezed their way into her lungs.

"Oh, I didn't mean to startle you." Bronson grabbed either side of her shoulders and squeezed. He pulled her in close and wrapped his arms around her body. His fingers grazed the bare skin of her back.

"Are you okay?" Beckett demanded in her ear.

She centered her thoughts, shoved away the panic, and honed in on the goal. Slowly, breath filled her lungs, expanding her chest. Bronson's high-dollar cologne burned her nostrils, and the nausea threatened to take her down. Again, she aimed everything at the goal.

"I'm fine." Larkin patted Bronson's back and shoved out of his hold. "How are you?"

"Ready to strangle that man if he doesn't get his hands off you," Beckett bit out.

The network of cameras Douglas rigged for the event worked too well apparently.

"I still can't believe everything that went down." Bronson popped the cuffs of his suit.

"It's only been two and a half weeks." Larkin shrugged. "It's a lot to take in. You think you know someone and bam." She smacked her hands between their faces. "All the things you thought you knew are a lie."

"Champagne?" Libby held two flutes. One she offered Bronson. He took the beverage, and Libby held hers up in the center of their small circle. "To true colors and true friends. May we know them when we see them."

"Cheers." Larkin finished her drink with a short gulp.

"Here. Here." Bronson tipped his glass and drained it

dry in a few gulps.

The smartest one among them drank only a sip.

"We need a picture," Libby cheered. She reached for a clutch that she'd purposely left upstairs. "Oh, I don't have my purse, which means I don't have a phone."

Larkin huffed. "I left mine upstairs since everyone who might call me is here." She turned to Bronson. "Take our picture?"

"Yeees!" Libby fist pumped the air. "Your arms are longer anyway."

Bronson fished his phone out of his inner jacket pocket. "What does that matter?"

"Men," Libby scoffed. "You have no idea about the angle."

"The angle?" Bronson's brows furrowed.

"Here." Libby swooped in to Bronson's side.

Larkin scooted in on his other side.

"You want to shoot from above. It eliminates double chins and nose hairs." Libby grabbed his arm and maneuvered the phone to the optimum height and distance. "Like that. Ready? Three. Two. One."

Bronson pressed the button. The flash burned bright.

"The flash?" Libby whined. She grabbed the phone from his hand and looked at him as though he'd committed a crime.

He had. And it had nothing to do with a camera flash.

"How do girls know about this stuff?" Bronson laughed.

"Women," Larkin corrected. "Not all of us do. Libby has a knack for it."

"Here we go." Libby huddled them together again. "Say champagne."

"Champagne," Bronson cheered not because he wanted to say it but because he wanted to be liked. They'd use that fault to their advantage.

Libby snapped the picture, then jumped to it on the screen. "Look." She maneuvered the phone toward Bronson. "That's yours."

"It's not bad," he defended.

"It's not good either." Libby switched the image. "Now this one."

"I'm man enough to admit when I'm wrong." His hand shot up in Scout's honor.

"See." Lib offered Larkin the phone.

"Look at us, looking good." She pretended to look at the image, and then looked at Libby and Bronson exchanging hip bumps. "I need a pic with Mar and Gen. Do you mind? I'll be right back."

Larkin smiled wide, waved, and took off with the phone before Bronson could protest. Not that he would have. His face was close to Libby's, looking for the subtle differences between her good and bad sides. Like she had a bad side. Like she knew anything about taking pictures beyond point and click.

The farther she got away from Bronson the louder her heart beat in her chest. She'd swear the small sea of people she maneuvered through heard the reverberations.

"You have time." Beckett's calm voice soothed. "You have nothing to hide."

She drew a deep breath and let it out slowly.

"Larkin?"

A woman she went to college with waved to her from across the room. Larkin waved and continued on as though all the woman had wanted was a friendly hello from afar. She approached the hallway. The girls weren't there. Sweat breached the pores above her lip.

"I don't see the girls," Larkin panted. She set the flute on a shelf. Her gaze shot left and right, seeking the girls.

"They're trying to get away from an old lady wearing a peacock." Beckett laughed.

"Don't laugh. I'm about to be sick."

"No, you're not. You handled Lucas. This is nothing."

"Ha."

"Lar." Marlis rounded the corner. She walked as though the ground were shaking beneath her heels.

"Marlis, are you drunk?" Larkin growled.

"No." Her friend waved off the accusation and nearly fell on her ass.

"Jesus. Where's Gen?"

"Trying to get away from Old Lady Gilbert, but she's determined to get free legal advice about a neighbor stealing her parking spot. She sent me to do ..." Mar grabbed her head with both hands. "What were we supposed to do?"

"Christ Almighty." Larkin ran to Mar and held her friend around her waist. "Smile and try not to look too plastered."

Marlis flashed a peace sign and squealed. Larkin snapped a couple of pics.

"I'm not cut out for this spy stuff."

"No shit." She turned Mar around and propped her against the wall. "Go find Gen. Tell her phase two."

"Phase two?" Marlis looked back as though Larkin had lost her mind.

"Yes." Larkin's knees quaked, but she drew a deep breath and bolted down the stairs to the kitchen. Douglas sat at the table in front of a laptop, sipping tea like this were any old night.

"Take a breath." Her dad smiled boldly, brightly. "You look amazing."

"So do you." She couldn't help but reflect his wide grin. He wore a suit. The first since the incident.

"I forgot how nice if felt to dress for an occasion."

"I'm sorry it's not a real one." Larkin stopped next to his chair and pressed a kiss to his cheek.

He patted hers. "Of course, it is. We're catching a bad guy."

Cue the jackhammer in her chest.

"It's fine. Hand it here."

Larkin handed over the phone.

"Now, get back to your party." He waved her off.

"How long until it's ready?"

"Twenty minutes max."

She'd known the answer, but hoped it had changed since she, Beckett, and Douglas had last discussed the details. "Good luck."

"I have skill." Her dad winked.

Beckett laughed in her ear.

"How are you both so calm?" Larkin snapped. "Never mind." This was their life. Covert operations. Sensitive missions. They flirted with death on a daily basis. She hated the thought of Beckett in harm's way, but it was what he did. He was one of the best at his job, and he helped make the world a better place.

"Bronson is on the move." Beckett's voice was tight. "He's clearing the room fast, looking for you."

Her stomach hit her heels. Douglas blew her a kiss. She hurried for the stairs. The party poured into the foyer. A man and a woman stood on the landing. Their hands intertwined. Their faces inches away from tongues twining. She grabbed the railing, added a little oomph to her steps and hoped they'd hear her approach.

"Excuse me." Bronson pushed through the middle of the couple and descended two steps before his gaze collided with Larkin's. "There you are."

THIRTY-SIX

LARKIN CLIMBED THE STEPS and stopped in front of him. "There they are." She rolled her eyes at the amorous pair. "I thought they'd come down here. Looks like I'll have to pay my housekeeper extra to clean the coat closet." Total bullshit, but she hoped it worked.

The guy who used to be her friend shrugged. Was he ever her friend, really? "We've both had our fair share of coat closet hookups."

"Speak for yourself. I prefer a bit of privacy."

"Where's the fun in that?" Bronson scoffed.

"He has no idea what it's like to have you to himself," Beckett purred.

"Nope. Nope." Larkin waved off the conversation, bobbed around Bronson, and headed toward the party.

Bronson's long fingers wrapped around her upper

arm, drawing her to a stop. "Where's my phone?"

"I gave it to Genevieve. She had a gaggle of ladies around her. You're bound to have a porno or ten on your camera roll."

"That phone has important information on it. If anyone can appreciate that, you can." His gaze narrowed.

Her head shook. "Nope. I drop my phone too often to keep anything important on it." Larkin headed up the stairs, past the couple, and into the party. "Two please." She grabbed the champagne offered from the tray and handed one to Bronson. "Did you ever figure out why Billy was following you?"

"Who?" Bronson drained his flute without thought.

Larkin sipped. "The guy from the park."

"You mean the guy from your hospital room?" Bronson set the flute on an end table. The glass smacked the wood so hard she expected the stem to shatter, but it held.

"That's right. I was so out of it." She lifted a hand to the back of her head. "It was one hell of a concussion. Not that I'd had one before."

"No." Bronson crossed both arms over his chest. "Are you with him?"

"What do you think it will be like in jail?" Her question hung between them for several seconds. It sucked the air from their bubble. Larkin breathed just fine.

"What are you doing?" Beckett snarled.

She ignored him and watched the sweat bead on Bronson's forehead. It was a small triumph. The color drained from his face. The butterflies hibernating inside her flew south.

"Excuse me?" He tugged at his collar and straightened his jacket.

"Tarin will have her day in court soon." A smile stretched her lips. "People who do wrong always pay in the end."

"I'm sure she will." Bronson cleared his throat. "I really need my phone."

"Sure. Let's go find Genevieve." Larkin took his arm and steered him through the party.

Several people stopped Larkin, wanting more face time, more details, more living vicariously, safely. She held Bronson's arm and included him in the conversations. In short order, his gaze quit roaming the room for Genevieve. Interest in his family's company and in his and Larkin's relationship kept his mind diverted from the phone. Until the group moved on to the next round of questions that had nothing to do with him.

"I'm going to find Gen." He grabbed her wrist and slipped from her hold.

"Okay." Larkin waved him off like she didn't care. Inside, her stomach lurched.

The moment he was out of sight, Larkin excused herself from the group and weaved through the crowd.

"They're by the long, funky chair," Beckett said through the earpiece.

"I see her hair." There was no missing the vibrant red. She neared in time to hear Gen say, "I gave it to Marlis." Larkin looked left and right. Her drunkest friend was nowhere in sight.

"Where is she?" Bronson barked.

Genevieve's chin rose. Her gaze studied the ceiling for half a second. It was her coping mechanism to keep from losing her cool. "First, simmer that tone. I'm not one of your bobble-headed bitches. If you want an answer from me, you'll ask civilly."

"It's my phone." Bronson stepped closer to Gen and lowered his face to hers.

Her friend's expression didn't flicker. Disinterest muted her gaze. Stubbornness held her mouth in a strict line.

"Dammit," Bronson huffed. He straightened, drew a

deep breath, and let it out slowly. "Genevieve, darling, where is Marlis?"

"Second, how should I know? I'm not her keeper." Gen's white teeth gleamed.

"You—"

"Gosh." Larkin crashed into their little face-off as though she had no clue it'd been near the point of explosion. "Those ladies wouldn't stop asking questions."

"We'll be like that in a few years," Gen quipped.

"I hope not." Larkin placed her hand on Bronson's arm. "Get your phone?"

"No. Marlis has it; at least, that's what Genevieve says." Bronson's angry gaze slid to her friend.

"She has no reason to lie." Larkin laughed. "Come, we'll go find her."

"You'll get caught up again. I'll find her." He took off through the crowd that showed no signs of thinning.

"Okay." She waved him off and turned to Gen. "Where's Marlis?"

"I'm looking," Beckett offered.

"I don't know. She told me two faces and then stumbled back in your direction."

"Why'd you let her get so smashed?"

"It was either get her drunk or watch her stroke out in the middle of NYC's finest." Gen shrugged. "You should have seen her, jumping at every noise, hyperventilating in general conversations. Better labeled a lush than have a psychotic break."

"I should have never included her in this."

"You couldn't have kept her out of it because she'd have gone crazy with curiosity. Mar's a big girl. She'll be fine." Gen grabbed her arm. "Come on. We'll find her."

"Before Bronson?"

"Four women move around a hell of a lot more than operatives or targets." Beckett groaned. "She's not in the living room. Not on the stairs. Not outside. I'm reviewing the last fifteen minutes."

"She's puking." Larkin knew it as surely as she knew her name.

"Yep," Gen agreed. "She'd make it to the guest room, if she could."

"You called it, but she teetered her way to your bathroom," Beckett corrected.

"Gross." Larkin sighed.

"What?"

"She's in my bathroom."

Gen looked at her like she was crazy.

"Beckett," she whispered.

"I'm here," Beckett said.

"Nothing." Lord, this spy shit wasn't as easy as it looked. She pulled Gen to her side and pointed at her ear.

"Oh." Gen's full lips made an exaggerated O. "Let's go se—"

"I've looked everywhere." Bronson's glistening brow had turned to a full-out sweat. "I can't find her."

"Jesus, Bronson. That's twice in one night you've startled me." Larkin threw her hands wide. "What's the deal? Do you already have porn on there?"

"I need my phone," he growled.

"If it has porn, I call dibs." Gen raised her hand.

His narrowed, hot gaze sliced to Gen.

Larkin placed an arm between them. "It's your phone, Bronson. It's in the house. We'll find it." Before they found Marlis, she needed an update on the transfer and Douglas's progress. "Is it done?"

"What done?" Bronson's nose crinkled.

"You two fighting?" She prayed Beckett got the message.

"Yeah. Whatever. Let's find Marlis and my phone." He headed for the foyer.

"Five minutes," Beckett answered. It wasn't the one she wanted.

"We have to stall him." Larkin pulled Gen with her. They caught up to Bronson at the top of the stairs. "Mar was pretty drunk. She probably went somewhere to puke."

"Delightful." Bronson's eyes rolled. He headed down the stairs toward Douglas.

"No." Larkin's bellow startled even her. Bronson stopped mid-step and glared at her. "She wouldn't puke in the kitchen." Not where Douglas was transferring information from Bronson's phone to a computer.

His gaze narrowed, and he darted down the steps.

Larkin felt every blood vessel in her body constrict. If Bronson hurt her dad, forget the eyes, she'd carve his heart out.

"Calm," Beckett warned.

Was he calm when his team was on the line? Maybe he was, but she wasn't cut out for this shit.

She shoved Gen after him. They clamored down the steps in a thunderous herd of heels. At least they'd give him ample warning.

"Oh. Douglas." Bronson stood in the middle of the kitchen staring at her dad who lifted his mug toward the murderer and smiled.

"Mr. Beauregard." Douglas pointed at the kettle on the stove. "Can I get you some tea?"

"No. Have you seen Marlis?" Bronson clipped the ends of each word.

"Can't say that I have." Douglas sipped from the steaming cup.

Before Larkin could take a cleansing breath, Bronson pounded up the steps.

"Follow him, please," Larkin begged Genevieve.

"On it." Her friend jogged for the steps.

"Is it—"

"Here." Douglas lifted the phone from his lap, removed the cable, and handed it to her.

"Thank you." She ran after them with the phone clutched in her hand.

The stairs stretched out before her, each flight taking longer to climb than she remembered. Larkin bobbed around the couple still hanging in the foyer and headed for the second floor.

Bronson slammed himself through one of the guest bedrooms. Genevieve crested the top of the stairs. He'd blown through the second bedroom by the time she reached the top.

"Well?" Larkin begged.

He didn't bother answering. The back of his suit heading up to her private quarters was enough. His single-mindedness worked. As it was, sweat slicked her palms and she held the phone so tightly she might crack the screen of his beloved device.

She and Gen ran after him.

"And I didn't think I would get my workout in today." Gen laughed.

"Thank you."

"Would go to the end of the world for my girls."

"I love when people think they have you figured out. They don't have a clue." Larkin smiled despite everything. She had the best people in her life.

They heard retching before they entered the bedroom.

"Marlis, give me my phone," Bronson bellowed the command above their friend's bodily revolt.

"Get out," Mar gagged.

"I need my phone now." He slammed something against the counter.

They rounded into the large marble bathroom in time to see Mar's sweat-slicked, chalk-white face peek out from the wall partitioning the toilet from the rest of the space.

"Go fuck yourself." Their friend yelled the edict and whipped her head back inside the small room.

Pride swelled in Larkin's chest.

Bronson stepped toward Marlis.

It turned to fury in that instant.

"Don't you dare bother her about your goddamned phone," Larkin growled.

His head whipped around, brow crinkled, ready to fight.

She lifted her hand and shook the phone back and forth in his face. "Take your precious phone and go."

"Where was it?" he snapped.

"On the bed, genius." If he looked, he could have easily missed it, had it actually been there. They'd left a mess throughout the room getting ready for the party.

Bronson snatched the phone from her hand and inspected it. The plastic and glass couldn't say it'd been violated. She tilted her head toward the exit.

"I just—"

She stopped him with a hand. "I just don't care. You don't treat my friends like that."

"I am your friend," he retorted.

"I thought you were," she bit back. "Turned out you and your family only wanted to use me for my business."

"That was my father's idea. I love you, Larkin."

Her laughter filled the gaps in Marlis's chucking. "You don't have a clue what love is."

"Oh, and you do?" He flung his arms wide.

"Yeah, I do." Larkin walked around him toward her sick friend.

His stomping tread sounded like tap shoes as he left. It surely defeated the purpose of his dramatic departure.

Marlis groaned.

"Can I get you something?" Larkin knelt next to her friend and held her nose.

Mar sat back on her heels and rested her head on her forearms … on the toilet seat. "Peace and quiet."

"I'll sit with her." Genevieve pulled Larkin to her feet and squeezed her hand. "Go make sure they get that as-shat."

"I will." Larkin pulled Genevieve in close, wrapped her arms around her, and held her tight. "Thank you for—"

"Mushy stuff later. Hurry." Patting her back, Gen shoved her off. "And take your phone with you. I want to see video of them taking him away in cuffs."

"I'm on it." Larkin grabbed her phone off the night-stand and headed for the stairs. She skidded at the top of the staircase. Beckett ascended the last of the steps. Heat radiated from her heart through her chest and warmed her entire body.

"You look even better up close." His voice echoed in the cavernous landing and in her ear.

"At least you could see me earlier. Where were you?" She took another step, meeting him and the top and elim-inating the distance between them.

"Do we need to review?" His fingertips brushed her lips and then slipped to her neck.

Her breath caught. "What about Bronson? He's getting away."

"It seems so." Beckett's hot fingers slid over her shoul-der and traced the length of her spine.

"Beckett, later." She grabbed his face and planted a quick kiss on his lips. "Bronson, now."

"I'm not allowed to operate in the US."

"Which means, what?" Her nose wrinkled. "You've been hunting here for a month."

"I can't take him into custody."

"So what …? He just gets away?"

His palm cupped her low back and pulled her close.

"The moment he steps foot on foreign soil, he's ours."

"That could take decades. What if he knows you're on to him and doesn't leave the country?"

"If there's one thing my people know how to do, it's cause a ruckus. They still have holding in South Africa and Botswana. He'll come. They'll all come. Brice, Bronson, and Cornish."

"Seriously?" Her mouth fell open.

"No. Sorry, Cornish is innocent of these crimes, but I'm sure I can find something on him."

Larkin pinched his ribs, and he danced out of her tiny grip.

"I still have loads of files to comb through, so who knows, he could be. There are more involved than the Beauregards."

Larkin blew a full breath through her lips and buried her head against Beckett's chest. She breathed him in and held him so tightly her fingers and arms ached. His lips brushed the top of her head. They stayed that way for a while. She straightened and looked him in his dark, dangerous eyes.

"When it all happens, you'll go."

"Larkin, I—"

She smoothed her thumb over his mouth. "You have to be there. You've worked hard. You need to see this to the end. Your teammates, you, deserve retribution. Closure will have to do."

EPILOGUE

LARKIN'S FINGERS SMOOTHED over the red gold of the Montblanc fountain pen atop the glass conference table on the seventy-ninth floor of The Ashford Building. The weight of it balanced easily between her thumb and index finger. Only now, she had no one to aim the pointy end at. A smile tickled her lips. Her gaze slid around the table from woman to woman.

Cornish wasn't the monster she'd hoped he'd been, but he'd been an old-fashioned asshole who didn't belong on her board. Benjamin had respectfully withdrawn from the board after the whole murder and mayhem debacle. It worked out for the best. Brice was in a foreign prison awaiting trial for his crimes, along with his son. It forfeited his position on the board.

The vacancies allowed four New York businesswomen to join Marlis and Genevieve on the board. Each raised their own companies on the back of hard work and their inability to accept the word no. They weren't multi-millionaires, and they didn't have Ivy League pedigrees, but each of the women was brilliant in their own right. The promise they held for Duo and Ditto's growth, the promise Larkin's company gave their own career lit a fire in her soul for her work that she hadn't experienced since the inception.

"Thank you, Darah." Larkin stood. "That's a heartening forecast."

"Heartening? It's fucking amazing." Genevieve danced a jig in her seat. Larkin was shocked her friend didn't actually climb on top of the table and start a strip tease. After all, her investment portfolio had doubled in the past two months thanks to the astounding amount of stock she'd bought into Duo and Ditto. She'd known that before Darah's treasury report because it was fucking amazing.

Larkin had made enough money that she started a nonprofit that with Beckett and her dad's help would change the world, ten disadvantaged children at a time. Move over Bill and Melinda. She really hoped the guys weren't recruiting for the CIA and Base Branch. After all, the first kid they'd selected started MIT in the fall. Another would enter the Citadel mid-semester.

"Whoop! Whoop!" Lenna lifted her hands to the sky and joined in Gen's seat dance.

The room erupted in laughter and cheers.

Larkin clapped. "Your confidence and support over the past four months has been invaluable. I cannot thank you enough."

"We're learning a lot from this experience," Kaitlin assured her.

"I'm thrilled." Larkin beamed.

"On that note, I move to close the meeting." Marlis

grinned too widely.

"Second," Darah saved Mar's hide.

"Meeting adjourned. Thank you, ladies." Larkin walked around to Marlis and propped a hip on her friend's coat that was draped across the table. "What's his name?"

"I don't know what you're talking about." Mar stuffed her laptop and phone into her bag without looking up. She grabbed her coat and tugged. Larkin didn't budge and neither did the coat. Her friend's gaze shot up and narrowed on Larkin's butt. "Marshal Gentry. He's not married. I double checked."

"Meeting at a neutral location?"

"Yes." Mar yanked on her coat. "Can I have my coat now? I'd like to change before I meet him."

"Is your driver taking you?"

"Yes." Marlis smacked her butt. "Gosh, you're as bad as Libby these days."

"After what I went through, I'm hyper cautious. You should be too."

Mar kissed her cheeks. "I am. I'll text you when it's over."

"Okay." Larkin lifted her chin and released her friend.

The other women hurried to catch the elevator with Marlis.

"Want to catch a quick bite with us?" Darah pointed at her and Lenna.

"I have to get the kids so Danny can catch his flight," Kaitlin explained.

"Thank you, but Beckett gets back tonight." Larkin couldn't hide her smile. It'd been three weeks without a word. She trusted him to be here tonight. If he wasn't … she'd try her best not to worry. It wasn't easy, but it was worth it.

"Enjoy!" Darah waggled her brow.

She waved them off and looked for Genevieve. Gen

was usually the first one out. Court hours didn't cater to her needs. Her friend hunched over her phone. Gen didn't hunch. Her posture was impeccable, just like her comebacks.

"Gen?"

Her friend slapped the air for Larkin to be quiet. Also not like Gen. Larkin stood and walked slowly to the other side of the table. Genevieve held the phone to her ear so tightly the smooth screen might leave button grooves on her cheek. Larkin listened intently without a word but heard nothing from the other end of the line. Gen was muting every tone with her ear.

Several more minutes gathered one atop the other. Nervousness she'd become too accustomed to after the Lucas incident bubbled to the surface.

"Yes. I'll be there." Genevieve dropped the phone into her lap and stared at Larkin without seeing her. She gave a thousand-yard stare. Her pale cheeks turned the color and consistency of chalk. Like one puff of air would blow her away.

"What?" Larkin begged.

Her head shook. No words left her parted lips.

She should wait. She should give her a minute. "Genevieve?"

"I have to go." Gen stood and grabbed her purse. Her phone tumbled to the ground, and she looked at it as though she'd never seen it before.

Larkin scooped it off the floor and held it out to her friend. "Let me call Douglas. He'll drive you."

"No. I can't wait." Gen snatched the phone and stuffed it into her purse. "I'll get a cab."

"A cab?" The Genevieve she knew would rather walk twenty blocks in heels than take a cab. She Ubered everywhere she went or rode with her or Marlis. "What's going on?"

"That was the office. Perry's family ..." Tears welled in Genevieve's eyes. She covered her mouth and breathed deeply. Her hand shook. A tear spilled over the edge of perfectly applied liner and mascara before she blinked furiously.

Larkin didn't know Gen's boss, the man who owned Carter, Cleary & McMellon. If he passed her on the street, she might not recognize him. She didn't have anything invested, but the word family and the tear from her rock-solid friend created a pit of dread that seeded deep in her belly.

Gen's chin lifted, and her shoulders straightened. Every hint of sorrow fled her about-business expression. "They've been murdered in their home."

"Oh, my God."

"He wasn't there to protect Pam or Claire. Not his precious namesake either. And now, the police are taking him to the station for questioning." Gen's heels made the floor her bitch with each strike she landed on her way to the door.

"He requested you as his counsel?"

"Yes." She grabbed the doorframe as though it was the only thing keeping her afloat.

"But Gen, you don't defend. You prosecute."

"I know," she said without looking back. "Perry knows that too."

"Let me go with you." Larkin's gaze slid to her things at the far side of the conference room.

Her friend's red hair shook.

"Why not? I'm ready. Let's go." Larkin headed for her purse.

"They won't let you back at the station."

"I'll wait out front."

"With the men in cuffs, addicts, and sex workers. No." Gen drew a breath and rushed through the door. The sound of her heels faded.

Larkin sat on the edge of the table and stared through the open door. Just when things settled for her, the world shifted on its axis for her friend. Of course, the only sure thing about Larkin's life was vulnerability. Going public had exposed her business. Things were good now, but there were no guarantees. Loving Beckett exposed her heart. She trusted he would never voluntarily hurt her, but his job bathed in danger. It suited him perfectly. It also gave no guarantees.

She grabbed her phone and dialed Beckett's number, the same number that had gone straight to voicemail for the past week. He'd warned her that he might be out of contact. Three weeks without a sound had broken her. Him not answering the calls aimed to destroy her.

The line clicked open.

Breath lodged in her throat.

A ring sang through the speaker.

Hope soared.

It rang again and again and again.

Each ring shot a hole in its wings. Hope's nose tilted toward the ground and gained speed. It increased with each shrill sound. At least the voicemail let her hear his deep, gravelly tone.

"You couldn't wait, could you?"

Larkin pulled the phone from her ear and stared at it for a second. Had she conjured him?

"Sweetheart? Larkin?" Beckett's voice bellowed through the line.

She put the phone to her hear. "I'd throttle you if I could get my hands on you. Wait? I've waited long enough and patiently, I might add."

"Not too patiently, I hope." She loved the laughter in his voice.

"Not at all." Larkin held the phone to her cheek, wishing it were his cheek touching her skin. "How much longer?"

"Five minutes."

"Seriously?" The squeal squeed from her throat unchecked and unabashedly.

"Meet me on the roof in five."

Larkin ended the call and bolted for the stairs. She'd be there, eyes open, arms wide when he arrived. First, she wouldn't be the one holding up their reunion. Second, and most important, she wanted to know how in the hell he got to the roof after she had new "un-pickable" locks and mammoth doors installed at all the access points.

A devilish grin stretched her mouth.

The thunder of her heels rumbled up the steps and down the hallway. Her lungs burned. She pushed harder to the ladder and scrambled up the rungs to the hatch.

"No, Larkin."

She heard him before she saw him standing over a table with a white linen cloth tied around each leg with what looked to be some heavy-duty cord. He held a bag of takeout in one hand and a flaming lighter to a low-profile glass jar.

"You were supposed to wait five minutes." He set the bag on the table and slid the lighter into his pocket. A tiny flame flicked and swayed in the breeze.

Love exploded inside her, leaving her a damn casualty of the never-ending war. It shot tingles to her toes and heated her hands that had been just a little cold since he left.

Larkin lifted herself out of the manhole, then ran at full tilt. To his credit, he opened his arms, crouched, and caught her midair. Her hands traveled up his shoulder and smoothed over his face, his scarred, stunning face. She pressed her cheek to his. Her fingers slipped into his hair.

Contentment smoothed her every rough edge. It

soothed the pain of her past. It brightened the future.

A rumble started deep in his chest. "Sweetheart, I never knew I wanted this. Now, I can't imagine life without you."

"Don't go getting sappy on me." She smothered kisses down his neck to the beat of his pulse. "I might not let you leave again."

"I'll always come back," he promised something he couldn't promise.

"No one can keep that promise, but I'm okay with that. I'll love you with all of me for all of my days."

He pulled her in close. "And all of mine."

If you enjoyed *Who*, please consider leaving a
review on Goodreads and your
favorite book vendor.
If you enjoyed *Who*, check out *Why* …

WHY

An attorney with a spotless record. A client with blood on his hands. How much will she risk to set the verdict straight?

Prosecutor Genevieve Holst lives for the thrill of putting bad guys behind bars. She owes her undefeated court record to Perry, her boss and mentor. So when he's accused of murdering his wife and children, she moves to the other side of the courtroom to defend the man who believed in her when no one else would. Her inevitable victory in court feels hollow when she catches Perry sneaking off to a secret meeting with a gorgeous woman and hosting extravagant soirees at the scene of the crime. Guilt-ridden at the thought of letting a possible killer go free, she follows her mentor's every move… and runs into the same NYPD detective who warned her against taking the case. When the detective threatens to arrest her for stalking if she doesn't stop, she's faced with an impossible decision—save her career and let an almost-certain killer walk free or risk everything to bring him to justice.

Why is the second standalone novel in an arresting series of psychological suspense thrillers. If you like tenacious heroines, courtroom drama, and a hint of romance, then you'll love Megan Mitcham's edge-of-your seat thrill ride.

Buy Why to take your seat at the witness stand for a suspenseful courtroom thriller soon!

BOOKS BY
MEGAN MITCHAM

ENEMY MINE

JUSTICE MINE

STRANGER MINE

WARRIOR MINE

DANGER MINE

PRISONER MINE

VERSIONS

VIRTUES

VARIATIONS

NEVER MINE

RELENTLESSLY MINE

FUIOUSLY MINE

CAPTOR MINE

BUREAU SERIES

FOR ALL TO SEE

PAINTED WALLS

STALKER SERIES

WHO

WHY

HOW

ABOUT THE AUTHOR

Megan Mitcham is a USA Today bestselling author who has penned more than 15 sizzling suspense novels. Her work is said to whisk you across the globe, wedge your heart in your throat, make your hands sweat and your skin tingle. Check out Megan's special forces heroes in the Base Branch Series. If you like the darker side of suspense, try her Bureau Series or her Stalker Series. She is a Mississippi native, living and loving it in the natural state.

Megan was born and raised among the live oaks and shrimp boats of the Mississippi Gulf Coast, where her enormous family still calls home. She attended college at the University of Southern Mississippi where she received a bachelor's degree in curriculum, instruction, and special education. For several years Megan worked as a teacher in Mississippi. She married and moved to South Carolina and began working for an international non-profit organization as an instructor and co-director. In 2009 Megan fell in love with books. Until then, books had been a source for research or the topic of tests. But one day she read Mercy by Julie Garwood. And Oh Mercy, she was hooked! For information on new releases and giveaways sign up for her

Readers' Group at **meganmitcham.com!**
Goodreads: **Megan_Mitcham**
Pinterest: **MeganMitcham5**
Website: **www.meganmitcham.com**
Facebook.com / **AuthorMeganMitcham**
Twitter.com / **MeganMMMitcham**